A
Season
of
Secrets

KATE LORD BROWN

ORION

First published as *The Christmas We Met* in Great Britain in 2015
by Orion Books
This edition published in 2020 by Orion Fiction,
an imprint of The Orion Publishing Group Ltd,
Carmelite House, 50 Victoria Embankment
London EC4Y 0DZ

An Hachette UK company

1 3 5 7 9 10 8 6 4 2

A CIP catalogue record for this book is available
from the British Library.

ISBN (Mass Market Paperback) 978 1 3987 0433 6
ISBN (Ebook) 978 1 4091 5996 4

Typeset by Input Data Services Ltd, Somerset

Printed and bound in Great Britain
by Clays Ltd, Elcograf S.p.A.

MIX
Paper from
responsible sources
FSC® C104740
FSC
www.fsc.org

www.orionbooks.co.uk

For GB – 'Born to Fly'

A
Season
of
Secrets

'She is more precious than jewels;
And nothing you desire compares with her'

Proverbs 3:15

PROLOGUE

'Take my hand,' he said. Well, what would you have done? I didn't mean to get involved; I just wanted to see the house where it all began, to learn the story of the diamond brooch. But I knew, you see, even in that first moment, the way you know about some people the instant they come into your life that they are going to be significant somehow. It was January 1979 when we met, the winter of discontent. The snow was falling hard, settling on his thick dark hair. He wore it longer in those days, brushing the collar of his jacket. It's white as the snow itself now, but then it had the blue-black sheen of polished obsidian. I remember the snowflakes catching in his eyelashes, the bloom of his breath blurring the intensity of those sapphire blue eyes of his. I knew I could trust him, and so I reached out.

It was one of those winter days when the ice is black and the road's a rink beneath the fresh snow and you don't even know it. The worst winter since 1963, they said, bitterly cold. He'd stopped a little way down the road. The headlights of his old blue Land Rover gilded the frozen drifts moulding the hedgerows like icing, the slanting spirals of flakes falling slow, a cloud of exhaust billowing white across the lane. The engine thrummed steadily, a Pink Floyd chorus drifting from the cab, breathing out across the silent fields. He was in silhouette at first, striding towards me out of the light, then as he came closer I could make out he was smiling, his eyes all creased up, trying not to laugh. I must have looked ridiculous,

1

stranded in the middle of the road in my sky-high boots and my shaggy old white sheepskin coat. The heels I wore in those days. My arms were outstretched like a tightrope walker, trying to catch my balance, the wind whipping my blonde hair around the edge of my black beret. My feet threatened to go from underneath me again at any moment. *Take my hand.* Those were the first words he said to me.

'I can manage,' I said. I was trying to edge backwards to where I'd parked my old red VW Beetle. It was as if the head-lights of my car were reaching out to his across the frozen air, criss-crossing like the spots on a stage in the snow before us.

'Sure you can. Dressed for hiking, are you?'

'I wasn't planning to. My dog . . .' I began, but his laughter was infectious. So I did it, I took his outstretched hand and held on so firmly that when I hit another patch of ice and my feet went and I fell, laughing, into the verge, he fell with me, trying to save me. I wasn't going to let him go, was I? We like to say we swept one another off our feet.

We lay in the snow catching our breath and I remember gazing up at the milk sky for a moment, the snowflakes all lit up like gold leaf drifting leisurely down on us. You can tell you are close to the sea in this part of West Sussex, there's a sparkle to the air and the light, even when you can't see the coastline. It was all fresh, then: this man, these roads, this land, and my heart was thumping with the newness of it all. When I turned to him he was already looking at me, smiling. It felt strange to me. I had been tired and sad for so long the fine muscles in my face had forgotten how a genuine smile lifted them, laughter bubbling up and free inside me. You know they say 'a weight lifted'? I swear that's how it felt, with him. Just a sense of relief and of joy – *I've found you.* That's what the still, quiet part of me felt, recognising him from somewhere, reaching out. It was like this heavy cold rock of sadness in me floated away, light as a balloon.

'I'm Jack,' he said, leaning over and offering me his hand.

'Grace,' I said, shaking it. 'Thank you for rescuing me.'

'Did a good job, didn't I?'

'I'm not normally this ridiculous.' I mean, I cope. That's what I'm known for. Good old Grace, always together, always prepared. The Fates decided to have some fun the day they set me into the path of the love of my life in sky-high boots on an icy road.

He raised himself up on his elbow and smiled down at me. 'Are you here to see Fraser Stratton?'

'Yes, I am.'

'He's going to love you.' That amused look in his eyes, again. 'But you're heading down the wrong road. This only leads to my place.' *How can that be the wrong direction?* was my first thought.

'You're not from here?' I said. 'Originally, I mean.'

'The accent?' he grinned. 'I grew up here, but I was born in the States.'

'That explains it.' He had American teeth as well, far too good for an Englishman in the 1970s.

'You know what this place is like – you have to have grand-parents buried in the churchyard before they'll accept you as local.'

'Do you?' I said.

'Does a great-aunt count?'

'Oh, definitely. What's Mr Stratton like?'

Jack laughed. 'You'll see. Let me give you a lift.' He got to his feet, dusted the snow from his legs and reached down for me. He tilted his head. 'You look like a snow angel,' he said, his face softening. I swept my arms and legs in an arc. I don't know what got into me, honestly. I hadn't done that since I was a kid, but with him – well, you know what it's like. I felt light in my heart for the first time in too long. 'Come on. You must be freezing. I promise I won't let you fall again.'

'Promise?'

'We'll tow your car down to the Manor.'

3

'I don't want to be any trouble. I was looking for the drive-way. My dog—'

'That crazy-looking lurcher I just passed?'

'Jagger. He was pawing at the door. I thought he needed to go, so I stopped just off the main road, but he shot off down here and I got stuck chasing after him.' I said a silent 'thank you' to my hound for bringing me down that way.

'Don't worry. I bet I know where he's headed.'

'Thanks,' I said, standing up. Even in my boots, I wasn't as tall as him. He hooked his arm around my waist and held me steady as we walked towards the Land Rover. Close to, I could see the first grey hairs at his temples – I guessed he was maybe thirty-five, thirty-six? He was wearing the kind of thick-knit white roll-neck jumper and an old blue wool pea coat you just want to wrap yourself up in. His blue jeans were clean but crumpled, and he smelt like the rain, like the earth, like something clear and real, like somewhere you could breathe easy. When he looked at me, it felt as if he saw me. *Really* saw me. It was the first time in years anyone had made me feel like that.

I still remember every detail of the drive down through the snow to Wittering Manor. The main driveway of the estate had been cleared, snow banked up against the riven oak fences. The cab of Jack's Land Rover was warm and smelt of oil and hay, and I felt safe. That's what I remember. I felt safe, with him, as if I had come home. It wasn't the swanky estate it is now with farm shops and cafés and holiday homes, of course. In those days you just passed a few cottages with woodsmoke pluming from their crooked chimneys, and farm tracks leading to old tumbledown barns. And then the Manor swung into view. The first glimpse caught me by surprise. I had imagined a pale, forbidding, pillared house, but instead saw a welcoming red-brick and timber building, set in beau-tifully landscaped grounds. The house seemed to have grown over time, with later wings extending out from the central

4

part, and the terracotta-tiled roof was charmingly wonky, dusted with snow. As we pulled into the yard, I remember noticing that even the weathervane on the stable building was skew-whiff and frozen, pointing in the wrong direction.

Maybe it was a sign. In the way of life, nothing was to be simple for us, but then, often what's most worth having takes some fighting for. Maybe that's how you get to appreciate things. And I thank my stars every day that my grandmother's diamond brooch brought me to him. Gogo has a saying: fall down seven times, stand up eight. It became a touchstone for me at the time, and I like that sentiment still. Jack caught me as I fell – and together we found our feet.

JANUARY

Garnet

Constancy · Fidelity · Patience

1

Grace runs through the dark woods; in the silence, her white breath plumes, streams behind her. The fresh snow is luminous in the moonlight and stars glitter above the trees, a field of diamonds. Her boots skid as she breaks through the trees and reaches the frozen road, chill twigs cracking beneath her swift feet. She gathers up the hem of her blue silk evening gown and glances behind her, her platinum hair blowing in the wind, a skein of silver. She has a few minutes, if that, when she can be sure all the villagers are indoors, when prying eyes turn away from net curtains to parties or the television and people sing Auld Lang Syne.

Twelve rings of the bell, counting down.

At the gate she pauses, gasping in the cold air. She rests her gloved hand against the stone sign, traces the familiar letters: The Old Rectory. Across the road, snow has drifted against the stiff box hedge of Mrs Miller's thatched cottage. It is dark, the curtains tightly drawn for once. The house reminds Grace of a bristling hedgehog, turned in on itself, its low, beady windows watching everything that goes on in the village.

Grace turns to the tree-lined Rectory driveway and walks, keeping to the shadows. She pulls up the hood of her velvet cape, breathes in the reassuring smell of her perfume, Opium, warm vanilla and patchouli. The house lies ahead, its elegant windows glinting blue in the moonlight, fringed by dark leafless trees, steady as the gaze of a woman sure of her beauty. It is waiting for her. When her family moved to Hampshire and she first saw this house, it made her think of the homes she had drawn as a little child – square and constant, safe. She pauses at the sound of voices, laughter, from a nearby house. Grace lifts her head and listens, quick and fearful as a deer in the forest. A door closes. All she can hear now is the distant rush of the silver river through the water meadows beyond Exford church. She runs on up the drive, the gravel silent for once, packed hard against the icy earth, muffled by the snow.

From her pocket she pulls the key and eases it into the lock with a shaking hand. It does not turn. She had anticipated the familiar slide and click of the bolt, the easy swing of the front door into the hall that she can navigate blindfold. She peers through the glass, sees the fanlight illuminated on the flagstones by the moon. *They've changed the locks already.* She yanks out the key, cursing. A car hisses by on the road and she steps back into the shadows of the sandstone porch. Her breath is short and shallow. She waits, then runs around the house to the back door. She tries the handle. *Locked. Think.*

The memories come to her in a rush, the life lived in these four walls. She lets them fly through her like a murmuration of birds. She remembers the endless summer they moved in, 1976. There was such hope, such ambition driving them on. The sun shone every day that summer, it seemed. She remembers jiving with Harry to 'Dancing Queen', her daughter's feet resting on her own. The radio echoed through the house as the movers carried their boxes in. It hurts, still, the joy she felt, swinging the lithe, light body of her daughter through the empty rooms. She wants that time back, desperately, the unguarded moments. She goes on, in her mind, through the house, the rooms illuminating one by one. She wants the heat of the fire in the hearth, the warm embrace of woodsmoke, cognac on her tongue. Or the cool blue of her bedroom, the caress of a breeze from open windows on a summer night. Her breath catches in her throat with longing. Grace balls her fist and thumps the door frame in frustration. There is no time for this. *Think.* It comes to her, then, the night in April that Sam had lost his keys at the cinema in Winchester. Friends had dropped them home, but they were locked out. 'We could sleep in the playhouse,' he said. 'Harry's staying with her mates for the night. It could be fun . . .'

'Are you mad?' she said. Sam pulled his Swiss army knife from his pocket, the porch light glinting on the blade. 'Be careful.'

'Don't worry.' He turned to her, his green eyes calm, unreadable beneath his blonde fringe. He went to the nearest window and slid the blade between the rattling sashes, edging the latch free. In a few seconds he was in and opening the back door for her.

'Where did you learn to do that?'

'You don't want to know.'

Grace flicked on the kitchen light. 'If it's that easy we should get better locks.'

'Who'd dare to break in?' he said, wrapping her in his arms. 'Nothing can touch us here.'

Grace stands looking at the back door. *Nothing can touch us.* Even then, she was unsure. She flinches, aware that she's been lost in the past again. She searches in her coat pocket for Sam's knife. It is one of the talismans she takes everywhere with her. She checks the time on his Omega watch. Five minutes to twelve. The first window she tries is latched too firmly, and the next. 'Sam,' she says, under her breath, 'I need your help.' Grace starts at the sound of people heading to the pub in the square, a snatch of 'You're The One That I Want' on the jukebox as the door opens, a chorus of laughter and singing: *oo-oo-ooh.* There's not much time. She strides over to the next window and forces the knife up, jamming the blade hard against the latch. Her fingers are stiff with cold, but she feels it give. 'Thank you,' she whispers and slides up the window.

Her footsteps echo on the boards through the house. She can hardly bear to look around her. She had never wanted to come here again. Grace wills herself not to look at the kitchen doorpost, at the marks they made for Harry as she grew, at the faint blue lines for herself, and just above her, Sam, at Harry's scrawled marks for Jagger the dog. She forces herself on through the hall, remembers standing at the door just before Christmas as her father Ted's van lurched out of the driveway with the last of the boxes, pulling to one side to make way for the dark Cortina. The bank's agent was businesslike as she handed over a set of keys, and she walked away without a backward glance, amazed at how quickly a life can fall apart.

At the door to the living room, she hesitates, afraid now to enter. Half of her expects everything still to be in place, the deep red velvet sofa, twin pools of lamplight spilling over the sheepskin rugs by the fire. *Do it*, she thinks, willing herself forward. The door swings open to empty space, a cloak of moonlight laid out beneath her feet on the bare floor. Grace hurries across to the fireplace and drags the firedogs clear. She squats down and pulls a small torch from her pocket, twisting it on. Placing it between her teeth, she squeezes herself into the chimney breast, feeling with her fingers for the loose brick above the stone arch. *There.* Gripping the knife, she hacks away at the wall, working the brick free. She squints, dust filling her lungs, smarting her eyes. The brick thuds to the ground and she reaches in, feels for the small wooden box with her fingertips. *I was right. It's gone.* The first church bell rings. Twelve, eleven . . .

Grace replaces the brick and eases herself out of the hearth. *Who could have taken them?* Headlights flare up against the far wall and she sees the lights waver as the car slips on the snowy drive. *Oh God, oh God,* she thinks, turning, running to the hall. Who saw her? She races down the moonlit corridor, her cape and gown trailing behind her. Perhaps someone called the police. Is it a crime to break into your own home? *It's not your home, not any more,* she thinks, running through the kitchen and scrambling through the window, sliding it silently down.

'What do you think you're doing?'

Grace wheels round at the sound of a man's voice right behind her. 'Dad? You scared the life out of me.'

'Hold still, your dress has caught.' Ted lifts the hem clear of the windowsill. 'I saw you leave the party and I had a feeling you might be heading to the house.' He pulls the sash down firmly. 'I know things are bad, but I didn't think you'd been reduced to burglary.' He takes the knife from her and pushes the latch back enough to secure the window. 'Wouldn't want just anyone breaking into the old place, would we?' He pats the wall affectionately. 'Are you all right?'

'I'm fine,' she says as they walk around to where Ted's red E-type Jaguar is parked in front of the house. 'I just had to check. They've gone.' Her face is pale, etched with fear. 'The birthstones have gone.'

The bells ring out across the frozen land. 'Happy New Year, love,' Ted says.

'You too, Dad. Let's hope so.' Grace shivers, tucks down into the collar of her cape. 'I could have done without 1979 starting off like this.'

'Who on earth would do something like that? Who?' Ted frowns. 'Do you want to go back to the party?' He edges the car carefully along the gritted lane, the tyres hissing through the snow. The flakes are a kaleidoscope, whirling towards them. 'Everyone will understand. No wonder that note spooked you. Don't you worry, love. We'll get to the bottom of this. You've been through quite enough already without—'

'It's all right, Dad.' She stares ahead at the snow, falling slow. 'Amazing, isn't it? I wouldn't have believed you this time last year if you told me I'd be homeless, a widow, a single mum—'

'You're not homeless, love. There's a place for you with us as long as you need it.' Ted reaches for her hand and squeezes it in his.

From her pocket, Grace pulls out a plain manila envelope

addressed simply with her typewritten name. Inside there is a small wooden box, and a card: *Faithful my love, and her heart. This garnet means we'll never part*. The rich red ribbon tied around the box falls to the floor of the car, unseen. She trembles with cold and adrenalin as she opens the box, running her fingertip over the eleven indentations until she reaches the garnet. Grace holds the gemstone up between her thumb and forefinger and it gleams red in the half-light. 'I recognised the stone at once. I remember cutting it.'

'Is that why you broke in, to check if the box had gone?' he asks. Grace nods, still watching the stone. 'I wish I'd seen who left it on the Mill's doorstep. I only saw the envelope because I went to let some people in to the party. Who'd take the stones?' Ted pauses. 'You don't think—'

'He's dead.' Grace watches a few fireworks soar above the streets of Exford: valiant rockets from the estate, a more sedate shower of gold above her parents' Mill House. It makes her think of the fireworks Sam arranged for their house-warming at the Rectory, the terrace thronged with people she didn't recognise. Afterwards, Sam called everyone into the living room, made a big speech before sealing the gemstones up in the chimney breast as a good luck talisman for their new home. When she suggested it, Grace had wanted it to be a private gesture, something just for her and Sam. Instead, he saw the chance for a big finish to the party. She remembers her cheeks burning, glancing around the room as Sam basked in his moment of glory, showing off the house, the family of his dreams. Close by, the smiling faces of her parents and Harry were lit gold by the firelight, but beyond she saw sharp eyes glinting in the shadows, faces she didn't know, people who to her looked anything but pleased at Sam's good fortune. *Like wolves circling a campfire*.

'Sam's dead, Dad,' she says. 'I've no idea how many people know that he bricked up the gemstones for luck, but there are plenty of people with a grudge against him. Sam's creditors, his family – the list of people his company owed money to is endless. I thought once the house went it would stop, but they still came after him and now they're playing games with me.'

'Do you want me to ask around? If someone's trying to hurt you . . .'

'Don't worry, I can take care of myself.' She turns, her head rolling against the headrest to look at him. 'Listen, I don't feel much like going back to the party, but Mum—'

'Your mother will understand when I explain.'

'Anyway, I promised Ben I'd help him out.'

'Ben? What's the old devil scheming now?'

'You'll see,' she says as her father pulls up outside the Old Mill and turns off the engine. Their driveway is full of cars and they weave their way through to the porch.

'Come on, love, let's go in. We'll talk about this tomorrow.' He opens the front door and a gust of warm air greets them, carrying the sound of music and laughter. The house is crowded with people, sparkling with coloured fairy lights, tinsel glimmering on the old beams. Grace hangs her cape up on the hooks in the hall and kicks off her wellington boots.

'Thanks, Dad.' She hugs him tightly. She wonders if the slight stoop he has in his shoulders these days is because of recent events or the low ceilings of the Mill. The star on the Christmas tree tilts against a beam, looking down on its shimmering lametta like a woman admiring her new dress. 'Happy New Year, Dad.'

'Where have you been?' Grace's mother pushes her way through the party towards them, clutching a silver tray of canapés. The billowing sleeve of her dress catches on the Christmas tree. 'Oh God, would you look how it's shedding, Ted.' As her mother sweeps aside the needles with her gold-sandalled foot, Grace catches the fresh scent of pine. Priscilla Manners' fuchsia lipstick matches her chiffon kaftan precisely, and her cheeks are warm with firelight and champagne. 'You missed the toast *and* the fireworks. I had to get Ben to help me. I thought he'd have his eyebrows off.'

'Happy New Year, darling,' Ted says, kissing her on the cheek.

'Look at you, you're frozen,' she says to Grace. 'What on earth do you think you are doing, going off like that?' Someone changes the record, interrupting Perry Como's magic moment, the needle scratching and bumping. 'Who's changed the music? I want a relaxed, refined atmosphere this year, not that disco rubbish.' Cilla cranes her head, trying to see through the crowd to the stereo. The opening bars of 'Stayin' Alive' pulse across the room.

'Don't fuss, Cilla,' Ted says. 'Everyone's having a good time.'

'Marvellous party, Edward,' a man says as he squeezes by, his index finger pointing at the ceiling, dipping in time to the music. 'Cilla's always the hostess with the mostess.' His other hand lingers on her waist.

She flushes and giggles. 'Do you think so? You're too kind. Have you tried the mini quiches?'

Grace watches her mother, senses the desperation in her question: *do you think so?* None of this has changed her at all. She wants to prove she's still queen bee of Exford.

'I've been coping single-handed,' Cilla says once the man has moved on. Her gaze scans the party. 'Ted, the vicar needs refilling.'

'Of course, my love,' he says, reaching for a bottle.

'And Mrs Miller wanted a port and lemon.'

Ted raises his eyebrows as he hands Grace a glass. 'I'll make her a weak one. I think she's already cleaned us out of Babycham. Splash of fizz, love?'

'Thanks.'

'Not real shampoo this year, but you'd never know,' he says, wrapping a linen napkin around the label as he walks away.

Grace reaches down as an old lurcher nudges her other hand with his grizzled snout. She absent-mindedly strokes his bony flank. 'Hello, Jagger. Have you been a good boy?'

'When is he ever?' Cilla says under her breath. 'I caught him with his head in the hostess trolley helping himself to the vol-au-vents.' The dog stares balefully up at her before loping off. He clambers onto an emerald green sofa, circles once, twice, and curls up in front of the fire. His gaze seems to say to her: *go on, I dare you. Tell me off in front of all these people.*

'What an adorable dog, Cilla. Is he yours?' a woman asks, taking a stick of cheese and pineapple from the tray.

'Jagger, oh no. He's Grace's, for her sins.' Cilla gives Grace a quick kiss. Her mother's blonde hair has the consistency of candyfloss pressed against her cheek, scented with Elnett hairspray.

'Sorry I missed the bells, Mum.'

'Never mind,' she whispers. 'There's always next year.' Her mother's face softens for a moment. 'I know it's hard for you, the first Christmas without Sam.' She fusses at Grace's hair, pushing a strand behind her ear. 'Never let them see you down.' Her eyes dart, looking to see who is watching, who is talking about them.

'Them? Mum, I don't care what people think—'

Cilla purses her lips. 'Harry's tucked up in bed, finally. I caught Ben giving her an advocaat and I thought it was time she went up. Talk of the devil,' she says, under her breath.

'Ah, there you are, Grace.' Ben shoulders his way through the crowd. He catches the wounded expression on her face as her mother walks away and puts his arm around Grace's shoulders, hugging her briefly to his side. 'Pay no attention. Your mother could teach St Joan a thing or two about martyrdom,' he whispers in her ear. 'Are we all set?' Ben smooths down his grey curls, heading towards the conservatory, and 'How Deep is Your Love' begins to play. 'How appropriate. A Good Sign, eh?' He looks down at Grace for reassurance. 'I haven't been this nervous since the Normandy landings.' He adjusts his cravat, and squares his shoulders. 'Margot!' he cries, pushing through the dancers, batting the last of the people out of the way using his walking stick. Grace's grandmother is dancing at the heart of the crowd, her movements sinuous and graceful. Margot's eyes are violet, clear, a colour Grace wishes she had passed down to her. As she turns, the soft waves of her grey hair shine, tinted with the jewel colours of the pulsing spotlights. Her dress matches the colour of her eyes exactly. On its collar, she wears a brooch, a wing of diamonds shimmering in the lights of the mirrorball turning overhead.

'I do hope you're not going to get down on one knee, Ben. You'll never get back up again,' she says, raising her voice over the music. Her accent is pure Paris still, smooth as the snow settling in the dark fields outside.

'How did you know?' he says.

'How long have we been friends?' She tilts her head.

'Margot, I have loved you more years than I can recall.'

'Twenty years this year.'

'Which deserves a celebration.' He raises her fingers to his lips, kisses them. 'We may not have another twenty years in us . . .'

'Speak for yourself!' Margot's laugh is rich, infectious.

'But I hope the years we have left, you'll spend as my wife.' The silence stretches between them like an over-tightened violin string, Grace sees the alarm flash in her grandmother's eyes. Ben leans in to Margot, rests his forehead against hers. 'I know you never wanted to marry,' he says quietly. 'But after this year, seeing Sam . . .' He pauses. 'It makes you realise you have to grab every moment, every chance of happiness you can.'

'Darling,' Margot says, poise regained, 'you know what they say. When a man marries his mistress, he creates a vacancy.'

'I promise you, my wandering days are over. I would have married you years ago if it hadn't been for Polly's illness. I could never have divorced her, but now she has passed . . .'

18

'You were a good husband,' she says quietly. 'If feckless and unfaithful.'

'I will be a good husband. A better husband. Marry me.'

'Ben, thank you—'

'I swear,' he says, raising his voice, 'marry me and I will spend the rest of my days making you the happiest woman on earth.' A cheer goes up. Grace sees a look in her grandmother's eyes she recognises – the wildness of a creature trapped and ready to fight or flee.

'Go on, Margot!' someone calls from the party. 'If you don't marry him, I will!'

Margot gazes at Ben. 'I can't. I adore you Ben, but I won't marry you.'

He lowers his eyes. 'Ah well, can't blame a man for trying.' He pats her hand. 'Think about it, though?' He glances around at the expectant faces, beckons to Grace. 'Let's still have a bash this year, to celebrate our anniversary?'

'It's your sixtieth birthday this year too. Why not?' Margot says.

Ben throws his arms into the air. 'And you're all invited!' As the crowd cheers, Ben kisses her tenderly. He waits for everyone to turn away. Grace sees the disappointment on his face, but he collects himself as she walks over. 'Now, I've been plotting with Grace. I thought this might be an engagement ring—'

'Oh, Ben. You're always racing ahead of yourself.'

'I haven't bought one, of course. I asked Grace if she would design it.' He squeezes Margot's hand. 'Twenty years of friendship, and . . . well, it deserves something special.'

'What a wonderful idea.'

Grace takes the small wooden box from her pocket and places the garnet on Margot's palm. 'Oddly enough, I may have the perfect stone.'

'How . . .?'

'Don't worry, it's mine,' Grace says. 'Or it was.'

'Beautiful,' Margot says. 'A symbol of fidelity.' She glances at Ben, a smile playing on her lips.

'Are you sure?' he says. 'Grace mentioned amethyst, to bring out the colour of your eyes. I thought we could all go to Hatton Garden, choose the gem together.'

'No, this is perfect.'

'Ben has talked to one of the men who rents a unit from him at the antiques centre,' Grace says. 'He's offered to let me use his jewellery workshop. In fact, it's just next door to your old stall.'

'Where the glass studio used to be? How amusing. It will be beautiful, I'm sure.' Margot turns the gem against the firelight, flaring red. 'I can't think of anything more perfect than my birthstone for my ring.' She watches Ben dancing stiffly off across the room to 'Night Fever', makes sure he is busy with their old friends. Margot leans towards Grace and whispers: 'Thank goodness that's over. I had a horrible feeling he was going to pop the question tonight. Now, where did you get it?'

'The garnet? It's one of the stones I collected in Jaipur when Sam and I travelled,' she says quietly. 'When we did up the house, we set them in the chimney for luck, do you remember? Twelve birthstones, one for each month.' Her stomach lurches with dread at the thought of someone taking them. She opens the box again and runs her finger over the empty spaces. *It's just begun, hasn't it?* she realises. *Otherwise why would they send the box with only one jewel?* Cold fear rises, prickling at the nape of her neck as she thinks of the months ahead. *What do they want? Money? Revenge?* She bites her lip, thinking of the note. *Me?*

'Grace?' Margot sits down in a velvet wing chair, and tilts her head, concerned.

'Sam was always talking about the things they'd find bricked up in fireplaces when they were renovating places – children's shoes, corn dollies, all sorts of little talismans.' Grace forces down her swirling thoughts, and takes the garnet back, clicks it safely in the box. 'I thought twelve stones would bring us luck, or protect us.'

'Like the breastplate of the high priest?'

'It seemed romantic at the time.'

Margot takes Grace's hand. 'You were worried, even then?'

'Of course I was. But you know as well as I do, Sam loved the Rectory his whole life. Every time we drove past that place he told me that when he was growing up on the council estate it was his dream house. I knew he was stretching himself but I couldn't shatter his dream.'

'Developers never know when to stop,' Margot says. 'Look at Ben. He's made and lost fortunes. More losses than gains, lately. At least he's still got the antiques market.' Grace could hear the weariness in her voice. 'Sam reminded me of him. Both charmers and chancers, always chasing the next dream, thinking their luck is going to hold out forever.'

The next song begins to play: 'More Than a Woman'. Grace remembers dancing with Sam to it at a disco in the village hall the previous year. He was dressed in an immaculate white three-piece suit. As they had walked back home, someone had leaned out of a car and yelled, 'Who do you think you are, mate? Tony Manero?' *A charmer, a chancer. Was he? Or is that what he wanted everyone to think?* Grace stares down at the box. 'Luck? Well, the stones didn't work for us.'

'Darling, there's always the brooch, you know.' Margot's index finger runs along the edge of the diamond wing near her collarbone. 'That charming fellow at the *Antiques Roadshow* said—'

'But it's all you have from your mother.'

'It's yours if you need it.' Margot glances across the room at Cilla. 'In fact, now is as good a time as any. Would you pass me my bag?' Grace leans over and gives her a supple black leather tote. Margot lifts out a battered blue Bouchet et Fils jewellery case and it tumbles from her lap to the floor. 'Oh dear, how clumsy, would you mind?'

'Why did you bring the case with you?' Grace kneels, reaching for it. 'Gogo, were you planning this all along? You mustn't.'

'Fair's fair.' She takes the case from Grace. 'You are making a ring for me, I am giving you what will be yours one day anyway. I know my daughter will be annoyed that I gave it to you rather than her, but Priscilla would only bring it out on high days and holidays to impress the WI.'

'Gogo, you are terrible.'

'We are alike, you and I.' Margot lifts Grace's chin, gazes at her. 'Be patient. You've been through too much these last months, but we are survivors. You'll get back on your feet, darling. Remember? What do I always say?'

'Fall down seven times, stand up eight.' Grace's smile crumples as she looks at her; she holds back her tears, her throat tight. 'How, Gogo? How? When I wake up in the morning, sometimes I forget what has happened, and then it all comes flooding back and I can hardly get out of bed. How am I going to get back on my feet?'

'You have Harry to fight for.'

Grace's brow furrows. 'I should have listened to my gut instinct. I *knew* Sam's company was going to pull us, and my business, under. What kind of mother am I?'

'A damn good one, and don't you ever let anyone make you feel any different.' Margot glances at Cilla's back and turns her steady violet gaze on Grace. 'You took a risk. Sometimes in life, you win. Sometimes, you learn. And you move on. Always. Always keep moving forward, darling.'

'I don't know how I'm going to support us. We can't camp out with Mum and Dad forever. I've lost everything – Sam, the house, my business. I lost . . .' Grace's face is anguished, she can't finish the sentence. 'I can't even work. The bank took all my equipment, the stock.' She takes a deep breath and forces a smile. 'The birthstones were the last gems I had, and someone's even taken them.'

'If I'd known he'd put the house and your shop up—'

'Gogo, don't start. It's my fault. I knew the chance I was taking, and there are people in a worse state than us.' *Who?* She thinks. *Who do we know that's in a worse state?* She looks down at her hands. *Never do anything by half, Grace, that's what Sam always said. If you're going to lose, you might as well lose everything.* 'Stop me, please.' She looks up at her grandmother, her eyes bright. 'I can't bear self-pity.' She stands, and smooths down her silk dress. The fabric ripples beneath her fingertips like water.

'You can start again, with the brooch.' Margot unclips it and places it in the box. 'Sell it. I want to help.'

'I know, Gogo. But I want to do it by myself.'

'Good for you. I told you, darling, when you insisted on marrying: never allow your destiny to rest in another's hands.'

'You told me to never trust a man.'

'Did I?' Margot's eyes gleam as she reaches for a Sobranie Black Russian. Grace picks up an onyx table lighter from the mantelpiece and lights the cigarette for her. Margot settles back in the chair and exhales. 'It comes to the same thing. You should have listened. Be the captain of your own ship, Grace. Sam's dead. The simple truth is you have to make a new life for yourself and Harriet.'

Grace flinches at her grandmother's directness, cannot return her steady gaze. She straightens the diamond wing brooch in the jewellery case, and runs her finger around the empty velvet crescent opposite. 'You can see where the tiara would have sat—'

'Grace,' Margot insists.

'I wonder what happened to the rest of it.'

'I have no idea.' Margot's expression softens.

'They were such clever designs.' Grace feels around the velvet case, finding a seam at the centre. 'Tiaras were for high

23

days and holidays, but if it was made in pieces, a woman could wear it as brooches or a necklace . . .' Her voice trails off. 'This is the compartment where they would have kept all the fittings.' She prises it open. 'They've gone, of course,' she says, peering into the case. 'What's that?' She notices a corner of yellowed paper peeping beneath the lining, and eases the brittle, folded square free.

'Good heavens,' Margot says, leaning forward. 'Has that been in there all this time? It must have moved when I dropped the case. What does it say?'

'It's the original receipt.' Grace turns it to the light. 'The ink's faded, but it's dated 1915, I think. Bouchet et Fils made it out to Stratton, Wittering Manor, West Sussex . . . That's only a few miles from here.' Grace looks at Margot. 'And why do I know that name?'

2

Fraser Stratton lay on the floor of his study with his feet raised up against the wall. His ankles were crossed, the wide legs of his ochre-coloured cords hanging loose, revealing a glimpse of smooth, tanned shins and purple socks above the edge of his suede Lobb Hilo boots. His right foot tapped in time to the music hissing from the black headphones clamped over his collar-length grey hair. The white fur coat he was wearing spilled around him like a hearth rug. An Afghan hound with platinum blonde hair lay beside him, her dark snout resting on his stomach. Scattered around them were scores of manuscript pages, crammed with spidery handwriting, some lifting in the draught from the old French windows, which rattled in the wind, snow drifting up against them. Fraser turned his head, searching for the pencil that he had thrown down in disgust a moment before, and the firelight glinted on the garnet earrings dangling from his lobes.

'More precious than jewels,' he said to himself. 'No, that's not right.' He reached for the abandoned page, and crossed out the last line. *What is that saying? No jewel is more precious than this woman? This boy?* he wrote, and closed his eyes.

'Fraser,' Jack said. 'Jesus, what happened?' He grabbed Fraser by his shoulders and hauled him up. The jack pulled out of the stereo, and T. Rex's '20th Century Boy' blared into the room.

'Nothing, my dear boy, I was just doing my yoga and my back went,' Fraser said, laughing. He pulled off the headphones and tossed them onto a teetering pile of paper and books on the nearest table. He ran his fingers through his hair.

'I thought you'd had a coronary.'

'Not yet.' Fraser clicked open a silver box on the desk and lit a black cigarette. 'Back exercises,' he said, inhaling deeply. He spread his arms wide, the coat swinging after him as he strode across the room, stretching his spine from side to side in time with the beat of the music. 'I know I'm frightfully behind the times, but this Bolan chap is marvellous,' he shouted above the pounding music.

'Yeah, he died a couple of years ago, but I'm doing my best to get you up to date now, like you asked.'

'Marvellous!' Fraser span round, and smiled at Jack, who was leaning against the desk, staring at a tailors' dummy propped up in the corner of the old Chesterfield sofa. It was dressed in the uniform of the 9th Lancers. 'I see you've met Daddy.'

'Dare I ask?' Jack leant across to the record player and turned down the volume several notches.

'Don't worry, I haven't gone completely bonkers.' Fraser took a deep drag of his cigarette and tossed his hair back as he blew a plume of blue smoke to the ceiling. 'I'm applying Stanislavsky's principles to my memoirs.' Jack looked blank. 'Method,' he said, striding over and slinging his arm over the dummy's shoulder as he settled on the sofa. 'I'm attempting to commune with the dead, you see, to squeeze all I can out of this story.'

'And you are . . . ?' Jack gestured at Fraser's ensemble.

He touched the garnet earrings dangling from his ears. The stones glinted, flared red in the lamplight. 'I am trying to be my mother.'

'Man, if we were in the States they'd have you in a shrink's chair faster than you could whistle Dixie.'

'I don't want to *be* her, I'm just trying to conjure her up, to imagine what it was like for her when my father returned home with shell shock, a satchel of jewels – and a newborn baby.'

'I still don't get why you're set on writing these memoirs. Why now?'

'Why not?' Fraser shrugged. 'I've retired, dear boy, and have far too much time on my hands. If not now – when?'

A smile twitched on Jack's lips. 'Are you sure it's not the prophecy?'

'Nonsense.' Fraser tossed him a look.

'Where was the old con artist–'

'She was a well-respected wise woman.'

'Moscow?'

'Leningrad. Her declaration that I won't live beyond the end of this year is motivating, to say the least.'

Jack folded his arms. 'OK,' he said slowly. 'You need help.'

'I told you, I am perfectly all right.'

'I don't mean a shrink. I mean a secretary. Did you like any of the ones this afternoon?'

'Hopeless, the lot of them. Wouldn't last a morning with me.' Fraser balanced a brass ship's ashtray on his knee and flicked his cigarette into it.

'I just bumped into the last one on the road. She's waiting in the kitchen to see you.'

'Is she? I really can't face yet another interview.'

'Trust me. You'll find this one . . . interesting.' Jack cocked

26

his head. 'Or I could always ask Ellen to tidy up in here.'

'Don't you dare,' Fraser said, widening his eyes. 'I have a precise system going on here. I'd never find a damn thing.' His eyes crinkled with amusement as he watched Jack look slowly around the room. Every surface was piled high with manila files, cuttings from newspapers and auction catalogues, scrawled sheets of notepaper. Fraser had commandeered the library too, and through a set of double doors two rows of trestle tables extended into the darkness like rowdy gatecrashers among the stately shelves of gilded leather books lining the cedar shelves. 'I know it may not look like it.'

'Whatever you say, Frase.' Jack stretched wearily.

'I hope your day was more productive than mine?'

'I'm just going to head out and check those fences before dark.'

'Are the horses OK?'

'Yeah, they didn't get as far as the road. Cy reckons we need to replace them all in the spring.'

'Horses or fences?'

'Both, probably.' Jack checked his watch. 'Listen, shall I send her in.'

'What's her name?'

'Grace.' Something in Jack's voice made Fraser look up at him.

'You like her?'

'You'll see.'

'Are you riding down?'

'Nah, too icy. I'll walk.'

'Watch the paths; it's like a rink out there.'

'I know,' Jack said, smiling, thinking of Grace.

'What's so funny?'

'Nothing. I've just got to tow a car down to the house.'

'Can't you get Cy or one of the lads to do it? You work too hard, Jack.'

'Yeah, well somebody has to.' His eyes crinkled as he smiled.

'That's the secret, you see, employ family. Better than slave labour. No one would work as hard for the estate as we do.'

Jack's smile faded. 'Have you got enough wood for the fire or shall I send Cy in with some before he goes home?'

'Hm?' Fraser reached for a pen and paper and scribbled something down. 'Sorry. Memory like a sieve. The moment I think of something, I have to pin it down or the thought flies away.' He smiled up at Jack. 'Wood, you were saying. No, it's fine. I'm going to tuck myself up in the den after I see this girl. A good book and a bowl of soup. Perhaps a little Scotch—'

'Frase, you know what the doctor said.'

'Oh phooey to the doctor. He's about twelve years old, what does he know?'

'OK. I'll see you in the morning.' He squeezed Fraser's shoulder and Fraser reached for his hand.

'Jack?'

'Yep.'

'You are all right, aren't you? You look rather tired, dear boy. You know if anything's worrying you . . .'

'Sure. I'm fine. Just got a lot on my mind with getting the estate into shape, and – well, you know.' He paused. 'Frase, do me a favour.'

'Yes?'

'Go easy on this girl. She comes across as confident, but there's something about her.'

'You've a soft spot for wounded creatures, haven't you? Just like me.' Fraser tapped the side of his nose. 'Understood. Right, send her in.' Fraser forced himself up from the sofa and clicked his fingers. 'Come, Biba.' The Afghan hound loped over and settled beside the desk. 'Dogs are much easier to understand than people, aren't you, my darling?' She lifted a paw and placed it in his hand.

'I'll leave you two alone, shall I?'

'Yes, run along. We shall be fine.' He watched Jack pad away across the study, his feet noiseless in their thick grey wool socks. 'No jewel is more precious than this boy, to me,' Fraser said quietly to the dog once Jack had gone. He smiled, lost in a kaleidoscope of memories. *I hope I have done right by him. Jack's always had the obligation of the estate. I wish he hadn't given up on exploring the world so quickly. He needs more passion in his life.* Fraser sighed. *But then, that didn't do me much good, did it?* 'He's not a child any more,' he said, lifting the dog's snout and gazing into her eyes. 'Where have the years gone, Biba? Where have they gone?' He glanced up at a knock on the door. 'Ah, Ellen.'

'I've just brought you a pot of mint tea.'

'Teazle?' Fraser said. 'Cake as well? Golly, we are pulling out all the stops. I take it you like this girl too, then?'

'She's just drying off in the kitchen.'

'Drying off?'

'Seems she and Jack have been playing in the snow.' Ellen hid a smile as she bustled around the coffee table, tidying up. 'Now you behave. You really do need some help with all this.' She gestured at the papers scattered around the sofa like confetti.

'Can't you interview her? You're a far better judge of character when it comes to young women than I am.'

'No.' Ellen folded her arms across her chest. 'I've found six perfectly qualified and charming young ladies and you've scared them all off.'

'I have been rather foul to them, haven't I?' Fraser's mouth twitched. 'What was that last one called? Tipper? Tippet?' Fraser launched himself across the room with the dignity of a clipper in full sail. '"I cannot be expected to work like this,"' he said in a falsetto voice. '"What you expect me to do for that, that book of yours—"'

'We did warn her you can be a little eccentric,' Ellen said. 'I was going to say, difficult,' she added under her breath.

'Difficult? *Difficult?*' Fraser pulled a blue Tuareg scarf from the sofa and flicked it over his shoulders. '"Mr Stratton needs

29

a saint, not a secretary. No secretary should be expected to . . . to . . . *dress up*.'"

'Six. Six secretaries in as many months.' Ellen took a deep breath. 'I don't know what you do to these girls. That's got to be some kind of record. Shall I run the ad in *The Lady* again, just in case this one doesn't work out?'

Grace turned to a mirror in the cloakroom, and wiped a smudge of mascara from beneath her eye. Her cheeks were still pink and cold, but she had dried off a little in front of the Aga in the warm yellow kitchen. She still wasn't sure what she was going to say to Mr Stratton. She took the diamond brooch from her pocket and unfolded the square of velvet, tilting it to the light, the stones shimmering. *Thank you, Mum.* She smiled, thinking of Cilla's surprise when for once Grace took her advice to apply for one of the jobs she had circled in *The Lady. I think she almost forgave me for the brooch.*

She flicked off the cloakroom light and walked on through the house, taking in the square wood-panelled hall at its heart. From the lie of the Persian rugs she noticed that the wide old boards sloped erratically. *It's like a museum*, she thought, wrapping her arms around herself. *And freezing.* A staircase with a threadbare red runner rose up to a first-floor landing, a colonnade of white arches looking down on the unused sofas and armchairs clustered around the large marble fireplace. Grace ran her fingertips over a tiger skin thrown across the back of a sagging red velvet sofa, and looked around at the ancestral portraits ranged around the room, the coffee tables cluttered with faded photographs, and blue-and-white Chinese vases. A grand piano with a faded Spanish shawl over it stood in the corner, unplayed. From a side hall came the sound of a door opening.

'Hello, dear,' Ellen said, popping her head out of the kitchen corridor. Her pink cheeks were framed by a halo of auburn curls escaping from a bun at the crown of her head.

Deep laughter lines creased her blue eyes, and Grace had the impression she smiled, permanently. *Like a little golden Buddha,* Grace thought. A draught of warm air and the smell of fresh laundry swept in with her from the kitchen as the green baize-covered door swung open. 'I was just looking for you.'

'I popped to the cloakroom to tidy up, I hope that was all right.'

'Of course. Are you ready to see Mr Stratton?' She was struggling to fold a large bed sheet, and Grace stepped forwards to help her.

'Yes, I am. Have you worked here long, Ellen?'

'Thank you, love. Always easier with two.' She nodded her head in approval as she looked at Grace and held the folded sheet to her plump stomach. 'I've been on the estate more years than I care to remember, since Jack was a little lad.'

'What's he like? Mr Stratton, I mean?'

'They broke the mould with that one, I'll tell you. The Strattons are an old family, from somewhere further upcountry. His grandfather was a Sir, and it looks as though Fraser will be knighted too.'

'Really?'

'He was a diplomat.' Ellen leant towards Grace and lowered her voice. 'Not that you'd know it to look at him half the time. Spent most of his life overseas he has, a distinguished career and all a bit hush-hush from the bits I know. He's just retired, and if you ask me he's got too much time on his hands.'

'Is there a Mrs Stratton?'

'No, dear, he never married, so there's no grandchildren to keep him busy either. It's a pity. From the way he was with Jack, he'd have made a lovely father.' Ellen glanced at Grace. 'Jack Booth, the chap who drove you down here? He's Fraser's godson.' The old brass clock ticking on the mantelpiece chimed and she checked the time. 'Now, let me show you through.' Ellen swung the kitchen door open and tossed the sheet into a wicker laundry basket. 'You still look half frozen.'

31

'Is it always this chilly in here?'

'Old house, you'll get used to it. Can I get you some soup?' At the muffled sound of a brass bell ringing in the kitchen, Ellen looked down the hall. 'He's waiting.' She led the way through the house and tapped on the study door.

'Come.'

Grace waited as Ellen swung open the door to a glorious room with red walls. Books teetered on tables laden with amber, ammonites, Tiffany lamps. Arabic calligraphy and Russian icons decorated the walls, set in fine gilded gesso frames. It was like walking from a black-and-white stage set into Technicolor. In front of the fire, two plump yellow sofas with needlepoint cushions flanked a circular brass tray table, set with Moroccan tea glasses, the colours gleaming like gemstones. A pot of mint tea steamed contentedly. Above the marble fireplace, a delicately painted nude reclined, her back sinuous and elegant, her hair upswept, her face unseen. Unlike the rest of the house, which seemed to be in suspended animation, this room had a beating heart. The kelims on the floor, the fire burning in the hearth – everything had an authenticity about it that chimed with something deep inside her. She had a sense of being in exactly the right place, at the right moment. And there he was, Mr Stratton, she guessed, a grey head just visible over the back of the leather desk chair, tanned hands with long fingers holding a broadsheet, turned away from her. A pink silk dress lay discarded on the sofa. *Interesting. Casanova or cross-dresser,* she thought, a smile playing on her lips.

'Young lady to see you, Fraser,' Ellen said.

'Name?' he said

'Grace. Grace Manners,' she said, using her maiden name. 'How do you do.' She waited for him to turn to her, but he continued reading the paper.

'Ha. I suppose that's a good start.' He turned the page.

'Sorry to interrupt, Fraser,' Ellen said. 'The milkman's due any minute and I haven't been down to the town to get out the housekeeping. Do you have £1.50?'

He patted his pockets. 'No, my wallet's upstairs. You – Grace Manners.' He waved his hand airily. 'Give Ellen £1.50 and I'll pay you back.'

'I can't.'

'What do you mean – can't or won't?'

'I mean,' she said, rifling in her pockets for some coppers, 'I don't have £1.50.'

Ellen caught the pride, the hurt in her voice. 'Don't you trouble yourself, love. I'm sure I can find it, or he can come back next week.' She could see from the angry, humiliated flush to her cheeks that Grace was on the point of walking away. 'Go on now,' she said quietly, ushering her forwards. 'Stand up to him. Good luck.' Ellen closed the door behind her.

'Well come in then, if you're . . .' Fraser paused. 'What perfume are you wearing?'

'*Opium*. Why?'

'A friend of mine wears the same.' He laid his head back against the chair. 'Do you have a résumé, references?'

'No.' If he was arrogant and rude enough not to turn around and talk to her properly, she could play that game too. 'The ad didn't say you needed one.' She faltered. 'I haven't . . . I mean, I've never been to an interview before.'

'Oh dear.'

'You see,' she said quickly, 'I've always worked for myself. I had my own business.'

'Can you type at least?' He still hadn't looked at her. 'For heaven's sake, are you here for this job or not? Come on, dazzle me with your shorthand or something.' Fraser's arm hung limp over the side of the chair. 'Good God I'm bored with this endless troop of girls in twinsets and pearls through here. I'm *bored*.'

'I've heard about interviews like this,' Grace said. She took herself over to the typewriter without looking at him, pulled a clean sheet of paper from the mahogany filing tray, and rolled it into the machine. 'What would you like me to do? Set fire to your newspaper so I make an impression?' *Was that a laugh?* She stared at the blank sheet for a moment. On it she typed: Grace Manners, age 29, mother, jeweller, basic typing, lots of common sense. She handed it to him.

'Good grief, look at the state of your fingernails,' he said. 'Have you never heard of grooming? At least it shows you're a hard worker.'

'I've come straight from the workshop.' She noticed the signet ring on Fraser's pinkie finger as he took it, an aquamarine glinting clear and bright. Fraser spun slowly round to face her. As he looked at her, she saw it was the exact colour of his eyes. He had changed into a heavily embroidered sky blue frock coat with gold braiding, and a pair of fur boots over his yellow cords.

'We match,' he said, pointing from her sheepskin coat to his feet. 'Are you a wolf in sheep's clothing, Miss Manners, I wonder?'

'Nice jacket.' She held his gaze steadily.

'My Sergeant Pepper phase.' He laid down the paper beside a copy of T S Eliot's *Collected Poems*, and looked her up and down. 'May I take your coat?'

'No thanks. It's rather chilly.'

'You'll get used to it.'

'That's what Ellen said.'

'Well,' Fraser said, stretching out his legs. 'She's right about that, as she is with most things. It's not normally this cold,' he relented. 'Worst winter since the big freeze of '62,' he said, putting on a broad country accent. 'Or was it '63? At least, that's what they were saying in the pub the other night.' Grace frowned, trying to imagine Fraser in his brocade jacket and sheepskin boots propping up the bar with the locals. 'Now, Jack was right. Aren't you an improvement?' He glanced at her CV. 'You did that quickly. Much quicker than the other girls, and I like your spunk.' Fraser tossed the paper onto the pile.

'I hate that word.'

'So do I.' Fraser's laugh surprised her. 'What on earth are you doing here?'

'I'm looking for work.'

'But you're a jeweller?'

'Yes. Hard times, got to fall back on your other skills, you know how it is.' *Or perhaps you don't.*

'My dear, as Confucius said, our greatest glory is not in never falling, but in rising every time we fall.' He pressed his fingers into a pyramid. 'Now, how do you feel about dressing up?'

'Sorry?'

'Costumes. I'm trying to stimulate myself . . .'

'Are you?' She raised an eyebrow.

'Not like that. I'm writing my memoirs. I've raided the attic to try and bring my ancestors to life.' He gestured at the cavalry uniform, the discarded fur coat and dress.

'Well, I won the drama cup at school.'

'Excellent.' Fraser weighed her up. 'I've seen more young women than I care to recall today, every one of them plain vanilla. I feel like dear old Prufrock,' he said, tapping the book of poems, 'utterly clueless about women. But I can tell Ellen likes you.' *And Jack*, he thought. 'Would you like some delicious teazle?' Grace frowned in confusion. 'Tea, my dear.' He gestured at the tray. 'Will you be mother or shall I?'

Grace poured two glasses – a cool blue for him, and a deep red for herself. 'Sugar?'

'Yes, six.' Fraser took the glass from her, and pursed his lips, blowing the steam away. He regarded her steadily. 'Thank you. Now, Miss Manners. You and I both know you're no secretary, so why don't you tell me why you are really here?'

3

'Can you keep a secret?' Grace said to Fraser, buying time.

'Now we're talking.' He leant forward, wrists resting on the desk.

She glanced down at the desk and saw a copy of *The Lady* peeking out beneath the copy of Eliot's poems. 'You're right, I'm not a secretary, but . . .'

'Beggars can't be choosers?' he said. Grace glanced warily at him, unsure, and Fraser raised his hands. 'No need to get your dander up, dear heart. Only teasing.'

'I saw your advertisement. To be perfectly honest, my mother did.' A memory of Cilla, sitting at the kitchen table just before Christmas, circling classified ads for Grace with a red biro popped into her mind. *Look, here's one: a private secretary. Apply to the Estate Office, Wittering Manor.* Grace couldn't believe the coincidence when she found the receipt in the tiara's case. It seemed too good to be true – a chance to find out more about the Strattons *and* keep her mother happy. 'I need a job,' she said truthfully. 'It was serendipity that I ran into Jack, or I'd have missed the interview.' She glanced at the window, wondering if Jack's men had managed to get hold of her dog yet.

'Perhaps it was lucky for us all,' Fraser said quietly. 'And do you?'

'Do I?'

'Like the look of us, Miss Manners?'

'I'm . . . intrigued.' A smile played on her lips as she thought of Jack.

'Well.' Fraser clapped his hands. 'By some glorious stroke of synchronicity – or sheer blind luck – the universe has sent you to me today, and you are just what I need. You see, at the heart of my memoirs are the Stratton jewels.'

'Tell me more.'

'Most of them are here, safe, but there are two pieces missing.'

'Two?' Grace's heart quickened.

'A rare asteria star sapphire necklace,' Fraser said, sipping his tea, pinkie finger extended. 'And, of course, the Stratton tiara. I'm hoping to discover what happened to it.'

That makes two of us, Grace thought, her palm settling over the bump in her pocket where the diamond brooch lay, waiting for the right moment to ask about it.

'Tell me, what do you think of those?' Fraser gestured at the garnet earrings lying on the desk.

'They're beautiful.' She put down her tea glass and turned one to the light. 'French, early twentieth century.' She recognised Bouchet et Fils' work even before she turned the earring over and checked the marks. 'Do you always take so little care of them?'

'I believe it is better for beautiful things to be used and enjoyed. This house may look like a museum, but it is a living, breathing family home that I am doing my best to preserve and pass on to the next generation, Miss Manners. I am simply its caretaker.'

'Please, call me Grace, I feel like I'm in a costume drama if you call me Miss Manners. What should I call you?'

'Sir.'

Grace glanced up at him.

'Only joking. We're an informal house. You may call me Fraser.'

'The setting is loose. May I?' She pulled out the Swiss army knife from her pocket and flicked through the tools until she found the closest she could to a blunt-ended pusher. She laid the earring on the desk.

'Heavens, were you a Girl Guide?'

'As a matter of fact, I was.' Gently, she adjusted the prongs, securing the garnet. 'There.' She handed it to him and flicked the knife closed.

37

'Very good. I like you, you have initiative.' Fraser clipped on the earrings. 'Now, shouldn't I tell you what the job entails?'

'I didn't say I'd take it yet.' Grace pretended it was the most natural thing in the world to see a middle-aged man wearing earrings. *There's no harm in playing along. I'll ask him about the brooch in a minute.*

'I'm writing my memoirs, as I said.'

'Is that what all this is?' She glanced over her shoulder at the row of trestle tables. 'It's quite a mess you've made here.'

Fraser placed his index fingers against his lips. 'Calls a spade a spade. I like it.' He stretched back in his chair and crossed his ankles. 'I need help.'

'I can see that.'

'In return, you get the going wage, accommodation—'

'Accommodation?' Grace paused, the tea glass halfway to her lips.

'An estate cottage. Did the advertisement not say it was a live-in position?'

Grace held her nerve and all thoughts of the brooch vanished instantly. She saw an escape, the chance for a new start. 'No, but – but that will be fine.' *Fine? That would be wonderful.*

Fraser glanced up at a knock on the door. 'Come.'

'Fraser, are you ready? Your car's here to take you to London.' Ellen walked into the study. 'And Cesca called. She's expecting you to pick her up on the way.'

'Damn,' he said, checking the clock on the mantelpiece. 'I'd forgotten all about the dinner. Can you tell the driver to wait while I dress? Listen, this is the one. If she'll put up with me. Think we'll have to watch her – she doesn't stand for any nonsense.'

Ellen stood in front of the fireplace with her arms folded, watching them. 'Good. That's exactly what you need.'

Fraser handed over the sheet of paper to her. 'If Miss – if Grace decides she likes the look of the place, can you ask Jack to take care of payroll and the usual?'

Grace chewed her lip. *Why not*, she thought, *why not? He's clearly as mad as a hatter, but if it gets me out of Mum and Dad's way, I can put up with anything for a while, and I can find out about the brooch later.* 'It will depend on the accommodation,' she said, straight-faced.

'Ellen will show you the cottage.' Fraser stood and offered Grace his hand. 'I hope to see you again. Do you have to give notice anywhere?'

'I have a commission to finish. If I were to take the job, shall we say a month?'

'Good. How does the first Monday in Feb, ten a.m. sharp sound?'

'Ten o'clock?'

'I'm writing my memoirs, Miss Manners, not building widgets.' He gestured that Grace should follow Ellen through the house, and closed the study door behind them.

'Do you plan to publish the book?'

Fraser laughed. 'I can't imagine my life is of any great interest to anyone but myself and my family.' Their footsteps echoed as they walked through the hall and Grace tucked her coat tighter around her. Fraser gestured at a painting of Jack as a child. 'No. It's for the future generations, so that they know where they came from.' He cradled his hands. 'I was a war baby . . .' He paused at the look on Grace's face. 'The Great War, my dear. No need to look like that. I look rather good for sixty-four, not like an addled thirty-something.'

Grace cleared her throat. 'Of course.' Ellen pushed open the heavy baize-lined door to the kitchen corridor and they followed her.

'I have certain questions about my life, that is all, and I am trying to solve them now that I have time on my hands. Jack can give you a full job description if you need one, but I will need you for a few hours a day. The rest of the time you can help around the estate, drive me occasionally—'

'You don't drive?'

'Never had to. You can walk the dogs, exercise the horses.'

'Horses?'

'You do ride?' A sleek grey cat jumped down from the old turquoise sofa by the Aga and rubbed up against Fraser's fur boots, purring. He leant down and scooped the cat into his left arm, lifting his chin as it nudged his jaw with its nose. 'It's never too late to learn new tricks.' He turned to Ellen. 'Do you have the key to the gamekeeper's cottage?'

'Yes, dear. It's somewhere here.' She sorted a hoop of keys hanging by the back door. 'I'll come over and let you in. The lock can be tricky.'

'Good. I hope we'll meet again,' he said to Grace, shaking her hand. Fraser turned back to the corridor, the cat slipping like mercury from his arm to the floor. 'There you go, Smokey.'

'We had a Bandit,' Ellen said to Grace, 'but he wandered off, as cats do, or the fox had him.' At the sound of the hall door closing, she nudged Grace. 'That's a good sign he wants you to see the cottage. I knew he'd like you.'

Grace stepped gingerly across the snow-muffled darkening stable yard following Ellen's hunched figure. She pulled a small torch from her pocket and swivelled it on. Ellen glanced over her shoulder in surprise.

'Good. If you're self-sufficient that will serve you well here.' The sleety rain beat down on them. A short way from the yard the paved road ran off into a wild and overgrown track. 'Here it is.'

Grace lifted the torch – she saw a small pink cottage. *Two up, two down, if that, but enough.* 'You're lucky, the last tenants moved the bathroom indoors.' Ellen unlocked the door and shouldered it open, the wood sticking against the flagstones.

'Selling it on its strong points, are you?' Grace said casting her a sidelong glance on the way past. The electric light flickered on from a bare bulb hanging over the centre of the room. The cottage was bitterly cold and it smelt musty, un-lived in, but Grace saw the wood-burning stove immediately, and imagined log fires. She walked back past Ellen and saw the kitchen had the basics – stove, sink, an old dresser in need of sanding down. She ran upstairs, the steep wooden steps creaking under her feet. *One – two bedrooms – enough.* The second bedroom was little more than a box room, but someone had built a cosy little cabin bed against one wall, and Grace could already picture Harry's pink rose quilt and cuddly toys in place.

'There's room for Harry, it's perfect,' she said.

'Harry?'

'My daughter – she's ten.'

'She never is?' Ellen said. 'You must have been a child—' She caught herself. 'Are you on your own then, love?'

'Yes. Yes, I am.' The tone of Grace's voice stopped any more questions.

'There's a lovely little village school for your daughter. Both of mine went there,' Ellen said. Grace peeked into the bathroom. 'It looks a bit grim now, dear. The last girl wasn't much for housework.' Desiccated flies lay in the bottom of the limescale-rimmed bathtub.

'It's nothing that a good clean can't handle.' Grace was already imagining long, hot soaks after Harry was asleep, candlelight, the scent of lavender.

'All right,' she said to Ellen. 'If Fraser wants me, I'm game.'

'He will be pleased.' Ellen paused. 'I'm sure we all will be.'

The sleet and rain beat down on the roof above them. *If he wants me? What am I doing?* Grace's hand settled on the diamond brooch in her pocket. *All I came here for was some answers.*

Jack paced across the estate office, shrugging off a mud-splattered Barbour jacket as he talked. 'No wonder one of the horses nearly got out onto the Birdham road this morning. The timbers are rotten, but I think the fence will hold for tonight.'

'Binder twine won't last. Them 'orses are taking lessons from

'Oudini.' Cy, the gardener, stretched back in the threadbare chintz armchair by the fireplace, deftly rolling a cigarette, a leather Stetson tilted back on his head. An eyepatch covered one eye, and his half-drunk mug of tea steamed on the table beside him. He licked the paper and pulled a stray strand of tobacco from his black moustache. 'Don't take much to get through a rotten fence. Reckon that whole stretch'll need replacing come the Spring—'

'Like everything else around here, Cy.' Jack stood looking at the old map of the estate pinned to the wall, his hands on his hips. He took down a clipboard from the wall and crossed 'feed', 'hay', 'cash and carry' off the to-do list. He thought for a moment and scribbled 'accountant', 'bank', on the bottom, and hung it back up. He ran his hand through his wet hair, shaking it dry. 'Is Fraser still interviewing?'

'What's she like, Miss Convertible Beetle?' Cy tilted back his hat and smiled at Jack's expression. 'Better-looking than the last one, then?'

'Did you tow her car down into the yard?'

'Yep. No sign of that dog of hers.'

Jack paused, thinking of the way he had seen Grace striding towards him out of nowhere like the road was a catwalk, calling after the dog. He saw her stop, raise her fingers to her lips – her whistle was surprisingly strong and true. She walked with determination, confidence, until she hit the ice. From a distance she looked like she was dancing. He felt laughter bubbling up inside of him again. *Grace*, he thought.

'I know that look.' Cy's eyes crinkled. 'You're soft on her.'

'No I'm not. She was . . .' He shook his head. 'She was stuck, I gave her a hand, that's all.'

'Do you good to have a bit of fun.'

'Nah. She's not like that.' Jack stuck his hands in his pockets, shrugging off Cy's comment. 'Can you unload the Land Rover before you go? I don't know how long the lorry drivers' strike is going to last, but I've got enough feed in to see us through, hopefully. There's a fresh load of hay in the trailer, too.' He looked up as he heard shouts from the house drifting across the yard. 'What now?' he said under his breath, reaching for his boots. Cy flung open the office door.

'What on earth?' Cy said. There, in the shadows by the kitchen porch, a dark shape writhed. Grace and Ellen were walking back from the cottage and she swung the beam of the torch across the sleet like a searchlight. They saw two pairs of eyes glow, one on top of the other.

'Damn it,' Jack said, struggling into his boot. Biba stood placidly, her nose in the air as Jagger pumped his scrawny hips, his front paws wrapped around her neck. 'Get off her! That bloody dog is smiling.'

'Biba!' Fraser called from in the house. He strode out into the yard, buttoning his dinner jacket.

'Biba!' Jack yelled, breaking into a sprint.

'Jagger, get down! I'm so sorry,' Grace said.

'Sneaky bugger. I looked everywhere for him,' Cy said, his voice tinged with admiration.

'He's yours, Grace?' Ellen began to laugh.

'It's not funny,' Fraser said, and folded his arms. Gold cuff-links glimmered at his wrists in the half-light. 'Jack, I told you to keep an eye out. Every dog in the neighbourhood has been sniffing around her this week.'

'I'm so sorry,' Grace said again, certain that it was over before it had begun. The dogs carried on regardless, Jagger's eyes narrowing, blissful.

Fraser flung up his hands in defeat. 'Luckily I've always liked lurchers, and this chap obviously has more brains than most if he managed what many have tried.'

'Can't you turn the hose on them?' Ellen asked Jack.

'No way. They could be tied. We'll just have to wait.'

'We don't want to damage his – ah – doghood, do we?' Fraser turned to Grace and offered her his hand. He smelt of fresh cologne, and in a dinner suit, with his hair freshly brushed,

43

he seemed to her suddenly every inch the retired diplomat, sharp and urbane. 'So? What did you think of the cottage?'

'It'll do.' She held his gaze and smiled. 'It's perfect, thank you.'

'Welcome to Wittering Manor, Miss Manners.' He thought for a moment. 'Is that really your name? God, what a burden to be good all your life.'

Grace laughed but she suddenly saw the truth. *That was exactly what Mum hoped for, and I disappointed her again and again.*

Jack stepped forward as Jagger finally dismounted. 'Go on, you've had your fun.' Grace dragged the dog back into the car by his collar.

'That's it, my friend. Time for the snip,' she said.

'Wow, remind me never to step out of line.' Jack folded his arms.

Biba glanced imperiously at them before trotting into the house.

'We shall see in a few weeks if your hound lives up to his namesake's virility,' Fraser said to Grace.

'Thank you for being so understanding.' She looked from Fraser to Jack. 'And thanks for fetching the car.'

'No problem,' Jack said, opening her door for her. 'Drive safely. No stopping for a quick hike, OK?'

'OK.' She smiled up at him as she started the car. 'See you in a month.'

They watched her drive away, the bubbling engine note of the old Beetle fading into the night. 'Are you happy?' Jack said to Fraser.

'She's the one. A breath of fresh air, and she didn't lose her step once in spite of my little performance.'

'Where is she from, though?' Jack said. Ellen searched in her pocket, and handed him the sheet of typed paper. 'Jeweller? *Mother?* What about a proper CV or references?'

'Don't need them,' Fraser said.

'Are you sure?'

'Well, they didn't do much for us with the other girls, did they? Frankly, I don't give a fig if she's been to Lucie Clayton's or not.'

Jack shook his head. 'Not bad, impregnating your boss's pedigree Afghan during your interview. Talk about making an impression.'

'Grace didn't do it personally, Jack,' Ellen said, laughing.

'You know what I mean.'

'Man, did you see the look on that dog's face?' Cy said.

'Ecstasy. Those were the days.' Fraser sighed.

'There's life in you, yet.' Jack lifted up the collar of his coat. 'Right, I'll send the car round to the front door for you.'

'Come on, Fraser, you'll catch your death out here without a coat,' Ellen said, ushering him into the house.

'Don't get him started on the prophecy,' Jack called to her.

'Lord, I'd quite forgotten. This is the year, isn't it?'

'I shall be lucky if I see another Christmas, Ellen,' Fraser said as they walked to the kitchen.

'Poppycock,' she said, rubbing her hands together. 'Is that what writing your memoirs is all about?'

'I simply want to tie up all the loose ends, before it's too late.' He glanced back, watching Jack walk away across the yard. 'And I think Grace is just the person we need to do that.'

4

Grace clicked the cover of the cassette player closed and shut her eyes, a gentle hiss filling her mind as the tape spooled round. The gale rattled the windows of the workshop, sleet lashing down. She was grateful for the loan of the space in Ben's Andrewsfield Antiques Centre to work on Margot's ring, but the mess, the careless way the tools had just been thrown around, annoyed her. It was cosy enough, with the old Calor-gas heater burning in the corner, but she thought of her own workshop, the bright, clear spaces in the room above the shop overlooking the cathedral square in Winchester, and her heart filled with longing. *Beggars can't be choosers,* she thought, remembering Fraser's words. She rolled her shoulders and tapped her thumb on the workbench in time to the opening bars of 'One Way Or Another'. The music drowned out the hum of voices from the antiques centre, the noise from the streets of the Hampshire market town, and she focussed on the work ahead.

She spun the stool round to face the workbench and pulled the magnifying lens closer. From a padded envelope stamped with her old logo 'GM' and two mermaids, Grace tipped out the box containing Margot's unfinished ring. It had come back that morning from the Goldsmiths' Company assay office in London, with its hallmarks in place. Grace slid the ring over a bench pin and inspected it closely, looking for any changes to the gold caused by the impact of the hallmark, any alterations she needed to make. It felt good to see her mark 'GM' next to the metal and year marks on the ring. *Just like old times,* she thought. She rifled through the tools and found an emery cone, sanded the gold gently. Grace studied the ring closely, her kohl-edged blue eye huge, magnified, blinking above it. Margot had asked for a gypsy setting – more of a cocktail ring than a design that might pass for an engagement ring. *Perhaps that's deliberate,* she thought, wondering why her grandmother was so set against marrying.

Grace had fashioned a wide gold band and the stone would lie flush with the gold, baguette diamonds salvaged from a pair of Ben's cufflinks flanking the garnet. Grace had reshaped the stones herself. It was the part of the process she loved the most. She could look at rough gem material and know instinctively the cuts to make to set the fire free. The garnet flared as Grace unrolled the leather pouch and moved it to the light. *Who sent you?* she thought. Every night when she woke at four, she ran through the possible names and the reasons they might have taken the stones, her mind running in circles until she slept again, exhausted, just before the alarm. Now she checked the size of the stone against the ring, then tucked it away. *It's hopeless*, Grace thought, reaching for the mandrel. *It could be any one of the people at the party that night, or someone they talked to. A lot of people envied Sam, or had it in for him.* She slid the ring down the tapered spindle, checking the size was perfect. *But why are they doing this to me?* Her brow furrowed at the thought of the eleven empty spaces in the little box and the months to come. *Stop it,* she told herself, and she cricked the tension from her neck, rolling her shoulders, ready now to finish the ring.

All the hours of sculpting the model, melting the gold, working the ring into shape, had led to this. Grace felt the familiar rush of excitement at the thought of setting the stones, finally, in the finished design. As she polished the ring on a buffing wheel, the hands of the clock wound on unnoticed and the last customers drifted out to the street from the antiques centre. She dipped the ring into acid for a final clean and rinsed it under the tap.

'Right,' she said aloud, once the finished ring was clamped on the setter's block, and she had given it a final polish with chamois. 'Let's see how you look.' She breathed deeply and reached for the stones with a steady hand, dropping them into place. Beneath the magnifying lens, she carefully folded the edges of gold over the stones to hold them in place with a blunt pusher. The garnet's fifty-eight facets shimmered, brilliant in the light, flanked by two simple diamond bars.

'Oh, it's beautiful,' Ben said, leaning over her. 'Margot will be thrilled.' Grace jumped and dropped the pusher. 'Sorry, my dear. I didn't mean to startle you.'

'I'm – I'm just a bit jumpy at the moment.' Grace wheeled the stool away from the workbench. 'Hello, darling,' she said as Harry swung her satchel to the floor. 'Is it home time already? How was your day?'

Harry shrugged, and settled on her mother's lap. She put her textbooks down on the worktable. Cilla had helped her cover them in remnants of wallpaper, and they were a kaleidoscope of swirling pink and purple flowers. Grace hugged her, snatched a quick kiss. The smell of her daughter's blonde plaited hair – warm, biscuit dry – reminded her of school. At ten, Harry was almost as tall as her mother. She wondered sometimes how long it would last, the easy way Harry would cuddle up beside her on the sofa at night, how long she had left of the child in her daughter.

'It was OK.' Harry pulled a face. 'We won at netball.'

'Well done. Were you goal attack again?'

Harry nodded. 'I'm starving.'

'I thought I might take you both out for tea?' Ben said.

'Please can we go to Alice's?' Harry jumped up from her mother's lap.

'Splendid idea,' Ben said. He watched as Grace lifted the ring from the clamp and slid it into a velvet box. The lid closed with a satisfying click and she handed it to him. 'Thank you,' he said. 'Margot loves the design. I said to her last night, if I get out of line it can always double as a knuckleduster.'

'Yes.' Grace looked him in the eye. She had always had her reservations about Ben, but had kept them to herself. *It's none of my business. If he makes Gogo happy, that's all I care about.* 'Better behave yourself then, hadn't you.'

'Of course, of course. Now, what do I owe you?' He reached in his breast pocket for his wallet.

'Nothing,' Grace said. She swung her patchwork leather bag over her shoulder. 'You gave me all the materials, and the garnet is my present to you both.'

'Grace, you must at least let me pay for your time?'

'I won't hear of it,' she said, gently pushing away the money he was trying to give her. 'The truth is, I've loved working on the ring.' She glanced around the workshop. 'It's the first time I've felt like making a new piece.'

'See? Didn't I tell you you'd want to create again, in time? You're an artist, Grace.'

They walked on through the antiques centre, past the pottery studios and furniture stalls. A stooped woman in a lavender nylon housecoat pushed an old Hoover backwards and forwards across the faded green carpet lining the aisles. Grace nodded in farewell at an artist lifting canvases back into his shop for the night. The stalls in the heart of the hall were closing down, lamps in the glass cases blinking out one by one.

'Frankly, I wish I could kick the chap out and give you the workshop space,' Ben said quietly, 'but his lease is paid up until the end of the year.'

'Thanks, Ben, but I'm starting a new job soon.'

'Ted told me. A secretary?' He looked at Grace with such pity that she had to turn away.

'I'm not proud,' she said, smoothing down Harry's hair. 'Harry and I are starting over, aren't we?' She smiled, thinking of Jack and the brooch. 'Besides, it should be interesting.'

'We're going to have our own cottage, too!' Harry said. 'Mum's going to paint my bedroom.'

'I'm sure you'll have a grand adventure.' Ben pushed open the heavy door to Andrewsfield high street and let the last people file out into the night. 'I'll see you in a minute. Don't get cold – why don't you go ahead to the café while I lock up?'

Grace and Harry walked on along the slushy, dark pavements, headlights washing the road. Harry chattered on about her school friends, about her homework, skipping on and off the kerb, her shoes splashing in the gutter. Grace found her mind drifting. *What would it be like?* she wondered, imagining setting up again in Ben's antiques centre. It was a far cry from her elegant shop in Winchester. She still avoided walking through the cathedral close when she was in town. It was a hairdresser's now, apparently. In her mind, she began to picture the jewellery she would craft, delicate filigrees of

49

gold, the dazzling colours, the fire of the gems. *If I can get enough cash together for a bit of gold and silver, I could try, couldn't I? Maybe I could ask a few old clients in London if they'd take something on sale or return . . .*

'Are you all right, Mum?' Harry said quietly. 'You look sad.'

'I'm fine, darling,' Grace said, hugging her close. 'Just thinking. Isn't it cold? Let's get inside.' She shouldered open the door to the café and a warm smell of toasted teacakes and coal fires embraced them. Red-and-white check tablecloths covered rattan tables, each with a polished green pepper pot and fresh flowers at its centre. Grace and Alice had been friends since meeting at drama classes in Andrewsfield as teenagers, and the café had all the theatrical flamboyance of its owner. Alice had commissioned a young art student to paint a mural based on the original Lewis Carroll illustrations, and the Mad Hatter's tea party played out on the walls behind the customers, while the caterpillar looked down benignly from his toadstool above the fireplace. A couple of young girls sat in the wicker peacock chairs beneath him, flicking through a copy of *Jackie*.

'Hello, girls,' Alice said, sweeping Grace and Harry into her arms. A pair of tortoiseshell glasses resting on top of her head held her glossy black bob back from her face. She wore a purple and green flowered apron with 'Looking Glass Café' printed in swirling white letters across her ample chest. 'You look frozen, the pair of you. There's a table free over by the fire. Why don't you go and get comfy, Harry? There are some crayons on the dresser over there. Do me one of your lovely pictures for the kitchen?'

Grace watched Harry's face light up. *I miss that smile*, she thought. *Sam's smile. His dimples, his charm. But none of his coldness.* Grace remembered how well he hid it, when they were first together. *At the end, it was as if he couldn't be bothered to hide any more.*

'Grace?' Alice said, touching her arm.

'Sorry.' She jumped. 'Miles away. I was just thinking that I can't believe it's seven months since Sam went.' Grace glanced over at Harry. 'Al, do you think she's OK? I mean, I worry what all this has done to her. I mean, she's lost her dad, and her home—'

'She has you,' Alice said firmly. She leant closer to Grace and whispered, 'If you ask me, she's better off without Sam. I know I shouldn't speak ill of the dead ...' Alice raised her hand to stop Grace. 'I know you'll defend him still, but you're my best friend. I know you. I know him. *Knew* him,' she corrected herself. Alice set a clean cup on the counter. 'Now, what can I get you? The usual?'

'Don't suppose you've got anything stronger than Earl Grey?'

'Are we celebrating – or is it one of those days?'

'Celebrating.'

'Well, in that case ...' Alice winked and ducked down behind the counter. She poured them both a coffee and added a shot of whisky. 'This will warm you up,' she said, handing one to Grace. 'Cheers. So, what's new?'

'I've got a job.'

'That's wonderful! Which jewellers?'

'I'm going to be a secretary.' Grace sipped the coffee, scalding her mouth.

'Aren't you a bit overqualified?'

'I just said to Ben, I think it will be interesting.' Grace couldn't help smiling as she sipped her drink.

'Graaace,' Alice said. 'What aren't you telling me?'

'What do you know about the Strattons?'

'You're going to be working over at Wittering Manor?' Alice raised her eyebrows. 'You don't see much of them in the village. Never did, even when I was growing up. Fraser Stratton was overseas a lot, I think, and Jack—' Alice paused as Grace glanced at her. 'Ahh – you've met Jack, haven't you?'

'Maybe.'

'I heard he was back. Good on you.'

'I haven't done anything!'

'My love, you're only twenty-nine. After all you've been through, it's high time you moved on and got on with your life.'

'It's too soon.'

'Nonsense. Sam gave up on your marriage long before he left.'

'He didn't leave,' Grace said quietly. 'He killed himself.'

'Oh, Gracie,' Alice said, squeezing her hand. 'You deserve to be happy.' She sighed and rolled her gaze to the ceiling. 'Jack Booth. He didn't go to the village school, but all the girls fancied him rotten. You'd see him out riding when he was at home. You know he's a big polo player?'

'Is he?' Grace stepped aside to let a couple pay and leant against the counter waiting for Alice to be free.

'I can't believe you're going to be working up at the Manor,' Alice said, closing the till. 'You know he's married? Jack, I mean.' *Of course he is*, Grace thought, trying not to show her disappointment. 'He was in Argentina, married to some lucky woman, last I heard, then he showed up at the pub in West Wittering a few months back. Rumour has it they split up, that's why he's come home.' Alice nudged her. 'Maybe you can cheer each other up.'

'I don't need cheering up. I'm fine.'

'Course you are. Look, you don't have to pretend with me.' Alice wiped down the counter. 'God knows, you've propped me up enough times over the years, and there's no shame in asking for help once in a while.' She leant towards her. 'If you need any money, I've got a bit tucked away . . .'

'No, I couldn't. But thank you.' She glanced down at the floor. 'You know me, I've never liked to owe anything to anyone.'

'I know, I know. It's not easy for anyone right now. You've just got to look at the news. It's enough to make anyone top themselves.' Her cheeks flushed as she realised what she had said. 'Oh God, I'm sorry!'

'No, it's fine. I'm sick of people not knowing what to say to me.' Grace shrugged off her poncho and hung it on the bentwood coat stand, running her hands through her hair. 'I know they're trying to be kind, but I just want to feel normal again.'

'Any word from the police? Have they . . . well, have they found anything?'

Grace shook her head. 'I rang them again this morning. They just said the same as usual – if there's any news, they'll let me know.' Her head fell. 'It's so hard, Alice. I'm just in limbo, I can't let go, not really.'

'I know, love.'

'They said to me that if there's been no contact in seven years, they'll declare him dead.'

'You can't be serious. Seven years?'

'Five years and they can officially say I was abandoned, so I can get a divorce.' She hugged herself. 'I can't . . . the thought of living like this for another year, even. Everyone says I should move on – you, Gogo, Mum and Dad. But I don't know how when I don't know what happened. How can someone be here one minute and then just disappear? It's unbearable.' Grace thought of her conversation that morning. The policeman had been patient with her.

'Ah, Mrs Morgan,' he'd said, a note of weariness in his voice.

'I'm sorry to bother you again.'

'It's quite all right. This is a distressing time for you.'

'Is there any news?'

'We would let you know as soon as we hear anything. I take it Mr Morgan has made no contact with you?'

'No. I can't— What am I supposed to do? We put up posters everywhere we could think, put ads in all the papers. I just can't stand doing nothing.'

'I understand. It's a horrible situation. If it's any consolation you are not alone. Over 200,000 people are missing in the UK every year, Mrs Morgan, for one reason or another. Of the cases I have this month, many of them have loving families like yours.' He paused. 'In cases like this where, from the evidence, the note he left, it is fair to conclude that Mr Morgan took his own life, and there is no estate to speak of, no life insurance—'

'I wish. I thought Sam had been paying the premiums. There are just a lot of debts and we're bankrupt. They've taken the house already, just before Christmas.'

'Again, you're not alone.' The policeman exhaled, his tone softening. 'I'd prepare yourself to try and move on with your life. I've seen whole families implode when one member goes missing. It's the aftershock, a ripple effect if you like. Think of your future, Mrs Morgan.'

'I feel like I've been going mad,' Grace said to Alice. 'One minute I'm upset, thinking about how desperate he must have been and how on earth I'm going to cope, and the next I'm so angry that if he walked through that door right now I'd kill him.'

'You have every right to feel like that. Do you want my advice?' Grace nodded. 'I know it sounds tough,' Alice said gently, 'but he left you either way.'

'He was under such horrible pressure. Towards the end, he wasn't himself at all. I don't know what happened. We had always been a team, you know, working to sort it all out. But it was as if he gave up.' She paused. 'He was hiding something, I know. There was something he wasn't telling me. I just keep thinking: what did I do wrong? What did I miss? There was nothing special the last time I saw him. He went out the front door in his work clothes, and I'd packed his lunch box and flask as usual, and he turned to me as he unlocked the truck . . .' Grace frowned, trying to remember. Did he look at her just a moment longer than normal? 'He said, "See you tonight, Gracie," just like always. That was it. Nothing special. No sign at all.'

'Grace, you can run yourself ragged trying to guess what was going through his mind, or you can concentrate on the here and now. Some of the best advice anyone ever gave me was to get on with what you have to hand. So many people are always thinking "what if", brooding about the past, or have their heads stuck in the clouds thinking about the future. You just do what you can now. You have to think about yourself, and Harry.' Alice hugged her. 'Listen, if you need cheering up why don't you come out tonight? My treat.'

'I don't know.' Grace was grateful for Alice's offer. *But I can't take handouts, not without being able to pay my round.* 'I start work on Monday, I've got a lot to sort out.'

'Whatever happened to you?' Alice laughed. 'We used to dance all weekend, don't you remember? I'll never forget the first night Sam saw you. He couldn't take his eyes off you. It was like you were the only girl at the party.' Alice turned away to take care of some customers, and Grace gazed out at the dark market square, at the sweeping lights of the cars heading home.

She remembered it still: 1967, the summer of love. She was seventeen, and the world seemed light and full of limitless possibilities. She had been away for most of the summer, staying with Margot's friends in Paris. She had returned to Hampshire with a new poise, a confidence she'd never felt before. It was Alice's twenty-first birthday, a few weeks before her own eighteenth, the night she met Sam. He was a friend of Alice's older brothers, and the boys had stood at the hotel bar in Chichester, drinking and talking, watching the girls dance. The room was strung with glowing pink and white lanterns, a silver key with '21' picked out in glitter dangling above the band. Grace arrived late, straight from the London train, still clutching her small white suitcase. Alice and the other girls screamed in delight, clustering around her, marvelling at her chic minidress, her elegant new hairstyle, her mousy school-girl plaits transformed into a gleaming swing of platinum hair. Grace had felt someone watching her and glanced across the room. The other boys looked awkward in their fathers' dinner suits, but Sam wore his open-necked, with a scuffed pair of tennis shoes. He was tanned from working outdoors all summer on building sites, his blonde hair bleached white. She saw him lean towards Alice's brother and say something. The boy looked over at Grace, and spoke quickly to Sam. The band began to play Frankie Valli's 'Can't Take My Eyes Off You', and Sam stared at her, his gaze unwavering, intense. He walked towards her, smiling, certain. *He chose me,* she thought. He seemed so much older, so sure of himself. She closed her eyes for a moment, remembering how it felt the first time he held her, the thrill when he took her hand in his. They danced easily together, a natural fit and rhythm to their bodies, the music swelling around them. She remembered laughing, how joyful she felt as Sam led the chorus: *I love you baby . . .*

'Mum,' Harry said, tugging on Grace's sleeve. 'Mum? Can I have another hot chocolate, please.'

'Sorry? Yes, yes, of course you can.' Grace forced herself back to the present, to the café, to Harry needing her.

'Make that two,' Ben said, his voice booming across the room. The brass bell on a long curved spiral jingled as he swept open the door and stepped down into the café, stooping beneath the beams. He unwound his scarf and squeezed his way through the tables to where Harry sat.

'I'd better go and join them,' Grace said to Alice.

'See you soon for a proper catch-up?' Alice stepped aside to let a waitress balancing a tray of steaming bowls of tomato soup and fresh bread sidle by from the kitchen. 'Grace, I am sorry for what I said.'

'What, the bit about topping yourself, or the other?' Grace tried to laugh. 'I do love you, Alice.'

'You know me, open my mouth any wider and I'll get both feet in.'

'I'm fine, I said. I'm tired of people tiptoeing round me like they are walking on eggshells.' Grace hugged her arms to her stomach. 'I'm looking forward to being somewhere where the first expression you see on people's faces isn't pity.'

'You're not going to tell them what happened, then? Don't you think it would be—'

'No. At least, not yet. I don't know if I can trust them.' *Or if they can trust me,* Grace thought, glancing across the café at the sound of her daughter's laughter. 'I've missed that. You know, she cried herself to sleep for months. I owe this to her. This is a new beginning for Harry – and me.'

FEBRUARY

Amethyst

Devotion · Intuition · Wit

5

Grace heaved the last of the suitcases across the worn stone step of the estate cottage. The snow had returned and in the evening light the windows glowed gold, a plume of woodsmoke rising from the chimney. The house smelt of beeswax polish and the rich beef stew cooking slowly in the old oven. The casserole was a house-warming present from Cilla, whose eyes had glimmered with unshed tears as she pushed the battered orange Le Creuset pot into Grace's hands when she left.

Grace was touched to find Ellen and the girls had already tidied the house and set a fire burning in the stove to welcome her. She looked out at the silent estate, bare trees silhouetted against the sunset, the first catkins trembling in the biting wind. It felt like a new beginning and she breathed the cold air in deeply. She closed the front door behind her and leant back against the post, sighing with relief. *We did it.* The thought of a quiet night in front of the fire once Harry was tucked up beckoned enticingly. *It's the first time in months I've been by myself,* she realised. The tension coiled in her chest like an overwound watch began to unspool. She heard Harry's high-pitched squeals of delight from upstairs, the sound of springs squeaking as she jumped on the bed.

Grace turned in surprise at the sound of a knock at the door. 'Come in?'

'Only me, love.' Ellen bustled through the door, her arms filled with a wooden crate of vegetables and a bottle of Bull's Blood.

'Hello, Ellen. Thank you,' Grace said. 'That's so kind of you.'

'Welcome, welcome.' Ellen heaved the box onto the kitchen counter. Grace gave her a hug. 'Goodness.'

'Thank you so much. I almost cried when I saw how lovely the cottage looked. I don't know what to say.'

'Glad you're pleased, dear.' Ellen stepped back, smiling. 'It's nice and cosy already and the damp will soon dry out now there's someone living here.' She warmed her hands in front of the log-burning stove.

'I always think houses are like people, don't you? You can tell when they're lived in by someone who loves them.'

'I'm sure you're right. Now, Jack's asked if you'd like to come over for a drink.' Grace's heart skipped. She was torn between seeing him again and luxuriating in the peace of her new home.

'To be honest, I'm shattered. I was just going to turn in for the night.'

'If I was you, I'd go over just for half an hour.' Ellen winked at her. 'Doesn't hurt to get off on the right foot, and he didn't ask any of the other girls over.' *Other girls?* Grace thought.

'Just how many secretaries has Fraser had?'

'Oh, only a couple.' Ellen hummed softly, reaching for another log for the fire. 'I'll be happy to look after your daughter. It will be nice having a little one on the estate again.'

Why would he want me to come for a drink? Grace thought. 'I suppose half an hour won't hurt.'

'Good for you, love.'

'Do I need to change?' She looked down at her jeans and boots, and adjusted the neckline of the old baggy black cashmere V-neck she was wearing, one of Sam's cast-offs.

'No, Jack doesn't stand on ceremony.' Ellen settled down in the old blue armchair by the stove. Grace ran her hands through her hair, and slicked on some lip gloss without looking in the mirror. She shrugged on her sheepskin coat and rummaged in her handbag for her perfume.

Harry skipped down the stairs, clutching a Pippa doll and

a small pink comb. 'Where are you going, Mum?'

'Just popping out for half an hour, Harry.' Grace dabbed her wrists with Opium. 'You can come if you like?'

Harry shook her head. 'I'm tired.'

Grace felt her forehead.

'You do feel a bit warm.'

'Must be all that jumping around,' Ellen said kindly.

'Darling, this is Ellen,' Grace said. 'She works for Fraser too.'

Harry offered her hand, her face solemn. 'How do you do.'

'Well, aren't you a lovely polite girl,' Ellen said. 'Now you have a look in that box on the counter there. I seem to remember seeing a packet of Spangles in among the veg.' She leant towards Grace. 'I hope that's all right?'

'Thank you. You've made a friend for life.'

'You will come back, won't you, Mum?' Harry said, tearing off the paper from the sweets.

'Of course I will.'

'I'll see you in the morning?' She hugged her mother tightly.

'Darling, I'm only going to be half an hour.'

'No, you have to say it, like every night.'

'I'll see you in the morning.'

'Love you.'

'Love you too.'

'See you in the—'

'For heaven's sake, Harry,' Grace said, laughing. 'This is getting worse.' She saw the crestfallen look on her daughter's face and hugged her. 'I'm sorry, I'm sorry,' she whispered, and kissed her head. 'You'll always see me in the morning, Harry, I'm not going anywhere. I'll always be here just as long as you need me.'

'Forever?'

'Forever.'

'Now then, Harry. Why don't you show me which boxes have got your board games in?' Ellen winked at Grace.

'Thank you for the sweets. The games are upstairs.' Harry ran up two steps at a time.

'She dotes on you, doesn't she?' Ellen said.

'She – she gets worried sometimes, lately,' Grace frowned.

'It's a big change for her, moving here. Children take a while to settle,' Ellen said, taking off her coat. 'She'll come round in her own time.' Ellen gestured at the box. 'Wasn't sure if you'd have a bottle in to take round, so I brought one for you. I don't know if you're one for wine? Mr Lloyd – my husband – likes a drop of Bull's Blood.'

Grace tucked the bottle into her fringed suede bag, and smiled, a little wistful at the thought of the cellar she had laid down in the Old Rectory. *All gone*, she thought, remembering how the arches echoed after the racks had been plundered by the receivers. 'Thanks, I'll replace it tomorrow—'

'Never you mind, love, you won't be paid until the end of the month. Think of it as a house-warming.' Grace sensed the kindness in her voice. Part of her wanted to say, '*I had a cellar full of wine, once, and a house full of antiques, and jewels . . . so many jewels. I wasn't always hard up. I worked hard for it all, and I lost it, that's all.*' But she snuffed out the flame of her wounded pride, just the whisper of her old strength rising up around her like smoke as she walked out into the night.

Grace strode down the lane, her wellington boots sinking, crunching in the fresh snow. She saw the silhouette of the old barn against the snowbound fields. The line of the roof dipped, as if it had been hand-drawn, and as she drew closer she saw that the bottom section had been plastered and whitewashed, new floor-length windows fitted between the old timbers. On the driveway, she saw Jack's beaten up Land Rover.

Grace banged the heavy iron door knocker against the studded wood door and waited, blowing on her cold hands. She could smell the rich scent of woodsmoke from the chimney and, as the door swung open, the first thing she saw was a crackling fire in the modern hearth, a beaten copper chimney rising to the rafters.

'Grace, come in,' Jack said. He was wearing a soft white shirt buttoned loosely over pale jeans, and the ends of his hair were damp from the shower still. As he held open the door for her and she stepped into the warmth, Grace caught the scent of good soap, clean skin.

'Thank you for inviting me.' She handed him the wine and pulled off her boots.

'You shouldn't have.'

'I have to admit, I didn't. It would have been a tin of beans, otherwise.'

'Mr Lloyd's finest?' Jack's eyes creased as he smiled. 'Ellen's a sweetheart.'

'Isn't she?'

'Let me take your coat.'

Grace turned her back to him and shrugged it off. She felt it again as she raised her gaze to his, a quickening. But then a burst of laughter from the kitchen broke the moment. *Of course*, she thought. *There are other people here. I'm so stupid.*

'Come on through and meet the guys. There's some wine open, somewhere.' He paused beside a low teak sideboard and sorted through bottles on the drinks tray. 'Would you like a glass – red OK?'

'Perfect,' Grace said. 'This place is amazing.'

Jack padded barefoot across the polished boards to her, the glass gleaming ruby in his hand. 'I've just finished it.' Their fingertips brushed as he handed her the wine. 'Welcome to Witters, as Fraser would say.'

'Thank you. Is he here?'

'Frase? No, poker's not really his style.'

The great room was sparsely furnished, a large, low brown sofa in front of the fire, with a Flos Arco lamp curving above it. Bookshelves lined one wall, and the opening bars of David Bowie's 'Heroes' pulsed from a record player. Grace hung back as Jack walked on towards the kitchen, wanting to take it all in, and as she turned she caught her breath at the sight of a ghostly young woman, watching her. *It's only my reflection.* Full windows lined the other walls, mirroring the room darkly.

'The views must be amazing in the daytime,' she said, following him.

'Yeah, I love it. The gardens will take a few years yet to be how I want them to, but you can see the sea on a clear day.'

'Do you like gardening?' Grace cringed inwardly. *What do I sound like?*

'Tell you a secret?' He tilted his head and Grace nodded. As he leant towards her, she felt the hair at the nape of her neck rise. 'Don't let on to this lot, but if I could do anything, I'd spend my whole time designing gardens.' He followed her gaze to the wall of windows. 'Cesca wants to do some drapes, not that anyone can see in. I kind of like it like this, simple.'

Cesca? Grace thought. 'Is that your—' She broke off as she realised her slip. *If he's split up from his wife, she'd hardly be picking out curtains for him, would she?* She felt the heat rising in her cheeks. Jack glanced up at her from beneath his fringe, and shook his head.

'Fraser's old friend. She's one of these society designers, you know? She's dying to do the Manor but he won't see it touched. She had to make do with this place. I was kind of worried it would be all swags and chintz, but she really listened.'

'It's beautiful. I was rather impressed by your taste.'

Jack laughed. 'I wouldn't have a clue about how to do this. Like I said, the garden is more my thing. You should come over and see it sometime when it's light.' He gestured for her to go through. 'Anyway, come on and meet the guys from the estate. I thought it would be good for you to meet them all before you start.' The scent of cigar smoke drifted to her, and the sound of male voices, laughter. At the heart of the dark kitchen a group of men sat in a pool of light around a circular oak table littered with beer cans and playing cards, a pile of poker chips in the middle.

'Hey,' Jack said, getting their attention. 'Everyone, this is Grace.' He introduced her to each of them, ending with a dark-haired man with brilliantined hair and an eyepatch. 'And this is Cy,' he said. 'You've already met.'

'How's that dog of yours?' Cy said, grinning, a cigar clamped in the corner of his teeth.

'Thoroughly ashamed of himself,' she said. 'Is Biba OK?'

'Never know with that one,' Cy said. 'If I 'ad to guess, she's knocked up. Hard to tell though. Stuck up, she is, looks right through you.'

'That's hounds for you,' Grace said. 'Always preferred lurchers myself.'

'Got their paws on the ground?'

'Something like that.' Jack dragged over a kitchen chair for her. 'Thanks,' she said, settling at the table.

'Hope you last longer than the other girls,' one of the men said, tossing a chip onto the table.

'Thank you. So do I.' Grace looked him in the eye.

'Is the cottage all right?' Jack said, reaching into a basket and tossing another log into the Rayburn.

'It's great, really cosy.' She gestured, self-conscious, at her jeans and old jumper. 'I was just unpacking.'

'Don't you always dress like that?' Cy's laughter creased his face. 'When Jack said the new secretary had turned up for the interview in jeans, I was curious. I thought that showed guts.'

'I'm not exactly a secretary,' Grace said carefully.

'So what are you?' A smirk played on his lips.

Grace's eyes narrowed, and she looked him straight in the eye, the table falling silent. 'I'm just making my way the best I can,' she said, her voice low and even.

'Come on, Cy. We don't need to give Grace the third degree.' Jack settled beside her, his arm brushing hers as he raised his glass to her. 'Cheers. I hope you'll be happy here.' She raised hers in return and sipped her wine. The game continued and she chatted with the men nearest to her, but she felt Jack's presence drawing her. There was a strength and ease to him that made her stomach tighten. She sensed he was completely at home in his own skin. Grace couldn't help comparing him to Sam, whose clothes, whose body, whose whole life, she realised, were trying to prove something. *The tennis shoes,* she realised. *Those bloody tennis shoes.* Her first impression of Sam at Alice's party had been of someone who was comfortable with themselves, of someone confident, who didn't care about conforming – like her. *It took me years to realise my idea of Sam didn't fit the reality. I was a kid. I fell for who I thought he was.* Memories from the past crowded in – Sam ironing a knife-edge crease into the arms of a blue shirt, his face set in fury because Grace had done it wrong, again. The shirt seemed to be flinging its arms open on the ironing board in surrender to his anger as Grace stood in shameful silence, determined Sam wouldn't make her cry. Anxiety balled in Grace's stomach, memories swirling and lurching inside of her. *The perfect life, the perfect wife, that's what Sam wanted.* She gulped down some wine, her heart racing. *He wanted to control everything.* Grace sensed Jack watching her, and she caught the concern in his expression. She smiled to reassure him and turned back, pretended to be listening to Cy's plans for the allotments. Grace glanced at Jack. She thought of her first impression of him, tested it to see if it was true: *I can breathe around him.* She felt herself relax and exhale. *All the years I was with Sam, I felt like I was holding my breath, on edge the whole time. Was everything good enough? Was I?* She glanced at Cy's flushed face, the amused look he exchanged with Jack, his darting look at Grace. She took a last sip of wine. She knew what some men could be like when they were together – she had overheard Sam and his builders talking about women often enough. She felt awkward, exposed.

'Come on then, Grace, if Fraser hasn't hired you for your typing, what has he hired you for?' the oldest of the men said.

Grace's jaw flexed at his tone. The insinuation in his comment and his lascivious look confirmed her worst thoughts and a ripple of laughter lapped around the table.

'Hey, come on!' Jack said.

'No, it's fine. I had my own jewellery company but it went bust last year.' Grace placed her glass carefully on the table, looked the man in the eye. 'If you want the whole story . . .' she said, staring him down, 'I lost everything. My business, my home, my whole life, and I'm starting again.'

'Grace, I'm sorry.' Jack glared at the man. 'It's none of our business.'

'Listen, thank you for inviting me, but I'm kind of tired,' she said. 'I'm going to go home now to unpack and I'll see you tomorrow.'

As Grace walked away, Jack scowled at the group. 'Thanks. Thanks for making her welcome. You all know how important this is to Fraser.' He caught the front door just as it was closing. 'Hey,' he said. 'Are you OK?'

'I'm fine,' Grace said, smiling. Her grandmother's voice came to her: *Smile, darling. Always smile as if you are having the most marvellous time, even if you want to scream.* She turned to him in the porch as she struggled into her boots, hopping on one leg. Jack's hair shone blue in the lantern light; his face was in shadow but she could hear the concern in his voice.

'I'm sorry. They're normally friendlier.'

I doubt that. I know that man's type – more protective of the big house and the estate than the owner. 'Sure. I'll see you tomorrow. Thanks again.'

'Listen.' Jack touched her shoulder. 'That guy's known me since I was a kid, I think he's just protective of Fraser . . .'

Grace laughed; it was as if he'd read her mind. 'That little scene had nothing to do with Fraser.'

'What do you mean?'

'Your friend's insecure, like a dog guarding a bone, doesn't like newcomers on his patch.' Grace pulled her coat closer

69

around her, shivering. 'Perhaps he thinks I'm going to seduce you and steal the estate away.'

Jack laughed. 'Seriously?'

Grace widened her eyes, smiling. 'Come on, you could at least pretend it's not that unlikely.' She nudged him, and strode off across the drive into the darkness. 'You can reassure him that romance is the last thing on my mind. Trust me, I just want to do a good job for Fraser and get back on my feet. Thanks for the drink,' she called and walked away without looking back, wondering if he was still watching her.

6

'Mum, please,' Grace said, the telephone hooked beneath her jaw.

'Absolutely not. You can't come running to us the moment you've left,' Cilla said. Grace could hear the metallic click of pins falling onto the counter as Cilla took out her heated rollers. 'For the first time in months I'm going to Winchester for lunch with the girls and your father is away on one of his defence courses. Lord knows what use that lot would be in the event of a nuclear war – they're like *Dad's Army*. He was saying if we were in Devon or Cornwall they'd barricade the motorways to stop people flooding in from the cities. What are we going to do here if they drop the bomb? Evacuate to the Isle of Wight?' The phone muffled as Cilla switched to the other hand. 'No, I'm sorry, Grace, you're on your own today. You'll just have to cope,' she said and hung up.

Grace looked at Harry, still tucked up on the sofa in her pyjamas. She was covered in red spots and calamine lotion.

'Mum, I'll be fine,' Harry said, plaiting her blonde hair, her face pale with nerves.

Grace hugged her. 'Thanks, sweetheart, but it's your first

day at the village school and I really can't send you in like this, can I?'

'I'm scared, Mum. What if they're mean, like the last school?'

Grace closed her eyes, held her closer. 'You'll be fine.' She cupped Harry's face in her hands. 'Just remember – you're a bright, kind girl. I'm sure you'll make loads of friends in no time.' Grace pulled Harry's duffle coat down from the pegs and helped her in to it.

'Will he be all right about this, your new boss?' Harry said as Grace opened the front door. A blue tit which had been pecking away at the frozen silver-top milk flew away.

'Of course he will. These things happen. I'll just have to explain to Mr Stratton.' Grace took a deep breath. 'Bring your school shoes and wear your wellies,' she said. 'Your feet will be soaked through by the time you get to the house otherwise.'

'Come,' Fraser called as Grace knocked on the study door. 'Jolly good, bang on ten,' he said without looking up from his desk. His hand was moving fast across the page, scrawling hurried notes on a yellow legal pad.

'Fraser, I—'

'Tell me about thrumming.'

'I'm sorry?' Grace was caught off guard. She held her fingers to her lips and gestured at Harry to wait. Fraser tapped the book beside him and Grace saw it was a dictionary of jewellery making. 'It's a term for buffing inaccessible areas with silk—'

Fraser snorted with laughter. 'I thought it sounded naughty.'

'Why do you ask?'

'No reason, I just like collecting words. I know nothing about jewellery making, Grace, and when I know nothing about a subject, I set out to learn as much as I can as quickly as I can.'

71

'Good heavens,' Ellen said, squeezing past them both with a tray of coffee. 'You should be in bed, Harry.'

'My daughter has chickenpox,' Grace said to Fraser. 'I didn't want to miss my first morning, and I couldn't send her in to school. I didn't know what to do except bring her with me. This is Harry. Harriet.'

Fraser looked up from his notes and burst out laughing as he saw the worried look on Grace's face. 'It's not the end of the world, is it, Ellen?' He tossed down his pen and strode over. 'Gosh, those spots appeared quickly.' He peered at Harry. 'Is it itchy?'

'It is rather,' Harry said.

'I remember. They're a right bug—' Fraser stopped himself. 'Ellen, could you take young Harry in the kitchen with you? Grace and I have work to do.'

'Are you sure?' Grace said quietly.

'Of course I am, love,' Ellen said.

'Thank you.' As the door swung closed behind them, she turned to Fraser.

'That young girl of yours is quite something,' he said.

'Harry?'

'Yes. I saw her in the stables last night, talking to the ponies. Charming girl. Most unusual eyes.' He paused. 'Once she's over the pox would it be all right with you if I start teaching her to ride?'

'I'm sure she'd love that. Thank you.'

'Very good.' Fraser clapped his hands. 'To work.'

At lunchtime Grace walked in to the kitchen to find Harry sleeping peacefully on the sofa by the Aga, curled up with Smokey. Ellen was singing along to 'Chanson d'Amour' on the radio as she bustled around, copper pans gleaming in the rack above her head, misting in the steam rising from the boiling pots on the stove. She sashayed across the kitchen swaying her hips, carrying one to the sink. 'Rat-ta-tat-ta-tat . . .' Ellen glanced up at Grace, and winked, giving a final wiggle.

'How's she been?'

'A little angel,' Ellen said, tipping vegetables into an old enamel colander. 'You are lucky. Mine were younger, but they screamed blue murder when they had chickenpox.'

'Thanks so much,' Grace said.

'No trouble at all. How was your first morning?'

'Eventful.'

'You look shattered. Don't you let him boss you around, dear. Now, will you be having some lunch with us?'

'I don't want to put you out.'

'I cook every day.' Ellen placed a pile of plates on the table. 'Fraser won't be in, but Cy and some of the stable lads will be along.'

'Let me lay up.'

'Oh it is nice to have someone who mucks in around. The last girl expected to be waited on like Lady Muck. Set for six of us today.'

'I hadn't expected this.' Grace laid out a plain white plate and a glass tumbler in each space on the scrubbed pine table. She reached for the old wooden caddy and counted out six forks and bone-handled knives.

'The Strattons have always taken care of their staff. Didn't you realise that we all have the run of the estate? He's never had children of his own, so he lets the families use the grounds, the pool and the tennis court.'

'Is that why everyone is so protective of him?'

'I heard you had a bit of a run-in with the lads.' Ellen set down a salt and pepper grinder and whispered, 'Pay no mind to them. Fraser has some liberal notions if you ask me, but he has a good heart and they're loyal to him and to Jack, that's all, especially after what Jack's been through lately.' Grace waited for her to explain. 'I'm not one to talk out of turn . . .'

'Of course not.'

Ellen glanced at the kitchen door to make sure no one was

coming yet. 'After school he went off round the world, bit of a rebellion, really. Fraser wanted him to go to university, I think, to learn how to run the estate. Jack travelled for years, did all sorts, worked on a sheep farm in Australia, crewed some big boat. He was proud, mind you, wouldn't take a penny from Fraser and worked his way round the world. He's only ever been interested in horses, really, wanted to be a big polo star since he was a little lad.'

'And is he?'

'Now? No dear, he's come back to run the estate. He played for a time, though, ended up in Argentina, and eventually he fell for some local girl.' Ellen leant closer. 'By all accounts, she was quite a madam—'

'They married?'

'Oh, yes. No children, thank goodness.' Ellen glanced at the door. 'I don't think she could,' she whispered, 'from what Fraser has told me. Jack brought her here once a couple of years ago, after the wedding.'

'What was she like?'

'A bit . . .' Ellen raised her nose, flicked it with her index finger. 'Too young and spoilt, if you ask me. She caught Jack at the time he was ready to settle down, I suppose.' Ellen clicked her tongue. 'But she wasn't the one. She was beautiful, of course, and thin as a whippet.'

Of course she was, Grace thought, her imagination filled by the image of some dark-haired Latina goddess. She looked down at her hands, short-nailed and toughened from the workshop. *That's the type of woman Jack likes?*

'I didn't take to her. Jack had always wanted a family, but he stood by her. Then she broke his heart, she did.' Ellen wiped some crumbs from the table. 'I don't know the details, but he came home a few months ago now, and they are divorcing. We're like one big family, you see. Jack's been hurt and the lads are just looking out for him.' She glanced up at the sound of voices, and nodded her head in greeting as a group of men came in from the yard, kicking their wellies off in the boot room. 'You'll grow to liking us, I hope,' she said, patting Grace's hand. Cy dumped a radio with a long aerial down on the table, and the men crowded round. 'Get that filthy thing off my clean table,' Ellen said, flicking it with her dishcloth. 'Whatever have you got now?'

'CB radio,' Cy said. 'Traded it with a mate for a bit of you know what.' He tapped the side of his nose and glanced at Grace uncertainly.

'Is that like *Smokey and the Bandit*?' Grace said.

'That's right.' Cy held out the handpiece to her proudly. 'Have a go, but don't use your real name, mind.'

'Thanks.' Grace raised her eyebrows at Ellen. 'Hello, hello. This is . . .'

'Rubber ducky!' Ellen whispered.

'This is rubber duck, over.'

They waited expectantly, the radio crackling.

Cy shrugged. 'Yeah, well it will be better when everyone gets them.'

Jack walked into the kitchen and swung his waxed jacket over the chair at the end of the table. He nodded at Grace and poured himself a tumbler of water, drinking thirstily. His hair, wet with rain and sweat, stuck to his forehead, and his jodhpurs were streaked with grass and mud. 'New toy, Cy?'

'You'll be glad of this if they drop the bomb, I tell you.' Cy switched it off.

'That and the bunker he's building,' Ellen said. 'Now get it out the way, Cy.' She placed steaming bowls of carrots and peas on the table. The willow-pattern china was chipped at the edges, winter sunlight spilling through the windows picking out the bright orange and green of the vegetables against the fine blue pattern.

'Dolly won't have it in the house, neither,' Cy said. 'All right if I rig it up in the shed down the allotments?' he asked Jack.

'Sure.' Jack pulled out his chair, the feet dragging on the flagstones. 'Could come in handy for your business.'

'Shh,' Cy frowned, nodding quickly at Grace.

'What else have you got in that bunker?' Ellen said, dishing up the cottage pie.

'This and that,' Cy said, passing the plate along.

Ellen settled down next to Grace. As they chatted through the meal, Grace glanced up at Jack once or twice. *I feel just like Harry: I'm the new girl at school.* She noticed the way the men joked easily around Jack, his natural authority. She heard Harry stirring, and she pushed back her chair, dabbing her mouth with her napkin.

'Excuse me,' she said. Ellen began to clear away the plates and the men milled around, refilling their thermoses with tea from the urn, ready for the afternoon's work. Grace sat beside Harry, and stroked her hair away from her hot forehead.

'Hello there,' Jack said, walking over.

'This is Harry,' Grace said.

'I know. How are you feeling?'

'I picked a good day to get chickenpox,' Harry said.

'Poor old thing.' Jack squatted down on his heels by the sofa.

'I'm sorry, I won't normally be bringing her in of course.' Grace glanced from Jack to Harry, wondering when they had met.

'No problem.' Jack smiled. 'When you're sick, you want your mum, don't you, buddy?' Harry yawned in reply, her head slumping down on Grace's shoulder.

'I do like to see a big strong man who's good with children,' Ellen said, bustling past with a pile of plates.

'Jeez, Ellen. You're about as subtle as Fraser's dress sense,' Jack said, standing up.

'Well, if you take my advice, you don't want to wait,' she said, dropping the plates into a sink of soapy water. 'Have them while you've got the energy still.'

'Give me a break,' Jack said, laughing. 'I'm thirty-five, Ellen.

I've got a bit of life left in me.' He glanced at Grace. 'You must have been a kid when you had Harry.' He caught her surprise. 'We had quite a conversation in the stables yesterday. She was telling me all about you.'

Grace's heart lurched. *What has she told him? Does he know?* 'If she's getting in your way, please tell me.'

'Nah, she's a good kid.' Jack ruffled Harry's hair, and zipped up his Barbour jacket. 'It must have been tough for you all,' he said gently. 'I hope this is going to be a new start for you.'

'Thanks.' Grace smiled up at him. 'So do I.'

'Jack!' Ellen called after him as he strode across the stable yard. She waved a tartan flask in the air. 'Take some tea, love. It's bitter out this afternoon.' He smiled at the concern on her face.

'You don't need to worry. I'm fine.'

'I do worry, Jack. You're like one of my own. You were just a little lad when Fraser brought you home.' She patted down the flap of his Barbour jacket, closing it against the cold. The wind whipped the gold curls framing her face. 'You were all dark looks and silences, but he won you round. He's always been good with wild things, especially if they're hurt.' She tossed her head in the direction of the kitchen. 'He's got a good heart and I knew he'd like her.'

'Grace?' Jack smiled, thinking of her wounded pride the night before, the flash of strength he saw when she stood up to the men.

'You know . . .'

'Not you, too, Ellen?' Jack laughed. 'I'm in the middle of a long and painful divorce and the last thing on my mind is romance.'

'Just strikes me you're both hurting—'

'Yeah? And that's always a great start for a relationship, right?' Jack stamped his feet to warm them up. 'I've got enough to think about with getting the estate into a good enough shape to survive the next year, let alone for the next generation. Fraser's been too busy in the last few years. We've got to adapt, move with the times.'

'It will survive, though, won't it?'

'The estate? Yeah, if I can get Fraser to concentrate on something other than his memoirs.'

'He'll settle down now Grace is here to help, you'll see. He's taken with her, I can tell.'

Jack flinched, surprised at the sudden flash of jealousy he felt. 'He's not the only one. I think you like her?'

'I do. She's the right girl for Fraser.' Ellen rubbed her hands together. 'And just so long as this book keeps him busy he'll stay one step ahead of the black dog.'

'He seems normal, doesn't he?'

'Normal?' Ellen laughed. 'Normal for him, you mean? Honestly, his dress sense doesn't improve. He dug out those horrible moth-eaten Afghan tribesmen's boots for the cricket at Burley, and I can't get him out of them now.' Ellen pulled her cardigan closer around her. 'It looks like he has a Yorkshire Terrier strapped to each leg.'

Jack laughed. 'Fraser said he played with a hot-water bottle down his pants.'

'I'm amazed he didn't catch his death, playing in the snow.'

'I think the whisky helped.'

'He was half-cut when they dropped him back,' Ellen said, growing serious. 'At least the doctor's put a stop to that.'

'I'm sure Cesca looked after him. It's the first year he's played without Alec and he didn't want to miss it.'

'Poor man. Losing his best friend has hit him hard.' Ellen shook her head. 'He's not sleeping, I know it, and he's always been a hypochondriac, but there's no pleasing him these days. Every ache and pain is a sign of impending doom.'

'Yeah, well it's the year of the great prophecy, isn't it? Fraser reckons his days are numbered. I'm sure that's what these memoirs are all about.'

'Happen you're right. Now, will you be in for supper?'

'No thanks, Ellen. I'm meeting a couple of old friends at the pub.'

'I'll put a plate in the Aga for you for later, then, just in case.'

Jack slung his arm around her shoulder and planted a kiss on her cheek. 'What would we do without you?'

'Don't you worry, I'm not going anywhere soon,' Ellen said, her cheeks flushing with pleasure.

The stable was still the place Jack loved best. The smell of warm hay, feed, and saddle soap embraced him as he dragged open the main door. Rain drummed faintly on the roof and he listened for a moment to the sound of hooves pawing at the stable floor, to the breathing of the horses, to something small scurrying along the rafters. He felt safe here. Jack heaved a burnished leather saddle into his arms in the tack room and slung a bridle over his shoulder. As he walked down the row of loose boxes, he looked up at the hayloft and pictured himself as a small, scared child Harry's age, hiding in the shadows up there twenty-five years before.

Fraser had simply let him be, had given him time to sit with his anger and grief instead of trying to buy his love with train sets and bicycles. He had told Ellen to put fresh food and water at the steps to the hayloft three times a day, and to let him be. The boy would eat if he was hungry. Fraser would sit with him at nightfall, never too close, his feet in their elegant Lobb polo boots dangling over the hayloft ladder. He told Jack all about his own childhood, his travels, his postings at embassies around the world. He always spoke gently, calmly. His voice was hypnotic. Jack often found he had drifted off to sleep, soothed by his stories. When he awoke there was always a warm blanket over him and a lantern at his side.

'You don't have to love this place as I do,' Fraser said to Jack one night, just as the ruby sun sank behind the horizon and the birds singing in the trees fell silent. 'But it's your home now, because as your godfather your parents chose me as your guardian.' He smiled at the boy. 'It's a great honour and I shall do my best to live up to that. My mother, your great-aunt, was fond of your mother. You know, you look terribly like Clemmie. You have the same colouring.' Fraser looked at the boy's black hair and widow's peak, and he paused when he saw the boy's blue eyes glaze with tears. 'You must miss your parents. I know I do. I can't pretend to know much about children, but I shall simply treat you as a young friend and I shall teach you all the secrets I know.' Fraser edged closer, as if he were confiding in him, and settled at his side. 'The world is full of marvellous things, Jack, and I'd love to share them with you.' He leant back against the wall, his movements slow, as if he was afraid that Jack would bolt. 'You'll have to go to school, of course, but in the holidays we shall have the most wonderful adventures. I can tell you like horses, but do you like boats?'

'I don't know. I never . . .'

'Well, I'll teach you how to read maps and charts, how to navigate by the stars. At home, I'll teach you to recognise every flower and bird on the estate, how to track wild animals—'

'Like wolves and bears?'

Fraser laughed softly. 'In England? Not recently, dear boy. But there are deer and foxes, all kinds of marvellous creatures.' He tilted his head and smiled. 'We'll read too, take anything you like from the library – Shakespeare, Rudyard Kipling, philosophy. We'll travel as well. Where do you want to go?' Jack started to say 'home', but Fraser interrupted him. 'We'll go to Europe and I'll teach you about art, and architecture, and show you where all the great battles took place.' He glanced at the boy to check he was listening. 'I'll teach you how to play blackjack—'

'And poker?'

'As you wish. And I'll show you how to fix a dry Martini James Bond would find acceptable.'

Jack hesitated. 'Will you teach me about girls?'

'Women?' Fraser rested his head back and gazed up at the sky. 'My boy, I can teach you everything you need to know to run this estate in time, but women . . .' He smiled. 'You're asking the wrong fellow.' His eyes were sad as he turned to Jack. 'I was raised by women, and I adore them, but I can't pretend to understand them. I've loved but one woman in my life, and I lost her. Perhaps I shall write a book about it all, one day.' Tentatively, he reached out and patted Jack's shoulder. 'Come on, let's go home.'

'This isn't my home,' Jack shouted. He blinked, determined not to cry. 'I want to go *home*, to my home, in Chicago.' His voice cracked. 'I want my mom. I miss my dad.' He buried his head against Fraser's shoulder and sobbed.

'There, there, dear boy. About time. You've been terribly brave.' Fraser stroked his back, rocking him gently. 'Let it all out, now.' He gazed out of the hayloft across the estate to where the sea glimmered, gilded by the fading sun. 'You know, we're all the same. That's all any of us want, to go home.'

7

Sunday, 18 February 1979

'Ted!' Cilla called. She sat on the sofa, her legs tucked beneath her. Her fair hair was swept up into a chignon, tendrils framing her blue eyes. She wore a sky-blue cowl-neck sweater and white flared slacks, a hopeful crocheted waistcoat disguising her waistline. On the coffee table at her side, a heart-shaped box of chocolates, half-empty, lay beside an empty glass of wine, illuminated by the light of a gold cherub lamp stand.

On the dining table, a dozen red roses bloomed their last, a petal dropping to the polished mahogany surface. The table was too large for the room, the chairs pressed up against the far wall as if they were trying to breathe in. 'Ted, it's on!'

Ted popped his head through from the kitchen, ducking beneath the beamed doorway. He was wearing a blue-and-white striped butcher's apron, the large collar of his pink shirt extending over the straps like protective wings. His cheeks were flushed from the washing up. 'I'll go and call Grace,' he said, giving a Midwinter Spanish Garden plate a final wipe. The scent of the Sunday roast lingered in the air and the heavy red velvet curtains were drawn now. Cilla had taken them up a couple of months ago and the hems bulged with folded material.

'You should have cut them down,' Margot said, waving a slender index finger at the curtain nearest to her. The gale rattled the leaded windows behind.

'The curtains? Why? This isn't forever. I don't want to tempt fate by shortening them. What if we lost this place, too?'

'You won't. Ted is cleverer than Sam. He didn't chance it all.'

'When I think of our lovely high ceilings at home . . .' She fingered the latest bruise on her forehead vaguely.

'This is home.'

'For now.' Margot paused. 'How's Grace? Is she coping with her new job – she seemed worried about something.'

'Worried? She's fine. Though it's hard to tell, she's so self-contained. I never knew what she was thinking, even as a little girl. Harry's the same. It will be easier for us all once the schools reopen – bloody lorry drivers, honestly. Thank goodness we're solid fuel here.' Cilla reached for her glass of wine and noticed it was empty. 'I don't mind looking after Harry while she's working, she's a lovely girl, but it's a bit of a houseful, and they've taken over the entire garage with all their stuff. What she's managed to move into that cottage has hardly made a dent in it.' Cilla's fingers hovered over the box of chocolates.

'Do you really need another?' Margot extended an elegant leg and slapped her thigh. 'You have to be careful at your age.'

Cilla ignored her, defiantly popping another chocolate into her mouth. 'I've no idea *what* Grace's doing out in the garage on a night like this.'

'She said she was looking for some papers.' Margot laid her head against her palm, and curled her toes in front of the crackling log fire. 'Do you really think she is all right?'

'Yes, she's *fine*. Did you see the huge bunch of white roses someone sent her for Valentine's Day?'

Margot shook her head. 'Who were they from?'

'No note.' Cilla chewed thoughtfully. 'It could be the vicar's boy.'

'Boy? He's over forty, Cilla.'

'No, can't be him. Grace was terribly rude to him at New Year.'

'No wonder. It was ghastly. He was all over her like a rash. You really mustn't try and set her up like that. She was embarrassed – and more importantly she's said she's not ready.'

'Well she's living in la-la land. She's a single mother with no prospects. It really isn't the time to be picky.' Cilla glanced up at the television as the *Antiques Roadshow* theme tune started. 'Oh, they're going to miss it!'

'Cilla.'

'Sorry, I know, I know. I'm just at my wit's end. She always thought she knew better than us, and look where that got her. I kept telling her before Christmas, just get a job, any job.' She tapped the copy of *The Lady* at her side. 'And I was right, wasn't I? Honestly, when I think of the money we spent on her education, not to mention secretarial training – at least that's come in useful, finally – but she still went and got herself knocked up.'

'Cilla, it's ancient history.' Margot's voice was sharp. 'I told her she was too young to marry, that I'll give you. Sometimes I wonder what we burnt our bras for.'

'Was that really wise, at your age?'

'Touché.' Margot raised an eyebrow. 'The past is past. She's more than capable of looking after herself, but Grace needs us now.' She watched the television as the camera panned over the Newbury Corn Exchange, showed the crowds of people queuing with their carrier bags of antiques. 'This is no time for "I told you so".'

'I told her, though. I told her Sam had stretched himself too far this time, but would she listen? Would Ted listen?' She selected another strawberry crème and nibbled the chocolate, levering a section free from the sugary centre with her tongue. Cilla glanced at Margot out of the corner of her eye and licked the chocolate. 'You've always had a soft spot for that girl,' she said, her words sticky and rich. Her gaze snapped to the television as the camera panned in on Margot's diamond brooch. 'Look at everything you've given her.'

'Which should have been yours? Are we still going to fight about that? Grace needs us, and she needs our help.' Margot raised a hand to stop Cilla's protest. 'I won't hear another word about it.'

'Grace!' Ted's footsteps crunched across the snow as he walked to the garage. 'It's on.' He saw her up ahead, silhouetted against the yard light. A fine sleet fell, sparkling across the tarnished carriage lantern.

'I can't watch it, Dad.'

Ted put his hands on his hips. 'Of course, love. I didn't think.' He smiled sadly. 'What on earth are you doing?' Grace had hold of the horns of an orange bouncy hopper and was trying to squeeze it back into the garage. The wind was whipping her hair, tendrils snaking silver in the light.

'Bloody thing,' she said, shoving hard. The cartoon face leered at her defiantly as the hopper bounced back down into

84

the yard. She kicked it, and it soared off into the shadows, Jagger in hot pursuit. Grace caught her breath and turned to her father. 'I can't get it back in. There's so much crammed into here.' She looked at the packing boxes and tea chests filling every corner, floor to ceiling. 'Our whole life, in fact.'

'Come on love,' Ted said, putting his arm around her shoulders. 'Keep it out. It would be nice for Harry to have some of her toys around when she comes over.'

'But Mum said—'

'I know you've got the cottage, for now, but I want Harry to be happy here. I've almost done building the Wendy house.'

'You're being so kind.' Grace felt her eyes pricking. She had overheard Cilla talking to one of her friends that morning on the phone. *You will watch the* Antiques Roadshow, *won't you?* Cilla had said. *I know . . . yes, I suppose so. Grace? Oh yes she's fine, and Ted's loved having them here. He's so good. He's built a little summer house down by the river. I might use it as a pottery studio eventually . . .*

'Take your time, love,' Ted said. 'There's no hurry to start again.'

'Mum thinks there is. Every little dig about the noise and mess . . .'

'Give her time. Your mum's used to having the house immaculate, and only me to look after. We've all had a lot to adjust to.' He looked up at the guttering on the garage as a trickle of water splashed onto the garage door. 'That'll need fixing.' The sleet drummed softly against the canvas roof of the Beetle. He patted the bonnet. 'At least we've got your old girl up and running again. The fan belt should do till you get paid.'

'I'm so sorry, Dad,' Grace said. She fought back the tears. 'If it wasn't for me, and Sam . . .'

'Now stop it, you hear? It's not like you to get upset.' Ted reached up and pulled the garage door down. 'It was my decision to back Sam.' The handle came off in his fingers and Ted paused, then burst out laughing. He tossed it down on the ground. 'Look, I took a calculated business risk and it didn't pay off, that's all. What's that saying of Margot's?'

'Fall down seven times, stand up eight?'

'Good advice.' He took his pipe from his cardigan pocket and sucked on the stem. 'I always said I wanted to retire to something smaller, didn't I?' He gestured with his arm at the Mill. 'Well, I've got the project I was looking for. No one wants these old places at the moment, with all the strikes and the petrol business, but I saw its potential straight away.' He looped Grace's arm in his, and they walked towards the house. 'With what I got for our place, we'll be all right for a year or so, and this will be lovely one day,' he said, looking across the untidy lawn. 'It's a much better size for me and your mum, anyway.'

'I can't believe how much you've done already. No one had lived in it for thirty years.'

'I remember coming down here with you when you were a nipper and catching frogspawn in a jam jar from the Mill pond. Do you remember? It took me right back, showing Harry the other day, and telling her all about tadpoles. It's making me feel quite young, starting over. There's not much on anyway – I was talking to one of the chaps who stayed on at the engineering firm.' They paused in the porch, the rain drumming down on the thatch above them. The snowdrops in the barrel tubs by the back door trembled in the wind.

'Mum doesn't seem to have realised how much things have changed.'

'I never could deny your mum anything, you know that.' Ted shrugged. 'She had a tough start in life, and if I can make her happy, it makes me happy.' He nudged Grace. 'Anyway, you're a fine one to talk about taking it easy. Did you find what you were looking for in the paperwork?' Grace nodded, her face etched with concern.

'Dad, I don't want to worry you—'

86

'That's what I'm here for, love. What is it?' Grace pulled a small manila envelope from her pocket. 'Not another one?' She handed the typed note to Ted and watched his face as he read. '*Devoted amethyst, free of strife . . .*' He glanced at Grace. '*Cherish one love all your life.*'

Grace tipped the purple gemstone into the palm of her hand. *One love*, she thought, her heart thumping with adrenalin. *What was it Sam used to say? 'There's only one girl for me. I'll never let you go.' It seemed romantic at first, so passionate.* She bit the inside of her cheek. *I'll never let you go . . .*

'When did this arrive? You didn't see anyone?'

Grace shook her head. 'Whoever it is, they're being careful. The envelope was tucked in that bunch of flowers that was left in the kitchen.'

'What? You mean they've been in the house? I thought it was a florist.'

'You never lock the doors, do you?'

'Well no, but don't tell your mother someone's been in.' Ted frowned. 'Who the hell is doing this?'

'I don't know, Dad.'

'It's like they're trying to court you.'

'Court me?' Grace smiled at the old-fashioned phrase. 'If that's the idea, they're doing a bloody good job of scaring me.'

'Oh love . . .'

'No, I'm fine.' Grace raised her chin. 'And to be honest, I don't give a damn. There are more urgent things to think about than someone playing – playing games with me.' Her voice caught.

'Love, are you all right?'

Grace raised her face to him, the porch light glinting on her eyes. 'It's just . . . the TV programme being on, it's brought everything back.' Grace straightened her shoulders. 'It's not fair, Dad. I'm doing my best to make a new start, and someone is dragging me back into the past.' Her jaw set. 'To hell with them.'

'That's my girl,' Ted said, stooping to kiss the top of her head.

'I thought I may as well make use of the stone. I was just getting some of my old client files out of the garage. I think I'll go up to town and see if Mr Goldstein would be interested in a new design.'

'Good for you, love. If I was you, see if he wants to buy that brooch your mother has been going on about non-stop. Use the money to start again—' Ted cleared his throat.

'Dad, don't upset yourself.'

'You're my little girl, and I hate to see you like this.' He screwed his eyes closed as he hugged her. 'I just wish I'd known how bad it was for Sam.' Grace rubbed his back. 'I'm sorry, love, you don't need to be comforting me.'

'Dad, you did everything you could. More than many, many people would have done. I mean, you lost your home too.'

'We're all right. Don't you worry. If I survived World War Two I can fight my way through this bloody recession.'

'There you are!' Cilla pulled the door open, the swollen timbers grating on the flagstones. 'You missed it!' she said, her eyes bright with excitement. 'It was wonderful. The family brooch looked stunning. I must ring Tiggy and make sure she saw it. If only we had one of those VHS players, we could have recorded it. We could have had a little drinks party, nothing big, a few select friends—' Her words cut off. 'Is everything all right?'

'It will be fine, Mum, don't worry.' Grace stepped past her, into the house. 'I've got to go up to London.'

'It's all right for some, gallivanting around—'

'Give it a rest, Cilla,' Ted said. Her words cut off at his uncustomary sharpness. 'I told Grace to sell the brooch.'

'Over my dead body!'

'Cilla. Margot gave it to her.'

'Don't we all know about *that*,' she said, storming inside. Cilla reached for the bottle of wine on the kitchen counter and refilled her glass, Liebfraumilch slopping onto the orange

Formica. She took a gulp of wine, and moved the handle of one of her Le Creuset pans fractionally on the wrought-iron stand, so that they were all perfectly aligned.

'Good for you,' Margot said to Grace as she came in. She leant against the kitchen door frame, her arm crossed loosely over her narrow ribcage. She pointed at Grace with her cigarette, a plume of blue smoke snaking into the air. 'I told you to get rid of the damn thing weeks ago.'

'But Mother, it's all we have, of Paris, of your mother—' Cilla began, but a sharp glance from Margot cut her off mid sentence. Cilla scooped up a well-thumbed Jackie Collins' from the kitchen table and raised her glass of wine. 'Well, good luck to you. No one seems to give a hoot what I think.'

'Mum, please don't,' Grace said.

'I'm going to bed.' Cilla walked unsteadily across the kitchen, swaying slightly as she negotiated the new breakfast counter that Ted had built that morning. 'No doubt you're expecting me to look after Harry when you swan off to town? Well, perhaps it's not convenient. Maybe I've got a hair appointment, or I might be playing golf with the girls.'

'I'll look after her,' Margot and Ted said together.

'Ted, you have enough on your plate here,' Margot said, watching Cilla leave. 'Grace, why don't you drop Harry round to me?'

'Or you could come and see the cottage? The estate is lovely.'

'No, I don't think so. Some paintings have just been delivered for me to restore. Harry can give me a hand with the frames.' She kissed Grace on the cheek and picked up her car keys. 'Thank my daughter for lunch, won't you, Ted?'

'Will do, Margot.'

'Are you sure about the brooch, Gogo?' Grace said to her.

'I've never been surer.' Margot cupped her jaw in her cool, dry palm. 'It's not really a brooch, anyway, darling.' Her eyes grew sad for a moment. 'As that young man on the television said, it's half a tiara. What use is that to anyone?'

8

'They've got this place tarted up like a cut-rate bordello,' Fraser said, batting a heart-shaped balloon out of his way from the hotel cloakroom. 'Valentine's Ball? Nonsense of a day if you ask me. I blame the Americans. No offence.'

'None taken. Remind me why we're here?' Jack said, buttoning his dinner jacket.

'Cesca twisted my arm – she's on the charity board. Is my dicky bow straight?' He raised his chin and Jack adjusted his tie.

'There, you look great. Talking of dickies, will Sir Richard be here tonight?' Jack asked as they walked up the wide, red-carpeted staircase to the ballroom.

'No doubt. Dicky's side of the family have always turned up for the opening of an envelope.' He paused at the table by the double doors and glanced down at the masks. 'Oh, God. Must we, really?'

'It is a masquerade ball.' Jack selected a simple black velvet mask.

'You'd think we were in Venice, not West Sussex.'

'You make me laugh. You spend half your life dressing up these days, and now, when everyone else is wearing masks . . .'

'You know me, never did like to follow the crowd. Oh, very well.' Fraser picked out a white mask and slipped it over his head. It covered all but his lips. 'How do I look?' His heart sank as he looked around the room. The ballroom's dance floor was edged with round tables of ten, draped with purple cloths. Elaborate gold-sprayed centrepieces decorated every table, and murals of Venetian masks hung from the walls. A local band was struggling its way through 'YMCA', and the dancers on the floor waved their arms in unison. 'Look at these buffoons. City money and country yobs, every nouveau one of them more interested in *noblesse* than *oblige*.'

'You're an old snob.'

'I have always detested climbers; they are quite bogus and sick-making. Talking of which, incoming on your right.'

'Jack!' a young woman called, weaving her way through the crowd. She wore a halter-neck silver evening dress and her red hair had been elaborately swept up and secured with mirrored clips. She wore a white lace mask and, as she offered her cheek to Jack to kiss, Fraser noticed her glance remained focussed on the room. 'Hello, Fraser,' she said. 'Let me show you where Cesca's table is.'

'I'm sure I shall find you,' Fraser said, executing a small bow. 'Why don't you two run along and have fun.' He suppressed a smile at Jack's wide-eyed grimace and made his way to a side room where the bar and buffet had been set up. He forced his way through the queue of people waiting to take their pick from the prawn cocktails, coronation chicken and teetering profiteroles, and leant gratefully against the bar, raising a finger to attract the barman's attention. 'Tonic water.'

'Hello, Stratton,' the man next to him said. Fraser recognised him as the hunt master. He held out his hand. 'We met at your cousin's a couple of years ago. I didn't think you were a hunt supporter.'

'I'm not,' Fraser sipped his drink. 'Sir Richard's lot are.'

'So you won't change your mind about allowing us on your land?'

'As I said last time I caught the hunt trespassing, I am far more likely to hide the fox than let you at him. I'm with Wilde: you are the unspeakable in full pursuit of the uneatable.'

The man smiled, but his eyes were hard. 'Excuse me.'

Fraser drained his glass and signalled for another. Out of the corner of his eye, he spotted his cousin bearing down on him. 'Oh God,' he said under his breath.

'Hullo, Frase,' Sir Richard Stratton said, clapping him on the back. 'Would you like a proper drink?'

'I would, but it would not like me, dear heart.'

'Ah, yes. I'd forgotten. Just the one?'

Fraser shook his head. 'Quack's orders.'

'If I'd known you were coming I'd have asked you to join our table.' He pointed across the room, and Fraser recognised several of the young people. 'The Strattons are out in force tonight.'

'How are you, Dicky?'

'In the pink.' He dug into the pocket of his blue brocade Nehru jacket, and pulled out a silver cigarette case. Sir Richard's long grey hair was swept back into a ponytail, and his salt-and-pepper beard reached the collar of his shirt. 'I've met a rather lovely young woman.'

'Another one? How many concubines does that make?'

'Frase, loosen up. They're not concubines. We all live together in harmony.'

Fraser laughed quietly. 'You amaze me. Is Lady Stratton still in South Africa?'

'Yes, in fact the boys have just been out to see her. She's perfectly happy.' Richard turned to Fraser. 'Listen, I heard you retired. Why don't you come over for dinner one night? I'm sure the girls have delightful friends we could introduce you to.'

'Thank you, but no.' Fraser picked up his drink. 'I am perfectly happy, too.'

'Now, Frase. The boys want to come down and talk to you. Is there a good time?'

'To talk about the estate, no doubt?' He gazed over at the table where Roger and Tristan held court, their braying voices audible above the music. 'Gilded youth loses its lustre not through age and trial but through apathy and smug certainty,' he said quietly. 'Roger's always assumed he'll get the title and the family cash, simply because I never married.' He had always reminded Fraser of a plump Persian cat that had belonged to his nanny. *Neither one ever knowingly turned down a good meal and they're both cruel bastards.*

'Frase, it would be good to have everything settled. After all, in your case there is no obvious heir.'

'Of course there is: there's Jack.'

'But he's not blood, Frase.'

'He most certainly is. He's a Booth, and he's my godson. If it weren't for Clemmie's family, Wittering Manor would have fallen apart years ago.'

'But he's not a Stratton. The Wittering estate may have been founded on Booth money but it's Stratton land, and Stratton company money helps—'

'We tick over,' Fraser snapped. 'I have never, ever taken more than my due from the Stratton firms.' Fraser slowly closed his eyes and counted to ten. 'You've never quite forgiven us that Clemmie chose Albert over your father, have you?'

'Daddy could have made her happy. Look at how bohemian she became after your nutcase of a father died.'

Behind his back, Fraser's fingers flicked against his thumb. He felt a cool focus. Instinctively he looked around for a weapon – the fruit scissors, perhaps? The heavy mock-Louis-XIV candlesticks on the mantelpiece? No – the heavy sash on the brocade curtain. He became quite swept away by the thought of garrotting his bloated, conceited cousin.

'Fraser?' Sir Richard pressed him. 'As I was saying, it's time for the Booth fortune to return to the family, as it was intended by our grandparents.'

'I don't think so, Dick.' Fraser's face was calm. 'I intend that Jack shall be my heir, and if you insist, I shall tell your charming sons Roger and Tristan face to face. Send them down to see me, but not at the moment. I'm up to my eyes – Ellen is away and the house is in chaos.' His lips twitched in amusement at the memory of their last meeting. *Mr Lloyd is taking me up the Black Forest for Valentine's Day, oh it will be romantic . . .*

'Of course, of course.' Sir Richard tapped a cigarette on the silver case and slipped it into the corner of his mouth.

'Allow me,' Fraser said, lighting a match from one of the books on the bar.

'Thank you.' He cupped the flame. 'We're not getting any younger, Frase. I hope you will reconsider, we have to think about the next generation of Strattons.'

'Oh, go and dance with one of your wifeys, Dicky,' Fraser said, waving him away. 'I'm bored now.'

'Bored and unreasonable.'

'I may not have the title, dear heart, but in this instance I do have the upper hand.' Fraser took his drink and walked around the edge of the heaving dance floor. He pushed open one of the doors to the terrace and stepped outside, breathing in the cold night air. A few couples were on the terrace already, kissing discreetly in the blue shadows. Fraser walked away from them towards the steps leading down to the lawns and leant against the stone balustrade, feeling the cold damp stone through the seat of his trousers.

'Penny for them,' a woman's voice said.

Fraser turned, and saw a woman dressed in a simple white Grecian dress walking towards him from the party. Her silver-grey hair was swept up into an elegant chignon, away from her high cheekbones. Her olive skin was tanned, even, the finest of wrinkles forming on her face as she smiled and lifted away a plain gold mask. 'Cesca, thank goodness for a friendly face.' He shrugged off his dinner jacket and laid it on the stone balustrade for her to sit down.

'Thank you, darling. I am glad to see you here.'

'Jack needed a wingman. Half the fillies in West Sussex are after his blood now he's getting divorced.'

'Do you like the party?' She waited for his reply. 'You think it's ghastly, don't you?' She reached for his glass and took a sip. 'Still, all in a good cause. Isn't it funny that we are now the aged hangers-on? The children forced me to come along too: "*Mum, you're on the board. When was the last time you dressed up and had fun*?" If only they knew.' She leant in to Fraser's arm. 'How are you?'

'Fine.'

'Truthfully?'

Fraser raked his hand through his hair. 'Bored, restless. Retirement is hideous, frankly. I'm trying to write these memoirs and I just don't know where to start.' He turned his face to her. 'I love that house, but I'm not used to being there all the time.'

'I know the feeling. I think the children would be quite happy if I took up bridge, or knitting. Children just want their parents to be seen and not heard at our age. I can't get used to that switch.'

'They're good kids. You and Alec raised them well.'

'It's only a year, you know,' Cesca laid her head against his. 'I thought it would get easier, but I seem to miss him more every day.'

'I miss him, too.'

'Alec was your best friend. When you think of everything we lived through together – Moscow, Washington.'

'Nostalgia is a trick, darling. They never were glory days.'

'I sometimes think no one else really knows us. All the secrets and lies.' Cesca looked at her hands. 'I don't know what's happening to the world. The Middle East, Ireland . . . It's terrible.'

'Not as terrible as this party. Listen, why don't we break out of this joint?'

Cesca's eyes sparkled. 'Do you think we could? It seems awfully naughty.'

'Go and make your excuses to your chums and I'll make an appearance at our table.' Fraser checked his watch. 'I'll be waiting outside for you in the car at 10.30.'

'Stay with me tonight,' she said, kissing his cheek softly. 'I don't want to be alone.' Her voice caught. 'I'm lonely, Fraser. I just can't bear waking alone, day after day . . .'

'I can't, darling. You know that.'

'Not even for Valentine's?'

Fraser raised her hand to his lips. 'Not even for that. But thank you.'

'Aren't you living on borrowed time?' she said, her voice as sweet and brittle as caramel. 'The great prophecy? The fortune teller in Leningrad said you'd be dead by the end of 1979. You should live a little.'

'While I can? I've lasted longer than many expected, and I always did get a kick out of tempting fate.' He smiled at her. 'You look beautiful, by the way. But then you always did.'

'I've often wondered, did you ever find me attractive, then? I mean, when Alec was still alive.'

'It never crossed my mind, because you were never available. You can always tell, somehow. I think it's like people have an inbuilt taxi light, you know? Even when some people are married it's as if they have the light on – that they're still available, if you want.' He looked into her eyes. 'Your light was firmly off all the years I've known you.'

'Alec was the love of my life.'

'You were both lucky.' He traced the line of her jaw with his index finger. 'And I feel lucky now that we can find some comfort with one another, as old friends.' Fraser kissed her cheek, breathed in the scent of her spicy perfume.

'Do you think of her, still?' Her voice, as cold as the night, made him flinch.

'Every day,' he said under his breath as he walked away. 'Every day.'

MARCH

Aquamarine

Courage · Creativity · Health

9

Grace checked her watch. Being in London again was exhilarating. Fraser was away travelling and she'd arranged with Jack to take the day off and make up the time. She'd missed the pulse of the streets, the energy, the glow of the lights at dusk. She paused on Holborn and waited as a taxi sped past, its tyres hissing on the wet road. She held the suede saddlebag to her side, and jogged across the road, her high wedges clicking on the tarmac. The hems of her bell-bottom jeans were damp from rain, and her white sheepskin coat shimmered. She felt alive and free for the first time in months.

At the corner of Hatton Garden, the windows of a brightly lit jewellers gleamed, welcoming. She paused to look at the display, one hand on the polished brass door handle. She recognised a pair of diamond earrings on the display. *They were some of the last pieces I made.* It felt like seeing an old friend. *A Good Sign, as Ben would say.* She shouldered open the door and stepped inside.

'Hello, Grace,' a young man in a purple shirt said. 'We haven't seen you for ages.'

'Hello, Maurice, how are you?'

'Not so bad. Business is tough, but we're coping. I heard you'd closed down in Winchester, I'm sorry.'

'One of those things. Is your dad in?'

'Yes, he's expecting you. Go on up.'

Grace pushed open the plush velvet door and walked through to the back of the shop. She passed a galley kitchen and squeezed through narrow corridors lined with metal shelving and packing cases. Grace paused at the mirror beside the cloakroom and checked her reflection. She ruffled her long, blonde hair, trying to bring some life to it, and swept it back from her face. *Maybe Alice is right,* she thought. *I should get a cut.*

'Gracie?' A man's voice drifted down from the first floor. 'Is that you?'

'Hello, Mr Goldstein,' she said, running upstairs, the toes of her boots tapping on the burgundy lino.

'Let me look at you,' he said, holding her at arm's length. His dark eyes were full of sympathy and concern. Grace gasped as he embraced her, squeezing the air out of her. 'Oh, my dear. I heard, I heard.' He took her by the hand, and led her into the back office. 'Come,' he said, settling her in an old bottle-green leather chair. 'Some tea? Something to eat?'

'I'm fine, really. I just had a bite.'

'But you look so peaky, my dear,' he said, falling back into the old captain's chair behind his cluttered desk. 'The last time I saw you, you were like Venus.' He mimed a voluptuous figure.

'A lot's happened since last spring.' She cut off any more enquiries, changing the subject quickly. 'I see you've still got the earrings?'

'The last ones, my dear. When those go, I'll have none of your work. When will you start again?'

'Funnily enough, I've just made a ring for my grandmother.'

'In business, I mean.' He made an arch with his fingers and leant his elbows on the desk. 'You must work, Gracie, it is the only way out of sorrow and . . .' He sighed.

'Debt? Destitution?'

'It's no laughing matter.'

'Oh, Mr Goldstein, I *have* missed you.' She leant across and squeezed his hand. 'Now, I know how busy you always are, and thank you for seeing me at such short notice.' She unbuckled the saddlebag and pulled out the Bouchet et Fils box and the manila envelope.

'What do you have for me? Not your own work?' He turned the fitted blue leather Bouchet et Fils box towards him, and clicked it open.

'No, this is my grandmother's. We're considering selling it. I thought you might like to have a look.'

Mr Goldstein reached for a jeweller's loupe and held the magnifying lens to his eye. 'Beautiful work.' He turned it over. 'Look at that attention to detail. Each hole in that filigree has been thrummed—'

Grace laughed. 'Sorry. A friend was asking about that the other day.'

'A sign of true craftsmanship. Hours of polishing that no one would ever see unless they removed the stones.'

'I always think it makes a difference to the quality of light in the stones.'

'You'd know about quality, my dear. There should be two, of course.' He traced the form of the velvet in the box. 'Have you checked to see if the other fittings are there?'

'All gone.'

'Sold off at some other desperate time for scrap, no doubt.' He set aside the loupe.

'The receipt's dated 1915. Does that sound about right to you?'

'Indeed, that places the tiara precisely. Our Mr Stratton evidently paid hundreds then, and it's worth several thousand retail now, in its entirety.'

'And the brooch as it is?'

He pursed his lips. 'What else do you have for me?' he said, gesturing at the envelope with his index finger.

'One cut gem,' she said, tipping out the amethyst onto the velvet pad on the desk.

'You cut this yourself?' He picked up the stone with a pair of needle pliers.

'Of course.'

'You've one of the best eyes in the business, Grace,' he said,

101

watching the fiery play of purples and reds. 'When I think of some of your fantasy cuts, when you give yourself free rein as a lapidarist . . . When they say phenomenal stones, they mean it with you. The spectral play of colours, of chatoyance . . .' He sighed. 'You're an artist, my dear. But art doesn't put bread on the table. I heard about your business. I'm sorry.'

'Thank you.' Her gaze was direct, determined. 'I'll build it up again.'

'One gem at a time? How much do you need?'

'How much are you offering?'

Mr Goldstein pressed his fingers to his lips. 'Gracie, I'm a businessman.'

'So am I.' Grace folded her hands and placed them in her lap.

'But we're friends. If I were you, with the brooch I would wait the market out. It's a unique piece, by Bouchet senior if I had to guess, a true artist.' He placed the diamond wing back in its box and turned it towards Grace. 'If you could find the missing wing, remount them, keep them safe in their nest for a few years.'

Grace knew the sense in what he said, but she felt the prickle of panic rising in her. She played for time. 'That's good advice. Maybe I'll wait and see what I can find out about the brooch.' She paused, tried to sound casual. 'And the stone?'

'Decorative, of course. You did a good job, as always.'

'What is it worth?'

'To me, as a cut stone? It's what, three carats? Lovely reddish purple.' He looked through his jeweller's loupe again. 'You've really brought out the brown tones, very rare. £15 trade.'

'Come on,' she laughed. 'It's one of *my* stones. You said your-self that you've sold everything I ever made for you. That's not enough, sorry.' She began to gather up her things.

Mr Goldstein pursed his lips, thinking. 'Wait. Perhaps there's a solution. If I were to loan you the gold to set it as a ring for me? Something Art Deco, or Art Nouveau? It seems to be what all the young men are looking for these days as engagement rings. Something fashionable?'

Grace tipped out the stone again. She turned the desk light towards it. The purples and reds glimmered, light flaring from the cuts she had made. She knew, instinctively, what she would do with it, designs forming in her mind.

'Is there a workshop you can use?' he said. 'You're welcome to use ours, but I know you have your daughter in the country.'

'No, thank you, it's fine. I can manage.'

'I don't know how you do it, my dear. So strong.'

Grace felt a lump forming in her throat at his kindness and she coughed, gently. 'If I set the stone, will you pay the usual price for one of my rings?'

'Gracie, Gracie,' Mr Goldstein shrugged. 'Times are hard and I have to consider the cost of the gold. But I do love your work. So many designers think of the ring first then struggle to find the gem to fit. You always work out from the gem. I think it's why your pieces are so harmonious and just . . .' He waved his fingers in the air. 'Right.' He jotted some figures down on the blotter pad on the desk. 'If I can sell the ring for £300, minus the gold . . .' He sucked his teeth. 'As an old friend, and as you are supplying the stone, I can give you £100 cash, today.'

A wave of relief rushed through her, but she tried to conceal it.

'£200 was my usual rate.'

'Gracie, you're killing me.' He spread his palms. '£150, in cash, today. I know I can trust you.'

That's a bargain for him, but it's enough to buy a little gold or silver to start working again. She tried to look disappointed. 'As a one-off, for an old friend, you have a deal. I'll send you some sketches tomorrow for approval, and I can get the ring to you by the end of the month.'

10

The Mill House was silent but for the sound of Ted's saw out in the workshop and the steady drip of rain outside. Grace carried a steaming mug of coffee across the yard and shouldered open the workshop door, the smell of sawdust and oil greeting her.

'Dad,' she called. 'Dad?' He looked up from the saw and swung the section of cut timber clear.

'Thanks, love,' he said, flicking the saw off. Laughter from a Radio 4 programme filled the silence, the old Roberts radio on the workbench crackling. Ted lifted back his goggles and smiled at her, a pink rim around his eyes. His thick greying hair was lightly dusted with sawdust and he had a smudge of grease across one cheek. 'How did you get on?'

'Mr Goldstein wants me to make a ring for him.'

'Congratulations, love. See, you'll be back on your feet in no time.'

'I just spoke to Ben. He said I can use the workshop on Sundays.' Grace ran her hand over the smooth arch of wood Ted had just cut. 'This is looking good. How's the waterwheel coming on?'

'Almost there. I'm going to call in a few favours and get some of the lads round to help me assemble it later in the year.' Ted took a sip of his coffee and tapped the sketches he'd pinned to the wall with his index finger. 'I reckon we'll be self-sufficient if I manage to get this up and running the way I want it to by next winter.'

'I'd better get on. Harry's having tea with Margot, but I need to pick her up on the way to Witters,' she said, imitating Fraser.

'Is that what they call it? Are you settling all right there, love?'

'It's . . . different. They're more like a big family.'

'Just so long as they're making you welcome.'

Grace hugged her arms to herself as she walked back to the house. She was restless and frustrated. A kaleidoscope of coloured gemstones and designs whirled in her mind. There was so much she wanted to do. *To prove what?* she thought. The sun was struggling to bring the day to life and Grace caught a glimpse of her reflection in the glass of the back door. *I look like a ghost*, she thought, studying her gaunt face and pale blonde hair before walking inside. On impulse, she picked up a pair of kitchen scissors from the draining board. She gathered up her long hair into a ponytail and began to hack at it, inches of silver falling silently to the floor like feathers.

'What on earth are you doing?' Cilla padded into the kitchen in an old housecoat, a towel wrapped around her own hair, turban style, and the ammonia smell of hair dye trailing in her wake. 'Your beautiful hair!'

Grace turned her head, scissors poised. 'I just felt like a change.'

'Well, if you're going to do it, do it properly. You look like you've just escaped from a loony bin. Sit down.' Cilla reached into a drawer. 'I'm going to set the timer for twenty minutes. If I haven't finished yours by then, I need to go and rinse this out.' She fluffed out Grace's hair and clicked her tongue – half hung to the middle of her back, the rest to her waist. 'Let me get my scissors.' She disappeared into the laundry and Grace heard her searching around in the drawers. 'I know they're here somewhere. Your dad could do with a cut, too. Here we are.' She unfurled a roll of hairdresser's tools on the kitchen table, and took out a wide-toothed comb. 'What were you going for?'

'Shorter.'

'I know that, but what kind of shorter?'

'Kate Bush, maybe?' Grace pushed aside Cilla's Avon catalogue and reached for Harry's copy of *Look In*. She flicked through the pages. 'Sam never liked me to cut it. There – like that.'

'Why not a bit more Farrah Fawcett? Some softer layers will suit you, I think. We can keep it long enough to put up – you just need something to bring a bit of life to your face.'

'Thanks, Mum.' She sank lower in the chair as Cilla swung a nylon cape around her shoulders.

'Sit up straight, love and raise your chin.' Cilla flicked on Radio 2 and hummed along to Gloria Gaynor. 'Right. Let's see what we can do.' Grace succumbed to Cilla's ministrations. The sound of the rain on the tiles, the gentle click of the scissors soothed her, and her eyelids felt heavy.

'Why don't you come along to the Soroptimists with me tonight?' Cilla said.

'I don't think so, Mum.'

'I know you mock my hobbies, but we do good work.'

'Mum, please don't start.'

'My mother gave me little confidence in myself, I can tell you, and I rely on my friends.' Cilla clipped up the top section of Grace's hair. 'I sometimes think I did the opposite with you. You always were a headstrong girl.'

'Here we go.' Grace rolled her eyes. 'You've never forgiven me for getting pregnant with Harry, have you?'

'It wasn't how we brought you up.'

'Have you ever thought it's got more to do with your own feelings about being illegitimate?'

Cilla hesitated, then carried on cutting, snipping away at the hair. 'Save me the pop-psychology. Mother always told everyone my father died in the war, and that will do for me. She never told me the truth and now, to be honest, I don't care.' Cilla sighed. 'You could have been so much more, Grace. You had a place at *university*, for goodness sake. We never should have let you go and stay with Mother's racy friends in Paris that summer. Turned your head, they did.'

'Mum, it's ancient history. It doesn't do you any good

106

fretting about the past all the time.' Grace hesitated. 'I wish you'd relax sometimes. We worry about you, Dad and I both do.'

'Worry that I'll get depressed again, you mean?' she said, her voice brittle.

'Listen, you've had a tough time lately and I wish you'd just let up a bit. It doesn't matter what other people think. To hell with them.'

'It does matter. It matters to *me*.' Cilla tugged a comb through a section of hair. 'Grace, you have no idea what I went through as a child. The shame of all that – that poverty. Being the one at school with holes in her shoes and nits in her hair because her slut of a grandmother couldn't be bothered to stop drinking long enough to notice there was a little girl suffering.'

'I'm sorry, I didn't—'

'Meanwhile, the great *Gogo* who you idolise so much was off doing God knows what with God knows who after she dumped me with her mother.'

'But then you met Dad.'

'He was my knight in shining armour. He is, still. I don't know what I'd do without him.' Cilla brushed through Grace's hair checking the fall of the layers. 'But God, it's so provincial here. I don't know how Ted persuaded me to move to the country.'

'Dad was worried, Mum. He thought it would be a good idea to be close to your mother in case you needed help.' Grace thought of the stories she had heard of Cilla's post-natal depression, how she became agoraphobic, anxious.

'I've never gotten used to it. When I think of some of the people in the village.' Cilla clicked her tongue. 'No style, no pizzazz.' She let down the top section of Grace's hair and brushed it through. 'Always looking to find fault . . . Well, they won't with me, I can tell you.' It was almost as though Cilla was talking to herself. 'I know you think it's a joke that

I try to keep going, in spite of losing our beautiful home.' *Because of Sam, because of me*, Grace added silently. 'Well, I won't let them see me down. You put on your slap and you hold your head high.' She caught herself. 'I am glad you're working again, you know.'

'It's not much, just secretarial work.'

'At least that course wasn't a complete waste, then.'

'The main attraction is the cottage – and I'm curious to find out what the link is with the brooch.'

'What's he like, the lord of the manor?'

'Fraser? He's . . . well, he's eccentric, but kind. I'm just using the job until something better comes along.'

Cilla shook her head. 'I know you, Grace, you've never used anyone in your life.' She glanced up at the warble of the Trimphone, and hooked the receiver beneath her chin.

'Hello, the Manners' residence.' Cilla's voice went up an octave. 'Mary! How *are* you?' She carried on cutting Grace's hair. The other woman's voice was so loud Grace could hear both sides of the conversation. 'You looked fabulous at the wine and cheese on Saturday.'

'Thank you, darling. I've found the most marvellous spa. It's terribly expensive but they're miracle workers . . .'

Ding, ding. Round One to Mary, Grace thought.

'I don't know how you find the time to spend on yourself. I'm helping Ted renovate our lovely new home. Do you know the Old Mill in Exford? Well we saw it and we thought, there's a project. I always wanted a project, you know. Ted's terribly clever, he's rebuilding the old waterwheel and we're going to have our own power source soon.'

A great comeback by Priscilla. Grace pressed her knuckles to her lips.

'I heard Ted had sold the company?'

Uh oh, right hook by Mary.

Cilla inhaled sharply. 'Early retirement. He's done so well, he deserves to take it easy. But he's investing in a computer firm. He says it's going to be the next big thing.'

And Cilla has her on the ropes.

'Did I tell you, Theodore, my eldest, has just been promoted to head of his branch? What about your Grace? How are you *coping?*'

Mary fights back, one, two, goes for the Achilles heel . . .

'Grace has the most marvellous new job.' Cilla's eyes narrowed. 'She's managing the Stratton Estate out at Wittering Manor. Do you know it?'

Knockout to Cilla.

'Must go, darling. See you at the golf club tomorrow?' Cilla clipped the phone into its cradle.

'That's not strictly true, Mum,' Grace said. 'I'm not managing the estate.'

'I wasn't about to let her win.' Cilla fluffed up Grace's hair. 'Bloody Theodore.' She stood back. 'Are you going to blow-dry this every day?'

'What do you think?'

'Thought not. Right, I'll style it so you can just wash and go, then you can zhoosh it up for special occasions.' She swept the front section of Grace's hair over her face. 'I'll keep the fringe soft, sweep it over your eyes.'

'That sounds good.'

'Well, you need it with your big forehead.'

'Mum!'

'Like your dad, lots of brains.'

Grace closed her eyes and felt fine hair falling on her cheeks. 'Do you ever think about going back to work?'

'Me? Why would I?'

'I just thought . . . you're such a good hairdresser and you trained in Paris. They'd snap you up around here, or you could set up on your own.'

'I don't need to work,' Cilla said. 'I haven't worked since I married your dad. He's my job, taking care of him and the house, and of course you, when you were small.'

'Do you ever regret not having more children?'

Cilla sucked her teeth. 'Not a bit. I went through hell having you. Once was enough.'

'Never quite forgiven me, have you?'

'No need for sarcasm, Missy. I know your dad would have liked more, but no thank you. And then there was that business afterwards too.'

That business, Grace thought. The months of depression that were only ever alluded to. She swung her head as Cilla stepped back to admire her work. 'That feels so much lighter.'

'It suits you.' Cilla cocked her head. 'I think it's a good thing. New hair, new start. Cut away all that sadness that's been dragging you down.' She shook the cape clear of Grace's shoulders and brought over a mirror. 'What do you think?'

Grace blinked at the stranger staring back at her and ran her hands through the thick blonde layers. The cut accentuated her high cheekbones, her wide blue eyes. 'I like it.' She stood and hugged Cilla just as the kitchen timer rang. 'Thanks, Mum.'

Cilla pushed her gently away. 'Go on with you.' Her gaze fell. 'So, did you sell it?'

'The brooch?' Grace shook her head. 'No. I gave it back to Gogo. I want to find out more about it first.'

'Do you think they have the other half? At the manor, I mean.'

'I don't know.' Grace reached for her coat. 'But I'm going to find out.'

11

'My parents met in 1911,' Fraser began, reading from his notebook. 'Good,' he said. Biba raised her head from the bed, and gazed down her nose at him. 'Not you, darling,' he said, reaching out a purple-socked foot and gently rubbing her swollen belly. 'Won't be long now, will it? The pups will soon be here.' Fraser settled back on the pillows in his four-poster bed, and gazed out at the rain falling across the misty estate. He cleared his throat and read on: 'My father, Albert Stratton, was the rebel of the family, which is not bad going in a flock of black sheep. He was the youngest son of a baronet, Sir Cosmo Fraser Stratton, an industrious and temperamental engineer whose contribution to the Empire was rewarded with a title, and who built a mausoleum of a house smack on the border of Hampshire and West Sussex. His sons were a great disappointment to him. After Cosmo's death, Aubrey, his heir, frittered away the family fortune on a variety of ill-advised business ventures, gambling and whores.' *Is that too harsh on Dicky's father?* He rested his pencil against his lips. *No.* 'Meanwhile Albert, his youngest son, had his mother's good looks, and her propensity for daydreaming. From a young age all he cared about was art and horses, and he set out to write the definitive anatomy of the horse.' Fraser broke off reading, and looked at the dog over the top of his half-moon reading glasses. 'Typical of his arrogance to think he could do a better job than Stubbs.' Fraser scanned the handwritten page, finding his place. 'He took a commission with the 9th Lancers fresh from school and when Clementine Booth met him I believe she thought he was her knight in shining armour.' Fraser chewed his lip, thinking of his family. *How remarkably different siblings can be. Look at Dicky and his useless sons, lording it over his sisters and daughters in that monstrous house. Any one of the girls would have been a better heir.*

Fraser shivered and pulled a blanket around his shoulders. 'I want you to picture the scene in that long, glorious spring and summer of 1911. Clementine was fresh off the steamer from New York. She found London in full swing for the coronation. All May, London smelt of sawn timber as they constructed the viewing stands along St James' Park.

'In those days, the wealthy left London for Saturday to

Monday house parties (there was no 'weekend'), and Clemmie came prepared with the finest fashions she could find in Chicago. She knew these parties meant six changes of clothes a day, outfits for games of tennis, bicycling and picnics. She was, she told me later, determined to make a splash.' Fraser turned the page.

'My parents met at a party thrown by Mrs Rosa Lewis in Grosvenor Square, though Albert might have glimpsed her among the sea of glittering tiaras at any number of social occasions that summer. Clemmie said he was squiffy on pink champagne, but dashing in his red and black uniform with all its gold braid. She was drawn to Albert's raw energy, she said, which matched her own – that night they danced to ragtime music, listened to Enrico Caruso on the gramophone.

'My mother . . .' He paused. 'Clementine was remarkably beautiful. She had ivory skin, lustrous black hair swept back from a widow's peak above a clear brow. In those days the girls powdered themselves with rice powder to try and achieve her natural pallor, used blue crayons to pencil in sensitive veins on their temple and cleavage. Clem had all this naturally. If anyone was designed to wear a tiara, she was.' His hand fell to the battered leather earring box beside him, and he traced the faded gold CBS with his hand. 'It was part of her charm that she never did, after the Great War.' Fraser cleared his throat.

'Yes, June 1911 was heady with romance. Cosmo's widow Lady Stratton courted Clem – ostensibly for Aubrey. They took her to Ascot; she saw Nijinsky dance at the Royal Opera House, lazed on the lawns of the Old Vicarage at Grantchester with Brooke, bathed on the beach with my father. Aubrey was no swimmer, so it was the first chance Albert and Clem had to be completely alone in the sea while their chaperones were safely on the sand. I remember her telling me about the heady sensation of changing in a bathing machine in the dark, knowing he was just next door, undressing, too. The days were drenched with the scent of lavender, clematis, and roses, she said. Their first stolen kiss was underwater.

'Albert had defied the family tradition of careless days of luxury and folly and scandalised his parents by joining the 9th Lancers. In spite of his good looks and success with women, he was a virile young man, uneasy at parties, happier on the farm, on a boat, or on horseback. When his father died and passed the title on to his elder brother, Albert took his small inheritance and bought Wittering Manor and a small estate in Tuscany. Everyone thought he was quite mad, but Albert was ahead of his time, and his independence only increased Clemmie's romantic attachment to him. Stratton money bought the properties, but it was the Booth fortune that made them what they are today.' Fraser picked up an early photograph of the Manor.

'Witters is not a remarkable house – Pevsner didn't consider the detour worthwhile when he charted West Sussex. The house dates back to the fourteenth century and is a hotchpotch of styles – but then, aren't we all?' Fraser paused. 'Albert loved it though. He built up the estate, the stables. It was, I think, the only thing that gave him satisfaction in his life.'

He scribbled a quick note to himself: *Backtrack, a bit. Let's add to Clementine's arrival.*

'Of course it wasn't like the great days around 1900, when my grandmother, Lady Stratton, came over from New York. Then, fifty American ladies populated the peerage thanks to their generous dowries. Women like Consuelo, daughter of William Vanderbilt, who brought a $2.5m dowry when she married the Duke of Marlborough. The Strattons weren't up to catching such big fish, but nonetheless my grandmother had decided that an American girl would be just the ticket for her eldest son – fresh blood and fresh cash, just as she had brought both to Cosmo. Clemmie told me later that my grandmother knew she didn't have long to live and she wanted her last act to be to secure the family's fortunes.

'Unfortunately for her, Clemmie was more of an individual than many girls of her time. Once she set her sights on my father there was no stopping her. She seduced Albert, made sure they were caught in flagrante in the stables. It was seen as the only possible solution that they should marry . . .' Fraser paused. The words were tantalisingly within reach, but he didn't know what to say next. It felt like a sneeze about to come, trapped, electrifying. At a knock on the door, he gratefully threw down his pencil. 'Come.'

'I thought you might feel like a bit of soup?' Ellen shouldered open the door, a legged tray in her hands. 'Get down, Biba,' she said, nudging the hound out of the way. 'If your chest is playing up, it doesn't do you any good having that dog in the bed. Nor those.' She gestured with her chin towards the overflowing ashtray at his side.

'Thank you, Ellen,' Fraser said, settling the tray across his legs. 'I can assure you that a warm dog in your bed is the best medicine known to man.' Fraser glanced down at the soup, steaming on the tray. 'It's terribly kind of you, but I really can't face a thing. They say it's one of the first signs—'

'Not that nonsense again. You're fit as a fiddle.'

'You might think so, Ellen. I'm quite sure it's stones of some sort. Kidney, or gall bladder. I feel like the wolf with a stomach full of rocks in that fairy tale.'

'You do go on sometimes. You must eat. You haven't had a bite since breakfast yesterday.'

'I'm not well, Ellen.' He sank further into the pillows.

'Dr Michaels said—'

'What does that quack know? He's younger than Jack, for heaven's sake. I shall go and see my doctor on Sloane Street next time I'm in town.'

'Very good.' Ellen tidied up the embroidered Turkish quilt and smoothed the red carnations. 'Why don't you get a breath of fresh air?' she said, collecting a heavy woollen dressing gown from the bed and draping it over the armchair. 'It did me the world of good, Mr Lloyd taking me up the Black Forest.' Fraser choked, stifling a laugh. 'Now, eat all that up. I want to see a clean bowl.' Ellen wagged her finger and closed the bedroom door behind her.

Fraser lifted the tray clear of his legs and placed the bowl of soup on the ground. 'Oxtail,' he said, as Biba took an exploratory sniff. 'No, I didn't fancy it much either, and I don't think you should risk it in your condition.' He tipped it into a potted fern and went to the Chinese cabinet between the tall sash windows. He slid out a battered leather wallet from between the bottles and crystal glasses inside and flipped it open. 'Gin.' he said quietly, staring at it. He took out a bottle of Gordon's. 'The sun's over the yardarm somewhere.' He fought the temptation, already imagining the liquor gliding over ice, the fizz of tonic, the taste of lemon on his lips. Biba strode over and nudged his leg with her muzzle. 'No, you're quite right.' He put the bottle back and picked up his notebook, taking it to a worn tapestry chaise longue beneath the window. He doodled a sketch of a leggy showgirl with an ostrich-feather aigrette in her hair in the margin, trying to pick up the story. 'My mother fell for Albert because he bore a passing resemblance to some fellow she'd seen in *Motion Picture Story Magazine*,' he said, writing quickly, 'and she mistook the early signs of depression for a smouldering artistic temperament. He painted her that summer, in 1911. She said later it was the best sex they ever had.' *Can I say that? Of course one knows one's parents did it, but still . . .* 'Clementine Booth of Chicago, Illinois, was emancipated well before that suffragette died at the 1913 Epsom Derby, and the surprise of real, romantic love took her breath away.'

The sun broke through the clouds, and Fraser looked up at the gardens. *Doesn't it always?* he thought. 'Perhaps Ellen is right,' he said to Biba. 'How about a bit of fresh air?'

*

Grace looked up at the sound of a knock on the cottage door and put down the roller. The few pieces of furniture had been pushed into the middle of the living room and draped with white sheets. She was halfway through whitewashing the walls and sunlight filtered through the window, casting shadows of the trees outside.

'Hello, Fraser.' She brushed a strand of hair from her face with the back of her hand.

'More spots?' He pointed at the dots of white paint flecked across her face. 'Not intruding, am I?'

'Not at all. Just freshening it up a bit. Hope you don't mind?' She looked around the room. 'Fresh paint always smells hopeful, don't you think?'

'New beginnings?' He poked his head through the door. 'Very good. I'm glad you like it enough to put your own mark on the old place. I was always rather fond of this cottage. Our gamekeeper lived here for years and years. He taught me everything I know about wildlife.' Fraser smiled.

The leading rein he had in his hand jerked and Fraser stepped back, patting the flank of the small skewbald pony munching on the long grass in the garden. 'Is Harry in?'

'You came!' Harry ran downstairs, her face lit up with happiness.

'Fancy starting those lessons we talked about?'

'Absolutely!' Harry pulled on a pair of boots and he handed her a black velvet riding hat. 'See you later, Mum.'

'Hold on a second,' Grace put out a hand to stop her. 'When did you two plot this?'

'I knew you would have said no,' Harry said.

'I assure you, she'll be quite safe,' Fraser said. 'We'll just go for a little walk to start with.'

'I don't know—' Grace folded her arms.

'Mum, *please*.'

'Harry tells me you dislike horses,' Fraser said.

116

'I don't dislike them.' Grace eyed the pony warily. 'I just had a bad experience when I was little.'

'We'll convert you, in time. Now, Harry,' he said, turning to her, 'the first thing you need to know about old Felix is that he's a tricky bugger.' Fraser glanced at Grace. 'Sorry. He's naughty. He breathes in the minute a saddle touches his back, and if you don't give him a good dig in the ribs and check the girth's tight enough, you'll be sliding off before you're out the yard. However, the best rule, as in life,' Fraser said, giving Harry a boost into the saddle, 'is that if you fall off you get straight back in the saddle again.' He held Grace's gaze for a moment.

'Good advice,' she said.

'There are no secrets, here, my dear,' he said, then led Harry off, the pony's wide backside wiggling like a Thelwell.

No secrets, Grace thought. She realised Jack must have told him about her outburst at the poker night. *Little do you know*.

12

'Are you ready yet?' Fraser called up the staircase. He was dressed in his father's old uniform and paced the hallway impatiently. 'I want to get work out of the way so I can get back to Biba.'

'Just a minute,' Grace shouted down. 'There are hundreds of buttons on this thing.'

'Ah, Jack.' Fraser looked up as the kitchen door opened.

'I know you're bored with retirement, but aren't you a bit old for the army?' Jack grinned, looking Fraser up and down. 'I take it you're taller than your dad.'

Fraser stretched out his arms and inspected the jacket cuffs. 'It seems so.' He clapped his hands. 'Did you hear? That reprobate Jagger is now the proud father of four rather charming pups.' He called up to Grace. 'Harry's already asked to keep one, did you know?'

'I think we've got enough on our plate with Jagger, don't you?' she said. 'Besides, I think the least we can do is let you sell the pups.'

'I'm just off to the bank. Do you need anything from—' Jack's words broke off as he caught sight of Grace, walking slowly down the staircase, her head held high. Her hair was swept up loosely and the pale silk dress accentuated her small waist and the curve of her hips as the fabric trailed behind her. He let out a slow whistle.

'Oh good, I thought it would fit.' Fraser offered her his hand.

'I can hardly breathe,' she said, blushing under Jack's gaze.

'The women all wore corsets in those days, of course.' Fraser stepped back, admiring the dress. 'You look quite lovely, doesn't she, Jack?'

'Sorry?' Jack took a step back. 'Sure. I'll – I'll leave you to your play-acting.'

'Right, shall we get on?' Grace said, smoothing the full skirt with her hands. 'I really wanted to get on with sorting the library out.'

'That can wait. This is far more fun.'

'Where do you want me?'

Fraser clapped his hands. 'There,' he said, pointing at the sofa. 'I rarely use this room, but Clemmie loved it. I imagine when Albert returned from the war she was sitting by the fire . . .'

'Hope it was a bit warmer in those days.' Grace shivered. 'Don't you think it would be better if we started at the beginning of the story?' she said, arranging the dress across the sofa.

'No. No, I'm not quite ready to do that yet.' Fraser marched across the room to the door. 'I've jotted down a few notes about how they met, but I feel inspired by this scene: my arrival at Witters.' He turned to Grace. 'Do you have a pen?'

She reached across to the side table and picked up a notepad.

'Not too fast, OK?'

'Few events in life are as pivotal as discovering you are not who you thought you are,' Fraser dictated. 'How does that sound? Less stuffy than if I start my memoirs: "Few events in life are as pivotal as discovering one is not who one thought one is." Or is it "was"?'

'Just talk naturally,' Grace said, not looking up from the notebook.

'I want to try and imagine the scene when Albert returned in 1915.' He paced the hall, holding his arms as if he were cradling a child. 'Perhaps Clemmie sat where you are now, holding the baby by the fire, playing with a silver rattle she'd bought for her own child, the boy she lost? "*Everyone told me it was bad luck to buy baby things so soon*," she might have said. Perhaps she paused, looked at Albert with those ice blue eyes of hers. Fraser held his hand to his brow, imagining her pain. He knelt in front of the fireplace. 'Albert falls to his knees. "*Clem, I'm sorry. Forgive me. This can be a new start . . .*" Oh bugger, he can't fall to his knees, can he? Not with his wounded leg.' Fraser scrambled back into the chair and considered Grace.

'Lieutenant Stratton gazed ahead,' he dictated, 'watched the flying lady on the bonnet of his Rolls Royce sweeping hypnotically along the frozen lanes. At least when they were driving, the child slept. He turned and glanced into the back of the car. The wet nurse he had hired in Paris dozed fitfully, her head lolling. She had been up all night with the boy, pacing the hotel room. Stratton had lain awake next door, following the path of her footsteps, wondering how to explain everything to Clementine. He had taken the coward's route and sent a telegram ahead, forewarning her about the child.

'"Not long now," he said, more to himself than the driver. They rounded the bend in the Birdham road and the car forged on through the gate. Albert glimpsed a figure in the lighted doorway of the gatehouse, his hand raised in salute.

Everyone was waiting for his return. He had half a mind to turn and run. *Nothing has changed here*, he thought, his fingers working anxiously at his side. *But everything has changed, for me.*

'"Welcome home, sir," the butler said, opening the passenger door the moment the car stopped. He held a black umbrella, protecting Albert from the freezing rain. Beyond him, Albert saw the housekeeper and cook and one of the youngest gardeners. *Of course, the rest of them are fighting*, he thought, remembering the days when twenty people lined the entrance steps to welcome him home.

'Albert swung his leg awkwardly from the car, and leaned against the door, pain coursing through his hip and back as he stood. The butler took a second umbrella from the housekeeper, shielding the nurse and child. Albert walked ahead and stood in the entrance hall, waiting for them. He closed his eyes for a moment, breathing in the reassuring smell of woodsmoke, beeswax polish and mothballs.' Fraser broke off. 'What else does this hall smell of?'

Grace looked up, breathed in the familiar scent. 'Roses. Pot pourri.'

'Add that in.' Fraser stretched out in the armchair. 'Albert walked through to the heart of the house. The lamps illuminating the square hall failed to light beyond the first floor and the room soared above him into darkness. Everything was in its place. The rugs were still reassuringly wonky, never lying true to the corridor walls. The tiger-skin rug draped across the back of one of several sofas arranged around the hearth still looked at him with a glazed look of surprise on its face. The grandfather clock ticked on. *I'm back, I'm back*, he thought, relief flooding through him.' Fraser jumped up. 'Walk down the stairs again, would you?'

Grace laid down the notebook and did as he asked, Fraser watching her movements. He picked up the pen and jotted down some notes, dictating aloud.

'"Welcome home," Clementine said, descending the stair-case, her pale silk skirts swinging around her. Her thick dark hair was piled high, swept up from her clear, pale face.

'Albert removed his cap, and tucked it under his arm. "My dear," he said.' Fraser strode over to Grace, still writing. 'He was not sure whether to venture a kiss on her cheek . . .' Fraser glanced up.

'Sorry.' Grace stifled a giggle.

'You told me you were good at drama.' Fraser folded his arms. 'Put yourself in her shoes. She lost a baby.' He hesitated as he saw Grace flinch. 'Her husband returns from war, wounded, and with a child, a boy—'

'You?'

'Yes, me. Keep up.' Fraser handed her the notebook and pen. 'Albert tried to read Clemmie's expression,' he dictated. 'Relief, fear. Wounded pride?

'"Come," Clem said to him. "Sit by the fire." She glanced at the nurse. "I shall take the child." She eased the sleeping baby into her arms.' Fraser looked at Grace. 'How was she feeling, do you think?'

Grace blinked. 'I imagine it was incredibly hard for her.' She looked at Fraser, her eyes glistening. 'I imagine, after you lose a child, to hold a baby breaks your heart.'

'I say, you *are* good at this,' Fraser said. 'You're really getting in to the part.' He picked up a photograph of his father from the side table. '"You look terribly well, Clemmie," Albert said once they were alone. He took down a silver box of matches from the mantelpiece, and lit a cigarette, buying time.

'"I am," Clemmie said, pacing before the fire, the child sleeping peacefully in her arms. "This ghastly war has given me a role, at least, helping at the hospital." She looked up at him and he saw her pain, clearly now. "I am so glad you have come home, Albert. I thought – I thought it was all over for us . . ."

'"If you will have me, perhaps it is just beginning." He went

121

to his wife, and embraced her. "I am sorry. I left you when you most needed me." He buried his face in her hair. "Can you ever forgive me?"

'Clementine reached for his hand, laced her fingers in his, their wedding bands touching. "Whatever you have been through," she said, "this *is* a new beginning for us." She looked at the child. "*He* is a new beginning." Her lips trembled as she smiled. "Perhaps in time, you will grow to love us both."

'"Clemmie, I never— "

'"It's perfectly all right, Albert. We share no illusions about our marriage. Your family needed money; mine needed some class. Our marriage was not her intention, but your mother's last act was to secure both families' futures." She waited for him to look at her. "But I love you, Albert. When I lost our child, and then you—" She gazed down at the baby as he stirred in her arms. "I don't need to know who his mother is, but is he yours?" Albert remained silent. "He is yours?"

'"Yes, yes, he is,' Albert said.

'"Did you love her?"

'"I—"

'"That doesn't matter." Clementine wiped at her eye with the back of her trembling fingertips. "You've come home, that's all I care about. You're alive, when so many aren't." Tears welled in her eyes. "Let us begin again." She lifted his hand, pressed her cheek into his palm. "Thank you. Thank you for coming back to me."

'"I have something to show you," he said after a time, lifting his leather bag onto the table before the fire.

'"My jewels?" She looked at the baby. "What gem could be more beautiful than him? But I've been dying to see what Monsieur Bouchet created."

'"Yes." He took a breath. "Well, most of them are here."

'Albert began by opening the smallest boxes. Garnet earrings glimmered in the firelight, a sinuous diamond bracelet, a magnificent parure of emeralds. He unfolded a velvet cloth and placed the diamond wing in her hand.'

Grace's pen hovered over the paper, her breath caught in her throat.

'"Where's the rest of the tiara?" Fraser went on, impersonating his mother's American accent.

'"I shall place an order for a replacement, just as soon as we can," Albert said.

'Clementine looked from the filigree wing in her hand to the baby. "He's so beautiful," she said. "If the tiara was the price, then it is the least I could pay."

'Albert reached for the final box in the bag. "There is one more, a gift I chose for you myself. I know how much you admired Lady Cotterell's sapphire. This Bouchet chap is a genius, and when I saw this jewel I thought of you immediately. I do hope you like it. It's most—" His words trailed away. "The asteria," he said, turning the empty box towards her. "It's gone. Christ, she must have stolen it."

'Clementine burst out laughing. "Good for her. It doesn't matter, Albert." She smiled as the baby opened his deep blue eyes and gazed at her. "What she has given us is beyond worth. This boy is more precious than jewels."'

Fraser sighed, slumped down in the chair. 'I wonder. Was it really like that?' he said to Grace.

'Unless we find an account by Albert or Clementine in among all your papers, we'll never know.' *The matching brooch*, Grace thought. *Albert brought it here during World War One with Fraser.* 'So Clementine wasn't your mother?'

'By birth, no. In every other sense she was the most wonderful mother any man could wish for.' A smile twitched on his lips. 'Of course, it might have been a different scene entirely. From memory, Clemmie was quite a thrower. I can picture Albert ducking as a vase flew past his head. "Where the hell is my tiara? I suppose you gave it to that tart in Paris?"' He shook his head. 'What really happened, Grace?' he said. 'I wonder if we'll ever find out the truth?'

123

13

'Damn it,' Grace said under her breath. The bonnet of the Beetle was up, and she was rummaging around in the engine.

'Morning,' Jack said, pausing to admire her legs. 'Fraser hasn't got you dressed up today?'

Grace bumped her head on the bonnet as she looked up in surprise. 'Ha ha – very funny.'

'Anything I can help with?'

'It won't start. I think it's the carburettor.'

'Wow. Jeweller, PA, mechanic, is there no end to your talents?'

'You're on form this morning.' Grace noticed the files under Jack's arm. 'Are you going into town? Fraser wanted me to get some copies made at the library.'

'Sure, I've got to go to the accountant. Do you want a lift?'

'Thanks.' Grace heaved a couple of heavy bags from the passenger seat.

'Here, let me.' Jack took them from her, and they headed across the yard. 'How are you getting on?'

'Good, I hope. It's rather hard to tell with Fraser. Nothing's very straightforward – I think it would be better if we started at the beginning and worked our way through chronologically, but he's all over the place.'

'You'll get used to him. How's Harry settling in? I saw them out riding together the other day.'

'She's loving it,' Grace said, smiling. 'And she's really enjoying being back at a smaller school.'

'Back?'

'I had to take her out of her prep school when I couldn't afford the fees.'

'That must have been tough.'

'It was. She found the big primary in Andrewsfield a bit overwhelming. I think she'll be happier at the little village school.'

Jack opened the Land Rover door for her. He threw the bags into the back and, as they drove out of the yard, Grace laid her head against the cold window, watched the fields speeding past, the riven oak fences undulating at their side marking out the Stratton estate. It felt as though the countryside was shrugging off the winter, with daffodils nodding in the breeze at the side of the road, birds hopping from branch to branch with twigs in their beaks.

'Look, there are a couple of hares boxing over there.' Jack pointed across towards an oak tree.

'Why do they do that?'

'It's courtship – he's trying to show what a tough guy he is, and the female is fighting off his advances. He's chosen her but she's not settling for it.'

'Good for her.' Grace stared at the hares, at the quick, calligraphic flash of their movements in the grass. *He chose her*, she thought, remembering Sam walking towards her at Alice's party.

Jack parked in Chichester and opened the door for Grace. 'I'll run a few errands first to give you time to do whatever it is Fraser needs. Where shall I meet you?'

'There's a coffee shop opposite the cathedral,' she said.

'OK, say a couple of hours?'

'Thanks,' Grace said, and she hopped down from the car. Her poncho swung around her hips.

'Will you be OK with those books?' He turned up the collar of his black wool reefer jacket against the cold.

'I'm stronger than I look,' she said, swinging the heavy bag out.

Up above them, on a new office block's scaffolding, three builders in yellow hard hats leant over to get a better look at Grace. An open copy of the *Sun* flapped in the breeze beneath one of their lunchboxes. One of them wolf-whistled.

'It might never happen, love,' he catcalled. 'Cheer up!'

'Oh, go away,' Grace said under her breath.

'Go on, show us your tits!'

Jack turned to them and lifted his sweater, wiggling his backside.

'Eugh, put it away, mate.' The builders quickly turned away and carried on working.

Grace stared at Jack, wide-eyed with surprise, and burst out laughing.

'See you later,' he said, and winked.

Walking along the high street from the library, Grace thought again of the glimpse of smooth-muscled skin she had seen when Jack was teasing the builders. Several times in the library she had drifted off into a reverie while she was photocopying, papers spilling onto the floor. *Stop it,* she told herself. *You've been without a man too long.* She thought back through the months, and her smile faded. *A year and a half? Sam hardly ever wanted me, even before that. Only when he'd had a drink.* The memory of his face, eyes screwed shut, forced its way into her mind. *It was never about making love with him, was it?* she realised. *It was about proving something, about power.*

It was the first time in months that she had been in town without Harry, and Grace felt as though she had left something important somewhere, had lost a limb, but the thrill of being by herself was exhilarating. She glanced at her watch and saw she had quarter of an hour before she needed to meet Jack, so she headed for the cathedral.

In front of the new Chagall window, she set her bags on the floor and sat down, gazing up at the luminous colours. The sun broke through the clouds, and jewel-bright ruby, gold, emerald patches of light from the stained glass shifted over her like a glimmering cloak.

'I thought I saw you walking along the road.'

Grace turned. 'Gogo, what a lovely surprise. What are you doing here?'

'I've just been for a dress fitting, for the party.' Her grand-mother stooped and kissed her cheek. 'How are you? And Harry? Pop round at the weekend – I have an Easter egg for her.'

'Thanks. We're doing well. The cottage is almost straight and I'm getting used to his Lordship.'

'Your mother said you'd started a new job. I'm pleased for you.' Margot paused. 'She said the house is on the coast somewhere?'

'West Wittering, the Manor – do you know it? You seem to have been to most of the big houses round here when you were trading antiques.'

'No, no, I've never been.'

'It was the funniest thing. You know that receipt in the Bouchet et Fils box? I knew I'd seen the name somewhere, and then I remembered the job advert Mum had showed me, so I applied. Once I saw the cottage, I just thought *why not*? It's not forever, but at least it lets us start over again.' Grace smiled at her. 'The funny thing is, I haven't felt this optimistic in ages. It feels so good to be in our own place again, and Harry is loving it. It really feels like a new start.'

Margot seemed to be on the brink of saying something, but she just smiled. 'I'm sure you'll be happy there. You're more than a match for anyone, darling.' She took her hand as she sat beside her.

'I'll ask them about the tiara soon.'

'I wouldn't, darling,' Margot said firmly. 'You don't want to rock the boat just as you are getting settled in. What does it matter? It's all so long ago.' She turned her face to the stained-glass window. 'I do love this. "Let everything that hath breath praise the Lord." It's so vibrant, so full of life. I love the figures, the little angels and musicians.' Margot's face shone. 'I believe he's done other windows in Jerusalem representing the twelve tribes.'

'That's why I came.' Grace turned to her. 'I was thinking

127

about the birthstones and it reminded me of the window. The colours are so beautiful, so alive. It's how I feel about gemstones, how I see them, when I think about designs.' Grace lowered her eyes. She didn't often talk about her work, found it hard to express in words how her ideas evolved. 'I've been given another commission recently.'

'Ben said you'd been using the workshop again.'

'It was an order for an old client in Hatton Garden. It's not much, but it's a start.' Grace glanced at her watch. 'Look, I have to meet my boss in ten minutes just across the road. Would you like to come and have a coffee?'

'Your boss? No, I don't think so.' They walked arm in arm down the aisle.

'Not Fraser Stratton, his estate manager, Jack. He doesn't bite.'

Margot hesitated. 'In that case I'd love to.' She glanced at Grace, sensing her curiosity. 'I'm hardly dressed to meet aristocracy, am I?' They reached the coffee shop just as Jack did, and he raised his hand in greeting.

'Well, hello,' Margot said quietly.

'Did you get everything done?' he said to Grace.

'Thank you. This is my grandmother, Margot. I just bumped into her.'

'Jack Booth, how do you do,' he said, and held out his hand.

'I hope you are taking good care of my granddaughter, Mr Booth.'

'Gogo,' Grace said, blushing.

'We're lucky to have her,' Jack said, holding open the door of the coffee shop.

'Americans have such lovely manners,' Margot said, walking through.

'Stop it, you're flirting with him!' Grace whispered.

'If you're not, I don't know why.'

'He's married,' Grace hissed. *And so am I.*

Margot chose a round table in the window and settled on a

wheelback chair. 'What would you both like, my treat?'

'Just a quick coffee, I'm afraid,' Jack said, pulling out a chair for Grace. 'We have to get back.'

'Very well. Three coffees,' Margot said to the waitress.

'I just ran into Gogo in the cathedral,' Grace said, slipping her poncho over her head.

'I was having a dress fitting for my party next month.' Margot extended her hand to Jack. 'Grace designed this for my anniversary,' she said. Margot puckered her lips at Grace as Jack looked down at the ring, as if to say: *he's gorgeous* . . .

'It's beautiful,' he said. 'How long have you been married?'

'Married?' Margot laughed throatily. 'No, it's a celebration of the day I met my friend, and his sixtieth birthday.' She looked from Jack to Grace. 'I've just had the most marvellous idea. The party is going to be a small affair, but I'm struggling to make up even numbers for the dinner. Why don't you come with Grace, Mr Booth?'

'Thank you,' Jack said, glancing at Grace. 'That's terribly kind.'

'Gogo, you're dreadful. Why on earth would Jack want to spend an evening with me?'

'No, I'd like to,' he said. 'It sounds as though you've had a tough time of it lately and social events can be grim enough anyway, without facing them on your own.'

Oh God, he feels sorry for me, Grace thought, scalding her mouth on the coffee.

'That's decided then,' Margot pulled out a blue Smythson notebook from her handbag and jotted down a note.

Jack glanced at his watch. 'I'm sorry, we really must be getting back.'

Grace pushed back her chair. 'Yes, we must.'

'Why don't you come up for supper tonight?' Margot said to her.

'I'd love to, but the PTA are having a cheese and wine do at the school and I thought I should make an appearance.'

'Cheese and pineapple on toothpicks?' Margot shivered in disgust. 'After all this time, I will never get used to English food. But of course, I understand.' She kissed Grace's cheek. 'I look forward to seeing you next month, Mr Booth. Grace has all the details.'

They drove in silence towards West Wittering. 'Listen,' Grace said finally. 'Please, don't feel you have to come to the party.'

'No problem. It was kind of your grandmother to ask me.'

'You don't have to feel sorry for me.' Grace's pride flared.

'I didn't mean it like that. It's just you're obviously alone.' He swung the car onto the road home. 'It's my job to make sure the staff are happy, and I do that as well as I can.' He glanced at her, frowning. 'Squiring you at some dance is no different from loaning Cy a lawnmower when he needs it to do some odd jobs, I assure you.'

'Great.' Grace folded her arms. 'As long as we are clear about that.'

'Leave a note in the office of the date and time and I'll send the car round for you.'

'Thank you.'

Jack paused at her tone. 'It must be heavy.'

'I'm sorry?'

'That suit of armour you wear all the time.'

Grace laughed and shook her head. 'Maybe I need it.'

'Maybe you should just accept an offer of help.'

'Help? What would someone like you know about what I'm going through?'

'Someone like me?'

'Someone who's had everything handed to them on a plate.' She swept her arm as they drove down towards Wittering Manor. 'The perfect house, the perfect life. Christ, I shouldn't think you've ever risked or lost anything, have you?' She heard him inhale sharply, but she stared ahead as they swept down the drive to the stable yard. Jack's words had stung.

He slammed on the brakes outside the cottage and Grace was thrown forward against the seatbelt. 'Is that what you think of me? Jeez, you try to do someone a favour—'

'I don't need any favours,' she said, not looking at him.

He reached across and threw open the passenger door for her. 'You don't have the monopoly on broken dreams, Grace.' She turned to him in surprise, and when he looked at her, close to, she saw the pain in his eyes. 'Maybe, just maybe, if you stop being so damn proud and wrapped up in coping with life single-handed—' He stopped at the expression on Grace's face. 'What's wrong?'

Grace was looking past him to the cottage. She jumped out. 'Harry shouldn't be back yet. Why's the door open?' *Something's wrong.* She pushed open the door and listened. It was silent, but in the half-light she could see that things were out of place. She flicked on the light. 'Someone's been in here,' she said, stepping back.

'A burglar?' Jack said, coming to her side.

'But why? We haven't got anything of value.'

'Wait there; I'm just going to check they've gone.' He picked up the brass poker from the fireplace and checked the kitchen before scaling the stairs two at a time. Grace looked up the dark staircase and listened for a moment, her heart racing. She crept upstairs after him. Jack checked the two bedrooms, pushing open the doors with the poker. In Harry's room, the door nudged the leg of a large doll balanced on the wardrobe and it flopped down to the floor. Grace cried out.

'Are you all right?' Jack put his arm around her.

'Yes, I'm fine.' She kicked it away. 'Bloody Holly Hobbie.' She leant against the wall, her hand flat against her chest. 'There's no one here.'

'Should we call the police?'

'I don't know. I can't see that anything's missing,' Grace said, looking around. 'You don't think one of the lads or Cy might have thought it's a joke?'

'Bit early for April Fool's. Anyhow, cling film on the loo seat is more his style.'

Jack led the way downstairs and checked the lock on the front door. 'Look, someone's jimmied it,' he said, pointing to the splintered wood. 'Man, they've got a nerve doing that in broad daylight. Didn't Jagger sound the alarm?'

'He's at the vets, having a little operation tomorrow.' Grace mimed *getting the snip*.

'Jeez, the one time that dog could make himself useful.' Jack looked around the living room, at the baskets and toys thrown around, at the kitchen doors and drawers pulled out. 'Right. We'll get a locksmith over in the morning, but in the meantime I'll put a couple of new bolts on the doors so you feel safe tonight.'

'You don't have to do that.'

'I don't like the thought of you guys being here alone with some creep around.' Jack strode through the cottage and checked the back door. 'I don't get it. We've had bits of kit taken from the workshops over the years, but no one has ever touched the cottages. Do you want me to call the police?'

Grace shook her head. 'Doesn't seem much point. They haven't taken anything.' Something clicked in her mind. *The stones*, she thought.

'OK. I'll tell everyone to keep an eye out, and I'll have a word with the village policeman tomorrow.' He began to walk away

'Jack.' She touched his arm. 'Thank you. I'm sorry about earlier.'

'Me too.' He looked down at her hand, raised his gaze to hers, relenting. 'Look, like I said, I'm not great with people. I don't . . . sometimes things don't come out right.' Her hand fell away. 'I'd be glad to take you to this dance.'

'Thank you. I'll even leave my suit of armour at home.'

He backed away from her, smiling. 'Sure you're OK?'

'I'm fine. Just a bit shaken.' She waited until he had gone, then ran upstairs and searched her bedroom. *Why?* she thought. *This isn't fair.* The cottage had felt safe, to her. It was hers and Harry's. She rifled through the wardrobes, pulled clothes from the shelves with shaking hands. *I don't get it. They haven't taken anything.* She flung back the patchwork quilt on the old brass bed, and there on the pillow was a plain manila envelope. Her hand trembled as she picked it up. As before, it said simply: GRACE, the typewritten capitals unevenly inked. Grace felt sick. She tore open the envelope and pulled out the card.

You think you can run, Grace? New start? So brave.
The strong wear aquamarine to their grave.

APRIL

Diamond

Innocence · Fortitude · Everlasting love

14

'Any news on your break-in?' Fraser said. He looked up from the orchid he was misting in the conservatory, his face in shadow beneath his battered panama hat.

'No, nothing.' Grace shook her head, and leant back in the pink Lloyd Loom chair, a blank notepad on her lap. She had been over and over it in her mind – why would they risk breaking in to leave the jewel when they could have posted it, or had it delivered in some flowers? *Because they wanted to show that they could,* she thought. *They wanted to show that they are in control, that I can't hide from them.* She tapped her pencil like a cat flicking its tail in warning. *Whoever it is can go to hell. I'm not hiding from anyone.*

Church bells sounded from the village, bright and clear in the fresh, still air. She looked out through the open door across the gardens. The trees and hedgerows were budding with new life, acid green leaves unfurling in the spring sun, glistening from the rain. Grace watched a songbird hopping from branch to branch, twigs in its beak.

'I just don't understand,' he said. 'If they were after money, there were other more valuable things they could have taken from the Manor. Why risk all that and leave empty-handed?' Fraser dug his hands into the sagging pockets of his blue linen jacket and strolled over, sitting at the table beside Grace. 'They did leave empty-handed, didn't they?' Grace felt him watching her.

'Yes. They didn't take anything,' she said truthfully. Grace thought about confiding in Fraser, but it felt as if she was hiding too much already. *How do I explain that someone has taken the jewels but they are giving them back one by one? It sounds crazy.*

'Enough boondoggling,' he said.

'Right. We were supposed to be making notes for the chapters on Clemmie.'

'Can't we do another bit? This is torture,' Fraser laid his head on his arms. 'I can't do it. This was a bad idea. Why should we be working on a Sunday?'

'Because I need to take a ring to an old client in London tomorrow morning.'

'I can't do it, Grace. Go home to Harry.'

'Harry's with Mum and Dad.'

'Can't we just *pretend* you need to go home? Every time I look at the blank page it's a reproach.'

'Forget about that. Let's try something different. Wait there.' Grace ran to the cottage. *What's got in to him today?* she thought. *He's up and down like a yo-yo.* A bright spring sun cut through the rain clouds, and the puddles on the road and fields shone like sky-glass, reflecting the clouds. The remnants of the cling film Cy had taped over their front door for April Fool's Day blew in the breeze as she pushed it open. Grace sat down on the floor and Jagger loped over to see what she was doing, nuzzling at her hair with his nose.

'Sorry old chap,' she said. 'Not time for your walk, yet. There's work to do.' She fast-forwarded through the *Top of the Pops* that Harry had carefully recorded from the TV the night before, sitting beside the television with the microphone, trying to click the recorder off the moment the DJ interrupted the songs. 'Finally,' Grace said as the recording ended, and she scooped up the recorder. 'See you later.' Jagger rolled his eyes and clambered onto the sofa.

Back in the conservatory Grace found Fraser still with his head on his arms. 'I'll get some blank tapes in town, but let's make a start with this,' she said, gesturing for him to follow her. In the study, she put the tape recorder on the coffee table. Grace pulled the curtains and flicked on a slide projector, clicking through images copied from the Stratton family albums until a photograph of Clementine filled the screen. The speaker on the tape recorder filled with white sound, as Grace pressed record. 'OK. Look at her. She's young, beautiful, wilful – you can see that from the way she's looking at the photographer. Tell me more about your mother.'

'Who do you think you are? Freud?' Fraser said.

'Look, do you want help or not? Go and lie down on the couch if you are feeling tired. Just talk. Pretend you're talking to Biba, if that's easier.' Fraser shuffled over and slumped down, hugging a cushion to his stomach.

'You're a slave driver,' he said. 'Shall I ring for Ellen? Oh, bugger, it's her day off. I'll go. How about some teazle? Mint, I think, with my stomach.'

'Fraser, we can stop for tea once we've done some work.'

'I feel ghastly. I have the most hideous ache under my ribs. I'm sure my liver is shot. Or is it my gall bladder?'

'Fraser!' Grace said sharply. She sat in an armchair, slightly behind him, and held up the microphone. 'I don't want to know what you had for breakfast in 1924,' she said. 'Or who won the Grand National in 1953.' She waited for him to laugh. 'I want to know what moved you.'

'Know a lot about writing, do you?'

'No, but I read a lot. I know what works.' Grace sat back in the chair. 'I always think the best memoirs read like novels. It's not just "he said, she said", they show what lies beneath.' She paused. 'You know, when I'm cutting gems, I look at the rough stone and know where to cut, to get something flawless.'

'Nothing is flawless but God.' Fraser waved his hand towards the floor. 'Look at Persian carpets – they deliberately drop a stitch because nothing is perfect but Allah.'

'Fraser, I don't make the gems; they're there already. I

139

just set them free. That's what we are going to do with your memoir. We're going to cut away the rough edges and show what lies beneath.' Grace looked at the tables piled with notes and photographs. 'We're going to cut and polish until your story is flawless.'

'And set me free?' He craned round to look at her.

'Yes, if you'll help me.' She tapped her notepad. 'Look. As I've said all along, I think we should break it down by decades, work chronologically. We can always move things around later, but why don't we start at the beginning?'

'No, I've done all that. How my parents met, etcetera, etceteraaaah.'

'Fine.' Grace took a deep breath, and drummed her pencil on the pad. 'Where have you got to?'

'1918. Albert dies.'

'Do you want to talk about that?'

'No. Too painful.' Fraser turned his head to the sofa. 'I was a huge disappointment to him and he died hating me.'

'I'm sorry. We'll come back to that when you're ready.' She waited him out in silence.

'Clemmie,' he said finally, and lay back, looking at the ceiling with one arm behind his head. 'She mourned my father and the end of all her dreams, but she was a resourceful woman and not one to give up on life and while away her days in widow's weeds. She reinvented herself. By the time she came round from her deep and all-consuming grief, she found herself in the era of the Bright Young Things, and with a willing accomplice: me.'

Grace flicked on through the slides until she found a photograph of Clementine and Fraser together. 'How old were you?'

'I was just a teenager when this was taken – the term was even then being used in America, and Clemmie adopted it, introducing me with "Have you met my darling teenager, Fraser?" I think perhaps she even introduced it over here, started the trend.'

'Tell me about these "bright young people".'

'I was rather in awe of the Stephen Tennants and Elizabeth Ponsonbys who had scandalised society with their parties and treasure hunts. I remember seeing Elizabeth top up her syringe of heroin with water from a vase of wilting lilies, once.'

'How grim.'

Fraser shrugged. 'They were a bygone *jeunesse dorée*. Their attitude was "forget the war, let's party", and a woman like my mother – beautiful, wealthy, tragic, fitted easily into their milieu. She shingled her hair, took to wearing trousers and started smoking Turkish cigarettes. Soon, our mantelpiece was bristling with stiffies – invitations to the brightest and the best parties in town.' Fraser took a breath, stared up at the ceiling.

'You see, many of the best hostesses were Americans, so Clemmie slipped perfectly into their circles. Mrs Corrigan (or Laura Mae Whitrock of Wisconsin as she was) and Lady Cunard (aka Maud, of San Francisco) became great friends of hers. We frequented nightclubs – the Cave of Harmony on Charlotte Street, the Blue Lantern, but my favourite was 69 Dean Street with its hookers by the front door and Matisses on the walls.' Grace sensed Fraser was getting into his stride and she relaxed down into her chair, trying not to make a sound.

'Artists and writers like Coward, Waugh and Beaton were drawn to them. Clemmie loved the glamour, the excitement of it, and the rather melancholy, restless rackety life suited her. These louche young people were only too aware of the sorrow in sunlight and of the good times gone. She had no interest in marrying again and had the maturity to skirt along the dangerous edge of their exploits without succumbing. While they rose late and adopted a louche daily routine commencing with cocktails at the Ritz before lunch, Clemmie never let herself go completely. One of the gossip rags noticed my ability to be there but not be seen, and offered me £3 a week to write a column. In those days you could rent a flat in Frith Street for 12s 6d a week, so I was quite tempted, but Clemmie warned me off.'

'So you spent most of your time in the London house, then?'

'On and off. But the parties at Witters became quite notorious for a while. I was treated like some kind of exotic pet – half-man, half-boy. I remember them all lolling around the house drinking the cellar dry, my mother presiding over them like a benevolent spirit. It was, to use one of their words, "bogus", a feckless generation, sick of the war but addled with guilt for the sacrifices the one before had made. If I learnt anything from them, it was that life is fleeting and expendable, that one must live in the moment.'

'Is that all they did? Lie around drinking and drugging?'

'No, no. That's how it was perceived. Clemmie and I became quite a good team for the treasure hunts across London in our motor car. It really was the golden age of motoring in England, and when we weren't chasing clues in town we explored all the villages in the south coast. It was a real England – green and remote and wild. But we would always tire of timeless countryside and return to the bright lights of London.' Fraser turned onto his side. 'On one occasion Beaverbrook even published clues in the *Daily Mail*. There is a cutting somewhere of Clemmie at the wheel, me at her side in a dashing tweed cap. The hunts titillated and excited the public, fuelled the gossip columns, the themed-dress parties fed the scandalmongers. Even after the 1925 financial crash, the young things continued to live beyond their means, burning bright, and there was Clemmie fluttering around the periphery like a gorgeous moth well into the 1930s.'

'How did you feel about your mother living like this?'

'I remember being terribly proud of her. I adored walking her to parties, a little Pierrot to her Pierrette. In the summer, when we were on the beach, I noticed how the older men looked at her. They stopped being fathers and husbands around Clemmie, but she never noticed, I think, so the other women did not hate her for it, and she gently rebuffed anyone who tried to cross the line. She was always fierce in her defence of me, too,' Fraser said, laughing. 'One or two of the men were rather taken with my youth and beauty, but she soon put them straight, not to mention the women of a certain age who took a romantic, maternal interest in me. Clemmie was always particularly harsh with them. One mother like Clemmie was enough for any man. She was less successful protecting me from the advances of some of the girls. I was not quite one of the £1000-a-year men, but I was catnip to certain types. I lost my virginity to a reckless girl with wild blonde hair. I don't recall her name, but her lips tasted of absinthe. I was cross-legged with lust for her.' Grace stifled a smile. 'I matured quickly as a result of mixing in these circles. By the time I went up to Cambridge with Alec I was a bit of a handful during my first year. If it weren't for Alec I'd have probably destroyed myself.'

'He died recently, didn't he?' Grace stopped writing. 'I'm sorry.'

'Thank you. We spoke most days, you know.' Fraser smiled. 'Funny isn't it, with friends like that. Life can send you to different corners of the earth, but when you are together again you just pick up where you left off.' He rubbed his brow. 'Where were we?'

'Bright young things.'

'Yes. I was quite comfortable around artists and writers, used to talking to my elders, unimpressed by hashish and cocaine, and confident talking to women. I had travelled through Europe with my mother, and spoke six languages. I was, in retrospect, in my prime. I sometimes think you become less confident – or less bullish perhaps – as you grow older and you realise what's at stake. I had learnt to blend in seamlessly, to be there but not there. No doubt that has a lot to do with why I was chosen for my profession.' Fraser cleared his throat. 'If you won't let me have tea, would you mind at least pouring me a glass of water?'

'Of course,' Grace said. She paused the tape, and went over to the drinks tray, pouring two glasses of water from the cut-glass jug. 'There you are,' she said, handing one to Fraser.

'Thank you.' He drank thirstily, then gestured she should turn the tape on again. 'I remember talking to Cecil Beaton one afternoon at Wilsford. I helped him with his cameras while a few of them were changing. His lens transformed them, immortalised them as exquisite creatures—'

'Wait,' Grace said. 'I have some pictures.' She flicked on through the carousel of slides.

'Stop – there they are.' Fraser's voice softened. 'They loved him for the magic his photos wove, in spite of the fact that he wasn't top drawer. Beaton had a genius for reinvention, and he told me about the uprise to come – how the future belonged to people like him, not the nobility.

'The next time I saw him was during World War Two. He pitched up in the Middle East, and it was rather marvellous to see him in the midst of such horror. Even his lens couldn't disguise the misery of war, but they were beautiful photographs.' Fraser paused. 'It all fizzled out, as these things do. Tennant became a recluse. Clemmie would go and have tea with him occasionally, but she confided in me she found him rather a drag, always going on about the novel, *Lascar*, he would never write. He intrigued me – and I must admit I adopted some of his otherworldliness as a disguise. He was androgynous, beautiful, spoiled. He had a glam-rock allure before it had even been invented – an extraordinary, artificial man. Few people saw beyond that and I realised it could be a useful mantle to adopt in my career.' A smile twitched on his lips. 'A certain flamboyance, wearing your hair a little too long ... Most men write you off as queer, or at least not a real threat. It's the equivalent of a woman having blonde hair and large breasts – it's so eye-catching they don't bother to see past the surface.' He glanced at Grace. 'No offence.'

'None taken.'

'The majority of people are so tied up in their own minds, their busy, busy little interior world, they don't bother to look beyond stereotypes. They make lazy assumptions and judgements – people like to place everything in boxes, it makes them feel secure. If you're smart, you can play with that.' He placed his index finger on his lips. 'I was quite the cat's whiskers in my younger years. Women certainly seemed to appreciate my persona, and I always took the time to appreciate them. I can't tell you the number of times I slipped beneath the radar to romance some bored, taken-for-granted, beautiful girl whose husband couldn't see me and certainly didn't see the jewel he had at home.'

'So it's all an act?' Grace's pencil hovered above her notes.

Fraser tilted his head, gazed at her upside down. 'Some of it. But I'm not going to tell you which parts.'

'Are you still in touch with these people?'

'No, most of them are dead. The Red and White ball in 1931 was like "the party at the end of the world", some said. They were decadent, doomed, irresistible, and I adored their peculiar democracy where a duchess and a painter were treated on equal terms. But unemployed workers were marching on the streets and the fun was over. We came off the gold standard, belts tightened, horizons diminished. There were less quails, more eggs and bacon, and many of us traded in our London mansions for mansion flats as the party ended. For Clemmie, too. I was home less and less, caught up in Cambridge with friends, with the hopeful pursuit of girls on bicycles.' Fraser paused. 'Each time I returned to Witters, she seemed a little less certain, like watching a photograph fading in the sun. We had such glorious, savage memories. Even in her last days she had a ferocity of elegance I've only seen in one ...' He twisted the aquamarine ring on his finger. 'Perhaps two other women.' He cleared his throat.

'She died shortly after Alec and I graduated.' He fell silent for a time. 'She hadn't wanted to tell me about her illness in case it affected my studies. She learnt I came down with a First, and that I had secured a position with the Foreign Office. I told her it was in the political section, and she was happy with that. Alec and I visited her just after graduation and he invited her to his wedding. She had always loved parties and it was when she turned him down that I knew something was wrong.' Grace waited in silence for him to go on. 'I remember the stuffiness of her bedroom, how the heat seemed to hang over the land that summer.

'"I've had to let the flower gardens go," she said. I watched the sheep grazing the front lawn. "And I've shut down the east wing."

'"Clem, what's going on?" I said, without turning to her, afraid to know the truth.

'"Come and sit down," she said, patting the bed beside her. She took my hand in hers. I felt like a petulant child again, as though the world were opening up beneath my feet. "Ra," she said.'

'Ra?' Grace interrupted.

'She was the only one who called me that, ever,' Fraser said, glancing up at her. 'When I was small I couldn't say "Fraser" and called myself Ra like the sun god.'

'Go on.'

'I said to her: "I know there's something wrong." I covered her hand with my own. "Why didn't you tell me?"

'"Nothing can be done, so what point was there, until now? I am so glad, and so proud of you. Your father would be too."

'"No he wouldn't."

'"He would," she said gently.

'"What can I do?"

'"Nothing." Her peaceful resignation alarmed me.

'"But there must be. We shall get every doctor in Harley Street here."

146

'"Dear Ra," she said, stroking my cheek. "I've seen them all, already."

'"No!" My anger flared in panic. "I won't have it."

'"I'm ready," she said. "I have seen you through to the time when you can take care of yourself."

'"I don't want to take care of myself." I flung myself down on her, and I felt her inhale with pain. "I'm sorry, I'm sorry," I said, uncertain what to do.

'"Lie next to me, here, for a little while," she said, and I curled up beside her. Clemmie stroked my hair as I tried not to cry. "Don't be sad," she said. "We've had such fun, haven't we? You brought such joy to my life. I love you, Ra. Be happy, for us both." I felt her breathe deeply. "It's time for you to go now."

'"No. I won't leave you, not like this."

'"There will be other times," she said. "But you and Alec must go to London and start your new jobs. I am so proud of you both. When I think of you as little boys in short trousers. Skinny legs and bruised knees . . ."

'"No, I won't go. I'll postpone the job."

'"I want you to," she said. "I'm tired, Ra." A nurse tapped on the bedroom door and came in with a silver tray of medicines. "Go," Clemmie said, shooing me away. "Come down again when you have a day free and perhaps you can take me for a drive?"

'"Are you sure?" I paused in the doorway.

'"Go," she forced a smile, but I saw her lips shake. I strode back across the room to her, and hugged her, kissed her cheek.

'"I love you."

'"I love you too, Ra."

'A few days later, I received a telegram. It was waiting on the hall table in our digs. Alec and I had gone out to a jazz club after work and I nearly missed it in my addled state. Clemmie died, peacefully in her bed at Witters. I never had the chance to say goodbye and she died without me at her side.' He cupped the heels of his palms against his eyes. 'I wish I had been there. God, you have to be careful what you wish for in this life, don't you? All Clem wanted when she was younger was her independence, her freedom. It's as if some malign creature said: I'm going to grant you your wish, but then I am going to take away your baby, the man you love, and your health, and you will die alone.'

'I don't think it works like that,' Grace said. 'And you're forgetting, Clem had you.' She waited for him to look at her. 'It sounds to me like your mother lived a full life. What more can we ask for?' Grace leant towards the coffee table and clicked the recorder off. 'Well done,' she said. 'I'll go and make you some tea.'

'Bugger the tea,' Fraser said. He wiped at his eyes, and looked up at Grace. 'Bring me a G&T, Miss Manners.'

'Are you sure? Didn't the doctor—'

Fraser waved her away. 'And just let the Gordon's sniff the tonic.'

Long after Grace went home, Fraser sat alone in the darkening study, flicking through the images in the whirring projector, stirring only to change the carousel or pour another drink.

He looked up at a photograph of himself in a sharp suit in Paris, his words slurring. '1939,' he said. 'The people in the village thought I was a conchie. Bloody white feathers through the letter box.' He flicked on through the images. 'They didn't know that I was in Berlin on the Kristallnacht in 1938, that I had seen the streets glittering with broken glass like fields of diamonds.' He raised his glass, gazed into it in confusion when he found it was empty. It rattled as he put it on the desk. 'My contribution was hidden in the shadows, wasn't it, Biba? Not on the front lines that they knew of.'

'I was in Paris, too, with Alec, on VE Day, that glorious 8 May in 1945 when young men and women embraced in the streets.' He smiled, rocking gently in his chair. 'Alec, God I miss you. The things we saw. Everyone thought we were just a couple of Foreign Office swells, embassy bods with little better to do than sign papers and play tennis out of the heat of the day.' He flicked on until he found the picture he was looking for. They were both dressed in tennis whites, clowning around for the camera on a court fringed with date palms.

Fraser lurched to his feet. 'What's it all been for, Biba?' The dog stirred in her sleep at the mention of her name, and the pups whimpered. 'I've returned to a country I barely recognise. Of course there were short weeks of leave, but you just scratch the surface of your home country in that time. I don't recognise the land I find myself in – with its motorways and high-street chains. I'm trying to teach myself about pop music, and punk, to understand hooligans and why the rubbish and the dead are rotting in the streets.' Fraser broke off, raised his hands to his head.

Jack tapped on the study door. 'I saw your light was on. Come on, Frase, isn't that enough work for today?'

'Yes. Yes, it is. How was yours?'

'It's good to be back playing again. The new ponies will take some work but they'll be first rate.'

'I'll come and watch next time.' Fraser stepped deliberately across the study, only swaying as he reached the door.

'Jeez, Frase.' Jack looked at him, concerned. 'You're pissed!'

'Don't start.' Fraser held his gaze. 'It's been a tough day.'

'OK.' Jack swung Fraser's arm over his shoulder, and helped him upstairs.

'Sometimes I wonder what it was all for, Jack,' Fraser said as he collapsed into bed. 'When you look at the chaos, the misery of so many ordinary people . . .' He exhaled. 'This Thatcher woman says she wants marriage, hard work and savings, and I bet you my last sou if she gets in what we'll get is mass consumption and a selfish "me first" generation.'

'We can talk politics at breakfast. Get some sleep,' Jack pulled the cover over him.

'Sleep? What's that?'

'Night.' By the time Jack reached the door and turned out the light, Fraser was snoring.

15

'Can we go to the beach next weekend?' Harry said, pushing her Chopper along. She was sucking a red lolly, and hollowed her cheeks, making a loud pop as she pulled it out. 'Look at me, I'm Kojak.'

'Very funny. Where did you get the lolly?' Grace ran her fingers over the fresh leaves in the hedgerow as they walked along the rutted lane from the cottage.

'Cy's wife gave it to me last night.'

'That was kind of her, but—'

'I know, I know,' Harry rolled her eyes. 'No sweeties in the morning? But you should see what's on the menu for lunch today.'

'Liver?'

'And sago.'

'Yum,' Grace said, laughing. 'Both your favourites.'

Harry stuck her tongue out. 'Frogspawn, yuck!'

'Still, better than semolina.' She paused as the lane branched off towards the Manor. 'Have a good day, darling.' She hugged Harry tightly, and waved, watching her cycle off up the lane towards the village, bent low over her handlebars, plaits bouncing behind her in the breeze.

'Morning, Fraser,' Grace said, striding into the study, the skirt of her gypsy dress swinging around the top of her tan boots. 'Fraser?' She looked around for him.

'Out here,' he said, his voice sounding muffled. Grace walked out through the open French windows to the terrace and found him doing a headstand against the wall.

'Are you all right?' she said, tilting her head. 'You've gone purple.'

'Yes, or I will be.' He flopped down onto his knees on the yoga mat, and straightened up, easing his neck from side to side, his palms pressed against the small of his back.

'Is it playing up again?'

'Bloody thing. It's a sign of something, I'm sure.'

'It's just tension, Fraser,' Grace said firmly. 'Right. If you want to get on with this before I have to drive Ellen to the market, let's make a start.'

'Must we? It's a glorious day. They say it's the finest Easter since 1949.'

'Fraser, you can play later.' She flipped through her schedule. 'Today we are making notes about your work.'

'Can't that wait for volume two?' He settled, cross-legged, on the ground, his hands resting lightly in his lap, thumbs against his fingers. 'Much of it involved grey men in grey suits.'

'Come on. You're not getting away with that.' Grace sat down at a bleached teak table beneath an arbour festooned with wisteria, and unscrewed the lid of her pen. 'Start at the beginning.'

'After my father died, Clemmie took my name off the list for Eton and packed me off to Bedales when it was time. It saved my life.'

'Did Jack go there too?'

'No, he was torn but he chose Stowe. He liked the follies.' Fraser breathed deeply, swinging his arms over his head.

Grace laughed. 'It's a different world when you choose a school for its follies—' She checked herself. *Jack's right. I need to stop being so defensive.*

'I thought it was a sensible choice. You've seen how much he loves the estate, and gardening. In another lifetime he could have been a Capability Brown.' Fraser glanced at her. 'Talking of which, have you seen him around?'

'He said he had a polo practice today.'

'Ah, of course. They're getting ready for the season.'

'Do you play?'

'Used to, until my back went.' He put his hands in the small of his spine and rotated his head. 'Jack's a far better player than I ever was. Polo takes an agile mind and an agile body. For hundreds of years men used it as a way to train for war.'

'How does it work? I mean, do you have your own team?'

'Too rich for us, my dear. Lord Vestey's Stowell Park team costs tens of thousands for the three-month season.' Grace whistled in surprise. 'Jack's got a good eye as a breeder. He's just starting out, but he's sold a few ponies this season. A good pony can change a man's game, you know.' Fraser stretched. 'No, the days of house party polo are over. There are more and more professionals coming over for the Gold Cup. Jack just plays for a patron, a local team. He'll be taking part in the Cowdray Park Challenge Cup later on – you must come along and watch.'

'I'd like that. I might bring my friend Alice, if that's all right. She has a thing for polo players.'

'Attractive, is she? Might dust off my jodhpurs.' He raised an eyebrow as he reached for his notes.

'Let's get back to the story.'

'Very well. Where were we?'

Grace glanced at her notes. '1938.'

He closed his eyes. 'As I said, my mother died—'

'How old were you?'

'I was twenty-three, old enough.' He sensed Grace's unasked question. 'Breast cancer. It was barbaric and ghastly and I would have given anything to have taken away her suffering.' Fraser inhaled. 'I became – what's the word? – nihilistic? I blamed myself terribly for not being there with her at the end. I threw myself into my work, drank heavily, took any woman who showed the slightest interest in me to bed, then cast her aside. I'm not proud of myself.' Fraser stood up and went to the drinks cabinet. 'But you learn. Tempt you with a drinkie?' He dropped some ice from the bucket on the trolley into two glasses, along with a sliver of lemon.

'Bit early isn't it? Just a tonic, thanks.' Fraser poured gin and a splash of tonic into his own. 'Thanks.' Grace chewed on the end of her pencil. 'Tell me about the Foreign Office?'

Fraser took a slug of his drink and nodded. 'They decided I would learn Russian in Paris, and I lodged with a marvellous old woman, exiled nobility. She used to cut up oranges with a knife and fork, and grew those little cucumbers in window boxes in her day room. She had twelve cats that used to pee all over the place. Bonkers, but utterly charming.' He stretched out on the bench opposite Grace. 'I returned from Paris at the outbreak of war, and my career took me all over the world, even to Washington eventually, for good behaviour.'

'But what did you actually *do*?'

'As I told you, Alec and I were recruited at the same time.'

'Recruited?'

'By the same clammy-palmed don at a drinks party in someone's digs in 1935.' He waited for Grace to catch on. 'British Intelligence, my dear.'

'You were a spy? I thought you were a diplomat.'

'I held a number of legitimate positions to cover my other activities, of course. I probably would have made Ambassador if it hadn't been more useful for me to be low-key. Cesca reckons I'll get the nod in the next honours list. You know?' He mimed a sword touching someone's shoulders, once, twice. 'I rather hope I do. It would annoy the hell out of Dicky if I had a title and the loot.'

'Are you still – I mean . . .'

'My dear, I shall be looking over my shoulder for the rest of my days. People have long memories.'

'How can you live like that? How do you sleep?'

'I don't.'

'Weren't you afraid?'

'Always. But I believed in King and country, and George V celebrated his Silver Jubilee in 1935. It all seemed terribly patriotic. And . . .' His eyes were bright, defiant, when he looked at Grace. 'It doesn't take much analysis to realise I wanted to prove myself as brave as my father.'

'I couldn't do it. All the lies . . .'

'A whole lifetime.' Fraser sipped his drink. 'Alec and I used to joke we were the founding members of the Two Wick Club.' He glanced at Grace. 'Burning both ends – get it?'

'Ah.' Grace cupped her jaw on her hand.

'Who would burn out first? I would have put money on it being me.' He blinked, came back from the past. 'Still, as I've said many times, it wasn't nearly as exciting as it sounds. We're not all James Bond, dear.'

'Licensed to kill?'

'Sometimes . . .' He paused. 'Sometimes it is unavoidable. We were fighting a war just as surely as the cavalrymen who charged across the fields of Belgium at my father's side on horseback.' He mimed aiming a lance with one hand, reins with the other. Fraser sank back, ran his fingers across his hairline. 'It's an edgy, rackety life and you make more enemies than friends. They are good at choosing their people – bright, ambitious, charming, little to lose, and lots to play for. It takes its toll, of course.' She sensed the mask fall away and knew that for once he was not play-acting. 'The greatest irony, of course, is that it was my job to uncover secrets, to find people out, and I have spent my life unable to find the truth about my past, or the one person I was looking for.'

Grace stared at her notes. 'Hold on. Who are you talking about?'

'Virginia West, my dear. The only woman I ever loved.'

16

'Harry,' Fraser called, waving to her from the Manor lane. Birds sang brightly in the trees as Harry strode up the lane to school, wheeling her Chopper bike towards the road.

'Good morning, Fraser,' she said. 'When did you get back from London?'

'Last night. Look, I've got something marvellous to show you. Come and see.' She glanced behind her to see if Grace was still watching from the gate. She threw down her bike on the verge and ran after Fraser.

'I won't keep you a moment. You mustn't be late for school.' Fraser pushed open the old wooden door of the woodshed. 'How are you settling in?'

Harry shrugged. 'You know.'

'I promise you, if you can survive the playground, you'll survive anything in life, my dear.' He squeezed her shoulder. 'It will get easier.'

'Can I come and see the puppies after school?'

'Of course.'

Harry followed him into the gloom of the shed, her shoes sinking into the splinters of wood and earth. It smelt damp and cool and her eyes took a moment to adjust from the bright spring sunlight outside. 'Now, I have a job for you,' Fraser said, pointing at a wooden cage in the corner. Harry leant down, and looked in. Two dark eyes ringed with white feathers stared back, and blinked.

'An owl?' she said, her face lighting up.

'This little chap has lost his mother. I reckon he was learning to fly, and took a hit against a tree or something. Biba and I found him in the woods at dawn. His wing is busted up, but I've set it for him. Do you think you could help take care of him, make him better?'

'Oh yes, yes, I'd love to!' Harry knelt down, pressed her fingers to the mesh.

'Be careful though, darling. He's a baby but his beak and claws are already sharp.' Fraser squatted down at her side, and showed her a fresh nick on the back of his hand. 'He's a wild thing, remember that.' He patted her shoulder. 'Come and have tea after school and I shall tell you all about what he needs to eat, and when. This can be your special job.'

'Can I tell Mum later? She told me never to keep secrets from her.'

'Of course you may.' Fraser dusted off his knees. 'Very wise advice. Hold still, you've got a cobweb on your blazer. Can't send you off to school looking like a ragamuffin can we?' He brushed her sleeve clean. 'Right, get a wiggle on. And think of a name for him,' he called after her.

'How do we know it's a him?' she called, sprinting up the lane. 'I'm going to call her Sindy.'

'Sindy,' Fraser said, laughing under his breath as he walked into the study. 'My God, what have you done?' Fraser's voice made Grace jump. She was on her hands and knees sorting the last of the papers into neat piles.

'Good morning, Fraser,' she said. 'How was your trip?'

'I can't— How on earth am I supposed to find anything now?' he cried, flinging down his briefcase. 'I had a system!'

Grace dusted off her hands. 'With respect, you did not.'

'For heaven's sake, I go up to London for a couple of days and this happens!'

'I just thought—'

'I'm not paying you to think. I'm paying you to organise *my* thoughts.'

'Which is precisely what I've done. I could hardly sit here twiddling my thumbs with nothing to do.' Grace raised her hand. 'Before you fire me, why don't I explain what I've done?'

Fraser clicked his fingers for Biba to follow him, and he

flung himself onto the sofa, his arms folded. 'Go on then, Miss Manners. Dazzle me.'

'Don't sulk. It doesn't suit you.' Grace waited for him to look at her. 'I read everything you have written so far—'

'You read it? In its entirety?'

'Yes. It took me all night to get your handwritten pages in some kind of order.' She tapped a small stack of manila folders on his desk. 'This is what you have to show for thirty-five years' work.' Grace paused. 'I checked the dates of your earliest notes.'

'Is it really that long?' Fraser blanched.

'This,' Grace said, sweeping her hand towards the rows of trestle tables with neatly stacked piles of paper, 'is your background research, all of your reference notes, cuttings and photographs.' She leant against the desk and crossed one ankle over the other. 'From what I can see, little of this has made its way into your memoirs yet.'

'No need to be brutal.'

'May I make a suggestion?'

'By all means.'

'I've sorted your manuscript into chronological order—'

'Oh God, not this again. I told you, I can't work like that.'

'—and all the reference material in the same way. Why don't we work through decade by decade, adding in the material you want, and then clearing it out of the way? No wonder you've been going round in circles with all this.'

'Very well. I give in.'

'And . . .'

'Out with it.'

'I don't quite know how to put this,' she said. 'Do you know that phrase of Virginia Woolf's: "We must seek the diamonds in the dust heap" or something like that?'

'I vaguely recall her saying something similar to my mother.'

A smile played across Grace's lips. 'See, there's a diamond

157

for a start. This,' she said, tapping the manuscript, 'needs the diamonds sorting from the dust.'

'Literary critic, now, are we? Is there no end to your talents?'

Grace held her ground. 'It's no good at the moment, Fraser. It's just a dry catalogue skirting around exactly what you got up to in Moscow in the 50s, and Paris and Washington in the 60s and 70s. How many meetings and cocktail parties can you talk about when you can't even tell the reader what you were really working on?'

'A fair point.'

'Look, I think there are maybe three key events in your life.'

'Is that all? Rather tragic.'

'I think the whole point of this exercise is you trying to reconcile with the past. Am I right? Forget your career, for now. I think it all begins with your father. We need to get to the bottom of what happened to him, why he changed, and why he said what he did to you. There are notes and paintings everywhere by Albert – are you telling me he didn't keep a war diary?'

'I've looked everywhere here.'

'Well, I'll look again.' She tapped the manuscript. 'We need to feel how he felt during the war.' Grace paused. 'Then there's Clemmie, your relationship with her, and her death. You're doing well with those sections.'

'Thank you. Do I get a gold star?'

Grace waited for Fraser to look at her. 'There's one more thing.'

'One more? Are you sure there's nothing else? Three key moments doesn't seem like much of an achievement.' Fraser murmured.

'It's time to stop skirting around. Let's talk about Virginia West, the one that got away.'

Fraser stared down at his hands. 'I don't know that I'm ready to write about her.'

'I think, in terms of your memoirs, that story is the

Koh-i-Noor.' Grace leant towards him. 'I think she's the reason you are writing this at all. You want to find her.'

'Well, aren't you full of surprises,' he said quietly. Grace felt as if she was seeing the real person for the first time: a layer of armour, a mask, falling away. She was shocked by the sharp intelligence of his gaze. *It is, it's all an act, this eccentricity,* she realised.

'I imagine that is why you are so good at your job,' he said, 'that clarity, the ability to see straight to the heart of a problem, a gemstone, to know what to cut and what to enhance.'

'Talking of jewellery . . .'

'I said to Harry this morning how wise you are.'

It was on the tip of her tongue to ask about the Bouchet et Fils brooch, but at the mention of Harry, she stopped. *It's all gone too far. How can I tell him the truth now?* Grace bit her lip. *Harry's been so happy since we've been here. I can't risk it, not yet.* 'I hope you don't mind, but I read the inventory of the Stratton jewels. As you said, there seems to be some missing items from the original order with Bouchet et Fils. The tiara—'

'And the asteria – star – sapphire? I know. I imagine some sticky-fingered housemaid probably had it away with her at some point over the years. I do keep an eye out for it at auction though. I have chaps looking for me all over Europe. Perhaps one day it will come up at sale. Tell me something,' he said, leaping up from the sofa and pacing towards the mantelpiece, 'I imagine you've heard of the lore of lapidary?'

'Of course, the meaning of stones.'

'Do you believe in all that? That each gemstone has a quality, an energy.'

'Yes, I do.' Grace's gaze followed him as he walked. 'Do you know that line in *Breakfast At Tiffany's* where Holly Golightly says how the store calms her down?'

'Of course. I adore that film.'

'I think that's what made me want to be a jeweller. I always loved going to Cartier and Tiffany's, to all those beautiful old stores with my grandmother. I loved how they were, so calm, so beautifully lit. I loved the magic of the gems. After all these years working with stones I think each of them has a definite energy, but I'm not sure about all the superstitions. I think you make your own luck.'

'Indeed. I've often wondered, you know, about all these old beliefs. Twelve stones of the breastplate of the high priest of the Israelites, twelve tribes, twelve months, twelve signs of the zodiac. I think most of it's poppycock.'

'Do you?' Grace's hackles rose, thinking of the twelve birthstones. 'But you believe in this prophecy business?'

'Heard about that, have you?'

'Isn't it why you're writing your memoirs now, in the hope that you can find Virginia before it's too late?'

Fraser shifted in his seat. 'It's not the only reason, but yes, she meant the world to me, and I still don't understand what happened. The thought that possibly time is running out for me has rather spurred me on to finish the memoirs and make peace with the past. If I were to find Virginia as well . . .' He paused. 'Do you think I'm an old fool, believing the prophecy? I know Jack and Ellen think I'm doolally.'

'Not at all.' Grace shrugged. 'But I think a lot of these things are . . .' She searched for the right word. 'About interpretation? Maybe there will just be big changes this year, rather than—'

'Kicking the bucket?' Fraser grew serious. 'I have seen the worst of man, and the best. Sadly it is the worst that keeps me awake at night, even now.' He pinched the bridge of his nose. 'I keep an open mind, Grace that is all. I hate to think we have all the answers, and you have to hope that there is more to all of this than us. Who knows. There are a lot of charlatans, and hokum with horoscopes and so on.'

'Which sign are you?'

'Aquarius – January 30.'

'I'd say you're fairly average.'

'Average? *Average*?' He fell back against the cushions and laid his hand against his forehead. 'How ghastly.'

'I meant for an Aquarian.'

'Let me guess – Leo,' he said and Grace nodded. 'Do we get on?'

'Not bad. Leo's better with Aries, or—'

'Jack's Aries,' Fraser said, stroking the arm of his chair with his index finger, lips pursed. 'In fact, it was his birthday the other day. Sorry, you were saying about superstition.'

'I tend to keep an open mind and think "why not" unless someone proves otherwise.'

'A good viewpoint. I made it my business to study many things, including the occult. It doesn't mean I'm skipping round Stonehenge at summer solstice, but I like to be informed.' Fraser looked at the aquamarine in his signet ring, turning it to the light. 'I sometimes think gems are nature's most perfect expression. I must fetch them from the bank and get you to have a look at our small collection, see what you think. It pains me that it's not complete. I'm still hoping to track the sapphire down. I read somewhere that Sir Richard Burton had an asteria as a charm.' Fraser made a steeple of his fingers and rested his lips on them. 'We could all do with some luck, at the moment. You know, Helen of Troy wore a star corundum too. The Greeks thought there was something magical about them.' He looked at Grace. 'Tell me, have you heard of lyngurium?'

'Vaguely.'

'Theophrastus wrote about it. Take a look in the library later, there's a copy of his *De lapidibus* around somewhere.' Fraser took a cigarette from a silver box, and struck a match. 'The thing is, lyngurium was supposed to be this magical jewel made of crystallised lynx urine or some such thing, but it never existed.' He leant forward in the chair. 'The early lapidaries wrote about its virtues and qualities, but no one has ever seen it. What do you make of that, eh?' He gestured

161

at Grace. 'This "diamond" you talk about at the heart of my story, is more like lyngurium. Virginia, the woman I loved, who I have spent half my life looking for, never existed.'

'There you go,' Grace said, reaching for a pen. 'That's your first line.'

17

Paris, Summer 1939

I leant against the bar in the club in Montparnasse. The walls were painted black, the original mouldings picked out in silver. Red light bulbs barely illuminated the tables. It was nothing new, going out boozing and picking up girls after work with Alec, but for some reason I was nervous, this time.

'May I introduce you?' Alec said. 'Gin, this is Fraser Stratton.' The dancers always made a beeline for him. He was good-looking, like a young Marlon Brando, and funny, and generous. When the girl turned to me, I saw she had the most remarkable eyes.

'Gin, as in Gordon's?' I said.

'As in Virginia. My friends call me Gin.' She edged onto the stool at my side, and I glanced down at her endless legs encased in fine fishnet tights.

'I hope,' I said, leaning closer to her, 'that we shall be more than friends.' She smelt wonderful – of vanilla, musk, fresh sweat.

'Tell me, are you something important? I see you and your friends in here every night, and they seem to defer to you.'

'Why don't you kiss me,' I said, my lips brushing her ear, 'and find out how important I will be to you . . .'

'Fraser,' Grace interrupted. 'Stop it. I can tell you're lying.'

He sighed. 'I wish I had been that smooth.'

'Start again and tell me the truth.'

'Oh, very well.'

Paris, 1939

Fraser and Alec lurched along the Boulevard du Montparnasse arm in arm, singing at the top of their voices. 'One for the road? I heard there's a rather amusing club nearby,' Fraser said, raising an unsteady arm to point at a black painted doorway in a dimly lit side road. 'Or will Cesca be waiting?'

'Nah,' Alec said. 'She'll be fast asleep with the baby.' He placed his finger in front of his lips and whispered: '*Shh.* 'S funny, I'm not interested in girls any more. Just don't see them. I tell you, Frase, there's no other woman for me now but my wife. From the moment I met Cesca, boom!' He mimed an explosion. 'I love my wife,' he cried out, setting a small dog barking in an apartment nearby.

'Shh!' Fraser laughed. The first feathers of dawn crept over the skyline of Paris, like a bird waking and stretching its wings.

'Thank God we share an office, eh? At least we can cover for one another if we need a little sleep later,' Alec said. His evening shoes slipped on the greasy fire escape leading down to the basement club. Two bouncers blocked their way. Alec straightened up, and Fraser smoothed down his windblown hair. The larger one relented and jerked his head and his friend opened the door. A waft of sickly-sweet, warm air swept out, and Fraser narrowed his eyes to see into the gloomy, red-lit interior.

Up on the narrow catwalk, a sallow girl with an appendix scar and a moulting feather boa was going through the last motions of a striptease. The men at the bar hardly bothered to look up as the band reached its thumping crescendo.

'Garçon!' Alec raised his finger, beckoning the barman

163

over. He struggled to get his wallet out of his breast pocket and fumbled with the sheaf of franc notes. In the end, Fraser took it from him. He noticed two men at the other end of the bar watching them, and he tucked Alec's wallet into his own pocket. 'Two whiskies,' Alec said. His elbow slid along the bar as he tried to rest his head on his hand.

'I don't suppose you'd like to make that three, would you?' The dancer beside Fraser turned to them, an unlit cigarette between her fingers. When he thought back over the years to the first time Virginia West spoke to him, Fraser remembered it as a missed heartbeat in time, a key change. Everything seemed suspended. He couldn't remember what she wore – was it satin, or sequins? Were there feathers in her hair? But for a moment it was only her, and him, and the world contracted around them. *You*, he thought. *You.*

'Certainly,' Fraser said, breaking the spell. He nodded at the barman, who reached for another glass. Fraser pulled out his lighter, trying to flick it into life. The girl took it from him, turned it up the right way and he lit her cigarette, the flame dancing between them.

'Your eyes,' he said.

'Tell me something original.' She exhaled a plume of smoke. 'English?'

'Fraser Stratton. And this is my friend, Alec. How do you do.' Fraser offered her his hand. Hers was slender, cool. It made him think of cupping a songbird in his fingers. 'And you are?'

'Virginia West.' She stepped closer so that they could hear one another above the pounding drums of the jazz band. She looked up at him, the bare red light bulbs above the bar gilding her black hair. Fraser longed to touch the shining waves, to feel them slip between his fingers.

'You're American?'

She smiled in reply. 'I recognise you.'

'Do you?' Fraser sipped his drink, playing it cool while his heart pounded. He felt light-headed with the nearness of her.

'From the evening art class. Your drawings are good.' *No wonder*, he thought, remembering how she had posed for his ragtag group of part-time artists a few days before. It was the usual crowd – foreign students and housewives, retired bank managers unleashing their creative side. It was dusk. The shops in the street below had closed for the day and the studio was silent, pools of grey Parisian light settling on them from the north-facing windows. He had been sharpening his pencil with a scalpel, lounging back on the rickety old bentwood chair before his easel when she walked past, a crimson satin gown trailing after her. Her black hair fell in shining waves to her shoulders, and a wide purple sash pulled the gown in at her hand-span waist. He stopped mid-stroke, the blade against the wood. Virginia stepped onto the podium and untied the sash of her gown as the teacher gave the class instructions. Fraser didn't hear a word he said, and the red gown slipped to the rough wood floor.

Fraser leant closer to her now. 'You're an inspiring model.' He remembered his hand shaking as he began to draw, the shock of her beauty. He had glanced around to see if any of the other students were as surprised not to be drawing the paunchy old man who usually sat for their Tuesday evening life class. The night had the unreal quality of a dream as Virginia struck pose after pose and the light fell, the gas lamps hissing in the silence, their smell, his desire, the nearness of her intoxicating his senses. After the last pose she had dressed and walked past Fraser without acknowledging him. But he sensed her pause and turn behind him, to look at his drawing. He had frozen, unable to talk to her, and when he had searched for her later she had already left.

Now she leant closer to him, her red lips brushing his ear. 'Is it a coincidence you are here?'

'Of course,' Fraser lied. He had pressed the art teacher to find out who she was, where she worked. The air between them seemed alive to him, shimmering with possibility. His body ached for her, drawn to her like a compass aligning to true north.

Virginia glanced along the bar, her shoulder brushing his chest. 'Your friend's tired?' she said. Fraser looked over and saw that Alec had fallen asleep on his arms.

'Long night.'

'Are you celebrating?'

'Wetting his baby's head.'

'Congratulations.' Virginia chinked her glass against Fraser's. He swayed as he raised the glass to his lips. 'Don't you think you've had enough?' She took it from him and went around to the other side of the bar, pouring him a black coffee.

'You're the most beautiful girl I've ever seen.' He leant against the bar, resting his chin on his hand. 'Will you marry me?'

Virginia laughed. 'Ask me again in the morning when you're sober.' She glanced over at a couple of men in dark suits, watching them. 'If I were you, I'd drink my coffee, and get out of here. It's not safe for you and your friend.'

'It's perfectly all right. I'm a spy,' Fraser whispered, tapping the side of his nose.

'I like you, Englishman, whatever you are.' Virginia's eyes crinkled as she smiled. 'You're not an artist then?'

'No, the classes are for fun. My father studied at the same art school, though he was more interested in horses than girls.'

'Fun? Is that all I am to you?' She raised her chin, gazed at him through kohl-smudged eyes. 'What do you really do?'

'It's very dull,' he said, draining his espresso. 'I spend most of my time cooped up in the visa section of the British Embassy pushing lots of boring pieces of paper around.' His cup rattled in the saucer. 'But I am having Russian lessons with a marvellous old girl in the Marais.'

'And then what will you do, Englishman?' She tilted her head. 'Go to the lands of the tsars?'

'You could be my tsarina.'

'You're funny. Drink up,' she said, glancing up as the music ended.

'Gin!' the owner called brusquely, beckoning her towards the stage.

'I'm on,' she said. 'Please, go.' The sudden vulnerability he saw pass over her face like storm-blown clouds moved him.

'Of course. Can I see you again?'

'Maybe.'

'Maybe?' Fraser laughed. 'Will you be at the class on Tuesday?'

'No. I was just helping a friend out.' She turned to the stage and glanced over her shoulder. 'If you really are a spy, you'll find me.'

Fraser smiled and shook his head as she walked away. He tossed down some coins onto the bar, heaved Alec's arm over his shoulder, and half-carried him out of the door. The cold morning air hit him like a slap, and the knowledge that the men were following him sobered him instantly. He dragged Alec up the stairs and heard their footsteps close behind. The street was deserted, not a taxi in sight, and it was too early for the cafés to be opening. Everything was shuttered, abandoned. They were alone. He parked Alec safely on a low stone windowsill, and turned to face the two men, pulling down the sleeves of his evening jacket. 'I believe,' he said quietly in French, 'it would be in your best interests to let me and my friend leave without any trouble.'

The smaller of the men sneered. As he took his hand out of his pocket, Fraser saw the glint of a short blade. 'Not again,' Fraser sighed. He went for the smaller man, using his own weight against him, swinging the knife around, hitting the other assailant as he came for him. Fraser's movements were swift, precise. He hit the small man on the back of his neck with the side of his hand. He fell to the ground, stunned. The other man backed away, blood trickling between his fingers where he held his stomach, and he began to run. 'When will you ever learn,' he said. He swung Alec into a fireman's lift, and set off the short distance to his riverside apartment. He rang the doorbell and propped Alec up.

'Great night,' Alec said blearily.

'Oh God, look at the state of you two,' Cesca said as she opened the door, her auburn hair spilling loose over her robe. In the background, Fraser could hear the sound of a newborn baby crying.

'Morning, Francesca,' Fraser said.

'I should know better than to let you two out together. You always drink him under the table.'

'You look beautiful.'

'I look like a woman who has been up all night with a baby,' she said, heaving Alec indoors. 'Goodnight, or should I say good morning, Fraser?'

Fraser ambled back along the streets, and waited in an alleyway opposite the club. The pavement was clear, the man had disappeared already. Just before six, Fraser saw the doorway open and the dancers troop out, dressed in plain beige overcoats and simple hats now, chattering as they headed home. He saw her among them, taller than the rest, and he followed her at a distance to a shady side street, lined with lime trees, and waited, seeing which door she went into.

Fraser strolled to his office via a café where he freshened up and bolted another strong coffee. By the time he reached his desk in a wooden cubicle with opaque glass, Alec was already sitting at the table opposite.

'I feel ghastly,' Alec groaned. 'Please, shoot me now. I'll stagger through the day, but there's no way I'm coming to Russian tonight.' He looked at Fraser with bloodshot, purple-ringed eyes. 'I don't know how you do it. You look like you've had eight hours sleep and a full English.'

'Mmm – lovely runny eggs.'

Alec covered his ears. 'Shut up.'

Fraser sat back in his wooden chair and put his feet up on the desk, hands behind his head. 'I feel marvellous,' he said, gazing out of the office window at the bright morning sky. 'Simply marvellous.'

That evening, after work, he stopped at his usual bar for a cognac, then retraced his steps to Virginia's street. He waited, leaning against a lamp post, smoking, for an hour. At last, the high pale blue door opened and she stepped out, looking up in surprise as he walked towards her.

'The Englishman.'

'The American.' He offered her his arm, and they walked in silence for a time.

'You found me. So you really are a spy?'

Fraser laughed softly. 'No, just a boring paper-pusher who likes to spin a line, I'm afraid.'

'You got home safely last night?'

'No trouble at all.' He could tell from the look in her eyes that she had heard about the man in the bar. Virginia paused at the corner of the street where the club was. She didn't back away when he stepped towards her.

'You are trouble, I think.' She looked up at him. 'First you follow me to the club, and now to my home? I don't know whether to be flattered or afraid.'

'Marry me, Virginia West.'

'The way you say it, it's less a request than a demand.'

'You told me to ask you when I was sober, and I am. Fairly.'

'Are you always this impulsive?'

'I believe in gut instinct.' Fraser pressed his palms against the wall, low down, near her waist. 'And don't tell me you haven't felt it, this attraction between us.' His lips grazed her neck. She smelt of violets. 'All those hours, sketch after sketch, looking at you, unable to touch you. God, how I wanted to touch you.' He leant in to kiss her. Her hands reached for him,

169

her fingers tangled in his hair, holding him to her. They broke apart, breathless. 'Marry me.'

'You're insane.' He let his right hand fall, releasing her. Virginia strolled on along the street, her hips swinging.

'Marry me!'

'Maybe, Fraser Stratton,' she said, glancing over her shoulder at him as she walked away. 'Maybe.'

'Maybe? What kind of an answer is that?'

'The best you are getting until I get to know you.'

'You know me,' he called after her. 'I saw it in your eyes, the first time you looked at me. You know me!'

18

Grace looked up at the sound of the cottage door creaking open downstairs. 'Only me,' she heard Ellen call. She exhaled and closed her eyes. She had been on edge for weeks since the break-in. Cy had fitted new locks to the cottage, but the shock of it was still with her. Each night she double-bolted the doors, and she slept now with an old cricket bat under the bed.

'I'll be down in a moment,' Grace called. She turned back to the mirror and finished applying mascara. 'That will have to do,' she said, turning her head from side to side, checking her hair. The golden light from the lamp on the dressing table gilded her skin, softened the dark circles and lines around her eyes. She thought of the night ahead with Jack, of the party to come. Something fragile and new fluttered in her chest like a butterfly. *Hope?* She imagined dancing with him, music, laughter . . . *I bet he's regretting agreeing to come. I mean, who'd want me?* She looked at her hands, then opened the dressing table drawer. The plain manila envelope she had found on the mat with the morning mail lay in the shadows. She tipped out the diamond onto the palm of her hand, and held it up to the lamplight.

A diamond endures through rain and sun,
From everlasting love you cannot run

Grace felt sick, trapped. *Who's doing this?* The address was typed, and the postmark smudged. *Who?*

'Are you ready, love? It's seven already – Jack will be here soon,' Ellen called, breaking her train of thought. Grace threw the stone into the drawer and slammed it shut.

'How do I look?' Grace asked, skipping downstairs. She wore a tailored white tuxedo that accentuated her waist.

'Like that Bianca Jagger!' Ellen hugged Harry to her side. They were setting up Yahtzee on the coffee table by the fire.

'I hope it will be OK. Margot altered the suit to fit me.'

'It does that a treat,' Ellen said. 'Here, let me tuck the flowers in your hair.' She pulled out one of the kitchen chairs and sat Grace down. Into the loose bun Grace had fashioned, Ellen threaded jasmine and gardenias. 'They do smell lovely.'

'Margot had them specially ordered for the party. They're her favourites. I helped her decorate the Tithe Barn today and there were a few left over.'

'Is that the barn over Andrewsfield way? I went there with Mr Lloyd to a Rotary do a while back, lovely it is.' Ellen stepped back to admire her handiwork and tucked a sprig of jasmine in a little further. 'So let me get this straight. It's an anniversary party . . .'

'And a birthday party.'

'But they're not married?'

Grace flashed a smile at Ellen. 'Margot was the other woman.'

'Ohh.' Ellen pursed her lips.

'It's not as bad as it sounds. Ben's wife was an invalid. He cared for her for over twenty years. He and Margot met through work and . . .' Grace glanced at Harry. 'They've been friends for a long time.'

Ellen frowned. 'I don't go in for all that carrying-on.'

'Ben's wife knew about it. She passed away last year, but Margot refuses to marry him now.'

'Heavens. How unconventional.'

'That's Margot all over,' Grace said, checking her watch.

'I am glad Jack's taking you.'

Grace felt herself blush. 'He just feels sorry for me.'

'It will do him good to go and have some fun. That lad works too hard.' Ellen clicked her tongue. 'I don't like seeing young folks lonely.'

'Maybe you can be alone but not lonely?'

'How long's it been?' Ellen said gently, reading Grace's thoughts. 'I don't mean to pry.'

'No, it's all right.' Grace looked at her hands. 'After the way Fraser has been opening up with his memoirs, maybe I should talk about it. It's been almost a year since Sam went.'

'Daddy could still come back,' Harry said, defensively. She stuck her hands in the pockets of her dungarees.

'I'm sure he will, love.' Ellen hugged her. 'Now listen, why don't you run upstairs and get your pyjamas on before tea, then we can settle down and watch *Doctor Who* together.'

Grace watched as Harry ran upstairs. 'It's normally me hiding behind the sofa when *Doctor Who* is on.'

'I don't believe that for a minute,' Ellen said, busying herself tidying up. 'You're a strong one, I knew it the minute I saw you.'

'Even the strongest person has a weak moment or two.'

'Is it the party that's upsetting you?'

'It's just ...' Grace thought about confiding in Ellen. *But what would I tell her? Someone's sending me jewels and scaring me witless?* She bit her lip. 'I guess the break-in shook me up, and I feel his loss more at a time like this. It should be Sam at my side, or fooling around dancing, or drinking too much so I have to drive him home.' Her brow furrowed. *When was the last time that happened? When was the last time we really had fun together? Years?*

'What happened, love? You never let on. Did he walk out, or . . .?'

'He disappeared, Ellen. I was out for the day with my dad, and when we got back to our old house, there was a police car waiting for me.'

'Oh, love.' Ellen sat down beside her.

'The police found Sam's car parked up in Eastbourne near the coast path to Beachy Head with his wallet and keys still inside.' She glanced at Ellen. 'When they were appealing for anyone who'd seen him, a couple of hikers got in touch. They remembered seeing him walking along the South Downs Way, along the clifftop.' Grace looked down at her hands. 'Someone spotted a pile of clothes out on the beach just round by Birling Gap. That's what alerted the police at first. He'd left everything – his watch, his penknife. He never went anywhere without that.'

'They think he drowned?'

Grace nodded. 'He left a note in the pocket of his jeans, said he couldn't take it any more.' She looked towards the stairs at a noise from Harry's bedroom. 'He was a builder, a developer. The recession really knocked his business for six. Our businesses. We lost everything, even my parents lost their house.' Her hands twisted in her lap. 'He said he couldn't live with the guilt. He'd planned to throw himself off the cliff, but he couldn't do it. So he said he was going to swim out to sea and just keep on going, didn't want to leave a mess for someone to clear up by jumping.' She pressed her lips together, and sighed. 'He was like that. Everything always had to be perfect, for Sam. No mess.' *But that's all he's left, one big mess.* Grace shook her head. 'They've never found a body, so they can't pronounce him dead for seven years. I'm in this limbo where I can't grieve, I can't move on. Harry's sure he's coming back, and I just don't know what to say to her.'

'Oh, Grace, I had no idea. Sam Morgan. I remember reading about him in the local paper. How terrible for you.

173

I hadn't put two and two together because of your name.'

'It's a fresh start for us, it just felt right to use my maiden name.' Ellen's kindness made Grace's eyes prick with tears, and her voice caught. She saw the concern on Ellen's face. 'I'm fine,' she said, forcing the tears back. 'We'll be fine. I guess . . . I guess part of me wonders if he'll turn up.'

'Do you? After all that?'

'I don't know what I'd do if he did . . .'

'I couldn't forgive anyone who put me through so much.' Ellen raised her head at the sound of a car horn. 'That'll be Jack. You run along now, dear, and we'll see you later.' Ellen stood and kissed Grace on the cheek. 'It's about time you both had some fun.'

Jack stood waiting for her by the open door of Fraser's Mercedes. The sight of him in a dinner suit caught her by surprise.

'You look—' they began to say at the same time, and laughed.

'Wow, we are travelling in style,' Grace said, sliding into the back seat. Jack closed the door for her, and came round to the other side.

'Fraser told me you were planning on wearing white and I didn't think the Landy was a good idea.'

'I don't know. A bit of mud and oil never hurt anyone.'

As Jack gave the driver directions to the party, Grace settled back on the warm leather seats, enjoying the luxury of the car, the closeness of him in the half-light. Jack turned to her. 'You look beautiful, that's what I was going to say. And you smell amazing.'

'It's not me, it's these,' Grace said, reaching up to her hair. He leant closer, breathed in the scent of gardenia. 'Here.' She plucked a stem, and tucked it into the buttonhole of his dinner suit.

'No one's ever given me flowers before,' he said, looking from the gardenia to her.

'There's a first time for everything.'

Fraser stood in the stable yard, and watched Jack and Grace drive away, a look of satisfaction on his face. He wandered down the Manor lane to where Ellen stood at the cottage gate, watching the tail lights of the car disappear. 'Make a fine couple, don't they?'

Ellen wagged her finger at him. 'Don't you go meddling.'

He pulled a face of innocence and held his hands up in surrender. 'Is Harry there? I think Sindy is ready to spread her wings.'

'She's just getting into her pyjamas, but I'll send her along.'

Fraser dawdled on the way to the woodshed, stopping to tie back a trailing honeysuckle plant on the archway to the kitchen garden.

'Fraser!' Harry called, waving. She had pulled a puffa jacket over her pink checked pyjamas, and Grace's wellingtons slapped on the ground, too big for her. 'Is it Sindy? Is she all right?' Harry caught up with him, slipping her small, slender hand into his. Fraser looked at her in surprise, touched that she trusted him.

'She's better than all right. Her wing's mended.'

'Oh good!' Harry's face fell as she realised what this meant. 'Are you ready?' he said.

'Do we have to?' Harry's voice caught. 'I'm going to miss her.'

'She'll have grown to liking you,' Fraser said, pulling open the door of the woodshed. He ushered Harry inside, and patted her shoulder. 'Owls have a wide territory, but I wouldn't be at all surprised if she didn't make this wood her home, to be close to you.' Between them, they carried out the cage and set it on the ground, deep among the trees. 'Would you like to say goodbye alone?'

'No, that's all right.' Harry's face was serious as she knelt down. 'Good luck, Sindy,' she said, loosening the bolt. 'I'm going to miss you.' She stood back, next to Fraser. The owl took an exploratory step forwards, ruffling its feathers.

'Good as new.' The bird hopped forwards and spread its wings, flapping free to the sky.

'She's flying! Sindy's flying!' Harry craned her neck back to watch the owl soar into the sky. Her smile faltered, and she blinked away a tear.

'Don't cry, my dear.' Fraser handed her a clean handkerchief, monogrammed with a purple S.

'Why did she have to go?'

'It's what happens with all things. Even the things we love. Change is the only constant in this life, Harry.' He put his arm around her shoulders as they walked back towards the cottage. 'Now, do you think Ellen has crumpets for tea?'

'Wow, this is more like a wedding reception,' Jack said as they checked the elaborate seating plan. The hum of voices and laughter lifted to the high, vaulted ceiling of the Tithe Barn as people made their way to the tables.

'I think that's Ben's wishful thinking.' Grace could just see the top of his white hair – he was sitting at a table on the far side of the barn, next to Cilla and Ted, but there was no sign of Margot. Grace looked around the barn. *There must be a couple of hundred people here.* She had no idea they had so many friends. *Perhaps they are more Ben's?* Her grandmother had always seemed to keep herself to herself.

Grace turned to Jack, aware of how close he stood in the crowded, warm room, scented with gardenias and beeswax candles at the centre of every table. The beams of the barn were swagged with fresh greenery threaded with jasmine, and the light from candle sconces flickered over the faces of the guests.

'I think we're over here,' he said. She felt his arm move against hers as he guided her through the tables, the weight of his hand against her hip. It was the first time she had seen him in anything other than muddy riding clothes, and the crisp white shirt, the tailored dinner jacket set off his broad shoulders and narrow hips perfectly. Even his hair looked artfully dishevelled for a change, rather than a thoughtless mess. He leant down to her as Grace pointed out her family, and she smelt the fresh, clear smell of good soap. At their table, he pulled out her chair for her.

'That suit is something else,' he said, sitting beside her.

'It's nice to be dressed up for a change, instead of frumpy old Grace the harried mother.'

Jack laughed softly. 'I never think of you like that. I remember the first time I saw you striding down the road in those kinky boots of yours. The way you shook your hair out in the snow . . .'

'Kinky?' She laughed. 'I was a mess.'

'You looked great.'

Grace felt her head swim with desire. 'Here she is,' she said, spotting her grandmother. She turned to Margot. 'Typical, Gogo, last person at your own party.'

'One has to make an entrance. Who *are* all these people?' Margot scanned the crowd. 'Jack, how lovely to see you again,' she said, resting her hand on his shoulder. Grace noticed she looked uncharacteristically nervous. 'Will I do?' Margot said, smoothing the heavy silver duchesse satin of her cocktail dress. The garnet ring Grace had made for her glinted on her right hand. She wore a high-collared bolero jacket embroidered with pearls, and the wide bell sleeves swung, catching the light as she reached up to touch her hair. Grace opened her mouth to say that she looked beautiful, but Margot had already walked on, her face an unreadable mask.

'Man, that guy Ben can talk, can't he?' Jack stretched out in his chair after the meal. The jazz band began to play, and people drifted towards the dance floor.

'I thought the speeches would never end,' Grace said. 'Perhaps he forgot it's not a wedding.' She watched Cilla

177

and Ted gliding among the dancers, Cilla's chin raised.

'Your guys are pretty good.'

'Ballroom dancing lessons. Listen, I'm sorry about Mum.'

Jack grinned. 'No need to apologise.'

'But she was ...' Grace groaned and put her face in the palm of her hands.

'Honestly, I was flattered that she thought we're dating.' Grace peeked at him through her fingers, laughing. 'C'mon. Relax.' He drained his glass of wine and beckoned to the waiter. 'Will you have another glass of champagne?'

'Why not?'

'You deserve it. Man, I thought I worked hard. When I look at you and Harry, and work, I don't know how you do it alone ...' He trailed off, awkwardly. 'Here,' he said, placing a fresh glass in front of Grace, then settled back beside her, his arm slung over her chair. The table was littered with empty bottles and glasses, the ashtray overflowing.

'Thanks.' She raised the glass to him. 'The way I look at it, when you hit rock bottom, the only way is up.' A smile played on her lips. 'Not that you'd know about that.'

'Hey.' He nudged her. 'I know what it's like to be at rock bottom.'

'You? How?'

'Jeez, not this again.' He fell silent for a moment. 'If you must know, I lost my parents in a car accident when I was a kid, so I know what it feels like to have your whole world fall apart around your ears. Fraser was the only one who would take me on. If it hadn't been for him, my life could have taken a different track.'

Grace wished she could fall through the floor. 'Oh God, Jack, I'm sorry.' She gave his hand a squeeze.

'Ancient history. I was lucky to have Fraser, and as you keep reminding me, "all this".'

'Sorry,' she said quietly. 'Maybe you saved him, too.'

'What do you mean?'

'The way he looks at you, sometimes. I think you gave him meaning, and purpose. You kept him in the present.' Grace thought for a moment. 'Maybe that's why he's struggling now. He's retired and you're taking over the estate. Maybe he thinks you won't need him any more.' She smiled. 'Then there's The Prophecy.'

'Told you about that, has he?' Jack laughed. 'I care about the estate, I care about Fraser, and he likes you.'

'Which is why you're here? Squiring the staff?'

'Jeez, Grace, give me a break will you?' He looked at her. 'I'm here because I want to be.' He looked around the barn. 'It looks amazing. Your grandmother should be a wedding planner.'

'What do you know about wedding planners?'

'More than I need to. Told you: you don't have the monopoly on broken dreams.' Jack sipped his drink. 'I was young, in love, it didn't work out.'

'I'm sorry.' She waited, hoping he would open up to her.

'If it had been up to me, I'd have headed to Gretna Green,' he said finally.

Grace tilted her head and smiled. 'It's not all it's cracked up to be.'

'You eloped?'

'We did.'

'And?' He turned to her. 'I mean, I wondered about Harry's dad, if . . . if you're on your own. You can't just leave it like that.'

'You were right. I was a kid.' She glanced at him. 'I was a teenager, and pregnant with Harry.' She watched him carefully for his reaction. She anticipated shock, scorn, but she saw something unexpected – compassion. 'I was young, and Sam never took no for an answer. My parents – well, Mum, really, had forbidden me to ever see him again but he turned up in the middle of the night and spirited me away. He'd arranged everything.'

'Aren't you full of surprises?'

'What do you mean?'

'Don't take this the wrong way, but you just seem so straight. I mean, the way you've cut to the chase with Fraser and kicked his ass into gear, the way you handle work, and raising Harry. I can't imagine you doing something so impulsive.'

'People change, I guess. I've had my moments.'

'I admire that. I don't think I've ever done anything impulsive in my life.' He turned the stem of the glass between his fingers.

'What about your marriage?' Grace said. 'Ellen . . . well, she said that was a bit of a whirlwind romance. I think it's one of the most romantic, optimistic things you can do, to get married.'

'Don't tell me you still believe in the fairy tale?' Jack looked at her.

'Sure I do.'

'Are you enjoying yourselves?' Margot paused by their table, her hands resting on their shoulders. 'Why don't you ask my granddaughter to dance, Mr Booth?'

'Thank you, I was just saying this place looks incredible,' he said. 'Congratulations. Twenty years is a long time.'

'Do you think it's about time you moved in with Ben?' Grace asked her.

'Move in?' Margot laughed. 'Heavens, no. We'd last five minutes. *Je suis un esprit libre dans un corps sage,*' Margot said, flicking her hand in the air. 'Talking of which, please get your gorgeous young bodies on the dance floor, and get this party going.' Margot waved at someone across the room, and disappeared into the crowd.

'Do you dance, Mr Booth?' Grace said.

'I thought you'd never ask, Ms Manners,' he said.

'Just wouldn't want to be stepping out of line, sir.' Grace tugged her forelock.

'Very funny.' He guided her towards the dance floor.

'The band's good, isn't it?'

'Say, if you like music, Fraser gave me a couple of tickets for my birthday, for the Kate Bush concert.'

'I love her!' She looked up at him.

'I don't suppose you'd like to come with me?' Above the band, a mirrorball twirled, bathing the dancers in a shifting cloak of light, sparkling like diamonds.

'I don't know what to say.'

'I mean, I don't want you to feel awkward, like you have to. I know you're married, Grace.'

'No, I'd love to, really.' Grace felt the weight of his fingers resting against hers. The music was a pulse around them. 'It's . . . well, it's complicated.'

'I don't mean to pry.'

'Let's just enjoy tonight. Shall we?'

'Sure.' His hand slipped around her waist and they moved together to the music. The soft linen of the suit slipped around her, her silk chemise whispering over her skin. She felt hot, suddenly, a prickling of the hair at the nape of her neck. 'I like your grandmother.' She felt his lips brush against her ear.

'So do I,' Grace said.

'She told me earlier to take care of you.'

'Oh, God, she didn't? I'm sorry.'

'I was flattered.'

'Maybe I can take care of myself.'

'I don't doubt it.' He held her closer. 'Let your guard down, Grace. You can trust me, if you want to.'

Grace felt the weight of the music, of the wine, on her. 'I want . . .' She hesitated. *I want it all to go away. All the sadness, the grief, the loss.* She looked up at the mirrorball, spinning. *I want to feel light, and alive again.*

Jack looked down at her; she felt his lips against her hair. 'What do you want Grace?'

'I want—' *You.* She realised suddenly as she looked at him that there was nothing she needed, nowhere she wanted to be apart from here, right now, with Jack. She wanted desperately to reach up and kiss him, to lose herself in him and the moment, but she felt someone watching, and as she turned she saw her mother, her face etched with disapproval. *It's hopeless*, she thought. *I'm trapped. I'm not a widow, I'm married, and it will be years until I'm free to love again. I can't do that to Jack. He's a good man; he deserves to be happy, not lumbered with me. I'm a mess.* She leant in to him, resting her head against his shoulder, enjoying the nearness of him while it lasted. *Everyone keeps telling me to move on, but I can't, not really.* She thought back over the last year, and the past tumbled around her like a child's building blocks. Her marriage, her love for Sam had died long ago, when she realised what he was really like. *I've been lonely for so long. But I have to think of Harry.* Grace closed her eyes, and an image of the twelve gemstones, glinting, came to her. *How can I think of the future when the past won't let go?*

MAY

Emerald

Fertility · Wisdom · Rebirth

19

'Hoi, Gracie, give us a hand,' Alice called, struggling to get a cardboard set of traffic lights out of her purple minivan, emblazoned with *Looking Glass Café and Catering* in swirling letters.

Grace was standing at the school gate, humming 'The Man With the Child in His Eyes', waving Harry off for the day. Spring flowers nodded in the hedgerow at her side as the children milled around in the playground waiting for the bell, and mothers stood chatting. 'What are you doing?' she said, laughing. She took the traffic lights from Alice and reached in to the van to pick up a couple of orange cones.

'You know my sister teaches nursery?' Alice heaved a box from the van. 'She only went and volunteered me to run the Tufty Club.'

'You?'

'I'll get my own back.' Alice's clogs clattered across the playground. 'How was the concert?'

'It was . . .' Grace smiled to herself at the memory of her trip to London with Jack. The Hammersmith Odeon had been packed, and the music, the performances, had transported her.

'That good, eh?' Alice nudged her.

'It was amazing. She's incredible, so creative. I stayed up for hours when we got back sketching new ideas for designs.'

'Ah, that's why you look so knackered? I wondered if Jack had you up all night.'

'Alice!' Grace whacked her with the traffic light.

'Well, I wish he had!'

'It was just ...' Grace's stomach fluttered at the memory of the night before, of Jack pressed against her, protecting her from the crush of people, the heat, the music embracing them. They were surrounded by hundreds of people, but to Grace it felt like they were the only ones there. 'It was a wonderful night.'

'You're not a kid any more, show a bit of confidence, woman! The number of times I saw some boy you had a crush on snapped up by another girl because you were too shy, and then Sam made a beeline for you, and it was too late—' Alice bit her lip, stopped herself. 'If you like Jack, show him.' Alice shifted the box in her arms. 'Listen, a few of the girls from the village are getting together for a Tupperware party and a bit of a drink on Friday night at my place to celebrate Maggie getting in – about time there was a woman Prime Minister. I'm sick of these strikes.'

'The Winter of Discontent?' Grace raised her face to the spring sun as they walked. 'Let's hope it's a new start for everyone.'

Alice shouldered open the school door. 'Milk's gone up to fifteen pence a pint, can you believe it? The amount we get through in the café, it makes a difference. Anyway, mustn't grumble. Come along on Friday. It's nothing special, just a bit of wine and a chat.'

'Thanks, I'd love to.' Grace smiled, leaning the traffic lights up in the hall. 'Can I bring anything?'

'Just a bottle – or two.' Alice raised her hand in farewell as the school Head rang the brass handbell.

'Ah, Ms Manners!' he called as Grace turned to walk away. 'May I have a word?' Grace was swept away by memories of her old school as she followed him along the school corridor. There were crates of little milk bottles by the door, and Grace breathed in the smell of gas fires, of plasticine warming on the heaters, of pine disinfectant and witch hazel. She saw Harry shoot her a worried look as the children lined up for assembly.

'Please, do take a seat,' the Head said, gesturing at a low chair opposite his desk. The noise of the hall fell away as he closed the heavy wooden door.

'I always feel as if I've done something naughty when they make you sit on these chairs at parents' evenings,' Grace said, settling gingerly on the little plywood chair. Her smile faded as he failed to laugh, and she folded her hands in her lap.

He filled his pen from a large bottle of Quink ink on the desk, wiping the nib on blotting paper. 'I won't keep you long.' He reached for a manila file marked *Harriet Morgan*. 'How do you feel Harry is settling in?'

'Very well. She's made some good friends already.'

'Excellent. We're very pleased with her progress. She's an extremely good pupil. Too good perhaps.'

'Meaning?'

'Ms Manners, we are not here to judge, but is there a situation at home we should be aware of?'

Grace inhaled slowly. 'We lost Harry's father last year.'

'I'm so sorry.' He closed the file and laced his fingers together. 'That explains it. I'm afraid there was an incident yesterday. She punched one of the older boys, knocked him to the ground.'

'Why? That's not like her at all.'

'We got to the bottom of it. It seems he has been teasing her for some time about being illegitimate. He said Harry had a different name from you, that you were – well, I won't repeat the word – and that you had "shacked up with Mr Stratton".'

'Oh good grief.'

'You work under your maiden name?'

'Manners, yes.'

The Head shrugged. 'It's a small village, I'm afraid. People talk.'

'Poor Harry, she hasn't told me any of this. I thought after Sam, her father, went that she might act out.'

'Girls often do at that age. It's a little glimpse of what you have in store when they are teenagers.'

'But she hasn't at all. If anything, she's done the opposite. It's as if she's trying to take care of me, which is all wrong.' Grace's head sank. 'I hoped I could give her her childhood back if we made a fresh start.'

'Give her time. Children are remarkably resilient. They are like plants, shower them with love and fresh air and they bounce back.' He stood and shook her hand. 'I have no doubt that you are a good mother, Ms Manners. Harry is a bright and lovely girl. She has guts too. By the time we knew what was going on, when it came to a head yesterday, six of the biggest boys in the school had her cornered. A lot of children would have broken down. She just went for the biggest one of them and flattened him with a right hook.' The Head winked at her. 'Not that I can condone that kind of behaviour, of course, but I think Robbie Green will think twice before he picks on another child.'

Grace stopped off at the cottage to change out of her wellies. As she pushed open the front gate, she noticed a manila envelope hanging from the letter box. She yanked it free, leaning against the doorpost to pull off her boots. Through the paper she could feel a familiar hard bump. Her heart began to race. She tore open the envelope and tipped out the gemstone onto her palm. *Emerald*, she thought. She held it up to the light, and checked the cut, the work she had done oiling and infilling the flaws to perfect the stone. Grace checked the envelope – there was a typewritten card: *In May you'll taste the caress, of emerald's promised happiness.*

She realised with a jolt that this time there was no postmark. *It's been hand-delivered.* She stood on the doorstep and looked out across the fields, up the lane towards the village. *Who's doing this?* she thought, shaking with anger.

'Where are we going?' Fraser dragged his feet crossing the yard to Grace's car. She had put the roof down and Jagger and Biba sat on the back seat, tongues lolling expectantly. Between them sat a wicker hamper with a faded F&M on the side, a tartan wool blanket folded on top. Two candy-striped deckchairs rested in the footwell.

'Not far,' Grace said, opening the passenger door for him. 'I just felt like getting out of here for a while, and it will do you good too.'

'I don't like magical mystery tours.'

'Trust me.' The Beetle's engine sputtered into life, and as Fraser wound down his window, she pulled up the driveway. Biba snuffled at his shoulder, her hair blowing in the wind. 'When are the pups going to their new homes?'

'Any day. Jack's keeping one, did you know?' He reached into his breast pocket for a pair of Ray-Ban sunglasses and settled back. 'He's said Harry can help train and walk him. Hopefully that will get her off your case about keeping one yourself.' He glanced at Jagger. 'I think your hands are quite full enough in the canine department.' Grace turned towards the coast road and flicked on the radio. The Rolling Stones crackled thinly. 'Ha. "Jumping Jack Flash". I like this one. Do turn it up.'

'You surprise me,' she said above the wind and the pulse of the music.

'Why? One must be of one's time. I can't bear people who say they never listen to pop music or watch television. What on earth is the point of being alive in the twentieth century and pretending you live in the seventeenth?' Fraser drummed his fingers on the door in time to the music. 'I love Chopin and opera, but I love Pink Floyd too. Jack has been educating me.' Fraser's shoulders shifted in time to the music. 'How did it go in London?'

'Fine, thanks. I had a meeting with an old client.'

'Are you working again?'

'Not really. I've just been using a friend's workshop to do a couple of commissions at the weekends. The guy who rents it from him has come back from India now, though, so I'll have to think of something else.'

'Oh good. I mean, I'd hate to lose you just yet. I'd love to see them.'

'There's a couple of photos in there,' she said, pointing at her leather bag on the floor. 'Take a look.'

Fraser lifted the bag onto his lap and swung open the flap. 'It always amazes me the amount of kit women get in their bags. It looks like you're going off to war.'

'I'm sure lip gloss and Sindy-doll shoes would come in handy.' She glanced down and saw that her wallet had fallen open. A photograph of her and Sam with Harry smiled up at them.

'Is that your husband?' He waited for Grace to reply. 'Good-looking chap. I'm sorry, I don't mean to pry.'

'No, it's fine. I don't talk about him because, well, it still hurts.' She gripped the steering wheel, her knuckles showing white. 'Did Ellen not tell you?'

'She, ah . . .'

'Does Jack know?'

'You can trust us, Grace. As I said, we didn't want to pry. Your private life is your own.'

'Thank you.' Grace exhaled. 'I just . . . I wanted a fresh start. But even here, some boy at the school has been teasing Harry about being illegitimate.'

'I know, she told me. Punched the little sod, good for her.' He folded his arms. 'Bring her round for tea tonight after school. I'll have a word with her.'

'Would you? She really looks up to you.'

He carefully moved the wallet out of the way and found the photos of the garnet and amethyst rings. 'Beautiful.'

'The rings? Thank you. The garnet was a gift for my grandmother, but Mr Goldstein sold the amethyst the minute it went in the window apparently.'

190

'I'm not surprised. I wish we'd known you when Jack got married. Something like this would have been far more becoming than that rock his wife chose.' Fraser smiled lazily as Grace swung onto the beach road. 'But then, sometimes size really is everything.'

'I get the feeling you don't rate her highly.' She hesitated. 'I apologise if I'm speaking out of turn.'

'Not at all.' Fraser laid his head back and gazed up at the sky, the wind ruffling his thick grey hair. 'I rather think Jack was chosen, rather than choosing for himself, that's all. It surprised me; she's not the kind of woman I thought he'd marry.' Fraser tipped his sunglasses back onto his forehead and pinched the bridge of his nose. 'After Jack left school, we had a bit of a falling-out. He ended up in Argentina, dead set on being a professional polo player.'

Grace glanced at him. 'I can't – I mean, he just seems too sensible. I can't imagine him doing something so . . .'

'Wild? I know. Of course, I had to pretend to be furious, but I was actually rather thrilled he had it in him.' He sighed. 'For a long time he was just focussed on playing polo, but he met this girl a couple of years ago. I don't know what they have in the water out there but Argentinians are stunning, the men and the women, have you noticed? He fell hard for her. She was passionate, wilful – too wilful. Not long after they married, Jack came back from practice early and found her in bed with his best friend.'

Grace whistled slowly. 'Poor thing.'

'I can't fathom it. Why she would cheat on a good man like Jack, I don't know. He's proud as hell – she's tried to win him back but he filed for divorce immediately. Can't say I blame him.'

'You care a lot about him, don't you?'

'As I would for my own son.'

'Any woman would be lucky—' Grace broke off, feeling awkward suddenly. 'Here we are,' she said, pulling up. West

191

Wittering beach car park was quiet this early, and she found a spot near the seagrass. She felt Fraser watching her, waiting for her to go on. 'Look, I shouldn't have said anything. It's none of my business.'

'No, I'm glad you did.'

Grace opened the door and pushed the seat forward to let Biba and Jagger out. 'Shall we head to the dog beach and give them a run?'

'Splendid idea.' Fraser opened the door for the dogs and lifted out the picnic. Jagger bounded ahead, Biba trotting sedately after him. Grace swung her bag over her shoulder and picked up the deckchairs. 'What a glorious day,' Fraser said. The spring sun shimmered across the open water as the dogs splashed in the shallow pools left by the tide. 'I haven't been down here for ages. Jack comes pretty regularly with some of the boys to exercise the horses. They love the water.' He turned to Grace. 'Have we got you in the saddle yet?'

'Me? No. Harry seems to be taking to it.'

'She's a natural, great seat.' He took the chairs from Grace and opened them out. 'But then you have a lovely posture too. Did you dance as a girl?'

'Every week.'

'I thought so. You still walk with your feet at ten to two.'

'Do I?' Grace laughed. 'How funny that you noticed. In fact, I wanted to be a ballerina until I got too tall and these, well . . .' She gestured at her chest. Grace flopped down in one of the chairs and the wicker hamper creaked as she opened the lid. 'I asked Ellen to make up a cold lunch for you, in case we're down here all morning. This must be for you.' She handed Fraser a hallmarked silver hip flask.

'She knows me well.'

'I thought the doctor said—'

'Bugger the doctor.' Fraser sat back in his deckchair and lowered his sunglasses to the tip of his nose. 'Now, what's all this about?'

'I thought a change of scenery might inspire you.'

'And?' Fraser waited. Grace hesitated. She wanted to confide in him, to hear his advice.

'And someone stuck this through our door today and I just felt like getting out of there.' Grace handed Fraser the envelope from her bag and watched his reaction. 'They didn't manage to get in, this time. The bolts Jack had put on the doors stopped them, at least.'

'Well. A mystery. Is this the first?'

'No.' She looked up at him. 'It's been happening every month.' Grace explained about the gemstones.

'Extraordinary,' Fraser said, turning the emerald over in his palm. 'Do you have any idea who's doing this?'

Grace shook her head. 'I can't . . . I mean, why would anyone do this?'

'Think. Who are your enemies, who would want to upset you?' Fraser pursed his lips. 'Or who might want to get your attention? An admirer with a penchant for the dramatic?'

Sam, she thought, instantly. *No. If it was him he wouldn't hide like this. He couldn't be that cruel, could he?* Grace's stomach tightened, thinking back over the years.

'The thing is, no one here knew about the stones except my family and the people at the party, who saw Sam put them in the chimney.' Grace pressed the knuckle of her thumb to her lips. 'I know Sam. I know people were intimidated by him, scared of him. Maybe now he's not here they're coming after me?' She shook her head. 'But even if Sam owed them money, they wouldn't do this, would they?'

'I doubt it. Why would someone who is owed money send jewels to you?'

'They're not worth a fortune.' Sam's words when she was choosing the jewels to set in the chimney came back to her: *Not the best ones, Gracie. It's only for show.*

'Even so.' Fraser drummed his fingers against his lips. 'No, this isn't about money. It's about power, manipulation. It's revenge . . .' He paused. 'Or seduction. There must have been someone – a friend of your husband's perhaps? A client at your jewellery store? There must be scores of chaps holding a torch for you.'

'For me? Who'd seduce me?' Grace burst out laughing and looked down at her hands.

Fraser fell silent. 'He must have been quite a piece of work, this Sam of yours, to knock your confidence so low.'

Grace looked at him in surprise. 'He never hit me.'

'And that makes it all right?' Fraser waited, but she wouldn't talk. 'There are many, many ways to hurt a person without using your fists.'

'Never mind, I'm sorry to drag you into this,' she said quickly. 'I don't know who's doing it, it's silly, really.' She busied herself lifting out the tape recorder and microphone. 'It's like some fairy story, gemstones appearing out of nowhere.'

'No, my dear, they're reappearing.' Fraser grimaced at the sight of the tape recorder and carefully folded the envelope, handing it to Grace. 'You killjoy. Not that blasted thing. It's all work, work, work with you. I bet your ancestors were pilgrims. Or slave drivers.' He took a slug from the hip flask.

'Nothing that exciting. French and English peasants.'

'Grace, dear heart, I am really not in the mood to work today.'

She looked steadily at Fraser. 'I don't want to talk out of turn . . .'

'But?'

'You hide it well, but I do know something about depression.' She watched his reaction, a slight defensiveness. 'My mother has been prone to it all her life.'

'Some of the most interesting people I've met are.' He ran his finger round the rim of the hip flask. 'You see things with great clarity, don't you? It's something I admire about you a great deal.' He took a swig and gazed out to sea, watching Biba and Jagger playing. 'There's little you can do about the black dog when he's on your heels.' He glanced across at Grace.

'Drinking doesn't help.'

'I assure you, it does.' He smiled grimly. 'I don't need a nanny, Grace. I know how to get through these episodes now. I've just found retirement rather challenging, that's all. I thought completing my memoirs might help ease the process, but it has dredged up all kinds of things I was too busy, or too scared, to work through at the time. Making peace with the past has proved to be harder than I thought.'

'But it must be helping, too?'

'Perhaps. I just . . . I can't bear the idea of slipping into another spell, and I can feel it waiting for me.'

'My grandmother always described it as seeing Mum wading through a fog-shrouded bog. None of us could reach her.'

'Fog in a bog.' Fraser laughed softly. 'That's good. Very good indeed. It's not feeling sad, or blue, you just feel numb. It's an absence of feeling – for me, at any rate. Life loses its colour. The temptation to lie down and sink is all-consuming.' He stuck his chin out. 'But you don't. You keep putting one foot in front of another, and walk your way out of it.'

'Have you ever seen anyone?'

'Shrinks you mean?' Fraser stretched. 'I've seen them all – shrinks, quacks, tried every med on the market. None of them have worked for me.'

'My grandmother always says exercise is the key. Yoga, meditation, fresh air.'

'Bit of a hippy was she? Girls like that seem drawn to yoga. Part of the reason I took it up.'

Grace smiled at him. 'Did you indeed? No, I don't think so. She's an antiques dealer – she does up bits of French furniture, textiles, drawings, that kind of thing. She used to sell some of her own work as well – you know, copies of old masters.'

'A forger too, eh? I should like to meet this grandmother of yours some day.' He cocked his head. 'Enough of this chit-chat.'

'Are you sure you're OK?'

'Don't worry about me, dear heart. I have summer and Italy to look forward to. That normally pulls me out of the doldrums.' He hunched his shoulders and settled down in the deckchair. 'Right, let's get on with it.'

'Tell me about her,' Grace said, clicking the machine on. 'Tell me more about Virginia West. Everything you can remember.'

'If you're trying to gee me up, this is going to be disastrous.' He exhaled. 'Tell me, do you ever take your own advice?'

'Don't change the subject.'

'It strikes me you're good at listening, at getting other people to open up.' Fraser stared out to sea. 'God knows, we all have secrets. And some of them are so painful it is easier to grow an exoskeleton to protect them. But old wounds need to breathe, to heal, don't you think?' He looked at her, waited until she met his gaze. 'Perhaps you needed your guard up, once. But to be happy and content you need to trust and let go.'

Grace felt hot; she swallowed down the tightness in her throat. It was as if Fraser had seen right through her. 'What if I can't trust again?'

'Dear heart, any wounded creature has to take that chance in order to recover. Risk the first step. Allow themselves to be helped.'

'Is that what you've done?'

'Me? God no, I'm as damaged as the next man.' He raised his flask. 'The only person you can trust completely is yourself. But life would be awfully dull if we played it safe, don't you think?'

'Tell me about her.'

'As I said, we met just before the war, in Paris.'

'She was your first love?'

'First and only. Of course there were girls before, and lovers after, but there has only ever been one woman for me.' Fraser turned slightly in the chair towards her, crossed his leg. 'I

196

never did find out how she ended up in Paris. There was a jazz band playing in that seedy club the night we met – I think they'd come over from the States and got stuck in Paris, so maybe she came over with them. The guy on the horn was a genius – I get goose bumps just thinking about those notes, the high C made the hair on my neck rise.'

'What did you do on your first date?'

'I took her to the Ritz for dinner. As we waited in the bar, I said, "May I buy you a drink?" "No, but I shall buy one for you," she said, and beckoned over the waiter. I was still expecting her to tell me to bugger off at any moment, and here she was handing me a glass of champagne.'

'I like the sound of her already. Describe her for me.'

'It's going to sound like Snow White, but she had ebony hair, glossy as the lacquer of a Steinway, a widow's peak, perfect rosebud lips. And her eyes . . . I can't begin to describe the colour. Like the night sky in the Middle East.' Fraser took a deep breath. 'God, even conjuring her up now, it hurts, the longing for her.' He sipped at the hip flask. 'The thing is, it wasn't how she looked though – there was an intelligence, a spark to her that blew me away. You know when someone has "it", that palpable charisma? Well Gin had it in bucketloads.' He tucked the hip flask in the sand and fumbled for his cigarettes. 'After that first date, we were inseparable, snatching a couple of hours whenever we could between my work and her performances. It was . . .' Fraser tried to articulate the days and nights in Paris the weeks before the war, the heady cocktail of exhaustion, fear, desire. 'You know, I'd been in Germany the year before, and I knew what was coming, what we were all facing.' He took a deep breath. 'But God, with her, I felt so alive.' His face took on a softness. 'It was a glorious summer. They were the most vivid days of my life.'

'So why didn't you live happily ever after?'

'I don't know.' Fraser's voice was tinged with sadness. 'We set a date for our wedding.'

'You were going to marry her?' Grace looked up in surprise.

Fraser nodded. 'She gave in after I had asked her about a thousand times. Alec and Cesca were going to be our witnesses.' Fraser crossed his legs, turning in on himself. 'That's why it's so painful to talk about her. Jilted at the altar, you see? I always knew she was hiding something from me, that there was a part of her life she wouldn't let me in on. I thought perhaps she had been married before.'

'Did you try to go after her?'

'Of course I did. I spoke to every taxi driver outside the hotel until I found the one who had taken her to the station. Eventually I tracked her as far as Bordeaux. Then she just disappeared.' His index finger followed the snaking line of smoke from his cigarette. 'Pfft.' His fingers splayed out. 'She disappeared like smoke.' He ground out the stub in the sand. 'With the chaos of the war, any tracks she left behind were thoroughly blurred. I spent years, afterwards, trying to find her, hoping each day that the mail would bring word of her. I could cope with her not wanting to marry me, and I think, with the benefit of hindsight, I came on too strong – I just couldn't bear not knowing if she was all right, if she was happy.'

Grace clicked off the machine. 'I'm so sorry.' She reached over and took Fraser's hand. 'Don't give up. I'm going to help you,' she said. 'Between us, we're going to find her.'

'But how? I've tried everything, and her trail went cold forty years ago.'

'It will be the perfect ending for your memoirs.'

'No, surely it's too late after all this time?'

'Never give in,' Grace said. 'We'll start with what we have to hand. All the papers in the library, is that everything you have?'

'Good heavens, no. There are boxes and boxes of photographs and letters up in the attic. It's in a bit of a state – I just grabbed anything that looked useful.'

'I'll make a start there. I promise you, Fraser, we'll find her.'

20

'Almost there,' Fraser whispered, guiding Harry. Cabbage White butterflies fluttered above the long grass swishing around their legs. Grace followed at a distance with the dogs. 'Be quiet, and crouch down here.' Fraser waited in silence, only the sound of birdsong and the wind in the trees around them. 'Ready? Open your eyes.'

'Where is it?' Harry said, blinking in the sunlight.

Fraser bent down to her level and pointed. 'There, in the reeds at the edge of the pond.' The surface of the water was gilded by the last of the sun, gnats landing, circular ripples radiating in the stillness. Nearby an iridescent green dragonfly hovered.

'A kingfisher!' Harry whispered. The bird's bright blue plumage flashed. 'I've never seen one before.' Jagger barked, spotting a rabbit, and crashed through the grass and reeds. Birds flew chattering into the rosy sky. Biba trotted after him, her curved tail held high, Jack's puppy gambolling at her side.

'Ah well, at least you saw him,' Fraser said, dusting off his knees. He put his arm around Harry's thin shoulders as Grace joined them. 'Now, your mother tells me you've been having a few difficulties at school.' He felt her stiffen.

'There's nothing difficult about it,' she said. 'Robbie Green is an idiot and he got what he deserved.'

'Good for you, my dear. If you're going to have a fight, hit first and hit as hard as you can—'

'Fraser,' Grace interrupted. 'That's not really the kind of advice I was hoping for.' Her tone was strict, but Fraser could see her eyes creasing with amusement. She was wearing a white gypsy shirt and a long embroidered skirt with sandals, her hair blowing loose in the breeze. *Attagirl – you are quite lovely when you smile. What a shame Jack couldn't join us,* Fraser thought. *This place is working its magic on you.* 'Sorry,' he said.

'The thing is, Harry, the way people treat you has far more to do with them than it does you.'

'I don't understand.' Harry frowned as they walked on along the overgrown path.

'Bullies are sad little people.' Fraser whistled for the dogs to follow them. 'They feel inadequate, so they surround themselves with spineless, cruel thugs and attack anyone they see as different, or anyone they think is weak, in order to make themselves feel big.'

'People like Robbie Green.'

'Exactly.' Fraser held his hand out to Grace to help her over the stile.

'Thanks,' she said, gathering up her skirt to climb over.

Good legs, too, Fraser thought, taking a peek. *I hope Jack declares himself soon, before he loses his chance.* Fraser lifted Harry over the fence and jumped down after them. Wittering Manor lay ahead of them now, just beyond the gentle curve of the golden field.

'Have you ever been bullied, Fraser?' Harry said, taking his hand.

'Not exactly, but I thought it might help you to hear my story.' He looked across the estate at the house. 'My father died eleven days after the eleventh hour of the eleventh day—'

'That would make a great line for your memoirs,' Grace said.

'It *is* in my memoirs,' Fraser said, and laughed. 'I thought you said you'd read the damn thing.'

'Must have missed that bit.' Grace glanced sidelong at him, smiling.

'The thing was, Albert saw us safely delivered into peacetime – his looks intact, only a limp from Mons, but no one knew how broken he was inside. To me he was a god, infallible. But like the internal injuries that cause a man to sicken and die when he looks whole, his death came as a great shock to my mother. Albert had the good grace to disguise his suicide as an accident.'

'Your dad killed himself too?' Harry looked at him in surprise.

'I think so, darling,' Fraser said, squeezing her hand. 'He had been around horses all his life, so I have no doubt he knew what he was doing the day he decided to ride out on an unbroken stallion when he still struggled to walk. Perhaps he was testing himself – who knows? One of them would break that day – the horse or my father. Of course, they had just begun talking of "shell shock", but he was bright and a good actor. Skills that I am grateful he passed on to me, for they saved my life many a time.'

'What was he like?' Harry said. 'Was your dad kind?'

'I have few recollections of him,' Fraser said as they walked, 'but my earliest memory is this: I was four years old and annoyingly precocious. I was a frantic, energetic child, a bright spark with flaming red hair and golden skin, an unusual combination that Clemmie loved, so opposite to her own pale skin and dark hair. Like most children, I broke things. I escaped my nannies, I played ball inside. Every smashed vase, every banging door shredded Albert's nerves.'

'Poor him,' Harry said. 'And poor you. That can't have been much fun.'

Fraser nodded. 'This is what I remember: it was the autumn of 1918. I can still see the fall of light through Witters' open front door. I was aiming for the garden. I remember the swing of my leg, my foot hitting the leather football, its trajectory. It missed the open doorway – I was never a terribly good shot – and the ball hit the fanlight. It was like an explosion – glass clattering down seemingly forever. I froze. As if in slow motion, I heard the sound of a chair falling in the study, my father's garbled cries. He seemed to be shouting from underwater. I remember the sharp pain of his hands on me. My mother, yelling at him to stop. He released me, finally, stood in the hallway screaming, his hands clamped to his ears. "I should have taken the girl!" he cried over and over again.'

'The girl?' Grace said.

'My twin sister,' Fraser said, his gaze clear. 'Clemmie pulled me to her, buried my head against the safety of her skirts. "*I should have taken the girl.*" I asked my mother later what he meant. She told me that I was special because my father had chosen me. She told me that my mother, my real mother, was called Josephine, that she lived in Paris, and that she had given birth to Albert's twins. He persuaded her to let him take me, to raise with Clemmie in England, because Clem had lost a baby, recently. He gave the girl child a diamond wing brooch.' Out of the corner of his eye, Fraser noticed Grace start.

'The tiara?' she said.

'Precisely. He took one brooch for me, and left the rest of the tiara with my twin sister. I imagine he gave Josephine more than that, but that is all I know, yet.'

'So you mean . . .' Harry said.

'Yes, I really was illegitimate. The realisation that Clem was not my mother broke my heart. I never recovered, never forgave my father for the brutal way he had told me. Albert left for Tuscany shortly after the war ended, and I never saw him again.' Fraser straightened his shoulders and took a deep breath as he looked at the house. 'I've always stood up to bullies, like my cousin Richard, just as you stood up to that little ratbag Robbie Green, Harry. God, how he taunted me about my "weak" father killing himself, and my Parisian whore of a mother . . .' Fraser quelled the tension he felt rising in his chest, even now, the memory of sing-song voices teasing him in the nursery. He turned to Harry, and held her shoulders gently. 'You are a smart and lovely young woman, and your mother is doing an excellent job raising you alone. I was also lucky enough to be raised by a clever, beautiful woman.' He glanced at Grace. 'You are lucky, Harry. Never let anyone make you feel any different.'

202

'But what should I do, if it happens again?' Harry's head fell. 'What if they tease me about my dad?'

'I am never one to condone violence,' Fraser said, walking on towards home at Harry's side, 'in fact, I detest it, but sometimes a short, sharp shock is entirely necessary. If you ever meet dear Cousin Dicky, why don't you ask him how he got his broken nose?'

21

The coloured lights whirled above the small parquet dance floor, 'Disco Inferno' pounding from the stereo as the women sang along. Grace danced in the middle of them, laughing, trying to keep step with the grapevine. The song ended and Alice ran to the stereo to put the next record on.

'That was brilliant,' Grace said, catching her breath.

'See? Told you we'd have a laugh. The lads all think we sit around talking about Tupperware all night. Little do they know I've built a disco in my garage now Rod's motorbikes have gone.' She tucked her arm in Grace's. 'I meant what I said. You're not alone here, Grace. My fella walked out on me and the kids a year ago, and we're doing all right.' Grace picked up on the brittle defiance, the determination in her voice. Alice looked around at her friends laughing, dancing. 'Anytime you feel blue, a bit of a dance sorts you out, that's what I say.'

'Thanks so much for inviting me.'

'You're not leaving already, are you?' Alice flung her arms in the air. 'The night's young! C'mon Grace. One more for the road?' She began to pump her arms to Sister Sledge.

'I've got to go,' Grace shouted above the music. 'Babysitter!'

'Pop into the café next time you're in Andrewsfield?' Alice called, backing away towards the dance floor.

*

Grace walked back from the village to the Manor, guided by the moonlight. There was no need for a torch. The fields and lane shone silver in the night, and ahead she could see the golden lights of Wittering Manor.

Ever since Fraser's further revelation about the tiara, her mind had been whirling. *I wish Gogo hadn't gone on holiday with Ben.* She was dying to talk to her, to find out what she knew about Josephine. *I'm sure she would have mentioned her.* Grace racked her mind; the name meant nothing to her, and when she had casually asked Cilla if Margot had ever mentioned a woman called Josephine, she drew a blank. *What if she changed her name? Lots of people do that during wartime.* As she walked, Grace ran through all the possibilities. *What if Margot's family just bought the brooch from Josephine? I can't suggest to Fraser that my grandmother may be his long-lost sister without evidence.*

She hummed a Gloria Gaynor track as she walked, her feet falling in time to the rhythm. She realised, for the first time, that she felt like she was coming home as she glimpsed the cottage lights in the distance. She smiled, thinking how the women from school had quizzed her over the owners of Wittering Manor. *I hadn't realised they kept themselves to themselves so much,* Grace thought. She had enjoyed the evening getting to know some of the mothers, and was glad to have a few dates in her diary for playdates and trips.

The wine glowed warm inside her and she swung her bag as she walked, the full skirt of her cotton dress blowing in the breeze. *It's going to be all right,* she thought, for the first time feeling like she had gathered the reins on her runaway life. She skirted past the manor, into the shadowy lane leading to her cottage.

It took her a moment to register the sound of footsteps running swiftly behind her and she wheeled round, her heart racing.

'Grace!' Jack called.

'You nearly gave me a heart attack!' She laughed, placing her palm against her chest.

Jack slowed his pace as he caught up with her. He was still wearing his team's polo kit – long, supple boots, pale jodhpurs, a dark blue T-shirt with white piping around the neck and sleeves. 'I'm sorry. I didn't mean to scare you.'

'That's all right. I'm just kind of jumpy at the moment.' She wondered if Fraser had told him about the birthstones.

'I was just heading to the cottage to see if you'd got home yet.' He put his hands on his hips, catching his breath. She walked beside him, caught the clear Vetiver smell of his cologne, the earthy smell of the horses.

'What's up?' She stumbled in her high boots as they walked along the lane and he reached out to steady her.

'Have fun with the school gates crowd, did you?' He had his arm around her waist.

'I might have had a spot of wine.' She looked up at him, and smiled. 'To be honest, I was dreading it. I'm not good meeting new people, but Alice's friends from the village were lovely.'

'Haven't you been friends for ages?'

'Since we were teenagers. But we went to different schools, and I grew up over in Hampshire, in Exford.' Grace nudged him. 'Seems half the girls in West Wittering had a crush on you.'

'I never noticed,' Jack said, laughing.

Grace was tired, and disoriented. The night seemed to fold around them as they walked in the darkness, and there, at the centre of it, she felt his warm, strong hand guiding her. 'Did Fraser need something?'

'No, actually it was Harry. She – well, she was at the stables this afternoon, mucking out Felix, when one of the mares went into labour.'

'Oh?' Grace stopped walking as they drew close to the cottage.

'The thing is, the foal didn't make it. Harry was pretty cut up about it.'

Grace glanced up at Harry's bedroom window, saw the lamplight seeping around the gap in the pink curtains. 'Poor thing.'

'We did our best to comfort her, but she kept on asking over and over why do the little ones always have to die? I asked her what she meant, but she said it was a secret.'

Grace screwed her eyes closed, realising what she had been thinking. 'Oh, Harry.' She touched Jack's arm. 'Thank you. Thanks for letting me know.'

JUNE

Pearl

Love · Charity · Beauty

22

At dawn, she woke. It was there, waiting for her in consciousness, the labyrinth of memories she walked each day like a penitent, round and round, leading to the grief she carried in her heart like a physical absence. It would be hopeless trying to sleep again on this day of all days, so she pulled on a pair of jeans and an old T-shirt. For months, she had felt as if the date was lying in wait for her. It was here now. *It's a date, just a day on the calendar,* she told herself, fighting down the feeling of anxiety that clutched at her stomach. But the raw grief that ran in her just below the surface broke through. It didn't take much, sometimes. The sound of a child crying in the supermarket. An advert on TV. The well-meaning words of a friend. She screwed her eyes closed, stemming the tears. She was afraid that if she gave in to it, she would never stop. The eggshell veneer would crack. All the 'I'm fines' and 'Isn't she coping wells' would be swept away in a tidal wave of animal pain. *I can't let Harry catch me crying, it's not fair on her.* In the bathroom, she splashed cold water on her face and brushed her teeth. *A year,* she thought, staring back at a face that seemed like the exhausted reflection of a stranger. A sentence from Fraser's memoirs came to her mind: *Love changes us; grief changes us.*

She checked Harry was sleeping peacefully and padded downstairs. Jagger stretched, paws extended, tail wagging high. 'Come on,' she said, opening the back door and pulling on a pair of boots. He ran ahead, joyous, oblivious, down the bridle path made narrow by overgrown ferns and wild flowers. Grace followed swiftly behind, walking fast as if she were trying to outpace her thoughts.

The fresh green trees sang, alive with the dawn chorus, and the rising sun held the promise of a beautiful day to come. *It was last year, too.* She remembered trailing her hand through the open window of her father's car, touching frothing cow parsley with her fingertips as they sped through the country-side near Winchester. The memories of that day were clear to her, polished like a stone that is touched constantly. She remembered Margot and Harry singing along together in the back seat: 'Alouette, gentille alouette . . .' Harry had an *I-Spy* book in her hand and was ticking off different cars as they spotted them.

'I've been worried about you,' Ted had said to her. 'It's no good for you being under this kind of stress.'

'Don't worry, Dad. The doctor is keeping an eye on me.' Grace had run her hand over her stomach. 'If it gets any worse, he said he'd admit me to hospital until the birth.'

'What's Sam doing today?'

'I don't know. He said he had some business down Chichester way, went off early.'

Grace strode on, following Jagger's regular route across the fields to the lake. Her breath was coming fast now, her heart beating steadily and limbs warmed. She forced herself to remember every detail, clearly. They had parked in the centre of Newbury and Margot helped Grace out of the car.

They had joined the queues snaking into the Corn Exchange. The old stone building on the marketplace was humming with activity. 'Last time I came here was back in '66 to see The Who play,' Ted said, looking up at the inscription beneath the portico as they waited on the pavement. 'There was a right punch-up. Keith Moon broke his ankle, I think.'

'I didn't realise the antiques fair was being televised,' Margot said, instinctively touching her hair at the sight of the camera crews as they finally reached the reception desks.

'Neither did I,' Ted said. 'Ben just mentioned there was

something called an Antiques Roadshow valuing items, and I thought it would be interesting to get that brooch of yours looked at.'

Margot slipped the blue leather tiara box from her basket and handed it to the young woman sitting behind the table marked 'jewellery'.

'Good morning,' the woman said brightly, clicking open the box. 'Oh, this is lovely,' she said. 'May I ask how you came by it?'

'It was a gift to my mother during the First World War,' Margot said. 'From a lover.'

'How romantic.' She inspected the hallmark. 'Was she CBS?' She tapped her finger on the embossed, faded initials on the case.

'No,' Margot said, a cool edge to her voice.

'Intriguing. I do love a romantic mystery.' She put down her jeweller's loupe. 'As I thought, Bouchet et Fils. Well, this is definitely the kind of piece we'd like to feature.' She beckoned to a young girl with a clipboard. 'Will you take them along to jewellery? I think they are filming over there now and this will be perfect.'

'Please come with me,' the girl said, ushering them into the hall. They wove their way through the crowd to a corner table, where a young man in a flamboyant suit was just finishing up with a middle-aged couple.

'Do you have this insured?' he asked them, turning the gold bangle over in his hand.

'No. Why, should we?' The man licked his lips. 'We thought it was just a bit of old tat my father dug up with the plough.'

'My God,' Margot whispered to Grace. 'Look at the greed on that man's face.'

'No, indeed, this is one of the finest Roman bracelets it has ever been my fortune to handle.' The man smiled encouragingly at them, their eyes glazed with expectation. 'If this were at auction, I imagine it would fetch somewhere in the region of £300 to £400.'

The woman gasped audibly. She glanced at the camera. 'Of course, we'd never sell it. Sentimental value.'

'My arse,' Ted murmured. 'I reckon they'll be down the auctioneers the minute they're out of here.'

The runner helped the couple up from their seats at the end of filming and ushered Margot, Grace and Ted forwards. 'Would you like to stand behind your mum?' she asked Harry.

'Splendid,' the young man said. 'What's your name?' he asked Harry.

'Harriet Morgan, how do you do.' She held out her hand.

'Well, Harriet Morgan, what do you have for me?' Harry pointed at the box in Margot's hand. 'Thank you.' He raised the lid of the box and smiled. 'Ah, this is beautiful.'

'They're ready to start filming,' the runner said.

'Thank you.' The jewellery expert waited for the signal from the cameraman, then turned to Margot. 'Now, tell me. How did this beautiful brooch come into your possession?'

'It was given to my mother during the Great War.'

'How romantic. It's rather dirty I'm afraid—'

'Beautiful jewels should be worn.' Margot flicked her lavender silk scarf over her shoulder.

'Of course. No, it's a good thing it hasn't been over-cleaned.' He removed an immaculate handkerchief from his breast pocket. 'May I?' He rubbed gently at the platinum setting. 'As I thought. Bouchet et Fils. You realise it is part of a tiara?'

'So my mother was telling the truth? For once.' Margot flashed a glance at the camera.

'Indeed. Tiaras were most in demand from 1901 to the Great War, so it was created during the heyday of jewellers like Cartier, Chaumet and Bouchet et Fils. Society was changing and the newly ennobled and nouveau riche needed jewels to reflect their status. Tell me what you know about the brooch. This is the original box of course.'

'How can you tell?'

'Well look at it rattling around,' he said, tracing the form of the velvet. 'As I said, what you have here is one of two – a pair. It would originally have been a tiara. All I can tell you is that the Curzon tiara of 1898 cost the princely sum of £1400. I have no doubt that if this tiara were intact it would have cost hundreds, and would now be worth thousands of pounds. It's possible that the stones were reset from an earlier tiara – Bouchet et Fils was known for stripping work down when it went out of fashion, or perhaps the owner's taste changed from Egyptian to Deco, for example. Styles changed, too, to suit the shorter hairstyles of the ladies. This brooch would originally have been set with its partner on a platinum bandeau, I imagine, looking at the setting.' He turned the diamond wing slowly, light dancing along the feathers of gemstones. 'They were artists, these jewellers.' The man held the brooch up to her hair. 'This charming piece would have been designed by Bouchet et Fils to rest against the lady's hair like the coronet of a goddess – they are the wings of love, don't you think? As a designer, he had a great lightness and naturalness—'

'As do my granddaughter Grace Manners' designs,' Margot said to camera, resting her hand on Grace's.

The expert smiled indulgently. 'One could almost imagine this brooch and its pair flying away.' He linked his thumbs and beat his long, slender fingers like a bird. 'The diamond, of course, symbolises endless love in the lore of lapidary. There is something terribly romantic about it, if you think that the jewels live on, but the woman they were designed for is gone.'

'Perhaps sometimes,' Margot said, 'diamonds can be a symbol for the coldness of a marriage, too.'

'Oh dear,' the jewellery expert said, laughing. 'That's rather cynical.' He turned the diamond wing to the light. 'I prefer to think of a love that lasts forever, don't you?'

Forever, Grace thought now, watching Jagger racing ahead.

She felt tears prick at her eyes. *Nothing lasts forever.* She laid the flat of her palm against her stomach and stifled a sob. The past seemed close to her now, biting at her heels. She had known something was wrong the moment Ted pulled in to the driveway of the Old Rectory. *The lights weren't on*, she remembered.

'I thought Sam would be back by now—' Her words had broken off as she noticed the dark car in the driveway. As Ted parked by the door, two men stepped out.

'Can I help you?' Ted said, getting out first.

'I'm looking for Mrs Morgan,' the taller man said. 'Inspector Todd, Sussex police.'

'I'm Mrs Morgan,' Grace said, leaning against the door of the car, her hand resting protectively over her stomach. She saw the policeman take in her pregnancy, his hesitation.

'Perhaps we should go inside?' Margot suggested, taking Grace's arm. 'Let me,' she said, taking Grace's keys. The wide door swung open to the hall, the porch light casting a gold parallelogram of light through the dark house towards the kitchen. 'Harry, why don't you go up and run the bath? I'll be up in a moment to read you a story.' Harry glanced suspiciously from Margot to her mother, and ran upstairs, her feet clattering.

Grace waited until she heard the footsteps retreat to the back of the house, and the sound of Harry's door opening. 'Please, come in.' She showed the policemen into the living room. Grace flicked on a pair of blue-and-white lamps on the red sideboard and stood by the fireplace.

'Mrs Morgan,' Todd said. 'I'm sorry to tell you that Mr Morgan's car was discovered near Beachy Head today.'

Her hand instinctively moved to the string of pearls that Sam had given her for their wedding. 'What do you mean, discovered?' She felt the room begin to sway.

'It was abandoned in a car park in Eastbourne, near the coast path, with the keys, his wallet and personal effects still in there.' The policeman glanced at Ted, who stood grim-faced by the hall door, watching for Harry. 'I'm afraid one of our officers discovered a pile of clothes on a nearby beach.'

'Perhaps Sam felt like a swim?' Margot interrupted.

'There was a note, Ma'am.' The policeman handed Grace a sheet of paper in a plastic evidence bag. She recognised his handwriting instantly, the awkward, printed letters. 'The coastguard is still out, and our lads are searching . . .' Grace lost track of what he was saying, his words fading as the blood sang in her ears.

'"I can't go on,"' she read aloud, her hand shaking. '"I'm sorry."'

Grace whistled for Jagger now, striding on towards the lake, the cool morning breeze drying the hot tears coursing down her face. *I can't go on. I can't go on*, she thought, the words tumbling in her mind in rhythm with her feet. She felt it all again, how her heartbeat skipped irregularly, her skin prickling with sweat, the pain and tension she felt searing across her stomach. 'Oh, God,' Grace whispered, reliving it. That's what she had cried out, as she doubled over in pain. The pearl necklace had snapped as her hand gripped it, and two perfect white pearls scattered across the polished wood floor, rolling away into the darkness.

'My babies,' she cried out, releasing her grief across the water like a bird taking flight. She fell to her knees at the edge of the lake as she wept, her head lowered, one hand clutching her stomach, the other reaching out, nails tensing against the earth. 'My babies!'

23

'Is this another one of your magical mystery tours?' Fraser asked, yawning, as Grace drove inland through sunlit valley lanes towards Exford that evening.

'Late night?' Grace said. She had hidden her red, swollen eyes behind a pair of Aviator sunglasses, and her blonde hair blew in the breeze as the Beetle puttered along.

'Ruddy dawn chorus. I wake every night at four as it is, and now with the birds there's not a hope in hell of getting back to sleep.'

'I know what you mean.'

When they reached the heart of the village, Grace couldn't resist the temptation to look at the Old Rectory on the way past, and saw the 'For Sale' sign had been replaced with 'Sold'. She craned her neck, and in the driveway she saw a removal van, with men in tan dustcoats and flat caps carrying tea chests into the house. *Life goes on*, she thought, pushing down the tight ball of sadness in her throat.

'So is it? A mystery tour?' he said.

'No, not exactly. I'm letting my guard down.'

Fraser turned towards her. 'Good for you.'

'Harry and I were coming out here this evening, and I thought it might help you, too.' Fraser craned his head as they drove past the pub.

'Any chance of a pit stop?'

She parked outside the church and went round to the boot. 'Maybe later,' she paused. 'I wanted you to understand why Harry was so upset by the foal the other night.'

Fraser glanced at her, curious. 'We gave the little fellow a good send-off, didn't we, Harry?' They had buried him in the orchard with all the other Stratton animals, and Harry had decorated the little grave with wild flowers.

'There you are, sweetheart,' Grace said, handing Harry a bunch of white roses. She followed Fraser and Harry as they walked along the sun-dappled gravel path to the churchyard. From the open window of Mrs Miller's cottage, she could hear the wrestling. The village was quiet, everyone indoors, watching the wrestling. *Go on, give it to him!* Grace heard Mrs Miller shouting at the television.

'I'll show you. It's over here,' she heard Harry say, and they cut across the grass to the corner of the churchyard. The sunlight filtered through the yew branches, gold dust motes dancing like glitter in a snow globe, a stray white feather drifting down. Pigeons cooed in the bell tower.

'Who are we visiting?' Fraser asked.

'The babies.' Harry pointed at a small white cross. She walked ahead and solemnly placed the roses beside the fresh flowers there already.

'It looks like Mum and Dad have been here with my grandmother,' Grace said, pointing at two bunches of pale pink roses. She froze as she noticed the blank envelope tucked among the flowers. She stooped down and felt a bump in the paper.

'Grace, are you all right?' Fraser said.

She tore it open and tipped a pearl onto her shaking hand. 'This isn't funny. This is sick!' Her heart thumped and she blinked, lights flashing in her eyes, a wave of heat crackling like wildfire through her.

'Mum?' Harry looked at her alarmed.

'It's fine. I'm fine.' Grace forced herself to sound calm. 'Darling, would you take that watering can and run to the back of the vestry to get some water for our flowers?' Grace read the card: *A Pearl for the babes of June, precious wealth, to crown them even in death.*

'Who's doing this?' She screwed up the card and looked at the pearl nestling in her palm. 'I don't want this. I don't want this at all.' She fell down on her knees, pulled Sam's penknife out of her pocket and flicked open the blade, gouging at the earth, near the headstone. 'If anyone deserves this little pearl, they do. It's their birthstone.' She dropped it into the earth and pressed the turf closed with her palm, resting it there, her eyes closed. 'It's perfect, like them.' Harry returned with the watering can, slopping water onto the dry earth.

217

Fraser put his hand on Harry's shoulder. 'Jemima,' he said quietly, reading the date: 8/6/78. He leant down and pushed aside the roses. 'Jemima and Rex.'

'It was Harry's favourite doll, from *Play School*,' Grace said, forcing herself to breathe slowly, evenly. 'I thought it was pretty, well, better than Hamble. And Rex was my uncle, Dad's brother . . .' Her voice shook. 'I still can't – I can't talk about them. I'm sorry.'

'No need to apologise, my dear.' Fraser put his other arm around Grace as she stood and held her tight. Grace nodded, unable to speak for a moment.

'They were tiny,' Harry said, her voice hoarse. 'They came too early, and they couldn't – the doctor couldn't save them.' She buried her face in her mother's sweater, hugged her tightly.

'I'm so sorry. You've been terribly brave, both of you,' Fraser said, stroking Harry's hair. He reached into his jacket pocket and handed Harry a packet of Polo Mints. 'Why don't you go and sit under that lovely tree and have a sweetie, darling? I saw some wild flowers you could pick for your press,' he said to her, and waited until she had skipped away. Grace took out the wilted carnations and Fraser poured fresh water into the simple white vase for the roses. 'Show me the card.' Grace handed him the balled-up paper. 'Not terribly original, is it? Whoever is sending these is adapting that old nursery rhyme.' He glanced at Grace. 'Shall we call the police?'

'And tell them what? That someone is giving gemstones back to me?'

'Grace, I'm worried for you.'

'Well, don't be. I can look after myself and Harry.' She reached out and touched Jemima's name on the little cross. 'You know, I look at her sometimes and wonder if Jem would have grown up to be like her.' Grace arranged the white roses. 'One of my friends was pregnant at the same time, and every time her little boy does something new, I think that

Rex would have been doing that too.' Grace rubbed between her eyes with her fingertips. 'I went to see a psychic, not long after. I don't even believe in all that, but I wanted to know if she could see the babies, and Sam.' She laughed softly. 'I think it was a bit of a dead giveaway when I burst into tears the minute she said, "I can see a baby"!'

'My dear girl, when I think what you've been through . . .'

'But we all have.' Grace turned to him. 'That's why I decided to tell you. You've lived all your life grieving the loss of the twin you never knew, of your mother, of Gin.' She looked up at him. 'Jack lost his parents.'

'If you get through life without grief, it means you've never loved,' Fraser said. 'I have no doubt these little souls knew they were loved, and that they are at peace. If it's all right with you, I'll bring flowers when I'm passing? I don't like to think of little ones without company.' He beckoned to Harry and they walked back through the churchyard. 'We're the lucky ones, Grace. However hard it is sometimes, imagine not knowing what this feels like. If there's one lesson I've learnt, it's this,' he said, watching Harry skip on ahead through the dappled sunlight, 'love and loss come in equal measure.'

24

Grace sat back on her heels and surveyed the trunks piled up in the far corner of the attic. Each had been opened, papers and photographs spilling from them like cornucopias. 'Blimey, Fraser,' she said under her breath. *If I wanted a distraction, this will keep me busy for days.* She pulled off her white shirt and adjusted the strap of her black vest, then crept forwards on her hands and knees. The air was hot, edible, toasted dust and mothballs. She sneezed. She worked through the trunks methodically, tidying away the papers into rough piles until she reached the last. Grace swung open the lid of the silver steamer trunk and lifted out a white leather wedding album. She put it on the floorboards between her hands and flicked through. *Jack's wedding. Wow, his wife was stunning.* Jack's happy, open smile touched her, the joy in his expression as he looked at his bride. *I wish he smiled more often.* She hesitated at a photograph of them kissing. Jack's eyes were closed, lost in the moment. The tug of envy in her stomach surprised her. She touched his cheek, imagined herself in the bride's place. She had never met her, but she hated this woman for hurting Jack. *How could anyone betray him?* Looking at the unguarded happiness on his face, she wanted to protect him. She realised she had come to rely on his kindness, to look forward to seeing him every day, even for a moment.

'There you are,' Jack said, poking his head through the attic's trapdoor.

'Jack? God, you made me jump.' Grace slammed the album shut, her heart racing guiltily. She glanced over her shoulder, and saw he was eyeing up her backside. 'Enjoying the view?'

He swung himself easily up through the trapdoor to the attic, and tilted his head. 'Not bad.'

'Not bad?' Grace widened her eyes. 'Not bad? Jeez, throw an old mother a bone once in a while, will you?'

'You have the finest ass in Wittering Manor.' He grinned. 'Better?'

'Ellen will be disappointed.'

'What have you found? Anything interesting?' He crawled over beside her, his face clouding as he saw where she had hastily hidden the wedding album. He threw it into the trunk.

'I'm sorry, I wasn't prying—' She caught herself. 'I suppose I was.'

'I thought Fraser had thrown them out.'

'It looks beautiful, Argentina.' Grace settled back, hugging her knees to her chest. *Why does this always happen? Every time I think he's starting to relax a little, he closes off again.*

'It is – it was. It was my dream, you know. I wanted to be

a 10 handicap pro player, with a beautiful wife and a troop of kids.' He ran his hand through his hair. 'I was green. I still believed in the fairy tale . . .'

'You don't now?'

He looked at her. 'I thought it was easy, you know, the happily ever after. You fall in love, and stay in love. I think you realise how hard it is to make it work as you get older.'

'Maybe anything worthwhile needs fighting for.'

'If your dream doesn't work out, you just pick yourself up and start again, right?'

'You've been talking to Fraser.' She laughed softly.

'Are you OK? He told me everything. I'm so sorry.'

'It – it was just a tough day to get through.' She forced a smile. 'I'm fine. How was your practice?'

'Good. It's the first season for a couple of the ponies, but I'm pleased with them.' Jack looked around the attic. 'Have you got to go through all of these?' He lifted the trunks clear so that she could get into the ones at the back. She noticed he hid the silver trunk behind a screen of boxes, as though he was trying to bury the past. As he heaved the largest cedar trunk down, she saw the muscles of his back ripple beneath his tight white T-shirt. Jack squatted down at her side and wiped the sweat from his brow.

'I've never even seen half of these. God knows what he has squirrelled away up here. I heard him say there's more in Tuscany.'

'I think it's that generation. Never throw anything away.' The lid of the cedar trunk creaked as she opened it. 'Look at this, a programme from a musical, Paris, 1945.'

'He never has told me exactly what he did in the war, or about this mystery woman.'

Grace turned to him. 'I think it's pretty romantic to love one woman your whole life.' He was close enough now for her to feel the heat of his body against her bare arm. 'Jack . . .' she hesitated. 'I need to talk to you.'

'How are you two getting on up there?' Ellen called, breaking the moment. She slid a tray with a jug of water across the boards through the trapdoor. 'I thought you might need some help lifting the heavy stuff, love, so I asked Jack to give you a hand.'

'Thanks,' Grace said, and she sat back against the trunks with Jack. He drank thirstily from a glass of water, condensation running down the side. As he wiped the back of his hand against his mouth, she saw the skin of his lower lip catch, freeing slowly. Grace tugged at the black vest she was wearing. It was wet with sweat, sticking to her back, her stomach.

'I'll leave you to it, then,' Ellen said, and disappeared.

'The look on her face. It was like she caught us making out up here.' Jack smiled. 'You were saying?'

'It's nothing. I . . .' Grace looked down at the open trunk beside her, scared now to go on. A photograph lay half tucked beneath yellowed typewritten papers.

'Grace,' he said, his hand inching closer to hers. 'I understand now. I can't begin to imagine what you've been through, losing your husband, and your babies. I hope . . . I mean, I've grown to—'

'No,' she said, setting her glass down. 'It can't be.'

'I know it's hard.' His face was close to her tanned shoulder now; she felt his breath on her skin. 'Your situation is complicated, but we can—'

'Surely not.' Grace pulled the photograph out, and stared at it.

'What is it?'

She handed the photograph to him. 'Fraser.'

'And this is the mystery woman?' Jack turned the photograph to the light. 'She's beautiful.'

'I have to talk to him.' She leant over and grabbed her shirt.

'Grace, wait,' Jack said, catching her arm.

'I can't, not now, I'm sorry,' she said, snatching the

222

photograph from him, and heading for the stairs.

'Fraser!' Grace shouted, marching through the house. 'Fraser!'

'Good heavens, what is it?' he looked up from the orchid he was repotting in the conservatory.

'This photograph.' She held it out to him. Fraser wiped his hands on his white apron and took it from her. 'Is this Gin?'

'Yes, yes, it is. It's the only photo I have of her.' He pulled his wallet out of his back pocket and flipped it open. Inside was a smaller version of the same photograph.

'*This* is Gin?'

'Yes, I said so. Is the heat getting to you up there?'

'When was this taken?'

'The night before our wedding. She always hated having her photograph taken, but there was a chap in the dining room that night taking photos for a few centimes, and he managed to get one before she could stop him.' Fraser gazed at it. 'I went back to the restaurant after she disappeared and bought the negative from him.'

'Fraser, this tiepin you're wearing?'

'That's the brooch I was talking about, the diamond wing. Clem never wore it, but I always liked playing with it as a child. She kept it in a button tin, if you can believe it.'

'Do you still have it?'

'Yes, haven't worn it since that night, but I have it somewhere.'

Grace stared at the photograph as he handed it back to her, at the matching Bouchet et Fils wing securing his cravat. 'I need to go out,' she said. 'I'll make up the time tomorrow.'

'Are you all right, my dear?'

'No, not really. But I think I may have some news about Gin.'

Fraser watched Grace leave, the plants brushing against her arms, the swing of her platinum hair. Her footsteps faded

223

away into the house and soon he was alone with the soft drip of condensation from the plants. 'I rather hoped you would,' he said, slowly folding the wallet and putting it back into his pocket.

25

'Sometimes I think we invented ourselves,' Fraser said into the tape recorder. He settled back into the hammock beneath the oak trees and gazed up at the shifting canopy of leaves above him. He rocked gently in the breeze, hearing the hum of insects in the long grass, Cy's lawnmower in the distance. Fraser held up the photograph that Grace had discovered in the attic. It felt like a sign to him, that he was getting close to the truth. 'Gin and I were like children in a fairy story, parentless, running free in a world of our own invention. I've always admired people who rewrite the script of their lives. There was something in her that I recognised the moment I saw her, a similar sense of sucking the marrow of life dry.' Fraser closed his eyes, conjuring up her image.

'She always wore a pale trench coat, a beret,' he said into the recorder. '"You look like a Frenchwoman out of central casting,"' I said to her once. '"Isn't this how the girls dress here?"' she said. I adored her accent. I hadn't travelled to America yet, and there was something about her that conjured up limitless possibility, and space.

'"Where are you from in the States?"' I asked her once. '"My mother was born in Chicago."

'"New York," she said. "My parents were French, so I ended up with this crazy accent."

'"I like it. Are they . . . ?"

'"Yes. Yours?"

'"So, here we are, alone together."'

Fraser clasped the recorder to his chest. 'We walked for miles, exploring Paris. I had never met anyone whose humour, whose thoughts were so in sync with my own.

'"I feel as if I've known you my whole life," she said, as we stood at the steps to her apartment building one morning.

'"I was just thinking exactly the same thing." I was really thinking: *I suppose this must be what love feels like.*

'"Will you come up? I can cook you some breakfast."

'I checked my watch. I had half an hour before work. "Thank you, another time. I have to get to the office."

'"When do you ever sleep?"

'"At my desk mostly. The visa section is terribly dull."

'She took out her key from her handbag. "Will I see you later?"

'"I could take you to dinner, tonight, before your show?"

'"I'd like that."

'"Pick you up at eight?" I walked away, backwards, stumbling on the cobbles. She laughed – I loved to make her laugh. My whole life I'd affected this guarded, rather soignée pose, and with her I could be a clown. I didn't have to worry about making a fool of myself.

'With Gin, it was like picking up a conversation that paused long ago. Like old friends who meet after years and gather up the threads of their friendship without missing a stitch. Paris before the war seemed Technicolor to me, everything heightened, the shadows crisper, the June fragrances more intoxicating: black tobacco, drains, cut flowers, coffee, the salty tang of shellfish on crushed ice. Gin's perfume – violets. It was as though the world had pulled into sharper focus around her.' Fraser smiled, remembering. 'Picture it, a Friday night, the streets were full, pavement cafés overspilling. Everywhere the sound of laughter, music, conversation. It felt like Paris was ours.

'"Do they make you work on Saturdays?" she asked, leaning across the café table to trace the dark circles beneath my eyes.

'"Not unless you've been naughty."

'"Then tomorrow you shall stay, and I shall teach you how to sleep. There is an art to it, you know."

'I have never slept as well as I did with Gin. She laid down the ground rules quickly – she may have been a dancer, but she was no call girl. Sleep meant sleep – a tantalising kiss if I was lucky. That weekend she made me cut back on the booze, the cigarettes, restricted my coffee to pre-lunch. Gin ran a bath each night, drizzling lavender oil into the steaming water. We bathed separately, her first, but it was one of the most erotic times of my life, lying on that soft white bed with the windows open to the narrow iron balcony, listening to the water sloshing around in the small bathroom, imagining her. Conjuring what lay beneath the showgirl costumes, the simple white cotton pyjamas she wore at night. And she cared for me – I loved the simple, intoxicating pleasure of someone looking after me. I don't think I had felt it since I was a child. Needless to say, I was quite beside myself with wanting her. She knew this of course, teased me about the thoroughness of my ablutions. By Sunday night I was hopelessly in love with her.

'"Marry me," I said, our heads lying close together on the down pillows.

'"You're crazy," she said, laughing. "Every day you ask me the same question. We are just getting to know one another, taking our time. What is the hurry?"

'"Gin, I love you. I feel as if I've waited my whole life to find you. I feel – whole," I said. She laid her palm against mine, and our fingers interlaced.

'"I love you, Fraser," she said. "I don't know who you are—"

'"We can be whoever we want to be, Gin. We can go anywhere in the world you want, just come with me." I saw her hesitate. "Be with me. Love me."

'"Very well," she said at last and I went the next day to arrange the marriage licence. I snuck out of work early with

Alec.

'"Are you sure about this, old boy?" he said as we strode through the lunchtime traffic.

'"Never surer. Wait till you meet her." I flashed him a quick smile. "Actually, you did meet her once, but you were so pissed I doubt you remember."

'"Very funny. You say she's a dancer? An American?"

'"I know what you are thinking."

'"Does she know what you do?"

'"Of course not." I glanced at him. "She thinks we're paper-pushers at the Embassy, just here to learn Russian—"

'"Which is true." Alec paused to light a cigarette, cupping the flame. "Good. I'd suggest you leave it that way until you are sure this is forever."

'"Forever?" I laughed. Pigeons rose from the square into the clear summer light. "Of course it's forever! I feel as though I've waited my whole life to meet her."

'"Frase, how long have I known you?"

'"I don't know. Since we were little boys."

'"I care about you. I don't want to see you make a mistake."

'"Alec, you're my best friend, and I adore you, but I know what I'm doing. You'll understand when you meet her." I jogged up the steps to the office. "OK, so she's not like Cesca, she's not from the right kind of family, or the same circles as us, but I'm sure you'll love her. You will both be our witnesses, won't you?"

'"I'll be godfather to every one of your twelve children if it will make you happy." Alec clapped me on the back.'

Fraser opened his eyes, and gazed up at the clouds scudding overhead, thinking of his old friend. *I miss you*. He tucked his arm behind his head, and went on:

'We arranged the wedding for that Thursday. I booked us in at Wepler, our favourite restaurant, for a celebratory meal on the Wednesday night with a few of our close friends. Gin and I were staying at the Hôtel Lutetia, in separate rooms, a suite booked for the wedding night. I had taken some of my mother's jewels from the hotel safe, trying to decide what to give Gin as a wedding gift. I had already given her my mother's emerald as an engagement ring. They would all be hers in time, of course. I remembered her birthstone was a garnet, so I settled on the garnet earrings, the stones that gleamed with all the fire of rubies. As I was closing up the jewellery case, I noticed the Bouchet et Fils wing brooch I had loved so much as a child. I discarded the simple pearl pin I had tucked into my cravat and instead put on the diamond brooch. It seemed perfect for a pre-wedding dinner: the wings of love.

'I joined our friends in the hotel bar. Alec and Cesca were the centre of attention as usual. She wore red, if I remember right, her hair upswept, a simple rope of diamonds around her neck.

'"Are you nervous?" she said. Cesca lifted my chin. "No you are in love, I can see. It is like a madness, a sickness."

'"Is that how it is with you two still?"

'"Of course it is," Alec said. He put his great hand around Cesca's slender waist and pulled her to him. "Can't get enough of her. Never will."

'Cesca tolerated his exuberance. There was always something feline about her, the one who deigned to offer the cheek rather than bestowed the kiss. She had always treated me like Alec's brother, indulgently, like a mother to a child. In retrospect, I think she got a kick out of stepping out with both of us on her arm, preferred it to the times I had a date. She certainly saw an equal, a rival, in Gin the minute she saw her.

'Gin could always make an entrance that would leave a room in suspended animation, as though someone had pulled the plug. She wore silver, some material that seemed to be woven from diamond dust, the lights refracting and sparking from her. There was a lull in the conversation, a collective holding of breath. "Is that her?" Alec whispered to me. I nodded and stepped through the crowd to take her hand.

'I'll never forget the look on her face, the moment when her gaze met mine. She was absolutely, powerfully present. I've never met anyone like that before or since. "There will never be another woman as beautiful as you are at this moment," I said.

'"You look handsome yourself." I saw her gaze settle on the Bouchet et Fils brooch for a moment. Her eyes opened wider, flickered in confusion.

'"Is it too much?" I said. "I wanted something flamboyant, celebratory." I touched it gently. "It was my mother's."

'"It's beautiful." She looked directly at me. I sensed, even then, that something was wrong, like music shifting to a minor key.

'"I have a gift for you," I said, desperately wanting to bring back that glorious moment when she walked into the room. From my pocket I took the garnet earrings.

'"Fraser, they are lovely," she said. I noticed her hand shook as she took off her simple pearl earrings and clipped on the garnets. "What do you think?"

'"Very beautiful," Cesca said, walking over. When I travelled later in Africa, and saw two lionesses squaring up, I thought of this moment. "How do you do. I'm Francesca, and this is Alec, my husband."

'"Delighted to meet you." Alec kissed Gin's hand.

'"Fraser has told me all about you," Gin said, her gaze hardening as she looked from Alec to Cesca. "It's a pleasure to meet his oldest friends."

'I saw Cesca flinch at the slight. She took Gin's arm as we walked through to the lobby to get a taxi. "Tell me, how did you meet . . . ?"'

'The meal was more strained than I had hoped. Alec kept the conversation going as he always did in those situations. I miss him terribly, still. He was the most good-natured bear of a man I have ever met. Cesca and Gin traded questions and answers as if they were parrying across the table with sabres. I remember feeling grateful that the women were separated by a towering iced bowl of *fruits de mer*. All we could do was watch. The taxi drive back to the hotel was as frosty as our meal.

'"Shall we dance?" I said, offering my hand to Gin the moment we reached the hotel. The band started up with "The Way You Look Tonight". She settled into my arms on the dance floor. "Are you all right?" I said.

'"I'm fine," she said, smiling.

'"Do you like them?" It mattered to me that she did. Alec and Cesca were the closest I had to family.

'"They're lovely. I think she is protective of you. Women can be like that sometimes about the single friends of their husbands. They are not used to sharing."

'"Give her time." My lips brushed her temple as we danced, and I inhaled the scent of her perfume. "I can't wait for tomorrow night," I said, and talked on about our future, how we would travel the world, make our home at Wittering Manor, and how happy we would be, the beautiful babies we would make.

'"Fraser," she said finally, "tell me about that darling brooch you are wearing."

'"Do you like it? I always loved playing with it when I was small."

'"Where is it from?"

'I hesitated. Would she be put off if she knew the story of my birth? I decided she had a right to know, so I took her hand and led her to the terrace, where it was quieter. I pulled out a chair for her at a table with a red-shaded candle light and sat beside her, taking her hand.

'"Once upon a time," I began, "a young British cavalry officer was in love with a woman in Paris who was not his wife." I felt her tense. "It was just before the Great War. She fell pregnant, and yet he decided to return home to his wife and do the decent thing by her."

'"Go on,"'she said.

'"My father went to see the woman one last time, to try and help her and the child. When he got there, he discovered there were two babies, a boy and a girl. I was that boy, and I have a sister I have never met."

'"What does this have to do with the brooch?" she said lightly. I unpinned it from my tie and gave it to her. I remember the diamonds sparkling in her slender fingers.

'"My father gave the matching one to my sister, and this one he brought home with me, for my mother."

'"Why did he leave the girl?"

'"He regretted it, later, I can tell you. My father died raging about his useless son, and said he should have taken the girl instead."

'"Oh, Fraser," she said. I was surprised to see tears in her eyes, and my heart swelled at her sympathy.

'"Please, don't upset yourself. Clemmie loved me, and that more than made up for my father. They've gone, and now I have you to love, forever."

'"Fraser—" she began.

'"We're going to head off and leave you lovebirds to it," Alec said, walking over with Cesca at his side. We stood and walked them to the lobby. I remember thinking it looked like a chessboard as we stood there, unsure of the next move. I kissed Cesca's cheek, shook Alec's hand. "We'll see you in the morning, bright and early." Somewhere a church bell began to toll midnight as they walked out through the revolving door to the street.

'"I should get to bed, too," Gin said. I'll never forget how beautiful she looked in the amber light of the chandelier.

'"Shall I walk you to your room?"

'At her door, she hugged me for longer than usual, kissed my cheek. "Goodbye, Fraser," she said.

'"I'll see you in the morning," I said, doubts pricking at me like wasps.

'That night, without her, I slept little. I seemed to hear the damn church bell strike every hour until seven. My room in the morning was a fug of cigar smoke and I threw open the windows to the square, to a glorious summer's day, clear and bright, birds wheeling in the cloudless blue sky above the pale grey roofs of Paris. I bathed and shaved, put on my suit, and paced my room until it was time to collect Gin at eight.

'I knocked on her door, my heart beating loud in my ears in the silence. I knocked again. "Gin," I called. Silence.

'I ran down to the front desk. "Has Miss West been out this morning?" The concierge had just come on duty and he shook his head. Perhaps she had already gone to the *mairie*, perhaps there was a misunderstanding. I forced my way through the revolving door, ran all the way to the Town Hall of St-Germain-des-Prés. Alec and Cesca were waiting for me on the steps, sunglasses protecting their eyes from the glaring sun.

'"Is she here?" I said, catching my breath.

'"No." Cesca stepped down, lowered her sunglasses. "Is she not at the hotel?" She glanced at Alec as if to say *I told you so*.

'We waited until the time allotted for our wedding. We waited until the next couple came, arm in arm, surrounded by exuberant friends and took our place.

'"Let's go back to the hotel," Alec said, clapping me on my back. "Maybe she has cold feet?"

'"Or a cold heart," Cesca said almost under her breath.

'The housekeeper let us into Gin's room. As I suspected, everything was perfect, the bed unslept in. The air still bore a trace of her perfume. On the bureau was a note, addressed to me, with the garnet earrings and the emerald ring on top.'

Fraser, my darling. I have to go away. I cannot explain, but know that I love you from the bottom of my heart, and I will love you forever. If I am right, we can never be together. If I am wrong, I will never be able to forgive myself for leaving you like this. You always said you never forget and never forgive those who hurt you, like your father. I couldn't bear for you to hate me. You will never see me again, but I will carry you in my heart always. Gin.

26

Grace pulled up in the driveway of Margot's cottage and climbed out. It was silent in the heart of the valley, only the rush of the river and the hum of bees in the long grass audible. She pushed open the pale blue iron gate, and walked up the brick pathway, her arms brushing against scented stocks and nodding agapanthus in the borders.

'Gogo,' she called through the open door. A rectangle of light illuminated the dark interior from the other side of the house. The television in the cosy living room was on, Grace heard the sounds of Wimbledon, the thwack of a wooden tennis racket and a ball bouncing on hard earth, a genteel cheer. A Burmese cat sauntered from the shadows, winding itself around Grace's ankles.

'Hello, Zazou,' she said, bending to scratch its back. 'Where is she?' Margot's house was full of antiques and textiles left over from her days selling French country antiques at the centre in Andrewsfield. In the hall, the hem of an antique silk kimono hanging on the wall lifted in the breeze. Grace poked her head into the living room. Comfortable sofas covered in antique ticking and linen flanked the polished grate, and prints of Redouté roses and fine calligraphy pages lined the walls. Margot had painted all the furniture white, and the room was both feminine and calm. By the bay window, Margot's drawing board stood with its ranks of coloured inks and fine pens, her copy of a Michelangelo nude taped down next to an open reference book, the pages blowing gently in the breeze. In the kitchen, Grace saw Margot's yoga mat rolled up on the counter and she guessed her grandmother had been doing her daily routine. From the garden, she heard the sound of Jacques Brel singing, 'Ne Me Quitte Pas' on the record player.

'I'm out here,' Margot called.

Grace strode through the house. She found her grandmother stretched out on a wicker lounger, a jug of lemonade at her side and a battered copy of *Bonjour Tristesse* cast aside, half read. She was still wearing a black leotard, a narrow belt around her waist. A wide-brimmed straw hat protected her face from the sun. 'Hello, darling, what a lovely surprise. Perfect timing. I've just finished meditating.' Margot lifted her white-framed sunglasses and looked at her. Grace smelt Ambre Solaire and coconut oil.

'Hello, Gin.' Grace's voice shook with anger. 'You *are* Virginia West?'

'It's been a long time since I heard that name.' Margot's expression didn't alter, still smiling. Only her gaze hardened. 'I can explain—'

'Why? Why didn't you tell me, when you heard I was working for him?' She dragged over an iron chair, and sat down.

'Don't upset yourself, darling. Lemonade?'

Grace pulled the photograph out of her back pocket and held it up.

'Where did you get that?' Margot calmly reached for her case of Sobranies and lit one.

'In the attic of Wittering Manor.' She waited for Margot's reaction. 'You knew, all this time, that I was working for Fraser Stratton and you didn't say anything?'

'By the time I heard you had taken the position, it was too late. I saw how Harry was blossoming again, and you seemed to have new purpose, and Jack—' Margot exhaled a steady plume of blue smoke. 'I hoped you would get a new job soon and move on.'

'I don't understand. I don't understand any of it.'

'Come on.' Margot pulled on a red silk dressing gown. 'This needs more than lemonade.'

They sat in the kitchen, a bottle of Gordon's on the table. 'Well this is appropriate,' Grace said, 'Gin.'

'Virginia West,' Margot said, looking at the photograph. 'I'd almost forgotten who she was.' She sipped her drink. 'It was a stage name. Some band got stuck in Paris before the war and I thought they would be more likely to take me on as a dancer if I sounded American.' Her voice slipped easily into an American accent.

Grace looked at her grandmother, as if seeing her clearly for the first time. 'I feel as if I don't know who you are.'

'Of course you do. Every single one of us lives many different lives in one lifetime. We all show different facets to different people. There's more of the chameleon about us than we would care to admit.' She looked at Grace. 'How much has he told you?'

'That you were the love of his life, that he never understood why you left him at the altar, that he thought you had a secret.'

'We all had secrets, then.' Margot sighed and rested her elbows on the table, swirling the ice in her glass. 'I never really knew what Fraser did. I could have found out. It's amazing what men will give away when they have a few drinks inside them and a hard-on.'

'Gogo!'

'Look, I was young, and pretty and useful. I made the most of this,' she said, sweeping her hand over her body. 'Once the Germans took France I helped the Resistance when I could. I don't think any of us knew what was truth or lies.'

'But you loved him?'

'Oh yes, always.' She drained her glass, set it down with a heavy crystal thud on the table. 'It's why I never married.'

'Fraser's the reason you won't marry Ben?'

Margot nodded. 'For once, I made the right decision. It would have been a case of marry in haste . . .'

'What do you mean?'

'Ben is a wonderful man, but he makes a hopeless husband.'

'He's not . . . ?'

'Playing around? Yes. I'm not surprised. I've known all along there have been other women over the years. The holiday was a complete disaster. Madrid was as lovely as ever, but Ben . . .' She frowned. 'I saw the hotel bill. He called her every single day of the trip. No fool like an old fool.'

'Gogo, I'm so sorry.'

Margot shook her head. 'No, don't worry. I'm going to break with him once and for all. I think I shall go travelling for a while.'

'Where will you go?'

'Wherever the wind takes me.' She gazed down at the photograph. 'Dear, sweet Fraser. He always said we could create any life we wished. What a mess we have made . . .'

'I don't understand, why didn't you marry him?'

'Darling, surely you've noticed the brooch?'

'It was the first thing I saw, after you.'

'I recognised it the moment I saw him wearing it that evening – he'd never worn it before. I suppose he was feeling sentimental about his mother or something.' Margot unscrewed the cap on the gin bottle, and topped up the glass. 'He told me that he had something to confess. That he was illegitimate. His father, Albert, told him during an argument that he regretted not taking the girl instead.'

Grace thought back to the manuscript, to Fraser's memoir.

'Fraser said that Albert told him he left the matching brooch for his twin sister.' Margot paused. 'Margot.'

'No?' Grace felt nauseous.

Margot looked at Grace. 'It was like something from a

236

Greek tragedy. I guessed that Fraser had to be the boy, the twin my mother had talked about when she was dying. I had to be sure—'

'That he was your brother? Were you – I mean, were you lovers?'

'No, thank God. Fraser was old-fashioned. He wanted his first night with his wife to be his wedding night. I'm quite sure he wasn't a virgin, but he wanted it to be different with us.'

'And you certainly weren't. Did he know about Mum?'

'No, no.' Margot looked down at her hands. 'How could I tell him I was raped when I was little more than a child?'

The breath caught in Grace's throat. 'Oh, Gogo. I had no idea.'

'No.' Margot couldn't look at her. 'And nor does your mother. She must never know. It would destroy her.' She looked up at Grace with tears in her eyes. 'It's bad enough that she thinks I was some kind of floozy.'

'What happened?'

'He was one of my mother's clients. A regular, I suppose, more of a boyfriend in that he didn't always pay.' Her voice was brittle. 'He was huge, a fisherman who would come into town occasionally. Mother encouraged me to call him "uncle". I suppose it was inevitable that once he had wormed his way in, one day she would leave us alone.' Margot screwed her eyes closed. 'Whenever I look at Priscilla, I see him. She has his colouring, his bone structure, his robust build. It's why even the smell of fish repulses me. This man, this creature,' she said, wrinkling her nose, 'stank of it. It was like the fish was in his sweating pores.' Margot dabbed at her lips. 'So, your grandfather was a rapist, and your great-grandmother was a whore and con artist.' Margot laughed bitterly.

'She sounds quite something.'

'I couldn't tell Fraser. He adored me. I loved seeing myself through his eyes.' Margot's voice shook. 'It was the first time I

237

felt clean. He made me new again.' She smiled sadly. 'I would – I would have told him about my daughter, eventually, pretended it was a foolish love affair. But Priscilla was safe enough with my mother's friend in Bordeaux.'

'Is that where you went? When you ran away?'

'Yes, I had to find out, you see, to talk to her and know for sure . . .'

'About your mother, Josephine?'

'Darling, you have to understand—'

Her words cut off as the telephone rang.

'Shall I?' Grace was closer, and she reached for the red handset, looping the cord free of the chair. 'Hello? No, this is Grace. Is that Mrs Miller? Yes? I'm sorry – slow down. You called Mum and she told you I was here?' She listened intently. 'Are you sure? I'll be right there.' Grace slammed down the phone and grabbed her bag.

'What is it?'

'She thinks she's seen Sam,' Grace said, running for the door. 'She says she saw him in the driveway of the old house.'

27

'It was him,' Mrs Miller said, folding her arms. Her dark eyes followed the path of a car along the high street. 'It was Sam, I'm sure of it. He was hanging around the gatepost a couple of hours ago.'

'How can you be sure?'

'I've known that boy since he was a lad.' Mrs Miller's chin jutted defiantly. 'I don't like to pry . . .' *Of course you don't*, Grace thought. 'But I feel it's my neighbourly duty to keep an eye on what goes on in the village. It was him.'

Grace had imagined so many times how it would feel to see Sam again. But she hadn't expected to feel this – anger.

'Thank you, Mrs Miller.'

'What are you going to do, love?' she called as Grace strode down the cottage path.

'I'm going to talk to the people at the Rectory,' she said, steeling herself. She felt Mrs Miller's gaze boring into her back as she strode up the familiar driveway. There were different cars parked by the garage, a new swing set gleaming red beneath the oak tree. Even the front door was a different colour – a new, deep crimson. She pulled the bell, her heart aching for her old home, and she waited.

'Hello? Can I help you?' A young woman with flushed pink cheeks and a baby balanced on her hip opened the door.

'I'm sorry to disturb you,' Grace said. 'My name is Grace Morgan.'

The woman tried to place the name. 'You used to live here?' She smiled warmly.

'This is rather awkward. I don't know how much you've heard?'

'Oh, Mrs Miller invited herself in for a coffee on the morning we moved in,' the woman said. Her gaze grew sympathetic. 'I'm sorry to hear about your troubles, and your husband.'

'Actually, that's why I'm here. Mrs Miller thinks she has seen Sam hanging around.'

'But didn't he—' The woman's words cut off awkwardly.

'I know, it sounds crazy.' Grace felt her cheeks burning and she looked down at her feet. 'It's just, they never found a body, you see, so you always hope . . . He hasn't been to the house?'

'No.' She shook her head. 'I haven't seen anyone, and no one has tried to get in. In fact, my husband is a bit paranoid about safety so he's just fitted a new burglar alarm and window locks.'

Grace smiled, thinking of New Year's Eve. 'Good for you. I always meant to get around to that.' She turned to go. 'I hope you'll be happy here.'

239

'I'm sure we will,' the girl said. 'I've dreamt of living some-where like this all my life. It's a bit of a commute for my husband, he's in the City . . .'

'A banker?'

'Yes.'

Grace tried to see the humour in it, that her beloved home had been repossessed by the bank and sold to a banker. 'Thanks. Bye.'

'Wait!' the girl called after her. 'I have something you might like.' She beckoned her over to the garage and heaved open the door. 'I couldn't bear to paint over it. When we redecorated I got a carpenter to replace it. I know it's silly, but it just seemed like part of the house's history.' She pointed at the far corner, and Grace saw the old doorjamb from the kitchen. Her eyes smarted as she stepped forwards and ran her finger down all the heights – Sam, Grace, Harry, Jagger, marking out another time, another life.

28

Grace knocked on the door of Margot's cottage, calling out to her. The sunset washed the windows gold, and swallows looped above the thatched roof. 'Gogo!' Grace called, ham-mering at the door again.

'No use, love,' the next-door neighbour said, turning off his lawnmower. He leant against the fence. 'Gone again, she has. Paid my wife to look after that cat of hers and gone.'

Gone? How could she run away now? On the drive back to the Manor, Grace's mind raced, trying to make sense of it all. *Is that why I felt a connection with Fraser? And I'm attracted to Jack? Because we're related?* Horrified, she mentally traced the family line and exhaled with relief when she realised that even if Fraser were Margot's brother, she and Jack were not related by blood. She gripped the steering wheel, racing along the familiar green lanes towards the coast. *I can't tell him, not yet.* Her brow knotted as she thought. *He'll be devastated. I can't tell Fraser until I've had it out with Margot properly.*

She swung the Beetle into the stable yard and pulled on the handbrake, sitting in silence for a moment to collect her thoughts.

'Hey!' Jack called to her, strolling across the yard from the estate office. Her heart lifted at the sight of him, in his familiar T-shirt and jodhpurs, at his wide open smile. She longed to confide in him, but knew that he kept no secrets from Fraser. 'I've been looking for you. Fraser has something he wants to talk to you about.'

He's not the only one, Grace thought as Jack opened the car door for her. 'Thanks.'

'Are you OK?' He touched her arm, and Grace lowered her head, waiting, part of her hoping that he would reach for her. She ached for him, wanted desperately to hold him, to be held. *Fraser's not the only one who will be devastated by this. I can't begin something with Jack when it could all fall apart. I can't do that to him.* 'I'm sorry if I came on too strong.' He stepped back, unsure. 'I guess—'

'Grace,' Fraser called from the kitchen door. 'May I have a word?'

She looked up at Jack. 'We can talk later?'

'Sure.' He nodded and strode away. But she knew from the look in his eyes that she had missed the moment, again.

Grace walked into the kitchen and pulled back one of the Thonet chairs. 'What's up?' she said to Fraser, while all the time her conscience was saying: *he knows, he knows . . .*

'Do you have a passport?'

'Of course.'

'Good. Pack a case. We're going to do some fieldwork.' Fraser laid down two tickets on the table. 'We're going to Paris.'

'Paris?' Grace's lips parted.

'It's all arranged. Ellen is going to look after Harry.' He clapped his hands. 'I've just called the Lutetia and booked the rooms. Bouchet et Fils are expecting us on Tuesday.'

Grace laughed. 'You amaze me.'

'Well? Don't hang around.' He shooed her from the kitchen. 'I thought we'd take a couple of days for some fun first. It's been all work and no play around here.'

Moments later Jack walked into the kitchen. 'What's this all about?'

'I'm taking Grace to Paris.'

'You're what?' Jack put his hands on his hips. His look of surprise changed. 'Don't you think she's rather young for you?'

'My dear boy, if I were thirty years younger, I wouldn't hesitate – and nor should you.' He narrowed his eyes, sensing Jack's anger. 'Good, you're jealous. You do care about her.' Jack's head fell and Fraser relented, patting his arm. 'Take my advice. Women like Grace are the rarest of gems. Declare your feelings before it is too late and someone else discovers her.'

242

JULY

Ruby

Passion · Nobility · Strength

'Fraser, are you ready? The car's outside,' Grace said, knocking on the door of the library.

'Yes, come on in. I was just showing Jack the little Bouchet et Fils brooch.' Fraser wore a purple Liberty shirt with a flamboyant silk cravat. 'Clemmie kept it in her button tin, of all things,' he said, showing Jack the diamond wing on his tie.

'It was a bit flash for the lawyer, wasn't it?' Jack said. He wore a simple dark suit and tie, his white shirt fresh against his tanned skin. He sat in the armchair in front of Fraser's desk, his head resting against his hand, legs spread wide. Grace could tell immediately from the way he was flicking the fingers of his left hand that he was angry. *Or hurt?* He barely glanced at her.

'A bit flash? Nonsense. I adore a bit of lawyer baiting.' Fraser shrugged on a blue velvet jacket. 'The cousins have managed to convince him I'm a hopeless fop and I intend to play up to it at every opportunity and wait until they make a mistake.'

'Is everything all right?' Grace asked, seeing the grim look on Jack's face.

'It will be,' Fraser said. 'Sir Richard's children are trying to make trouble. I've declared Jack as my heir and they are fighting their corner for the estate and the Booth fortune. I have no brothers or sisters, no children, so they feel they have more right as blood relatives. I don't want them giving Jack any trouble after I'm gone, and I don't have long left . . .'

No brothers or sisters, Grace thought. *But what if you do?* Panic fluttered in her stomach. *I can't tell you, not yet. Not until Gogo comes back.*

'Jeez, not this again,' Jack said. 'You've got years ahead, Frase.' He leant forward in his chair and glanced up at Grace, his dark hair flopping over his eyes. 'You've heard about this? He was suckered by some old hag in a Leningrad street market—'

'She was a well-known mystic,' Fraser interrupted. 'Related to Rasputin.'

'She read his palm and told him that his life would end in 1979.'

'It's nonsense, isn't it?' Grace said, but her blood ran cold. She realised Fraser would be destroyed if she told him that Gin was his sister. *When the time comes, I need to think carefully about how to do this . . . it could kill him.*

'Are you ready?' Fraser asked her.

'Can't wait.' She busied herself tidying some papers on the desk. 'Do you need to bring any of these with you?'

'No, I have everything I need. Will you see us off, Jack?'

Jack looked from Fraser to Grace as he stood. 'I've got to get on.'

'Jack—' Grace began.

'Have a great time.'

As she watched him walk away, Grace's eye was caught by a new silver frame on Fraser's desk. 'Virginia West,' she said under her breath, looking at her grandmother's face gazing at Fraser in the photograph, with love in her eyes. From her pocket she took out the envelope she had just found on the driving seat of her car, and a ruby tumbled into her palm. She read the typewritten card: *The ruby stole a spark from heaven above, July will bring you fervent love.*

30

Grace sat at a small circular café table on the Place Vendôme, waiting for Fraser. A sketchbook lay open on her lap, and her freshly manicured fingernails drummed on the paper in time to the bossa nova tune drifting from the café. She slipped a pair of large tortoiseshell sunglasses on, shielding her eyes from the bright sun. She was wearing a new dark blue trouser suit from Le Bon Marché, and high tan heels, and she enjoyed the admiring glances of a couple of men at a nearby table. She smiled quietly to herself as she continued sketching new ideas for jewels inspired by her visits to Chaumet, Cartier, Van Cleef & Arpels and Boucheron that morning. It had done her good having time alone to enjoy the city, to walk and think without the worry that she was being watched or followed by whoever was sending the stones.

The magic of the streets pushed aside Grace's guilt at concealing what she had found out about 'Gin' from Fraser, and her sorrow at the knowledge that everything could soon end. The markets, the cafés, the elegance of the architecture and the beauty of the parks, the Seine walks reinvigorated her. She realised that when the time came she would tell Fraser everything herself. Until she had talked to Margot she could do nothing. She missed Harry and found herself wishing that Jack were there beside her as she watched lovers strolling arm in arm through the leafy avenues, or kissing at café tables. But Grace decided as she sketched a new idea for a necklace with the ruby at its heart to enjoy every last moment of the trip.

After a time, she looked up across the elegant square and saw Fraser strolling towards the café. Pigeons rose, a flurry of wings around the column at the heart of the square. He raised his hand in greeting as he drew closer.

'Don't you brush up well?' Fraser pulled out the cane chair at her side. 'That chap at the next table is practically panting. Go on, let's have a bit of fun. Pretend I'm your sugar daddy.' He threw his arm along the back of her chair. 'How was the spa?'

'You have no idea.' She laughed as she leant across and

pecked his cheek with a quick kiss. 'I think I've grown three inches after that massage. Thank you so much.'

'I love what they've done with your hair.'

Grace turned her face from side to side so that he could see the loose chignon properly. 'I can't tell you how glorious it was. I feel like a new woman.'

She looked up as the waiter came over. 'Coffee?' she asked Fraser, and ordered in fluent French. He looked at her in surprise.

'You didn't put that on your CV.'

'French grandmother.' Grace tossed the sketchbook onto the table. 'I spent a lot of time in Paris, before I met Sam.' She gazed out across the square. 'In another lifetime, I dreamt of living here.'

'I must say you look at home. Tell me what you've been up to?'

'I've had the most wonderful time. Shopping, museums, just walking for miles and miles. I've been in every jewellery store you can think of. God, I love this city.' Grace smiled, her eyes bright. 'I feel so . . . inspired.'

'It's lovely to see you like this.' Fraser patted her hand. 'I thought a change of scene might be just the boost you needed.'

'I thought this was a working trip?'

'Oh, there's time for that today.'

'Have you been back to the hotel at all?'

'Me? No, I've been having fun too, a trip down memory lane. I went to Gin's old bar.'

'You spent the night at a strip club?' Grace's lips parted in surprise.

'It's more of a burlesque cabaret, dear heart. Full of old codgers like me, hankering after the old days.' The waiter arrived with their order, and Grace ladled six teaspoons of sugar into Fraser's bowl of coffee.

'You must be shattered.' Grace checked her watch. 'Are you sure you want to go to Bouchet et Fils?'

'Of course! I can sleep at home, what a waste to lose a moment of Paris.'

A doorman welcomed them beneath the blue and gold awning of Bouchet et Fils, the brass fittings glinting in the midday sun as the heavy wooden door opened. In the showroom the noise of the square fell away and a luxurious silence embraced them.

'This is beautiful,' Grace said, gazing around the elegant panelled room. A few people milled about among the glass cases, admiring the jewels, and a large chandelier with ropes of sparkling crystal hung from the high, stuccoed ceiling. Their voices were softened by the rich blue carpet and gold velvet drapes which hung from the soaring windows looking out on the arcade fronting the square.

'I have an appointment with Monsieur Bouchet,' Fraser said to the young girl who came to greet them. 'The name is Stratton.'

'Please, follow me, Monsieur Stratton,' she said, taking them through the showroom to a set of high doors. She knocked and ushered them into a side room.

As Grace looked around, her eyes lit up. 'I've never seen anything so beautiful,' she said, walking across the room. It was furnished in elegant eau-de-Nil shades, with silk upholstered gilded chairs, and the high French windows overlooked a private courtyard garden with manicured orange and lemon trees.

'I am glad you like it. My great-grandmother chose the furnishings nearly a hundred years ago.' An immaculately dressed man in a grey suit stood up at the desk in the corner. 'Welcome to Bouchet et Fils.'

'Delighted to meet you, Monsieur Bouchet,' Fraser said, shaking his hand, 'and thank you for agreeing to see us. This is my secretary, Miss Manners.'

'Enchanted,' the man said.

'Grace is also a jeweller.'

'Ah? Then you will enjoy seeing some of our finest designs.' Bouchet walked across to the panelled wall opposite the windows. One by one, he turned the panels to reveal rows of glittering tiaras. As each hidden display turned, concealed spotlights illuminated, showing the designs to perfection.

'It feels like Christmas,' Grace said.

'I can see from your delight that you are an artist.' He smiled indulgently. 'These are just a few of the designs that generations of my family have created over the years.'

Fraser slipped his glasses from his top pocket and studied the tiaras. 'These aren't the real things, though, are they?'

'No, these are the models. The originals are owned by aristocratic families around the world, such as yours.' Bouchet ushered them towards a table near the open doors to the garden and held out a chair for Grace. 'May I offer you some coffee, or tea?'

'No, thank you.' She smiled, and glanced back at the display. 'I don't see the Stratton tiara?'

'Indeed, no.' Bouchet returned from his desk with an old leather-bound ledger and a file of papers. 'After my conversation with Mr Stratton, our archivist went back through the company records. I am glad to say that I have found the original correspondence with your father, Albert Stratton.' He looked up at Fraser over his reading glasses, and passed him the file. 'I have made copies for you, here.'

'Thank you,' Fraser said, flicking through the paperwork.

'You may be interested to see the original sketches for the design.' He turned the ledger towards Grace and she stared down at the exquisite life-size painting of the Stratton tiara.

'So that is how it would have looked,' she said.

Fraser gently placed his winged brooch on the drawing. 'Perfect.'

'This is the brooch you talked of?' Bouchet leant in to take a closer look. 'If I may, I'd like to take some photographs?'

'Of course.' Fraser reached into his briefcase and handed Bouchet a file. 'You may like to take copies of these, too. I have photographs of all the Stratton jewels, apart from the tiara and the missing asteria sapphire necklace.' He looked down at the winged brooch. 'I must admit it was in an old button tin . . .' Bouchet inhaled sharply. 'My mother adored the other jewels, but never cared for this.'

'You do not know what happened to the rest of the tiara?' Bouchet asked, lifting the telephone.

Fraser shook his head. 'Old Albert was more generous than I thought. It looks like the band – or whatever the technical term for it is – was inlaid with diamonds too. What do you think, Grace?'

'Yes,' she said. She stared at the drawing, imagining Margot's wing in place. 'Monsieur Bouchet would know, but I think the diamonds probably detached as well, and they could be used as a necklace. It's an exquisite design.'

'Good,' Bouchet said. 'Our photographer can take the pictures now. May I?' He lifted up the winged brooch and placed it on a deep blue velvet tray.

'Do you mind if I have a look around?' Fraser asked.

'Please, be by guest.'

'Grace, will you be all right?' Fraser asked.

'Couldn't be happier,' she said. 'I'm going to take a good look through the designs and paperwork.'

Grace worked methodically through the sketches, noting down all the details of each piece of jewellery purchased by Albert for Clementine. She came to the missing asteria sapphire and studied the design closely. Grace sorted on through the paperwork until she found Bouchet et Fils' receipt for the tiara. *That can't be right*, she thought, remembering the folded bill she found in the tiara box. The letterhead was entirely different, and the company stamp all wrong. Her stomach plummeted. Fraser's words came back to her. *Bit of a forger, too?* Grace shook her head as the truth came to her. *Gogo used*

251

me. She set this whole thing up. She forged the damn receipt.

'All done,' Bouchet said, returning with the brooch. An assistant brought over a new blue leather case and he carefully set the brooch at its heart, clicking it shut. 'Thank you, Mr Stratton,' he said as Fraser walked over. 'Please, as a favour to me. No more button tins.'

31

'Montmartre,' Fraser said to the driver. As the car pulled away from the Place Vendôme along the Rue de la Paix, he checked in his wallet for the folded piece of paper and made sure of the address. 'Take us to the Place du Tertre.'

'Yes, sir,' the driver said, and turned the car towards the Opéra.

'Where are we going?' Grace said.

'Where it all began. We are retracing Albert's steps.' Fraser wound down the window and the hot, succulent air of the city filled the taxi, blew away the trace of eau de cologne left by the previous customer. 'Imagine it. 1915. He was on the way home to England now that he was well enough to travel. Whatever happened to him during the battle at Mons, he was a changed man. He had decided to do the decent thing and give up his mistress, and return to Clemmie. But he loved this woman, this Josephine, Grace.' Fraser turned to her. 'Imagine this last drive he took, how torn he must have felt.'

'He was about to break her heart.' Grace's brow furrowed. *He was about to break my great-grandmother's heart.*

'It was winter, of course.' Fraser gazed out of the window. 'Among the men and women strolling the streets in their dark winter coats, Albert would have seen the colours of uniforms leaping out at him – crimson Zouaves, dark blue gunners, azure Chasseurs d'Afrique.' He looked up at the clear blue sky. 'I love Paris in the winter. Perhaps it was snowing, dense flakes of snow billowing among them.' Fraser took a small notepad from his breast pocket and began to scribble down notes. 'The buildings looked the same as ever – the elegant, grey streets leading up the hill.' He thought for a moment. 'Albert would have seen the newly finished Sacré-Coeur.'

'I wonder what she was like,' Grace said quietly.

'Josephine? All I know is that in the spring before the war, when Clem lost the baby, she and Albert had a terrific falling-out. He couldn't help her, couldn't express his grief at the loss of their child and Clem sent him away. It seemed like the end of the marriage. So he ran straight into the arms of his one-time mistress.' Fraser sighed.

'Then the war separated them?' Grace asked.

Fraser nodded. 'When he came back to collect Clem's jewels and break with Josephine, the cafés were full of men like him, soldiers convalescing in the Red Cross hospitals in Paris. He must have lost count of the number of crutches and sticks he saw propped up beside café tables and bars. The wounded were an everyday reminder of the war entrenched on the Western Front.' Fraser flicked on through the pages of his notebook. 'Did I show you this?' he handed Grace a tattered, folded piece of paper.

'It's from Josephine?'

'From the date, he would have received it in hospital.'

'The heart of Paris is a flame, burning steadily, like my love for you,' Grace read, staring down at the paper. *Poor you. You must have thought he had come back to Paris for you and the children, not for his wife's jewels.*

'There,' Fraser said, 'number three.' The car pulled up outside a red double door, set back from the street beneath a stone pediment. Fraser glanced upwards at the flaking wooden shutters of the apartments above as he waited for the driver to open the door. 'Oh God, I'm forgetting myself.' He swung open the door himself, and helped Grace out before he paid the driver.

The ground floor of the building was a café at street level, and the scent of roasting coffee, of onion soup and fresh bread made Grace's mouth water.

'So?' Fraser turned to her. 'Up for a bit of re-enactment?' He mimed walking with a stiff gait. 'Albert would have stepped awkwardly out onto the pavement, stumbling on the uneven, slushy cobbles. I know from Clem that he carried the jewels in his old leather satchel.'

The grandeur of the street entrance belied the simplicity of the apartments behind. The dim courtyard was strung with a spider's web of washing lines, and from the open doorways Grace heard the sounds of raised voices, wailing children, the clatter of pots. Her nostrils flared at the overpowering scent of garlic, urine, drains.

'*Oui? Je peux vous aider*?' The concierge opened her window.

'Ah, hello.' Fraser turned to Grace. 'Your French is better than mine, my dear. Could you explain? I know she lived at number four, from the letter.'

Grace explained that they were researching a book, and asked if it was possible to see apartment four. 'We're in luck,' she said, as the old woman sorted through some keys. 'It's empty at the moment.' They followed her across the courtyard. Fraser gave her a few francs, and waited, his hand on the doorknob.

'It gives me chills, imagining my father here.' He tilted his head back and looked up at the square of sky above. 'This is where I was born, Grace. In this crowded, filthy apartment block that smells of cat piss and cabbage.' He exhaled. 'God, I didn't think I'd feel so nervous.' He shifted the weight of his briefcase, and Grace took his arm.

'We'll do it together,' she said.

'Yes. Yes we will.' Fraser squared his shoulders. 'So, Albert stood here, waiting for Josephine to answer. He was in pain, no doubt, from where his leg had been badly set after the battle, each step a small torture. He waited here, heard the

254

sound of footsteps through the thin wall, and then she was there.'

Fraser flung open the door. He stepped into a cramped, single room, a stove and sink in one corner. The dusty floorboards creaked under his feet as he strode across the room in three steps and flipped back a faded floral sheet pinned across an alcove at one end.

'Are you OK?' Grace said gently, seeing the expression on his face.

'Yes. It's . . . God, it's pitiful. Poor woman.'

'How did she feel?' Grace said, hugging her arms to her chest. 'I mean, from your notes she thought he had been killed at Mons. She'd given birth alone, had gone all those months without word until she heard from him in hospital.'

'You're a woman—'

'Thank you for noticing.'

'How would you have felt?'

'Relieved? Overjoyed? If I thought he had come back to me, and I loved him, I would have held him so tight I'd never let him go again.'

'Good. Excellent,' Fraser said, making a quick note. 'Now, he had left Josephine in Paris at the outbreak of war in 1914 to join his Division in England and he was sent back to France as part of the Expeditionary Forces. It all happened terribly quickly.'

'So it was nearly a year since she had seen him and conceived the twins? She would have wanted to know what he had been through,' Grace said.

'Yes.' Fraser paced the room. 'I know my father. He would have been anxious, shaking, the effects of the battle still with him.'

'Shell shock?'

Fraser nodded. 'He wouldn't have wanted to open up at all. How would that have made her feel?'

'I . . .' Grace thought about how Sam refused to talk, towards the end. How shut out and frustrated she had felt, how use-less. 'She would have wanted to help him, to reach him.' She remembered all the nights she had cried herself to sleep with worry and exhaustion before Sam went. *I'd forgotten,* she re-alised. *I'd forgotten how unhappy I was for months.* 'Perhaps she cried.'

'He would have hated that.' Fraser folded his arms, ran the pen against his lips as he thought. 'That's what he was hiding from with Clem – all that emotion. This was his mistress, his good-time girl. There are no photographs of her, but from the colour of my own hair when I was younger, I imagine she was a redhead.' *Good-time girl?* Grace's pride rose up on Josephine's behalf. *Poor thing. The man she loves, the father of her children, thought that of her?* 'They met when she was modelling at the art school Albert attended when he was on holiday in Paris.'

'Like you and Virginia West,' Grace couldn't help saying.

'History repeating itself, eh?' He closed his eyes and waved his hand in the air, thinking. 'Albert and Josephine had a whirlwind affair, a holiday romance, some time before he met Clem, but he returned to Josephine when he fell out with his wife.'

'And she became pregnant immediately?'

'Perhaps she was trying to trap him?'

'Not everyone who falls pregnant is trying to trap a man. Maybe she was more than a "good-time girl". Perhaps they were passionately in love.' Her eyes flashed as she looked at Fraser. 'Don't you remember how that feels?'

'Of course, my dear. My apologies.' He raised his chin and closed his eyes. 'So, think how he felt. After the horror of battle, here he is with his lover – exhausted, full of desire. I'm quite sure all he wanted was to lie down with her and sleep in her arms forever.' Fraser looked around the room. 'Was this the best she could afford, with the money he had been sending her?'

'Perhaps she had to stop working after she had the children?'

'Of course! The babies. Perhaps he found her changed? Dark circles beneath her eyes, a fierceness in her gaze. When war broke out, the artists left, so there was no work for her at the art school.' Fraser checked his notes. 'Josephine was unemployed, living in poverty, and Albert was about to break her heart.' He looked at Grace, adopted his father's clipped tone. 'It's my duty to go back to England.' He waved his hand, encouraging Grace to play along.

'To her?' Grace said.

'To my wife, yes, and to my Division.' He gestured at his leg. 'I was wed to the cavalry long before I was wed to a woman. This is just a Blighty – a *bonne blessure* as you say, a good wound. It's bad enough to put me out of active duty, but not bad enough that I can't be useful, somehow. I'm not much use in the cavalry any more, but, by God, I shall do what I can at home.'

'But I love you, Albert.' Grace stifled a laugh.

'Come on, Grace,' Fraser said, putting his hands on his hips. 'Take this seriously, please?'

'Sorry,' she said, and cleared her throat. 'What's changed? Before you went to fight, you said you would stay here, with me. Think of our children, we could make a life—'

'Darling, I've had a lot of time to think over the last months in dock. I've been forced to, lying in bed with my damned leg in traction.' Fraser looked at Grace. 'And consumed by shell shock, poor sod,' he said. He limped across the room, taking on his father's character again. 'Clementine and I had our troubles. She suffered more than I will ever know losing our child last year. I was a coward to run away. I didn't know how to reach her.'

'She can't give you an heir now, Albert. I can, I have.' Grace imagined Josephine's anguish, and to her surprise felt tears prick her eyes. 'Stay with us.'

'I owe Clemmie everything.'

'You don't love her. She is just a rich American heiress

257

buying herself some class by marrying an aristocrat. You needed one another, that's all.'

'Don't be cruel. It doesn't suit you.'

'I was here before her. You could have married me.'

'My time in Paris with you was the happiest of my life. Do you remember? Days of white linen, walking in the Jardin des Tuileries, the scent of lilac—'

'Where were the babies while they were talking?' Grace interrupted.

'The children!' Fraser said. 'I was getting quite carried away.' He looked around the room. 'Perhaps she had her bed here?' He swept aside the curtain and stared at the small alcove. Grace walked over to his side.

'A boy and girl, Albert,' she said, taking Josephine's part. 'Three weeks ago.'

'Twins?'

'Which is which?'

'Fraser Albert . . .' she said, pointing at an imaginary crib.

'After my father?'

'And Margot . . .'

'Margot Helene. After her mother I assume?' Fraser hesitated. 'I've never experienced this, Grace. What's it like? When you look at a child – children – you have created together. Grace?' He turned to her. 'Oh my dear.'

'I'm sorry.' Grace wiped at her cheek with the heel of her hand. 'I was just remembering my twins, Jem and Rex.' She bit down hard on her lips, stifling a sob. 'They lived for a little while, you see. They held hands, as I held them. Maybe you held hands with your sister, like that?' Fraser embraced her. 'They died in my arms, Fraser.'

'Let it all out, dear heart.'

'I'm sorry, I'm so sorry.' Her breath shuddered. 'The poor girl. Her heart must have been breaking once she realised Albert was leaving her. I could never, never give away my child.'

258

They stood in silence for a time, until Grace composed herself. 'Are you sure you want to go on?' Fraser handed her a clean handkerchief, and she nodded. Fraser walked to the window, waiting for Grace to tidy her face in the cloudy mirror above the basin. 'Perhaps he thought that life was hard enough here for her without two children to care for.'

'No.' Grace shook her head and took a step back. 'She was used to taking care of herself. I bet she was proud.' She thought of the way she had struggled to keep going after Sam left. 'She was no kept woman.'

'How would he have put it?' Fraser turned to her. 'Let me take the boy?' Fraser placed his briefcase on the counter. 'At some point he would have reached into the satchel and lifted out the boxes embossed with Clementine's initials: CBS.' Fraser opened the box containing the diamond wing. 'Maybe he thought back to the spring of 1914 – visiting Paris to order the jewels had been his escape from his grieving, distant wife. Perhaps he hadn't even intended to take up with Josephine again, but he couldn't resist the temptation to see her.' Fraser turned the diamond brooch to the light. 'In his young life of duty, of *noblesse oblige*, his occasional weeks in Paris with Josephine were his one taste of freedom, of joy. *Now, I must leave her. The least I can do is take care of her and give the boy legitimacy.*' Fraser's eyes lit up. 'That's it. I know him. That's how he would have sold it to her. Then he showed her the tiara, two delicate diamond wings arched above the platinum band, seeming to float as effortlessly as the wings of Eros.' He looked at Grace. 'He unclipped the right wing, easing it free of the platinum setting. He placed the wing in his pocket, and offered the tiara to Josephine.' Fraser reached out his hand to Grace. 'Please, take this, for the girl. It seems appropriate, somehow, that both of them should have half. Keep the brooch for her, but you can sell the setting I'm sure. It will help you for a few months.'

'Jewels, love, a life. They can all be broken apart,' Grace said. 'Something doesn't make sense. Why just the boy?'

'Albert wasn't interested in children, or a family. He just wanted an heir.'

Grace put her hands on her hips, impersonating Josephine again. 'Our son will have a life of wealth and ease, while the girl will struggle, with me? It hardly seems fair.' Her eyes flashed as she looked at him. 'Take both children.'

'I don't need both.'

'Then do what is right by the girl. She needs a better home than this.'

'Of course,' Fraser said, clicking his fingers. 'The allowance that was paid to a bank in Paris for years and years. That explains it.' He glanced back at the alcove. 'I hope my sister inherited Josephine's strength and beauty.' Fraser put the diamond wing back in his case.

She did, Grace thought. A wave of nausea swept over her at the thought of having to tell Fraser the truth soon.

'How do you think she felt, handing me over?' Grace caught the vulnerability in Fraser's voice. 'I've often wondered. Do you think she cared?'

'Cared?' Grace thought of the last time she held Rex, before he was taken away, and her chest tightened. 'Your heart breaks when a child is taken from you.' When she looked at Fraser, her eyes glistened.

'Please, don't upset yourself again.'

'No, it's good. I'm glad to talk about it.' As she smiled, her lips trembled. 'I didn't have a chance at the time. With everything that happened with Sam, and the banks swooping in to take everything we'd ever worked for, and comforting Harry, I didn't have a chance to talk about them.' She laughed bitterly. 'Some people treated it like I'd just miscarried, not like Jem and Rex were people, who lived, even for an hour or two.' Grace looked down at her hands for a moment, collecting her thoughts. 'Something happens when you love a child. I know this from talking to friends who have adopted children as well – it's the same. You lose a part of yourself to them. When you love them, it's a physical, visceral thing. When I'm apart from Harry, I feel like part of me is missing. And it is. And a part of me will always be missing, because it's with them.' Her voice shook. 'I feel them, you know, I miss them. I miss everything that could have been.' She tried to force down the tightness in her throat. 'When Josephine held you for the last time, I bet she held you to her like she never wanted to let you go.' Grace cradled the air, remembering her own goodbye to Jem and Rex. 'I bet she rocked you in her arms, and wrapped you up warm, and told you that she would always love you.' Grace screwed her eyes closed as the tears fell. 'She would have tried to remember everything about you, every detail of your face, your hands, how you smelt, how your skin felt . . .' Grace looked at Fraser. 'If I were her, and I had to let you go, I would have thought of you every single day for the rest of my life.'

32

Grace stood on the balcony of Fraser's room, sipping a glass of champagne. The lights of Paris sparkled below like a field of gemstones, and in the distance, the Eiffel Tower. The hem of her black silk Madame Grès dress lifted in the breeze. She leant against the wrought-iron railing and raised her face to the sky, closing her eyes.

'How are you feeling now?' Fraser strode out onto the balcony, adjusting his tie.

'A little raw still,' she said, turning to him.

'I apologise, Grace. I should have thought—'

'No, really.' She smiled. 'I feel better. Rather like I've come round from a fever. A bit shaky, but . . .'

'Purged?' Fraser lifted the bottle of Perrier-Jouët Belle Époque from the silver champagne bucket and topped up her glass. 'This will soon have you right as rain.' He poured himself a glass. 'Well? Give me a twirl.'

'You sound like Bruce Forsyth,' Grace said, turning around to show him the dress. The column of fabric draped beautifully across her body, cinching in at her waist, two bands flowing from a low neckline across her shoulders to a plunging back. 'There was no need for this.'

'There was every need. You look divine. And it was fun, wasn't it? Madame Grès is a genius.' Fraser sipped his wine.

'That vintage shop was gorgeous. I could have chosen any one of the dresses – the woman who helped us has wonderful taste.' Her eyes creased as she smiled. 'In men as well? I take it you're old friends.'

'Yes, my dear. Very good friends.' He smiled. 'At least, we were before she married. I learnt a great deal about fashion from her. Jack's never been interested in clothes, but I adore shopping.' He raised a finger. 'Hold on, I almost forgot.' He put down his glass and disappeared back into his room.

Grace could sense he was excited about something. *He's being so kind. I can't bear the thought of hurting him.*

'Now,' he said, striding out onto the balcony with a blue leather Bouchet et Fils box in his hands. 'Don't have a heart attack. This is just a loan for the night. Monsieur Bouchet was most taken with you. He thought you might enjoy this.' Fraser opened the box and turned it to her. A fine triple band of diamonds sparkled in the lights on the terrace.

'It's beautiful!' Grace placed her hand flat against her breastbone.

'It's yours for the night.' Fraser watched her slide the band onto her hair, securing the combs in the chignon. 'May I?' He teased a couple of strands of hair loose, letting them frame her cheekbones. 'You are a vision.'

'Thank you. I feel like a princess.'

'It is I who should thank you, Grace.' He took her hand. 'I want you to know that you, and Harry, have come to mean a

262

great deal to all of us.' She couldn't look at him, felt sure he could see how guilty she felt.

'Thank you.' Margot's advice came to her. *Smile. Always smile, darling.* 'Where shall we go? It's our last night in Paris.'

'Yes. Unfortunately—' He broke off at a knock on the door. Grace strode after him, frowning.

'What do you mean, unfortunately?'

'I have to fly back to London. Some business has come up and they need my advice. Honestly, and they call it retirement.'

'You're leaving?' Grace couldn't hide her disappointment. 'Then why am I all dressed up?'

'My dear, as if I would leave you here alone.' Fraser swept the door open.

'Jack?' Grace said, her eyes widening.

'Perfect timing, dear boy. I'm just going to get my case,' Fraser said, excusing himself.

Jack stood on the threshold of the suite, transfixed by Grace. His pale linen suit and white shirt were crumpled from the trip, his tanned face bruised with five o'clock shadow. He stepped forwards, shaking his head. 'Man. When Fraser rang and said he'd upset you, I didn't expect to find you looking like this.' He touched her arm. 'You OK?'

'I'm . . .' She laughed with surprise. 'You came all this way?'

'I was worried about you and didn't like the thought of you here alone.' He smiled, looking at the floor, and raised his gaze to hers. 'Besides, Fraser told me I'd regret it if I didn't.' He stepped back, his hand still lingering on her wrist. 'He was right.'

It would have felt like the most natural thing in the world to Grace for their hands to slide together, fingers lacing. *I can't believe he came all this way, for me.* She wanted to hold him, to be held. *I can't, I can't,* she thought, fighting the temptation to reach out to him. *I can't start something when I know it's going to end badly. I can't hurt him.* 'Come through,' she said, stepping away. 'Would you like some champagne?'

263

'I'd love some.' Jack followed Grace through the room.

'Where's your luggage?'

Jack reached into the pocket of his jacket, and waved a red toothbrush at her. 'Travelling light. I almost forgot.' He handed her a folded piece of card. 'Harry gave me this for you.'

'Is she all right? I've missed her terribly.' Grace looked at the drawing on the card. It was still warm from where it had lain against Jack's chest. 'Bless her. It's all of us, even the dogs.' She read the message and smiled. Jack followed Grace outside and whistled.

'Wow. What a view.' Jack looked out across the glittering panorama of Paris, his eyes settling on Grace as she poured him a glass of champagne.

'Beautiful, isn't she?' Fraser whispered, nudging him. 'Right, Jack,' he said, draping his coat over his arm. 'I'm relying on you to make amends to Grace.' He waved a slim silver camera at them. 'Indulge me.' Jack and Grace edged together. 'Come on, closer, I've chopped half Jack's leg off and I can't get the Eiffel Tower in if you stand a foot apart.' Jack glanced at Grace and put his arm around her waist, holding her close. 'That's better.'

Grace leant in to Jack, and closed her eyes for a moment, enjoying the closeness of him, the warmth of his arm around her. She felt safe. *I could stay like this forever, never mind all night.* The flash startled her.

'That's no good, you blinked, Grace,' Fraser said. 'One more. Say cheese, or fromage . . . Excellent.' Fraser pecked her on the cheek with a quick kiss, and shook Jack's hand. 'Paris is yours for one night. Go wherever you like – the opera, ballet, just charge it to the room. The concierge will take care of returning the diadem to Bouchet et Fils in the morning.'

After he had gone, Grace and Jack stared at the closed door. 'Do you really think something came up at work?' Grace said.

'Nah. We've been set up.'

'Do you think?' Grace looked up at him through smoky lashes. 'I feel like a fraud. I don't deserve this.'

'Hey, never say that about yourself.' He turned to Grace. 'You know, when I went off to school, Fraser told me what Socrates or Aristotle or some guy said once . . .' Grace laughed. 'Yeah, you know what he's like. He said if you act brave, you become brave. I think you're about the bravest person I've ever met.'

'Jack, I'm not—' Grace longed to tell him the whole story, to share her suspicions. *But he'd be devastated. I can't hurt him.*

'So, where would you like to go? I feel kind of underdressed in a lounge suit.' He tilted his head towards her. 'But I'll even sit through an opera or ballet if that's what you'd like?'

Grace looked up at Jack. 'You know what? I don't think anything could be more perfect than this. Paris will always be there for me tomorrow. You're here tonight, and that's all I need.'

They sat side by side on the terrace, talking late into the warm night, the sounds of the city, the traffic and music from below drifting up to them. One by one, their defences loosened like the tightly wound petals of a rosebud blooming beneath the sun.

'Do you think we could stay like this forever?' Grace said, watching the first apricot blush of dawn creeping over the silver roofs of Paris. 'Hide away on this terrace high above the world.'

'No worries, no past, no future.' He watched her profile, the triple band of diamonds glittering in her hair. 'God, you look beautiful.'

Grace let her head fall towards him, and smiled sleepily. 'Thank you.'

'I mean it.'

'I know. And I can't tell you how much it means to me that you didn't drag me out on the town tonight. That you were just glad to be here.'

'With you? Of course.' He laughed softly. 'Why wouldn't I be? I wish everything was as easy and peaceful as spending time with you.'

'And fun. No one's ever made me laugh like you.' Their faces were so close, if Grace moved a fraction, they would kiss. Her head swam with desire, and lack of sleep. She forced herself to move away, tucked her legs up underneath her. She saw the disappointment on his face, but Jack said nothing.

'Are you cold?' He walked into the bedroom and returned with a blanket, draping it over her.

'Thanks.'

'Look, Fraser left his cigarettes behind.'

'Gitanes?' Grace took the packet from him. 'I smoked those when I lived here for the summer. Thought I was terribly sophisticated.'

'Want one?' Jack's eyes crinkled. He searched on the drinks tray for a book of matches and lit two cigarettes, passing one to her.

'I didn't know you smoked.' Grace inhaled, letting her head fall back as she blew a plume of silver smoke into the air.

'I don't.' Jack settled beside her, his arm resting along the back of the seat. 'Well, only on nights like this.'

'You're a bad influence,' she said, glancing at him. 'Cigarettes, staying up all night . . .'

'I'm the boy your mother warned you about.'

'No,' Grace shook her head. 'I married him.'

'Bad boy, eh?' Jack tilted his head. 'Was it like this with him?'

Grace ran her thumb along her lower lip. 'No. Nothing like this. Sam would have wanted to show me off tonight. *Look at my beautiful wife. Look at my beautiful life. Look at all I have achieved.*' She pressed her lips together. 'What's that poem?

The one about some great king, who was showing off, and all that was left was a bit of broken statue in a desert?'

'Ozymandias.'

'Exactly. That was Sam.'

'It must have been . . .' Jack chose his words carefully. 'It's not easy living with someone like that.'

'No.' Grace took a sip of champagne. 'It was never easy or peaceful with Sam. And it wasn't any fun.' She looked at Jack. 'It hadn't been, for a long, long time, even before he disappeared.'

'I'm sorry.'

Grace stubbed out her cigarette, and checked her watch. 'We've got a few hours before the flight. Do you feel like taking a walk?'

'Sure. I'm starving, too. Maybe we can find a bakery.' Jack shrugged on his jacket, and Grace slipped her feet into a pair of silver sandals.

They walked through the silent hallways of the hotel, Art Deco lamps casting golden pools of light on the wood panelling. On the street, they were alone, the brisk morning air bringing them back to the world. Jack offered Grace his arm, and they walked on towards the river. On a side street, they stopped at a café, drank an espresso at a zinc bar among the night workers returning home after their shift. Jack bought a couple of newly baked croissants and they walked on towards the Pont des Arts, sharing the warm pastries. In the middle of the bridge they paused, and Grace let her head fall to his shoulder.

'Grace,' Jack said, 'I don't want there to be any secrets between us.'

She closed her eyes, felt him turn towards her. *He knows*, she thought.

'I'm going to Argentina next month, to finalise the divorce.'

'Oh?' She looked up at him.

'The thing is, I'm willing to give her anything she wants,

267

just to get out of the marriage. I know she was the one screwing around with my so-called best friend, but half her brothers are lawyers and I don't rate my chances much. I wonder sometimes if that's what she was interested in all along – the money, not me. I just want a clean break, now.' He hesitated. 'The thing is, it may well wipe me out, financially. And whatever Fraser says, when those Stratton cousins get to work on his lawyers, blood is thicker than water. We may lose some of the estate when Fraser goes. At the moment, I'm not ... ' He looked at her, his eyes clear and blue in the morning light. 'I'm not a great prospect, Grace, that's what I'm trying to tell you. I know Sam lost everything, and I understand if you're holding back because you don't want to get involved with someone who can't give you the security you deserve.'

'Oh, Jack,' she said, reaching up to touch his face. 'It's not that at all.'

He cupped her hand in his, pressed his lips to her palm. 'You've come to mean the world to me. I don't want to push you, or rush you.'

'Jack, I just can't. Not yet.' She laid her head against his chest, gave in to the hunger to be close to him as he embraced her.

'You do care about me, then?'

'Of course.' She wrapped her arms around him, the sure pulse of his heart beating against her cheek. 'Of course.' Grace inhaled the fresh morning air deeply and looked out across the shimmering river, the first boats drifting along the water, dog walkers and joggers dark specks on the banks beneath them. 'It's just – I want to do it right, this time. I was a teenager when I met Sam, and green as anything. Harry – I mean, I love her with all my heart, but she wasn't planned. I had no idea.'

'But your husband was older?'

'Sam knew what he was doing.' Grace looked up at Jack. 'I

want it to be different. I don't want to rush. You're still married. I – I can't divorce for years.'

'I'll wait.'

'And Harry. It would break her heart to see me with you, like that. She still thinks her dad is going to come back.'

'But we get along.'

'As friends, yes, but children are funny. They like everything to be above board. I don't know what she'd do if we were—'

'In love?' Jack put his hand to Grace's neck, his thumb tracing her jawline. 'I will do whatever I have to do to be with you. I'll hide how I feel about you, and I will give you all the time you need. Just promise me you will always be truthful to me, no lies. If your feelings for me ever change . . .'

'They won't, they won't . . .' Grace leant in to his touch.

'It took me a long time to put my heart back together again.' He frowned, and when he looked at her she saw the vulnerability there. 'Trust me, let me trust you.'

'I promise,' Grace said, wishing she could tell Jack everything. 'I promise that whatever happens, this has been the most wonderful night of my life.'

33

Grace carried the last tray of scones towards the white tea tent at the Pony Club gymkhana. Rows of cars and horseboxes snaked away down the West Sussex hillside, bunting fluttering in the breeze above the stalls as people milled around, starting to head home. She glanced up at the sound of a commotion. 'Robbie!' she heard someone shout, 'Robbie Green, get down at once.' A small red tractor bombed down the hillside from the children's area. 'Who the hell left the keys in it?' a woman cried, as a small crowd raced after them.

'Looks like that Robbie's up to his usual,' Grace said, setting down the tray on Alice's stall.

'I pity his poor mum.' Alice's face was flushed with heat. 'Thanks, Gracie,' she said, unwrapping the cakes. 'I don't know what I'd have done without you this afternoon. I really want to make a go of this.'

'You'll get loads of bookings, I'm sure. Masses of people took your card. Everyone needs a good outside caterer.'

'God, I hope so.'

Grace turned to see what had caught Alice's eye. A young man with a halo of blonde curls was walking away from the bar. 'Stop it, you're practically drooling.'

'He's the new gardener up at Wittering Lodge. I went round there to quote for a christening the other morning and he was in the shrubbery, shirtless, like some young Adonis. Of course, her husband is never there – we all call him Captain Universe – he's something in the City, up at the crack of dawn and back after the children are asleep. I think she feels rather neglected. Good for her – who cares if he's not Percy Thrower. Imagine being able to look at that every day from the comfort of your conservatory.' Alice folded a tea towel and clutched it to her chest. 'Do you remember it, Grace? Boys with golden skin, young and tanned and lean?'

'Steady on Mrs Robinson.' Grace ducked down under the trestle table to get more cups.

'Where do the years go?' Alice turned to the next customer. 'Hello, Fraser.'

'Alice, my dear. Splendid feast.' He leant against the tea table. 'How are you? Whenever I see you and your sisters you're always surrounded by children.'

Grace popped her head up. 'Fraser, behave. I can practically hear your hooves pawing the ground.'

'Didn't see you down there, Grace. A little flirtation goes a long way, doesn't it, Alice?'

Grace pushed her hair back from her face as Jack wandered over to join them. 'Hello, Jack. What can I get you?' She hadn't seen him since they had returned from Paris, and the memories of that night flowed between them. She blushed, smoothed down the floral sundress she was wearing. 'Alice does a mean cream tea.'

'Just the tea, thanks.'

'Did you enjoy the Gold Cup?' Grace said, reaching for the urn.

'It was a good final. Songhai won.'

'Prince Charles was playing for Les Diables Bleus,' Fraser added. 'Mountbatten gave out the trophies, shame they didn't win.'

'Sounds like fun,' Alice said.

'Grace told me you like watching polo.'

'Me?' Alice roared with laughter. 'I know nothing about polo. I just like fit blokes in tight trousers. Now then, Fraser. Why don't you make yourself useful and help me carry these orange squashes over to Harry and her friends?'

Once she was alone with Jack, it seemed to Grace that the noise of the tannoy and buffeting flags, the cars and voices fell away.

'Hi.' Jack brushed the edge of Grace's hand with his thumb. She looked across to check that no one was looking. His gaze mirrored hers, tender, unsure.

'Hi,' she whispered, their fingers interlacing, just for a moment. She reached for the teapot as a group of people wandered over. 'So is that the end of the season?' she said clearly.

'No,' Jack said, glancing at them. 'There's the Challenge Cup to come, before everyone leaves for Scotland. You should come along.'

'Fraser mentioned it.' Grace handed him the tea. 'It would be good to see what you've been up to.'

'It's fun. Why don't you make a day of it?' Jack waited for Grace to serve the next customers. 'What are you doing now?' he said as they walked away. 'I'm supposed to be going to Cesca's with Fraser for a fondue supper to meet her niece.' He grimaced. 'You know the kind of thing, "casual" and anything but.'

'Fondue? Mmm – lucky you,' Grace said. *Niece? What's Fraser playing at?* She hid the flash of envy she felt at the thought of Jack with another woman.

'Truth is, I'd rather be with you.' He leant towards Grace and a warmth radiated through her like the summer sunlight gilding the hills. 'Don't suppose you need me to drive the horsebox back while you finish up here do you?'

'Cy's already offered, sorry. You're not getting out of it that easily.'

'C'mon, give a guy a break?' he said, laughing.

'Once we've cleaned up here, I'm taking the girls up to the Downs for a picnic to celebrate Harry's rosettes if you fancy it?'

'Stay there.' She watched him stride over to Fraser and gesture at Alice's van. Jack slipped off his jacket as he walked back to her and tossed it onto a chair. 'Right, what do you need help with first?'

Grace glanced over at Fraser and caught his expression. *You old fox,* she thought and laughed to herself. *If you're trying to make me jealous, it's working.*

Grace's red Beetle puttered through the green summer lanes with the roof down. Harry and her friend sat in the back, singing along to 'Brown Girl in the Ring' on the radio.

'It is squashed back here, what a funny little car. My daddy has a Range Rover,' the friend said.

'How nice for you.' Grace raised her eyebrows at Jack.

'How big is your house, Harry?' the girl's piping voice carried through to the front of the car. 'Is it one of those funny squished-together houses? Or is it a thousands of pounds house? Ours is *huge*. Our house is as big as that.' She pointed at a large stately home in the distance.

'God, this one won't be coming for a sleepover again,' Grace said under her breath to Jack.

'Actually,' he said, turning to the girls, and affecting a cut-glass accent, 'Harry lives at Wittering Manor, don't you, my dear.'

Grace stifled a giggle. 'You sound like Fraser.'

'This is a runabout. When Harry goes to town, she tends to use the Bentley, don't you, Harry?' Grace glanced in the rear-view mirror and saw her beaming with delight. 'That is, of course, when she's not riding her pony.'

'You have a pony?' The little friend's eyes opened wide. 'I have to share with my sister.'

'His name is Felix, and he's lovely,' Harry said.

Jack winked at Grace as the girls chattered on.

'Not like you to bail out on Fraser,' Grace said, changing gear as the car climbed the hill.

Jack ran his hand through his hair and rested his elbow against the open window. 'Fondue. Honestly.'

She glanced at him and smiled. 'Where's the best spot for kite-flying?'

'You brought a kite?'

'See, now you're glad you came.'

'Take a right here,' Jack pointed at the white crossroads sign. The lane narrowed to a single track as they climbed upwards. 'If you pull up just where there's a break in the hedge, I'll open the gate for you.'

'Is it OK? Won't the farmer mind?'

'I'm sure they wouldn't care less.'

Grace pulled to a halt. 'This is Stratton land?'

'No, but they're old friends.' Jack jumped out and heaved open the five-bar gate. Grace drove just to the edge of the field and parked the car. The girls scrambled out and went racing down the hill, arms stretched wide. The South Downs fell away beneath them, a patchwork of greens and golds.

'Oh, this is glorious,' Grace said. She spread out a picnic blanket on the soft grass and lay down, gazing up at the clouds scudding overhead in the blue sky. Her mind raced constantly these days, thinking about Margot and Fraser, about the birthstones. The silence and space embraced her and she felt still and present for the first time in a long while. With Jack she felt no need to talk, just a deep sense of peace. *Maybe that's how it's meant to feel, when it's real?* she thought. Life with Sam had always been a roller coaster. *I never knew what his mood would be,* she realised. *I was always walking on eggshells.*

Jack opened the boot of the car. 'You don't travel light with children, do you?' he said, emptying out the kite and hampers. He untangled a long tail of bows and handed the kite to Harry, and the string to her friend. They raced away, and launched the kite, fluttering and buffeting in the breeze.

'You get used to it.' Grace rolled over onto her stomach to look at him. 'Are you hungry? There are some sandwiches in there and a flask of Pimms if you feel like it. It's a bit weak, I'm afraid.'

'No, I'm fine. You go ahead though. You've been on your feet all day.' He sat down beside her and poured a glass for Grace, ice chinking. 'How's Fraser getting on with his memoirs?'

'I think we're getting to the heart of the story,' Grace said carefully.

'This secret love of his?' Jack rolled on his side towards her. He smiled, watching the looping path of a tortoiseshell butterfly in the meadow flowers. 'Do you think you'll find her?'

'I just hope Fraser finds what he needs.'

'What about you? Any more mysterious notes?'

Grace swirled the glass. 'Funny you should say that.' She glanced at him. 'The ruby turned up in my car just before Paris. I was going to mention it to Fraser, but I didn't want to spoil the trip.'

'Yeah, he's kind of worked up about the whole thing, got Cy on high alert.' He tilted his head. 'He's protective of you.'

'I don't want to upset him again. Would you keep it under your hat?' Grace raised her glass. 'Sure I can't tempt you?'

'You?' The air seemed to contract and shift between them. 'Any time.'

'Jack . . .'

'I know.' He checked Harry wasn't looking. 'Do you think we'll ever get any time alone?'

'In this place?' The girls ran closer, whooping and screaming.

'Pimms?' he said clearly. 'No, thanks. You go ahead, I'll drive back.'

'I think you're the most sensible person I know.' She took a sip of her drink and chewed the fresh mint.

'Man, that sounds boring.' He settled back on the picnic rug and plucked a stem of grass.

'I like it.' Grace brushed away a strand of hair from her cheek. 'It makes a change to have someone I can count on.'

Jack bent his arm behind his head. 'I don't drink and drive because it's how my parents were killed. Dad was pissed.'

'I'm sorry.' She turned to him. 'I didn't know.'

'No one does, but Fraser.' He looked at her. 'I've never told anyone that. Grace—'

Harry sprinted towards them and banged Jack on the shoulder. 'You're it!' she cried, and ran away laughing. 'Come on, Mum!' Grace scrambled to her feet and ran after the girls, Jack in pursuit. They ran fast down the hill, long golden grass and scarlet poppies snatching at Grace's bare shins, the wind whipping her face, her hair. Her heart thundered and she heard the girls scream as Jack sprinted after them, lunging, just out of reach. Grace felt as if she was flying, breathless, and then he was there, his arm around her waist and they were falling, falling into the soft grass, tumbling together. Grace lay on her back, Jack's hip resting against hers, his hair falling around his face as he looked down at her. 'You're it,' he said, and grinned before scrambling to his feet, leaving Grace alone beneath the soaring blue sky.

34

'It's just typical of mother,' Cilla said, 'gallivanting off without a by your leave. I love her, but she's the most selfish woman I know.'

'Come on sweetheart, you don't mean that,' Ted said.

'Well, where is she? It's all Ben's fault.'

Ted watched Harry playing with a crystal prism by the window, the light refracting into a rainbow that danced across the dining room. 'There you go, love,' he said to her. 'That's what I was talking about. You just have to be a bit patient with it, but once you get the light just right—' He broke off at the sound of an engine. 'Talk of the devil,' he said, glancing up from the dining table as Ben's bright blue Rolls Royce pulled into the driveway of the Old Mill. Grace began to tidy away the plates from the Sunday lunch. 'Leave them in the sink, love. I'll wash up later.'

'What do you think he wants?' Grace said, her gaze following Ben as he walked towards the front door. 'Do you think he's heard from Gogo?'

'I don't know what he wants but he's going to get a piece of my mind.' Cilla pushed back her chair.

'Rather him than me,' Ted said.

'You've got a nerve!' Cilla flung open the front door before Ben had a chance to ring the bell.

He stepped back in surprise. 'Cilla, my dear.'

She grabbed an umbrella from the basket by the front door and pointed it at him like a fencing sabre. 'If I were less of a lady, I'd beat you black and blue with this for what you've done to my mother.'

'Is Margot here? I must talk to her.'

'Here? No, she's not here.' Cilla took a step forward and Ben retreated. 'How could you? With that bottle blonde floozy from the Fox and Badger.'

'I'm a fool—'

'Yes, you are,' Ted said. He put his arm around Cilla and took the umbrella from her hand. 'Shall we put this away before you do something you'll regret, my love?' He slotted it neatly into the basket and reached for an envelope on the post tray. 'Margot left this for you,' he said, handing it to Ben.

'Left this? Where is she?' he said, ripping it open. His eyes darted as he read the note. 'She's gone back to France, it seems.'

Grace joined her parents on the doorstep. 'Does she say where exactly?' Harry tried to poke her head through the door, but Grace gently guided her away. 'Darling, go and put on the TV.'

'It's so boring,' Harry muttered, walking away. 'You never let me in on any grown-up stuff.'

'She doesn't say where she is,' Ben said, turning the letter over.

'She always was a drama queen,' Cilla said. 'Probably hopes you'll go running after her.'

'I must talk to her!' Ben cried.

'Good luck,' Grace said quietly. 'You're not the only one who'd like to do that.' She thought of the conversations to come and felt nauseous. 'You'll just have to wait until she's ready to come back, we all will.'

Ben put the letter back in the envelope and Grace glimpsed her grandmother's familiar, lovely calligraphic script in lilac ink. 'It makes no sense at all. She says it would never have worked with us, that she deserves to be cuckolded after all the years of being my mistress. She says there was only one man she ever loved and she couldn't marry him.' Ben broke off, his voice anguished. 'What does she mean? What *can* she mean? Is she talking about your father?' he asked Cilla.

'Your guess is as good as mine,' Cilla said.

Grace looked down at her feet. 'I don't know,' she said. *Just go*, she thought, biting the inside of her cheek. *Go, before I say something I'll regret.* She looked up at Ben. 'If Margot comes back, we'll let you know.'

'Grace, I'm sorry. I'm an old fool. I'm just no good without a wife, and Barbara—'

'Barbara the barmaid?' Grace said, shaking her head. 'You couldn't make it up.'

'She needs me. She wants a settled home life as I do, whereas Margot—'

'Stop right there. I won't hear you say a word against my grandmother.' Grace took a step forwards. 'I feel sorry for you, Ben, I really do,' she said. 'You've just lost the most remarkable woman you'll ever meet in your life.' Even as she spoke, she wondered why she was defending Margot after the way she had used her. *Because I love her.*

Ted took her arm. 'Come on, love,' he said, guiding her inside. He closed the front door and waited to hear Ben's car start up. 'Well done, girls. Margot would have been proud of you.'

'When has my mother ever been proud of me?' Cilla said, sitting at the dining table. Ted laid his hand on her shoulder as he refilled her wine glass. 'This family's falling apart. I can't keep track of things these days.' She sipped her wine. 'There are people coming and going all over the place.' She looked at Grace. 'Have there been any more supposed sightings of your husband?'

'No, there's nothing. I told the police, of course, and they spoke to Mrs Miller. She's the only one who says she's seen him.'

'Probably after a few too many Babychams,' Ted said. 'You mustn't give up hope, love.' He glanced at her. 'Grace? Are you all right, love?'

'I was just thinking that I can't imagine seeing him again. I spent months hoping Sam was all right, that he was alive somewhere, even if he didn't want to be with us, and now, I . . .' She paused. 'I feel angry. Is that crazy?'

'No, that's exactly how you should be feeling after everything he's put you through.' Cilla's fuchsia nails tapped against the glass.

'Leave it, Cilla,' Ted said. 'I won't hear you say a word against that boy. He loved Grace, and Harry, and – and the babies. If he disappeared, he had good cause, and if he's alive – if he's come back, he's come back for them.'

Grace's stomach tightened at the thought. *I'll never let you go, that's what he said.* Her hand went to her throat. *I'll never let you go.*

AUGUST

Peridot

Success · Peace · Luck

35

'Thank God,' Fraser said, beckoning Grace and Alice over. 'I need reinforcements. Cesca's niece and her parents are on the prowl. I still haven't been forgiven for the fondue disaster when Jack didn't show up.' He sat at the edge of the polo lawn at Cowdray Park, a panama hat tipped low over his eyes. Biba sat regally at his side, watching a couple of labradors walking by with their owners. Alice swung the wicker hamper to the ground and Fraser stood, pulling back a cream director's chair for her. 'Do have a seat, my dear.'

'It was kind of you to invite us,' Alice said, unpacking the picnic.

'You did say you have a thing for chaps in jodhpurs.'

'Fraser!' Alice reached over and smacked his leg as Grace sat down, laughing.

'Makes me feel quite young, seeing all these dashing chaps and fillies flirting away.' He waved his arm at the line of cars lining the field, the picnickers and polo groupies, girls in long cotton dresses, the sunlight in their hair, chatting to tall, tanned players as they trampled down divots of earth on the field between chukkas. 'Does take me back. Those were the days . . .'

'Nonsense. You're still in good shape, I can tell.'

'I believe in an excess of everything, Alice.' Fraser reached into his linen jacket for his hip flask. 'Fresh air, exercise, vitamins, whisky . . .'

'Women?' Alice said.

'Will you two behave?' Grace slipped on her sunglasses. 'Has Jack played yet?'

283

Fraser listened to Terry Hanlon announcing the next match. 'You're just in time. His team are up next.'

'So, fill me in,' Alice said, when Fraser went to talk to some friends. 'Any news from the police?'

Grace shook her head. 'I told them about Mrs Miller, but they can't do anything with that.'

'What about these notes you're getting?'

'They could be from anyone. What am I supposed to say? The stones from our old house were stolen and now someone is giving them back one by one?'

'When you put it like that . . .' Alice scratched her head. 'I just don't get it. I mean, they're not threatening, are they, the notes?'

'Far from it. The notes aren't Neruda, but they're beautiful.'

'So it's almost like someone is trying to seduce you with them. Someone romantic,' Alice said. Grace followed the path of Jack's horse as he rode on to the field. 'Who do you know that's attracted to you, but can't be with you for some reason?'

'Al,' Grace interrupted, 'do you remember the night I met Sam?'

'Of course.'

'He was wearing tennis shoes.'

'God, he never forgave that kid with the red hair for that.'

'Which kid?'

'I don't remember his name. Sam and the kid and my brothers came straight to the party from some job they were working on over near Winchester. You know how particular Sam was about how he looked. Well, this kid threw Sam's shoes and bow tie out of the van window for a laugh. He was new and I think he was trying to make a place for himself in the group.'

'He didn't know about Sam?'

'He learnt his lesson.' Alice shook her head. 'Apparently Sam made the kid look for his shoes for an hour. That's why they were all late.'

'What do you mean?'

'Sam only turned up at the party a few minutes before you.'

Grace frowned, fragments of the past falling in to place. 'And the tennis shoes?'

'The kid had the same size feet as Sam. Sam wasn't going to turn up in work boots, was he? So he took the kid's shoes and left him on the side of the road rather than dropping him home on the way to the party. Sacked him, as well, from what I can recall.'

'There we are,' Fraser said, appearing with a silver ice bucket and three glasses. He poured a glass of Veuve Clicquot for Alice and handed it to her.

'Thank you – what a treat.'

'Least I could do after you brought this delicious feast.'

'Now, will you please explain what's going on here?'

Grace settled back in her chair and stretched out her tanned legs in front of her, one sandal hanging loose from the arch of her foot. *How can you be so wrong about someone?* she thought, chewing her lip. *If Sam hadn't been wearing those shoes, if he had been as buttoned-up as he normally was, I never would have looked twice at him. All those years, I had that first impression of him stuck in my head and I didn't see what he was really like . . .*

'Right,' Fraser said. 'They are playing for the Cowdray Park Challenge Cup. There's really only two things you need to know. Firstly, polo's all about tactics, it's a high-contact team sport.'

'Like rugby, but with horses?' Alice said.

Fraser laughed. 'Something like that.'

'Who are those two?' Alice pointed to a couple of riders in distinctive shirts.

'They are the umpires. Now, the object of the game is to score the most goals.'

'Through the posts, using those mallet things?'

'Exactly. Each player supports the team effort offensively

285

and defensively – but you have to be careful not to incur a foul and penalties.'

'Like football?'

'You're getting it.' Fraser sipped his champagne.

'And what's the second thing?'

'The line of the ball, my dear, the imaginary track of the ball from A to B.'

Grace tuned out of the conversation, and concentrated on Jack's match. It was thrilling – ponies thundering along, churning up the earth, the exuberant cries of the commentator echoing from the tannoy system, the excitement of the crowd as Jack's team scored. Grace watched the deft movements of the lean, tanned men. Her gaze returned to Jack again and again. He moved with a focus and determination that drew her. For once, she could enjoy watching him.

'Why have they stopped?' Grace asked Fraser.

'They take a break between each chukka,' he said. 'Those ponies have been galloping practically non-stop for seven minutes, they need a break. The pros change horse with each chukka.'

'How many chukkas in a game?' Alice asked.

'A full game has eight.'

'God, it's complicated,' Alice said, folding her arms. 'It's like that tongue-twister: how much wood would a woodchuck chuck . . .' She snorted with laughter.

'Are you tipsy already?' Grace said, smiling.

'I'm just going to drink my champagne quietly and stare at all these lovely men.'

A couple of minutes later the players rode back onto the field. 'Ah, Jack's riding one of the new ponies,' Fraser said.

'Are they special, the horses?' Alice asked.

'Absolutely. They need a good mouth, and a good turn of speed.' He broke off as the players thundered past, mallets clicking. 'Now, Jack's playing in the No 1 position,' Grace heard Fraser say. 'His main job is to concentrate on scoring

'...' The speed, Jack's easy strength, thrilled her. Grace's eyes closed as she remembered how it felt to be held by him. At a cry from the crowd, she snapped back to the present.

'Jack Booth is on the ground!' the commentator shouted. 'An ambulance? No ... wait, he's on his feet. He's OK, ladies and gentlemen.'

'What happened?' Grace sat forward. 'Is Jack all right?'

'Foul!' Fraser yelled. He listened to the commentator. 'There we go. The umpire's awarded a free goal to Jack's team. An opponent blocked him and Jack's pony reared up.'

'But he's OK?' Grace got to her feet. Jack squatted back on his heels on the field, catching his breath.

Fraser stood beside her, waiting. Jack leapt up, swinging his arm, flexing his shoulder. 'Just winded,' Fraser said. Grace felt him exhale with relief. 'I told him that pony needed more time, but he wouldn't listen. Bloody-minded—'

'Wonder where he gets that from,' Grace said quietly. Jack caught hold of his horse and swung back up into the saddle to the cheers of the crowd. As he thundered past Fraser and Grace, he tipped his cap.

'A good effort, Jack,' Fraser said, clapping him on the back.

'We'll get the trophy next year,' he said.

'I'd go and get yourself checked out. Could be your collar-bone again?'

'Nah, it's fine. The shoulder's just bruised.' Jack gingerly put his arm across his stomach. 'And maybe a couple of ribs.'

'Never would listen, even as a child,' Fraser said to Grace. 'He had a fractured wrist once, wouldn't let me take him to the doctor. Wasn't until his hand blew up to three times its size and went bright purple that I managed to get him to A & E.'

'Right, I'd better be getting back to the restaurant,' Alice said. She shook Fraser's hand. 'Thank you for a lovely after-noon. Now you call in next time you're in Andrewsfield.'

'My dear, I shall. The picnic was divine. You're a genius.'

'Can I drop you?' Alice said to Grace, kissing her on the cheek.

'Thanks, but I'll drive Fraser home.'

'I'll see you later,' Jack said to Grace. 'At the party?'

'Do you have a costume?' Fraser said.

'You didn't say it was fancy dress!'

'It's something of a tradition on the estate, and this year Jack's taken over the task. A Thousand and One Nights, my dear.' He glanced at her, his eyes travelling from her feet to her chest. 'You're the same size as my mother. I'm quite sure we have something in the attic which will suffice.' Fraser raised his chin. 'Cinderella *shall* go to the ball.'

36

'I say, aren't you the cat's pyjamas,' Fraser said as Grace and Harry walked into the study. He wore a peacock blue silk Nehru jacket over wide white trousers and a gold turban on his head. He placed his hands together and bowed to Harry, who was dressed in a red fez and white robe, a thin black moustache pencilled above her lip. Harry giggled and bowed back. 'Lovely to see you all dolled up,' he said to Grace, his gaze travelling from her gold Moroccan slippers, up her wide scarlet harem pants to the gold bustier she was wearing. As she gave him a twirl, the silk costume dipped at the back, revealing the dimples at the base of her spine. 'Clemmie wore that costume to a party in 1929, you know. It's funny, you do remind . . .' He paused, and shook his head. 'I'm being a silly old fool.' Fraser drummed his fingers against his lips. 'There's just one thing missing,' he said, swivelling a blue leather jewellery box around on the table.

'I thought it was quite good?' Grace checked her reflection in the mirror. She had spent an hour twisting her hair into an elaborate updo.

'Try this,' Fraser said, draping a ruby and diamond necklace around her brow. Gently, he took out a couple of hairgrips and secured the necklace.

Grace touched the stone dangling above her brow and smiled. 'I feel like a princess.'

'Precisely how you should be feeling for the Thousand and One Nights.' He held out his hand to Harry. 'Come, Aladdin.'

The garden of Jack's barn was illuminated with strings of paper lanterns, and the summer air hummed with mingled voices, the scent of lamb and garlic barbecuing, the pulse of disco music. Harry spotted some children from the village and ran off happily with them.

'He has flair, my boy,' Fraser said.

'Who's that?' Grace said, watching a slim brunette flirting with Jack.

'That's what's-her-name from the pub. Always had a soft spot for Jack, but she's not his type at all. I made the mistake of popping round unannounced earlier to pay for the booze with Ellen and she was out basking naked on the roof terrace, like a lizard.' He clapped Cy on the back as he joined them. 'She has a stomach you could bounce sixpence off and the arse of a twelve-year-old boy.'

'Yeah,' Cy said. 'No tits neither.'

'Yes, well we all know your tastes, Cy,' he said, miming a full pair of breasts. 'Is Dolly here tonight?'

'Nope, she's got a gig in Winchester. Picking her up later.'

'Have you heard Cy's wife sing?' Fraser said to Grace as Cy walked away. He raised his hand in greeting to Jack and they made their way to the bar.

'Jack, dear boy, you've surpassed yourself.'

'Do you like it?' Jack smiled at Grace. 'You look beautiful.' He leant down and kissed her chastely on the cheek, his hand resting lightly on the curve of her waist, just for a moment.

*

289

The night worked its magic on Grace as she explored the grounds of Jack's house. He had created 'rooms' off the main garden, intimate, unexpected places where she could imagine whiling away an afternoon in a hammock, or dozing on a picnic blanket beneath scented curtains of jasmine and roses. She kicked off her shoes and wandered barefoot across the cool, dew-wet grass away from the party. The night sky above was a clear, deep blue with silver stars, a thumbnail crescent of a moon. She swung the gold slippers in her hand and sipped at her drink. A snatch of music drifted out to her, and she followed the familiar tune. *Pink Floyd?* she thought, recognising the melody of 'Breathe'. She heard a low whistle, and Grace pushed aside a low branch of scented Madame Alfred Carrière roses, revealing a small clearing.

'You look like some princess from a fairy tale.' Jack's voice was low. She saw the flare of a cigarette, the dim lights of the stereo.

'Are you hiding?' She paused as she smelt the sweet smoke and he offered her the joint. 'Oh.'

'Go on, live dangerously.' Jack tucked his arm behind his head. He patted the blanket with his other hand and Grace settled down on the pillows beside him.

'Where did you get this?' She inhaled deeply, the music, the closeness of him, washing over her.

'It's a bit of a secret, but Cy grows it on his allotment.' He glanced at her. 'Don't normally indulge, but my back's killing me.'

'I was worried about you.'

'I felt like a complete idiot, coming off.'

'Does it hurt?'

'My shoulder?' He laughed. 'Not any more.' He took the joint from her.

'It's very strong,' she said, holding her breath.

'Yeah, he's got a bit of a sideline going, has Cy. One of nature's gentlemen.'

'Is that his real name?'

'No. His real name's Archibald, but he's been Cy as long as I've known him.' He covered one eye with his hand. 'Cyclops. He lost an eye when he was a kid, somehow. He got his nickname in the playground and it's stuck.'

'I wondered.' It felt as if the garden was contracting around them. 'This is so beautiful.'

'You found my secret place.' He turned on one elbow, closer to her.

'Everybody needs a place of their own.' Grace gazed up at the shifting sky above them. 'My grandfather – Dad's dad – had a shed that no one was ever allowed in. He kept it padlocked and my grandmother never went in there until he died.'

'What was in there?'

'All kinds of stuff – it was like a cabinet of curiosities.'

'Maybe he needed somewhere to escape. Guys from that generation went through a lot in the wars. We're lucky we didn't have to make the choices they did.'

'If you could choose anything, what would you do?'

'Apart from the estate and the horses, you mean?' Jack exhaled a plume of smoke and handed her the joint. 'If I had my chance, I'd design gardens all the time. Maybe you feel the same way about jewellery?'

'Sure. I love it. The stones are magical. They're decorative but they're mythical, and curious, and sexy.'

'Sexy stones?' Jack laughed.

'Yes,' she said, nudging him. He moved closer. 'They can be—' She paused, wincing as she tried to inhale.

'Is it too hot?'

'A little.'

'Let me.' He held it to her lips and she felt the warm skin of his finger, his thumb. He held it there as she exhaled, watching her.

'Jack,' she said, her head swimming with desire. He flicked away the glowing coal of the joint and kissed her then, the dark line of his shoulders, his head eclipsing the moon, the stars. Grace's back arched up to him, her fingers tangled in his hair. He pulled her to him, his hand against her hips, strong and sure. 'Jack, oh God, we can't, we can't . . .' She caught her breath as he kissed her neck, her collarbone. 'Jack,' she said, taking his head in her hands, waiting for him to look at her.

'I've wanted to do that from the moment I saw you.' He held her close, their foreheads touching. She placed her right palm against his chest, felt the steady beat of his heart.

'It's a mistake,' she said, nestling her face beneath his jaw, afraid that if he kissed her again, everything would be lost. 'We can't.'

'Don't say that, please don't say that. Look at me.' He cupped her jaw in his palm, lifted her face. 'I have never felt the way I feel about you with any other woman.'

'Jack, please don't.'

'Tell me you don't want me.'

The night seemed to shift and close around them, his face so close to hers, she felt herself falling, falling. 'I do,' she said, and he kissed her, his breath hers. 'I do,' she said, as his lips fell to her neck. Grace tensed, hearing someone call her name. 'Jack, Harry's looking for me. I can't, not like this.'

'I'm sorry.' His head rested against hers as he caught his breath. 'Hell, what am I saying? I'm not sorry, but I said I wouldn't rush you. It won't happen again, if that's what you want. Blame the moonlight, blame summer madness – blame it on falling in love.'

'I wish . . .' She closed her eyes. 'I wish it could be different.'

'Mum!' Harry's voice was urgent, closer now.

'I'll go,' Jack whispered. He ran his hand against the nape of her neck, kissed her one last time. 'God, you're driving me crazy.' Jack leapt up on silent feet and broke away through the trees. Grace lay back on the blanket and listened.

'Hello, Jack,' she heard Harry say. 'Have you seen Mum?'

Grace heard them pass by the clearing, she held her breath, pressed her fingers against her lips, bruised and swollen from his kisses. She sat up and let down her hair, shaking it loose. She wished she could curl up and sleep here, sleep for a hundred years, to wake to a world that was clear and straightforward. 'Go away,' she whispered. 'Go away all of you.'

'I vant to be alone?' Fraser squatted down and peered into the clearing. 'Thought I might find you here. Are you all right, my dear? I just saw Harry looking for you.' He held back the branch. 'Come on, let's straighten you up a bit.' He dusted the grass from Grace's costume and secured the ruby necklace on her hair. 'There.' He looked at her and smiled. 'God, you two make me feel young again.'

'He told me he's falling in love,' Grace said.

'Falling? Fallen, more like. About ruddy time,' Fraser said, triumphant.

'You knew?'

'I guessed. What were all those years with British Intelligence for if not to notice everything? Why do you think I hired you? It certainly wasn't for your shorthand skills.' Fraser looped his arm in hers. 'I knew the moment I saw you that you'd be perfect for Jack – and the house.'

'You've been playing matchmaker all this time?'

'I admit you've come in surprisingly useful with the memoirs, but yes, I hoped you'd bring him back to life.' His voice dropped as they rejoined the party and Harry ran over.

'Mum, where have you been? I was worried.'

'I wasn't far away.' Grace looked across the crowd of people to where Jack stood watching them. 'Are you tired, darling? Let's take you home.'

'See you in the morning for our ride, Fraser?' Harry said.

'No, my dear, I'm off to Tuscany first thing. You're in charge of Felix.'

'All by myself?'

'My dear, you are perfectly capable of taking care of that naughty pony. If you do a good job, I may have a surprise for you when I come back. A little dicky bird told me it's someone's birthday in September?' Fraser turned to Grace. 'Talking of which, I shall be away for your birthday. Jack came up with a splendid idea for your gift, didn't you?' he said, as Jack wandered over.

'I've left Harry and Ellen in charge of that one,' Jack said, putting his arm around Harry's shoulders.

'I know you told me not to keep secrets, Mum, but this is a good one.'

Grace held Jack's gaze. 'Thank you.'

'Poor Grace, you'll be all alone,' Fraser said. 'Will you miss us?'

'I shall be fine.' Grace felt Jack watching her. She couldn't trust herself to look at him. 'There's plenty of work to get along with.'

'Thank you, Jack,' Fraser said. 'I'm going to escort these young ladies home. It's been a glorious evening. Quite enchanting, wouldn't you say? Now, what time are you leaving for Heathrow?'

'First thing, same as you.'

'It'll do you good to have the divorce finalised,' Fraser said, looking from Jack to Grace. 'And time away will give you a chance to think, make plans for the future.'

37

'Where are you taking me?' Grace laughed, feeling ahead with her outstretched hands. The strap of her white sundress slipped down her tanned shoulder as she reached out, the full skirt swinging around her bare legs.

'Not far now, love,' Ellen said. Biba and Jagger trotted along at their side, with Jack's puppy Floyd. Grace could hear them, their claws on the yard, the puppy's snuffling. Harry had to stretch to keep her hands over Grace's eyes.

Ellen had been waiting for them in the kitchen when Grace arrived for work on Monday morning. The house seemed strangely silent without the music drifting from Fraser's study. Jack's Land Rover was parked in the yard, and for a moment her heart leapt at the thought of seeing him, until she remembered that he, too, was travelling. Grace ran her hand over the warm metal of the bonnet as she passed, remembering the night of the party.

'Grace!' Ellen's excited shout shattered her daydream. 'Happy Birthday! Come in, love, and I'll make us some coffee. Jack and Fraser left a note for you.' She was buzzing with excitement.

Grace sat down at the scrubbed kitchen table and tossed her sunglasses aside. She was dreading a quiet month ahead with nothing to stop her endless, circular thoughts. Ellen passed her a heavy envelope and Grace recognised Fraser's flamboyant script. She flipped it over and slid her thumb along the edge. The paper was thick, the flap edged in royal blue. 'Thanks,' she said, as Ellen placed a steaming blue-and-white striped mug of coffee in front of her.

'My dear Grace,' he began. 'I should hate to think of you bored out of your wits until my return ...' Typical, she thought, smiling. 'So Jack suggested we prepare a little surprise to keep you out of mischief. Ordinarily, I would save your bonus until Christmas, but we thought you deserved a little 30th birthday present. Ellen has the key. Yours, F.'

They stopped outside the door to the old workshop in the yard and Grace heard Ellen turning the key in the lock, smelt the aroma of oil and sawdust that had marinated the timbers over decades. She heard the pop and fizz of a strip light flickering on, and then Harry said, 'Open your eyes.'

'I don't believe it!' Grace's eyes adjusted to the light. 'How did they do this?' She stepped towards the workbench and touched the anvil like a long-lost friend.

'Are you pleased?' Ellen's voice was trembling with excitement. 'Fraser has contacts everywhere. He got hold of a copy of the inventory from the sale of your shop and workshop and bought back what he could.'

'You should have seen them, Mum,' Harry said. 'Fraser and Jack were so pleased with themselves, sneaking all this in without you knowing.'

Grace shook her head, dumbstruck. 'I don't deserve this.'

'Of course you do, love!' Ellen put her arm around her. 'Fraser wants you to be happy here, he wants you to stay, and he thought if you had a little workshop here you could do a few commissions in the evenings and at the weekends.'

'This is too much.' The weight of what she knew bore down on her, guilt twisting in her stomach.

'Nonsense. Fraser said to me that when he gets back he expects to see a new Grace Manners collection. He said you have a few stones, and he's donated these.' Ellen pulled open a shallow wooden drawer and Grace saw odd gold cufflinks, tarnished silver necklaces, single earrings. 'You know what a dandy and a magpie he is; he's collected for years and he's had a proper clear-out for you.'

'This is the kindest thing anyone has ever done for me.'

'Come here, love,' Ellen said, enfolding Grace in her soft arms. 'Don't start blubbing or you'll set me off. You take this gift in the manner it was given and make the most of it. Make him and Jack proud. Do what you can with this lot and sell them on. You'll build yourself back up in no time, I just know you will.' She stepped back. 'Now then, Harry and me have made a little cake for you as a surprise, so when you're done here we'll have tea in the kitchen later.'

*

Grace sat quietly in the workshop for a few minutes, taking it all in. *I can't believe they did this, for me.* She hugged herself. *I can't control the future, whatever is going to happen when Gogo returns, but I can do this. I can start small, work hard, one piece at a time.* She worked through the day without stopping for lunch, cleaning and sorting the workshop how she wanted it, placing the grinding wheel, her saw for rough-cutting gem material and the faceting machine along one wall. On the bench at the far end she set up the crucible for melting metals and her ceramic soldering block, and then the lap for polishing gems with diamond dust. Grace borrowed a drill from Cy and hung boards on the wall to store her hand tools – the pliers and bezel pushers, hammers, burnishers, files. As Grace stood back to inspect the workshop, it was as if she felt her heart expanding. She had come home. Harry poked her head through the door at teatime.

'What do you think?' Grace's voice was bright with excitement.

'Yeah, it's great,' Harry said impatiently. 'Come on, Mum, we're waiting!' she said, and ran back to the house.

As she walked to the kitchen, she felt a new lightness in her step. The sky was the colour of faded denim and the earth seemed to hum with life, swallows chirruping on the telephone wires above her. It was there; she felt it, a glimmer of happiness, a hint of how she used to feel.

'Here she is,' Harry called to Ellen and they began to sing 'Happy Birthday' as Grace stepped through the door.

'Thank you.' Grace leant down to kiss Harry.

'Do you like it? Do you?' Harry handed Grace a knife. 'Make a wish,' she said as she cut into the cake.

'I *love* it. Smarties, my favourite.'

'We kept your cards back.' Ellen handed her a pile from the dresser.

'I wondered why I hadn't got any.' Grace smiled as she

ripped open the first, from Harry, a shower of glitter falling onto the kitchen table.

'That next one's from me and Mr Lloyd. Go and treat yourself to something nice from Boots.'

'Thank you.' Grace smiled up at Ellen. The next card was from Ted and Cilla, she recognised the handwriting. But beneath it she saw a familiar sliver of manila paper. Her heart lurched. 'Who delivered this?'

'I don't know, love. It was in with the rest of them on the mat this morning.'

Grace tore it open, and tipped the peridot out onto her hand. The typed note read: *My August maiden in her white dress, wears peridot, gem of success.* 'He's here,' she said, dropping the note as though it burnt her fingers. She lifted the skirt of her dress. 'Whoever it is has been here, today, watching us!'

Every day, after finishing her work in the house, Grace spent a couple of hours in the workshop before collecting Harry. It was her space, a room of her own. She felt safe there. The latest note had set her on edge. At night she lay awake, her thoughts running round and around. During the day she found she was watching every car following her on the winding lanes. Every distant figure in town or on the beach became suspicious to her. Closed safe in the workshop, though, she knew no one could see her, or watch her. She set to work stripping the old pieces of jewellery, separating the metals from the stones. She knew immediately what her first pieces would be – a thank you to Fraser and Jack.

After working up the sketches, she melted some scrap gold in the crucible and poured it into the mould she had made. Once it had set, almost instantly, she tapped it clear and set to work filing and hammering it until she was happy, before polishing it to a high, clear shine. She remembered her old jewellery tutor telling her that some polishers apprentice for ten years in the big jewellery houses. *That would drive me nuts,* she thought. *Being a jack of all trades suits me – designer, cutter, polisher, setter. I like doing it all myself.* That was what she had told herself all the years, in work and in life. Now she wondered for the first time whether that was true any more.

For Fraser she fashioned a tie stud to match his signet ring. As the gold setting polished in the magnetic tumbler, she looked at the aquamarine she had salvaged from an old pendant. It would need to be adjusted. Sometimes Grace lost as much as fifty per cent of a stone in the cutting, but it was always worth it to bring the best out of a piece. *Quality not quantity, that's the way,* she thought. Grace attached the gem to a dop stick, and set to work filing and polishing it down with diamond dust until it was perfect. Once she was happy with it, she set the stone, and tucked the tiepin into a small brown suede box.

For Jack, she was unsure. *His birthstone is either a diamond or an aquamarine,* she thought, *but I want him to have something different. He's more of a jeans and T-shirt type.* She sorted through the scrap jewellery and laid out the stones in front of her. *Three wishes,* she thought. *What would I want for him? Prosperity, happiness, success – turquoise.* She knew then what she wanted to make for him, a tiepin that he could wear out at horse shows, an arrow piercing the stone, not his birthstone, but one that seemed right for him. *The colour of the deepest flecks in his eyes.*

Grace created a new mould in the shape of an arrow and cast the gold. She fired up the gas torch and soldered on a pin fitting. *A stone of character,* she thought, setting the turquoise at the heart of the arrow. When they were finished, she took them in to show Ellen. She sat in the kitchen with a mountain of peas before her, podding them into Tupperware boxes to freeze for the winter while she watched *It's a Knockout*. Through the open windows, the sound of Cy's lawnmower drifted in.

'Look at the state of them,' Ellen said to Grace. 'I reckon we should get a team up, don't you? I could just picture Cy in one of those big foam costumes.'

'There's a thought.' Grace placed the tiepins on the table in front of Ellen. 'What do you think? I wanted to say thanks to Fraser, and to Jack too. They've both been so kind.'

'They're beautiful,' Ellen said. 'I can't believe you made these.'

'Do you think they'll like them?'

'Fraser will wear his every day, I'm sure, and I do like Jack's. He's not really one for flashy things. I'm surprised he hasn't called to wish you a happy birthday.'

'Argentina is a long way.'

'What does the arrow symbolise? Cupid?'

'I just thought it was a good design for the stone,' Grace said, busying herself with the boxes. Her cheeks were burning and, as the phone rang, she jumped up from the table. 'Wittering Manor,' she said.

'Grace, my dear!' Fraser's voice boomed down the line. 'Happy Birthday. How are you enjoying your surprise?'

'I don't know what to say. Thank you. As I said to Ellen, it's the kindest thing anyone has ever done for me.'

'See, some people think I'm kind,' he said to someone at the other end.

'Do you have a guest? I thought you said you were alone?'

'Cesca doesn't count— Ouch!' Fraser's voice muffled with laughter. 'Damn woman kicked me in the shins.' Grace heard her voice, faintly. 'She just dropped in for the weekend en route to Naples. She's off to Capri.'

Grace's mind filled with visions of pine and cypress trees, a clear blue sea, scorched earth. 'I'm glad, I've been worried about you all alone there.'

'Oh, I'm having the most marvellous time. I always feel twenty years younger here. Now listen. I have been poking

300

around in the attic and I've found Albert's notebooks and sketchbooks. You know he's buried out here? Clem must have sent a lot of his personal effects out here too. She was sentimental like that, probably liked to think of them being near him. I've found all sorts – books, paintings, and I've finally found out the truth about what happened to him at Mons. No wonder the poor bugger was in such a state.'

'Mons?'

'World War One, Grace, keep up. Have you heard the legends about the "angels" that appeared to the beleaguered soldiers?'

'I'm afraid I haven't.'

'Well, grab a pen and paper. Not only does he write about Mons, but he describes exactly the scene we played out when he took me and left my twin sister Margot behind.'

Ice water ran through Grace's veins. 'Right,' she said, settling down at the kitchen table. 'Why don't we talk about that later? Shall we concentrate on Albert? I've got a pen. Where would you like to start?'

'You can read the diary yourself when I get back, but I'd like you to do a bit of research into Mons for me, fill in the details.' She heard Fraser flicking through the pages. 'The old dog. The day Archduke Ferdinand was assassinated, Albert was in Paris with Josephine.' Fraser laughed. 'It's incredibly touching, really, a confession more than a diary. He had no illusions about himself. He wanted to become the sort of artist, officer, gentleman and sportsman he admired – in other words, everything my grandfather, Sir Cosmo Stratton, Bt, was not. That's why he joined the 9th Lancers.'

'When did he meet Clementine?'

'He was nearly thirty, a confirmed bachelor as they say.' Grace heard Fraser laugh. 'This is interesting – in spite of the money, she wasn't quite the catch she seemed.' Fraser paused. 'According to this diary, she was, to use a harsh term, "damaged goods", and barren, they believed, to boot.'

'But Albert married her anyway?'

'He admired her passion. He agreed to marry her and give her her freedom, thinking that all would continue as before – his occasional relationship with Josephine in Paris suited him fine because he was wedded to the cavalry, you see. They all were.' Fraser laughed softly. 'I remember him talking about it when I was small: "Bury me with my horse if I fall." Too many of them were, of course. Nine million died in the Great War, and nine hundred thousand horses of one million didn't make it back.'

She gasped. 'The numbers are staggering, aren't they? Imagine being caught up in all that.'

Fraser cleared his throat. 'It seems Albert gave Clem a sweetheart brooch of the 9th Lancers insignia and asked his Colonel for permission to marry. After a simple service in the local church, Clem established herself at Wittering Manor, while Albert returned to his barracks at Tidworth.' Grace heard pages turning. 'As we know, they had a falling-out after Clem lost her baby, and he took some leave, went off to Paris to Josephine. But he didn't learn she was pregnant until he had returned to Tidworth. By then they were in the midst of preparing to join the British Expeditionary Forces, ready to move out the moment Britain declared war on Germany on the 4th of August.' Fraser exhaled. 'They're incredibly moving, the passages he's written about the French and Belgians cheering them on. No one had yet anticipated the horrors to come of trench warfare, and cavalry reigned supreme. They were the pick of the troops of Europe and ready to fight to the death.' The phone muffled as Fraser switched the receiver to his other ear. 'Ah, here it is. Are you writing this down?'

'Yes, go on.'

'I'm going to transcribe the diary when I get back.' Fraser cleared his throat. 'Listen to this: *August, 1914. Days that changed my life forever. Nothing was the same after Mons.* There are pages and pages about the battle,' Fraser said, 'but this is the bit I want you to find out about:

'By May 1915, people were saying that the angels that appeared at Mons were proof of divine intervention, that the soldier on the front line who cried out to St George for help summoned up holy warriors against our enemy. "Adsit Anglis Sanctus Georgius – May St George be a present help to the English". This story filtered through to sermons and newspapers – God knows, we needed a morale boost. Some said it was propaganda and it was easy enough for the editors to say they couldn't reveal their sources "for security reasons".

'But here's the thing. When you have fought, when you have seen the men, the friends around you die, when you are so exhausted you don't know whether you yourself are alive or dead, is it any wonder that men might hallucinate? Experience mass hallucinations even? But why is it that men from all the ranks should report such similar sightings? If I told you I saw the Angel of the Lord on a white horse with a flaming sword, would you think me mad?

'In the hospital, later, I met a man who had been down in the trenches with the enemy only 300 yards away. He spoke of a line of shapes beyond the trench, of Agincourt bowmen and a cloud of arrows that blocked the sun from the sky. He said he saw the corpses of enemy troops with arrow wounds. What are we to make of that? It was a furnace of torment – we were 80,000 souls against 300,000 in Belgium. Perhaps we were all driven quite mad. Another of the Old Contemptibles I knew from before the war told me of three angelic figures hovering over the enemy lines. He was a man who had regularly drunk me under the table, but after Mons he never touched another drop.

'As for my part in the retreat from Mons, we were unbowed, undefeated. The 9th Lancers made a final push at the end – we rode over fields of grass torn by shells, fogged with smoke, towards their guns. We held fast and broke their line. Batteries of rifles caught us on the return, and many fell. I was wounded, and Grenfell, though wounded in both legs, saved us, and between us all we saved the guns. We caught our breath beneath a railway embankment and he got the remnants of our squadron away. Grenfell was a fine man, and a fine polo player too. Little wonder he received the VC. He was a gentleman, a sportsman, a hero. Everything I wish I could have been.'

Fraser broke off. 'Poor Albert.' He flicked on through the diary. 'How incredibly brave he was, and how modest. He makes no mention of how severe his own injuries were. His leg was shattered – I don't know whether it was a fall, or whether he was shot during one of the charges.' He took a deep breath. 'I realise I have done my father a huge disservice. There are pages of stuff. He's talking about seeing thirty-foot pillars of fire, how huge figures began to appear over the German lines, winged like angels.'

'Maybe it was a mirage?' Grace said.

'Whatever it was caused the enemy to stop and allowed the British to retreat in safety. It's fascinating. There are too many accounts to discount it as mere fancy. Certainly Machen's story "The Bowman" was just that – a story, but it helped to establish the legend of the Angels of Mons.' Fraser took a sip of his drink. 'Can you look into it, Grace? Go to the library. If I remember rightly, there are accounts by Begbie and a nurse called Campbell who recorded her conversations with wounded soldiers who had seen the angels.' Fraser flicked on through the pages. 'There's more about this chap Grenfell here,' he said, and read on: *'The Duke of Westminster took him in his Rolls Royce to the nearby town of Bavai where he was treated by French nuns in a convent hospital. This is where I too recovered, and where we heard he had been awarded the Victoria Cross.'* Fraser paused. *'When he died later, at Ypres, his last words were, "I die happy. Tell the men I love my squadron."*

'When I saw selfless, noble men like Grenfell in action, I realised what a waste my life had been so far. I was the rebellious youngest son of a baronet, a spoilt man with a pregnant mistress in Paris and a devoted wife at home that he didn't deserve.

'Everything I had learnt as a man, as a soldier, had not prepared me for Mons. Among the countless losses of this war to end all wars,

the millions of war dead, this was my small loss. I grew used to the sight of dead men, but I never could become accustomed to the sight, the sound, of wounded horses. These noble creatures I had loved all my life – their suffering seemed the very symbol of man's inhumanity. When the order came, it fell to us to deliver the coup de grâce to hundreds of horses.

'The 9th Lancers fought as cavalry only until the end of the year – machine guns, barbed wire and trenches did for them as they did for me. The thought of men charging one another on horses armed with lances seems to belong to a fairy tale now. Does it really matter, the truth or lies about Mons? Or the White Cavalry at La Bassée? I know what I believe. If it helped men through Loos, the Somme, Passchendaele, what is the harm? I believe what I saw that day, in Belgium. It decided me to return and do the right thing. I have never spoken of any of this. I have tried to return, in silence, to a better life than I led before. I carry what I saw in my unquiet heart. I will be a good husband to Clem, and a better father to the boy. What does it matter that when I sleep I hear the screams of horses still?'

38

In the last week of August, the estate seemed to re-radiate the sun, the earth hard and warm, the clear blue skies heat-hazed and shimmering. The hedgerows were a riot of nodding ox-eye daisies and poppies, frothing with cow parsley, the long grass alive with the sound of crickets. Down on the beach, Grace and Harry grew golden from long evenings combing the beach for shells and playing in the surf with the dogs. Jack's puppy, Floyd, was happy to pad along the shoreline beside them, taking explorative sniffs of the surf, racing away as it reached his paws.

Grace made herself relax into long days of simple pleasures. She revelled in the light evenings, swimming in the sea or the pool with Harry. Floating, weightless, beneath a summer moon, the stars reflected on the water around them, she felt herself coming back to life, to her self. She had taken a Polaroid of Harry sitting on the side of the pool in a flowered bikini, eating a heart-shaped choc ice, her legs dangling in the water. The photo seemed to her to capture the whole summer and she framed it.

She had spent days typing up her notes from the library, and the story of the Angels of Mons haunted her. Looking out through the open French doors of the study, across the grounds to a hillside of newly planted trees, she thought of everything that drove men like Albert – sacrifice, honour, family. *Men like Jack and Fraser*, she thought. They believe in the future, in something bigger than them. They would never see the trees they had planted full grown, but their grandchildren and great-grandchildren would. *This place needs a family*, Fraser had said. *That's what I've always said to Jack.*

Is that what Jack wants? she wondered, as she swam one evening, arms outstretched beneath the cranberry sky. A flock of birds flew above her, changed direction, pulsing like a heart. She remembered Fraser had laughed once – *If it hadn't been for the estate I would have gone off to Haight-Ashbury in the 60s. But my father left me all of this, and it's not just about me. I have people, families, depending on me, and I have to make it work for all of them.*

This quiet time had restored her and the workshop was festooned with new sketches for designs, fresh flowers blooming in the window boxes. She had scrubbed the space from top to bottom, had breathed new life into it and made it her own. The old doorjamb from the Rectory stood in one corner, a link with the past, a promise for the future.

One Friday evening after everyone had gone home, Grace was working late as Harry was sleeping over at a friend's, making the most of the time left before Fraser and Jack returned and the estate regained its normal rhythm. She was listening to Judie Tzuke, lost in her thoughts of Jack and the future. 'Stay With Me Till Dawn' reminded her of Paris and her stomach fluttered with anticipation as she made sketches and notes about the Stratton asteria sapphire. She daydreamed about another time, another hotel where she and Jack could be alone, together. In the distance, Grace could hear birdsong, the sound of a tractor some fields away. Then, closer, she noticed the sound of a V8 engine pulling into the stable yard, doors slamming.

They're back! Grace thought, laying down her pencil. She wiped down her hands on her apron and went out to the yard, shielding her eyes against the low sun. Two men stood there and she felt suddenly nervous, aware that she was alone, the dogs shut up in the kitchen.

'Can I help you?' She stretched up to her full height.

'Who are you?' The larger of the two men stepped forwards.

'I could ask you the same.' She squared up to him.

'Bloody cheek. You must be the new girl Uncle Fraser has helping him with the great memoirs.' He began to walk towards the house. 'Is he in?'

'He won't be back for some time. You've had a wasted journey.'

'What's your name?' The other man slunk towards her, smoothing his moustache between thumb and forefinger.

'I'm Grace Manners, Fraser's assistant.'

'I thought you might be going parachuting.' He gestured at Grace's jumpsuit and snorted with laughter.

'Not today.'

'Is that what they are calling style these days?' The first man turned to her, and in the light she could see a passing resemblance to Fraser, but this man had a shot-away chin, a thinness to his lips. 'Give me a good old miniskirt any day.'

'If you don't mind, I have work to do. May I tell Fraser who called?'

'Tell him Roger and Tristan dropped by to say hello.'

307

'What's a pretty young thing like you doing working in a dump like this?' The one with the moustache was close enough for Grace to detect the unmistakable smell of Brut.

'I told you,' she said, using the patient voice she used with Harry sometimes. 'I'm working with Fraser.'

'Manners. Doesn't that ring a bell with you, Tristan?'

'Wasn't there a jewellers in Winchester called Grace Manners?' Tristan cocked his head. 'My wife seemed to live in there. Cost me a bloody fortune. Thank God it closed down.'

Grace folded her arms. 'We went bust, lost everything, usual story.'

'That's it!' Roger's gaze swivelled to Grace and she thought of a cat toying with a mouse. 'Your name came up at work. You really did lose everything, didn't you?'

'What do you mean?' Her skin prickled and she felt hot. Roger obviously knew exactly who she was and she could tell from the tone of his voice he was enjoying having the upper hand.

'Has Fraser not told you how the family makes its money these days? They play around with the estate, of course, but if it weren't for his stake in the family finance business it would all go tits up.' His eyes narrowed. 'We invest and trade, of course, but one of the things we do is buy property and stock the receivers have seized from bankrupts, strip down companies, sell the assets on. It's lucrative.'

'I bet it is.' Grace put her hands on her hips.

'We made a pretty penny on the Old Rectory in Exford,' Tristan said. 'Shame to see a family house—'

'*My* family house,' she cut in. Grace felt sick. 'How ironic. Once, the Strattons made a fortune building things, and now they rip things to shreds.' She held her ground, but she felt as though her legs were going to give way. 'As I said, I'm busy. If you'd like to call ahead next time, I'll make an appointment for you to see Fraser.'

'No hurry. The old goose seems to think he's going to pop

his clogs any day now and we'd just like to get things sorted out as soon as possible.'

Sort things out? Get your cut, more likely, Grace thought.

'Pop's lawyer had no luck, so we thought we'd have a little chat.'

Roger glanced over her shoulder into the workshop. 'See you've got your feet well under the table here. Must say I hadn't taken Fraser for the sentimental sort, but the minute he saw your name on the purchases list he was on the blower to London to find out what we'd bought.' His eyes were cold as he looked at Grace. 'He got every bit of machinery and stock we hadn't yet auctioned off. If I had that turn of mind, I might think there was something going on here.'

'How dare you.' Grace had controlled her temper, but now it flared, the colour rising in her cheeks. 'I work for Fraser and I have grown fond of him, of all of them—'

'Wouldn't be the first time a young gold-digger wormed her way into a will at the last minute,' Tristan said. 'Just how fond of you *is* Fraser?'

'For your information, I'm married. Maybe we were just a name on a list to you. Did your precious estate-stripping inventory not tell you that, when you took my business, my home, my dad's investment, destroyed my husband's company? Did it tell you what the banks did to us? How they hounded us day after day? How they destroyed *him*?' Roger and Tristan stepped away in unison. 'Bugger off. You've had your fun taunting the staff. Just clear off, before I really lose my temper.'

'Tell Fraser we called.' Tristan retreated to the car.

'Crikey.' Roger jumped into the passenger seat beside his brother. 'She's a firecracker.' He stared at Grace from the safety of the car, wiped the sweat from his top lip. 'Bet she's a tiger in the sack.'

'I'd be too scared to find out.' Tristan pulled out of the yard, dust flaring beneath the tyres. 'I'm sure I've seen her somewhere before.' He put his foot down and they sped away from the house, and all the while he could see Grace standing, hand on hips, in the driveway, watching them go. 'It will come to me.'

SEPTEMBER

Sapphire

Serenity · Truth · Honesty

39

Grace heard the taxis arriving in the night. First Fraser's, the sound of tyres on the driveway, slamming doors in the courtyard, the swing of lights across the bedroom wall. Then, later, she heard a second car driving past towards Jack's house. *They're back*, she thought. It had been easier while Jack was away, not worrying about bumping into him, trying to hide how she was feeling. Now the thought of him, so close, tormented her. *The thought of him, in bed.* She rolled over and thumped the pillow, turned it over to a cooler patch. Grace stared at the envelope on her bedside table. In the morning she would give it to Fraser. *And then what?* She dreaded telling Harry that they had to leave. *And Jack.* Grace threw back the covers and picked up her pillow, hugging it to her chest. *There have been too many lies. I have to tell Fraser the truth about Margot soon, and I can't stay, knowing the Strattons helped destroy Sam.* She padded downstairs, careful not to make a noise as she opened the front door.

The trees were alive with birdsong. She walked barefoot through the dew-wet grass to the side of the cottage where she had strung a hammock between two apple trees. Grace settled back in the hammock, her arms behind her head, and stared up at the swaying canopy of trees and dawn-lit clouds above, letting the cool breeze lull her into a light sleep.

When she awoke some time later she had the sensation someone was watching her. Her head jerked up and she gasped.

'How long have you been standing there?' she said.

'Not long.' Jack was leaning against an apple tree, his arms folded. His skin was deeply tanned and his eyes seemed a brighter blue than ever. His hair was softer, longer. 'I couldn't sleep.'

'Me neither.'

'You looked so peaceful; I didn't want to wake you. I was just on my way to the stables when I spotted your feet.' He ran his index finger along her toes.

'How was your trip?'

'I missed you.'

Grace smiled and rubbed her eyes. 'Me too.'

Jack glanced up as the wind ruffled the leaves above him. 'These are almost ready for picking.'

'How can you tell?'

'You just cup it in your hand,' he said, reaching up to the nearest fruit, his gaze not leaving her. 'If it comes easily, it's ready for plucking.'

'Plucking?' Grace laughed as Jack took a bite. 'Good?'

'Very.' He tossed her the apple and came and sat at her side on the lawn, laying his head against her stomach. 'God, it's good to be back.' Grace stroked his hair, the hammock swaying in the breeze. She felt the tension in him fall away at her touch. 'I was just imagining what it would be like to wake up beside you every morning.'

'And?'

'Right now, I would give anything to take you to bed.'

'That would be dangerous,' she said, smiling. 'I might not be able to control myself. What with how irresistible you are, and all.'

'I promise you, when we're married—'

'So we're getting married now, are we?' Grace curled round so that they were eye to eye. 'We're already married, just not to one another.'

'Speak for yourself.' Jack kissed the ridge of her ribcage, raised himself up onto his knees to kiss her breastbone, her throat. 'I'm a free man at last.'

'Congratulations.' Grace closed her eyes, her head tipping back. She felt weightless, as if she were flying with the rocking of the hammock and his touch sparking a warmth deep in her stomach.

'There's no hurry,' he said, his lips against her ear, his hips pressed hard against her. 'But when we are together, I promise you, I will make love to you like—'

Grace's eyes opened wide at the sound of a door opening in the cottage. 'Oh God, Harry!' She struggled up with Jack's help and swung her legs to the ground. 'You have to go.' She kissed him quickly. 'I'll see you later?'

'Harry's party?' He looked uncertain. 'What did you think of the workshop?'

Grace touched his face. 'Thank you. No one has ever done anything like that for me before.' Her head rested against his. 'But I know. I know about the Strattons . . .'

'Grace—'

'I can't stay here.'

'What? Why?' Jack sat back on his heels. 'I had no idea that they'd cashed in on your husband's bankruptcy till Fraser told me. It's what they do – buy up distressed stock and property and sell it on.'

'It's not just that. It's all become too complicated.'

'That's ridiculous, you can't leave, not now.' They heard Harry calling upstairs in the cottage.

'I'm coming!' Grace shouted to her. 'We can talk later,' she said.

'Where were you?' Harry said, hopping from one foot to the other in excitement at the top of the stairs.

'It's a surprise. Happy birthday, darling.' Grace ran up two steps at a time and swooped her into her arms. They cuddled up together on Grace's bed, and Jagger loped in, sidling onto their feet. 'See,' Grace said, kissing Harry's head, 'even Jagger wants to wish you a happy birthday. Do you feel like an eleven-year-old?'

'Yes, I do,' Harry said. She tucked up against her mother and Grace breathed in the wonderful toasty smell of her. 'What's that?' she said, pointing at the envelope. 'Is it a birthday card?'

'No, it's a letter for Fraser.' Grace sat up and rubbed her eyes. 'Why don't you go downstairs while I brush my teeth?' Within moments she heard Harry squeal with excitement. Grace tied her hair back and rinsed her mouth, splashing her face with cold water.

'Do you like it?' she said to Harry, walking downstairs.

'Mum, it's wonderful!' Harry sat at the head of the table in the chair Grace had decorated the night before. Ribbons and tissue-paper flowers wound around the spokes, and balloons with a hand-drawn banner saying 'Happy Birthday Harry' floated above. 'I can't believe you remembered the birthday throne!'

'You missed out last year, so I wanted it to be extra special.'

Harry went to turn on the television. 'Please can I put *Tiswas* on?'

'Sure, as a special treat.'

Harry pressed the button for ITV, but the screen was blank. 'Crap, I keep forgetting the network's down.'

'Harry, please don't swear. You're picking up bad habits at school.'

'Sorry, Mum. These strikes are *so* boring.'

'See if *Swap Shop*'s on instead?' Grace suggested. 'Aren't you going to open them?' She nodded at the pile of presents and cards on the table. Grace flicked on the kettle and reached for the coffee pot. 'Cards or presents?' she said, knowing the answer.

'Presents!' Harry tore open the largest parcel and yelled with delight. 'Proper jodhpurs and boots! Thanks, Mum.' She leapt up and hugged her mother quickly, eager to get back to the gifts. 'Where have you hidden these? I looked everywhere.' Harry picked up the next parcel. 'It's from France.'

'Must be Gogo.' Grace cut some slices from the fresh granary loaf and put them in the toaster. 'Would you like bacon sandwiches as a treat?'

'Yes, please.' Harry read the card. 'She says that now I am such a grown-up horse rider I need a proper scarf and she hopes I like it. And look.' She flashed a handwritten ticket in fine sepia script. 'Gogo's given me an IOU for the cinema and cake.'

'Is that it? No mention of when she's coming back, or where she is?'

Harry ripped open the orange tissue-paper parcel to reveal a silk scarf. 'It's lovely, look at the horse pattern.'

'Good grief, typical Gogo,' Grace said, looking closer. 'It's her vintage Hermès. You *are* lucky.'

'I shall wear it next time I go riding with Jack.' Harry tied the scarf over her pyjamas and moved on to the next card. 'This one's from Grandma and Grandpa. They said they'd give me my present at the party later.'

'Are you looking forward to it?' Grace put four rashers of bacon into the hot pan and the air filled with the rich scent.

'Yeah, but I can't believe I have to wear a dress.'

'Darling, *all* the girls will be wearing dresses.'

'Can I at least wear my new Kickers?'

'All right. As long as you don't get them scuffed up before school starts.' Grace glanced at her. 'I think we're all ready. I got Cy to cut the lawn yesterday so we just need to decorate after breakfast.'

'I can't wait!' Harry turned to a final brown-paper wrapped parcel with a typewritten label. 'Who's this from?' she said, untying the string.

'I don't know. I wondered if Fraser had sent you something.'

Harry ripped open the box, and pulled out a small leather

jewellery box. She flipped it open. 'It's beautiful,' she said, turning the box towards Grace.

The wooden spatula fell from Grace's hand. 'It's mine! I mean, I made it.' She pulled the frying pan off the heat and wiped her hands.

'There's a little card: *For Harry. A beautiful surprise, a gem the colour of your eyes.*'

'It's got to be Fraser.' Grace shook her head incredulously. 'I told him about making the ring for Mr Goldstein and he's the only person we know who could afford it.' She grabbed her old Burberry raincoat from the door. But she had recognised something in the typeface on the parcel's address, an unevenness. Grace looked at the packaging again, and noticed a plain envelope in the bottom of the box. Her hand shook as she ripped it open. *Grace,* the card said, *Out of the depths shall sapphires come, bringing September's child wisdom.* A sapphire tumbled into her palm.

'What's wrong? Are you cross, Mum?' Harry looked crestfallen. 'Please don't be cross.'

Grace caught herself and slowed down, not wanting to scare Harry. *Whoever it is, they are right about one thing. Harry does have beautiful violet eyes, just like Gogo.* She leant over and kissed Harry's head, shoving the note into her pocket. 'I'm sorry, darling. Don't worry, everything will be fine.' She picked up the box containing Fraser's tiepin on the way out the door. 'Now eat your breakfast. I'm just going to pop over to the house, OK?'

'Morning, Ellen,' she said, striding through the kitchen with her pyjamas poking out from the bottom of her raincoat. 'Is he awake?'

'He's in the breakfast room.' She pointed at the *Daily Mail*. 'They reckon that Ripper's struck again. You don't feel safe in your own bed.'

Grace squeezed her shoulder. 'We're a long way from

Yorkshire.' She marched through the house and knocked briskly on the door.

'Ah, Grace, how lovely to see you.' Fraser looked up from the *Telegraph*. 'I'm just catching up on the news while I've been away. It's a bad business about Mountbatten—'

'Fraser, I'm handing in my notice.' She handed him an envelope.

'You're what?' The newspaper crumpled to the table.

'Do you think you can buy me? All this time your family business had stripped mine clean.'

'Oh dear. How did you find out?'

'I can't believe you're involved with this. It destroyed us.'

'Your husband overreached himself. We just—'

'Cleaned up at my family's expense? Vultures rather than lions?'

'It sounds ghastly when you put it like that.' Fraser's face was calm. 'Scratch the surface of any wealthy family and you'll find muck. I had no idea when we met, I promise you.'

'But you still take the money from Strattons?'

'Don't be naïve, Grace.' Fraser folded his arms. 'The work-shop was Jack's idea and I hoped this went some way to atoning for our sins.'

'No secrets, eh? No lies. Roger and Tristan were here.'

'Those two oleaginous creatures. What did they want?'

'The usual – their cut of the estate and to humiliate the staff.'

'Oh dear. Your dander *is* up.'

'Tell me something, Fraser. You told me Gin's eyes were the colour of the night sky in the Middle East.'

'What on earth made you think of that?'

'I imagined they were dark, like her hair,' Grace said, her voice shaking with emotion. 'What colour is the sky?'

'Violet, in places,' a female voice said from the sofa facing the fireplace. 'Deep, deep violet. Most unusual.'

Grace turned. 'I'm sorry. I didn't know you had company.'

She felt self-conscious and tugged the raincoat closed.

'Have you met Cesca?' Fraser said.

Cesca sat up on the sofa and smiled at Grace, her chin resting on her arm. 'Fraser's told me all about you. I'm so glad to meet you at last.'

'How do you do,' Grace said.

'I convinced Cesca to let me give her a lift home.' Fraser scraped his chair back from the table. He walked over to Grace and gently took hold of her arms. 'I'm sorry. I should know better by now than to keep secrets from you. Grace has the most amazing ability to cut to the chase,' he said to Cesca. 'She has a perfect eye for detail. A terribly clear mind.'

'I imagine that's useful in your line of work?' Cesca said.

'Talking of which, do you know anything about the ring?' Grace said.

'The ring?' Fraser said.

'The one I showed you a photo of. Mr Goldstein's amethyst ring – which someone's just given Harry for her birthday.'

'Nothing to do with me. Jack and I are going to make her a gift of little old Felix, if that's all right with you? She's grown terribly fond of the pony.'

'Thank you, she'd be over the moon, but we're leaving.'

'Harry can still visit, surely? You've seen how happy she is here,' Fraser said. 'You can't take that away from her, not after everything she has lost.'

'No, you're right.' Grace's brow furrowed in confusion. *The sapphire was with the ring, so whoever is sending the stones has money, and now they've involved Harry.* Any doubts she'd had that it could be Sam went. *We were broke. There's no way he'd buy the ring. So who did?* She looked down at the Persian carpet. 'I'll work out my month's notice,' she said, unable to look at Fraser. 'Everything has become too complicated.' She felt Cesca watching. 'There's more we need to discuss.'

'You can jolly well tell Jack,' Fraser said. 'I'm not breaking the news.'

'I'm sorry. I've loved – we've loved being here, but I have to go.'

'If it's my ghastly cousins, I'll sort them out. Whatever they said to you—'

'No. It's not them. I'm sorry.' She rifled in her pocket, and handed him the box with the aquamarine tiepin. 'This is for you. A thank you, for everything.'

Grace walked away and Cesca came over to Fraser's side.

'It's lovely,' she said, pinning the stone to Fraser's cravat. 'Virginia West. There's a name I haven't thought of in a long time.' Her face was unreadable as she looked at Fraser. 'I was terribly jealous, you know?'

'Of Gin?'

'Of you both.' She straightened his collar. 'Did you ever care for me, even a little?'

'Cesca, you are a dear friend, and I should hate to lose that.' Fraser's voice softened. 'Who was it said "friendship is love seen in profile"?'

'Perhaps you've never really looked at me.' Her gaze faltered. 'You care a great deal about that girl, don't you?'

'Not like that, dear heart. I do hope she reconsiders.'

'She's been through a lot and she's proud,' Cesca said. 'I'll talk to her.'

'Grace,' Cesca called, striding across the yard after her.

'I'm sorry. I have to get back. I left Harry in charge of the breakfast.'

'I'll walk with you.' Cesca glanced at her. 'You can't leave, you know. Has Fraser told you about the fortune teller?'

'He's going to die this year?'

'No, not that nonsense. I've been telling him for years he got that bit wrong.' She paused at the path to the cottage. 'She told him that a jewelled woman will reveal the secret to his past.'

'So I'm some kind of lucky charm?' Grace laughed at the

irony. 'I wonder if that fortune teller is still there. I could do with a few answers myself.'

'Couldn't we all? If I were you, I'd reconsider. Sometimes we don't realise how precious people are until it's too late. Fraser and Jack care for you a great deal, and there's a life here for you and your daughter. They were simply trying to protect you.'

'I can look after myself.'

'Of course you can.' Cesca walked away, raising her hand in farewell. 'The question is, do you want to?'

40

Young girls in long party dresses ran across the sunlit lawn. Grace had asked Cy to leave a border of long grass and wild flowers and the last of the poppies and daisies nodded in the breeze. She had put up a pole at the heart of the lawn, and multicoloured ribbons trailed from there to the trees and the garden wall like a maypole. The village Punch and Judy man had set up in the corner of the garden, and boys and girls sat cross-legged on the lawn, giggling and shouting at the puppets: *He's behind you!*

'Where shall I put the sausage rolls?' Cilla said, pushing aside a bowl of Waldorf salad.

He's behind you, Grace thought, feeling cold suddenly.

'Grace, love?'

'Sorry? Just over there, Mum.' Grace looked down at the buffet table. The peace of the last few weeks seemed a distant memory and her mind was whirling. *I can't make sense of any of it – the stones, the Strattons or Margot's link with Fraser.* It felt like one of the intricate gold puzzle boxes she had seen, where each part had to fall in exactly the right place for the secret to be revealed.

'Darling, everything is all right, isn't it?' Cilla said.

'Yes. Yes, it's fine. I think that's everything. Oh, the hot dogs!' Grace ran towards the kitchen just as Ted opened the front door. *Hello*, she heard him say. *Yes, we met briefly. I'm Grace's father, Ted.*

Grace pulled the sausages out of the oven and slipped them into the fresh cut buns. 'Who was that?' she said as Ted walked into the kitchen.

'A man about a horse.' He took the platter from her and they walked to the table outside. 'I told him to go round the side.'

'Is it Lord Stratton?' Cilla said, craning her head above the children.

'He's not a Lord, I told you that,' Grace busied herself squeezing the last plate onto the little table. 'And I doubt it. He doesn't like parties much.'

'Hello, Grace.'

She looked up to see Jack standing at the edge of the garden. He held Felix on a lead rein, a large red satin bow tied at the side of the bridle. 'Jack.' Grace smoothed down the bodice of her white dress. 'Thank you,' she said as she walked over to him. 'Fraser told me about your idea, but—'

'If you insist on going, Harry can visit anytime she wants to. You both can.' She heard the hurt in his voice and he couldn't look at her. He rubbed the pony's forelock. 'Harry loves this old boy.'

'Thank you.' Every cell in her body yearned for him. She remembered the feel of his lips against her neck that morning, the weight of his head on her stomach. Being away from Jack for weeks had only made her want him more. The pony nudged her side with its head and she stepped closer.

'Please, don't go,' he said quietly. 'I've thought of little else but you.'

'We can still see one another, sometimes.' She tried to hide how much the thought of leaving hurt. 'I have something for you.' She reached into her pocket and handed him the box with the turquoise pin inside. 'It's just, well, I wanted to say thank you. The workshop—' She broke off, bittersweet feelings of gratitude and regret welling up in her. 'It's the most wonderful thing anyone has ever done for me. I know you meant well.'

'Surely you can understand why Fraser didn't tell you?'

'Felix!' Harry yelled, racing across the garden towards them, young girls in her wake. 'You came to my party!' She flung her arms around his neck and buried her face in his mane.

'Happy birthday, Harry,' Jack said. 'Fraser and I thought it was about time we made things official. Felix is yours now.'

'Mine?' Her eyes widened and she hugged Jack, knocking the wind out of him. 'Thank you, thank you, thank you!'

'Steady on,' Jack laughed. 'It's a big responsibility having your own horse. From now on, you'll have to do everything for Felix. Muck him out before school, exercise him every day . . .' He paused. 'At least, when you can.'

Grace felt Jack's gaze on her as she worked, setting up the plates and glasses on the picnic blanket beneath the maypole.

'That dishy fellow was at Margot's party, wasn't he?' Cilla said, dropping a party blower onto each plate.

'Who?' Grace glanced over. 'That's just Jack.'

'Can't keep his eyes off of you.' Cilla watched Grace's reaction.

'Mum, stop it. I'm married.'

'Do you well to remember that. People talk.' The girls came racing back from the stable and Cilla clapped her hands. 'Right, everyone grab a plate and help yourselves.'

'Your mum's in her element,' Ted said as Grace walked over. He sat on the old bench, a dimpled pint mug of bitter in hand. 'He's a nice chap.'

'Who?'

'Jack.'

'Oh God, Dad. Not you too?' Grace turned sideways to squeeze the tray of juice through the back door. 'He's my boss, that's all.'

'Didn't mean anything by it, love . . .' Ted began to say.

She walked through to the kitchen and dumped the tray on the table, started to load it with more jugs of orange squash.

'Is that all you think of me?' Jack said quietly.

She spun round at the sound of his voice. He was leaning against the dresser, in the shadows, the window bright with the golden sunset at his side. 'You almost gave me a heart attack.'

'I'm just your boss?' He walked across the kitchen and pushed the door to slightly.

'No. I . . .' Grace turned to the table. She began placing eleven candles on the cake.

'What's happened? Everything we said? Everything we promised in Paris?'

'What am I supposed to say, Jack?'

'Don't go.' He was standing close behind her now, his hand on her waist.

'I have to. I can't explain, not yet, but I can't do this.' His lips brushed the nape of her neck. 'Jack, please.'

'I told you, I'm free now, Grace. Broke, but divorced.' He smiled, hopeful, unsure. 'Grace, I love you.' He pulled her to him. 'Being away from you made me realise that even more.' He kissed her, lifted her up into his arms. Grace's back flattened against the wall, her leg encircling his, her light white dress slipping over her thighs.

'Jack, we can't, we can't—' she said, her breath short and fast.

'What are you doing?' Harry's voice was shrill. She stood, arms rigid, beside the kitchen door.

'Darling.' Grace pushed past Jack. 'It's not what you—'

'What are you *doing*?' she yelled.

'Harry . . .' Jack said gently.

325

'It's disgusting.' Tears pooled in her eyes. 'What about Daddy?'

'Darling, Daddy left us. He's gone, he's probably—'

'Dead?' Harry yelled. Grace saw Ted and Cilla cross in front of the window on their way in. 'That's what you want, isn't it? So you can do this – this, with Jack. Maybe Daddy ran away because you didn't love him enough. You killed him!'

'Harry, don't talk to your mother like that,' Ted said, his voice stern.

'I hate you!' Harry yelled. She tore off the amethyst ring and threw it at Grace and Jack. 'I hate you both!'

41

Grace tapped on Harry's bedroom door. She tried the handle. It was still locked. 'Harry, it's time for the Harvest Festival.'

'I'm not coming.'

'Please, Harry.' Grace rattled the door handle. 'Let me in.'

'Go away!'

Grace padded downstairs. 'It's been like this for days,' she said to Fraser.

'She's angry, my dear. I wonder where she gets her stubborn nature?' Fraser sat in the old armchair by the stove, his fingers pressed into a steeple.

'Her father.'

'Would it kill you to forgive us, Grace? Jack's as proud as you and he won't beg you to stay. I could knock your heads together.' Fraser's chin rested on his thumbs and he looked up at Grace. 'I, however, am shameless, and will beg until I wear your defences down.'

Grace laughed. 'It won't make any difference.' She squeezed his shoulder. 'It's not just the Strattons. There's a lot we need to talk about.'

'Not now, you'd better run along or you'll be late.' He picked up Grace's knitting. 'I'll stay here in case Harry comes down.'

'Are you sure?' She took her blue velvet jacket down from the coat rack.

'Of course.' Fraser shook out the long striped scarf Grace was knitting. 'Do you think this is long enough?'

'It's for Harry. *Doctor Who*.'

'Do you think you might make one for me afterwards?' he said, starting the next row. 'Or perhaps I shall. Clem taught me when I was little. Most relaxing.'

'It's on tonight – 'Destiny of the Daleks', or something. Harry was looking forward to it.'

'Then we shall watch together.'

As Fraser expected, the moment Grace's car pulled away he heard Harry's door unlock and the creak of her feet across the landing. He waited in silence as she crept down then jumped up from the chair: 'Boo!'

'Fraser!' Harry staggered back. 'You scared the life out of me.'

'How are you?' He put down the knitting.

Harry shrugged, dug her hands into the pockets of her flared cords.

'That bad, eh?' Fraser offered his hand. 'Come on. I have something that might cheer you up.' They walked along the path behind the cottage. 'Would you like to talk about it?'

'Not really.'

'Harry, sometimes grown-ups are hard to fathom.' He lifted his head, following the looping path of a flock of migrating birds. Fraser stopped to pluck a plump blackberry from the hedgerow and offered it to Harry. 'Go on. You have to eat.' He popped it in his mouth, savouring the sweetness. 'They're at their best.' He picked a handful, waiting for her.

'If it will make you happy,' she said, taking a berry. 'Thanks.'

They ate the berries in silence, walking along the overgrown path. 'Harry,' Fraser said finally. 'Grace and Jack . . .'

'I said I don't want to talk about it.'

327

'Fine, you will just do me the courtesy of listening then.' She glanced down at her feet, her cheeks colouring at the sharp tone he used. 'Your mother and Jack have both had a tough time of it lately, and if they have found happiness it is not up to us to spoil that, do you understand?'

'Yes, Fraser.'

'It's up to them to decide their future. Your mother loves you, and so does Jack, I believe. Neither one of them wants to hurt you. Why do you think they hid their growing feelings for one another from you? Jack is a free man, now, and your mother is alone. Do you love her?'

'Yes, of course.'

'I love Jack as I would my own son.' Fraser looked at Harry. 'You and I must simply love them and support whatever they decide. You are a bright girl, but you are young still and there is a lot you will learn about the human heart.' He thought for a moment. 'Then again, how much do any of us really know? Every person on the planet is ridiculous in some way.' He put his arm around her shoulders and hugged her to his side. 'When your mother comes home, I want you to give her a big hug. Will you do that? You don't have to understand what she's feeling, because they are grown-up emotions. Frankly, I am as clueless as you about affairs of the heart.'

'What do I need to do?'

'Nothing. There's no need to apologise – it's understandable you were shocked and needed some time. You just need to let her know you haven't turned away from her. Keep talking to one another.' He looked up as they reached the end of the path. 'Right, we shall say no more about it.' He stopped by a gate and pointed across the field. 'Look over there.'

Harry clambered up onto the five-bar gate. 'A straw house!' she said, climbing over. Fraser plucked a stem of pale grass and leant against the gate, watching her race across the stubbly field.

'Reckon she likes it, then?' Cy said, scrambling to his feet from where he lay dozing in the hedgerow with his Stetson over his eyes. He ran his hand through his receding, curly hair, which seemed to hover on his head with a temporary air. Cy settled his hat in place and turned to Fraser.

'Just finished it? Well done, Cy. I think that's the best you've ever built. I knew it would cheer her up.' Fraser chewed on the stem of grass. 'Your predecessor used to build one every harvest for Jack with the bales.' Fraser's expression darkened. 'I have a feeling that with the mess the so-called grown-ups are making of everything, it will do Harry good to have a refuge.'

42

Grace helped Alice with the Harvest Supper, manning the village hall's kitchen as teenagers served the long tables of people. She found herself scanning the rows of faces, hoping to see Jack there.

'No sign of him?' Alice paused to wipe her forehead with the back of her hand. Grace shook her head. 'Why don't you call it a night? You've been working non-stop since this morning, helping Ellen decorate this place, and giving me a hand here.'

Grace slipped her white apron over her head and smoothed down her simple denim shirt. 'It's such a mess, Alice.'

'Go on,' Alice said, steering her out of the kitchen to the hall. Men were clearing away the tables for dancing, and people sat on hay bales at the sides of the room. Ellen waved to Grace from a place near the stage, beckoning her over. 'Go on now.'

The stacked heels of Grace's cowboy boots tapped on the wooden floor as she crossed the hall to Ellen. 'There you are, love, come and sit down for a bit.' Ellen offered her a bottle of cider from the table at her side.

'Thanks.' Grace sat on the bale with Ellen. 'It's better to keep busy.'

'Is she talking to you yet?'

'Harry?' Grace shook her head. 'She's practically moved into that straw house, taken her favourite cuddly toys with her.'

'Bit of space will do her good. She'll be safe enough there, bit of an adventure, and the lads will keep an eye on her tonight. Just you watch, she'll come back when it starts raining.'

'I don't know what to do, Ellen. I feel like I've let her down so badly.'

'She'll come round, love. Children don't like to think of their parents as anything other than that. She's had a shock, that's all. Well, we all have.' She smiled kindly at her. 'Though I've seen the way he's been looking at you for months. I didn't think you were interested.'

'I'm confused, Ellen, that's all.' Grace picked at the label on the bottle with her thumbnail, peeling it back. 'The way I feel about Jack . . .' It was like a visceral tug in her stomach as she thought of him. A Dolly Parton tribute band took to the stage and the crowd whistled and cheered. Grace clapped her hands and stretched out her legs, crossed one over the other. 'She's very good.'

'That's Cy's wife,' Ellen said, her head rocking in time to the music. 'Everyone round here always called her Dolly even before they started the band.' She mimed a voluptuous chest and laughed. Grace craned her head to look for Cy. He was standing at the bar, gazing adoringly at Dolly as she sang.

'She's brilliant. Cy's always reminded me of Burt Reynolds.'

'He'd be tickled pink to hear that.' The couples on the dance floor danced in lines, stomping and clapping to the country and western tune. 'So, you were saying about you and Jack.' Ellen leant towards her, raising her voice over the music.

'I just don't know what to do.'

'You deserve to be happy, Grace, remember that.' Ellen sipped her cider. 'Strikes me you've done what we all do, put the happiness of your husband and your family ahead of your own.'

Jack strode into the village hall, weaving his way through the crowd towards the bar. He wore faded blue jeans over cowboy boots, and a loose white shirt. 'All right, Cy? Dolly's sounding good.'

'She's my angel,' Cy said, tapping his foot to the music.

'Buy you a pint?' Jack signalled to the bartender.

'Don't mind if I do. And another packet of peanuts.' He glanced over his shoulder as the barman yanked a packet off the cardboard stand. A grinning brunette glamour model with her arms reaching to the sky still had her modesty covered by the remaining packets. 'He does that on purpose,' Cy muttered. 'Never have seen what's behind the packets.'

Jack laughed. 'They're always wearing a bikini, Cy, every single time.'

'Man can dream, can't he?' Cy nodded towards Ellen's table. 'Talking of which, you seen Grace tonight? Looking fine, if I may say so.'

Ellen looked up as Jack walked over. 'Talk of the devil. Your ears must have been burning, Jack.'

'Ellen, Grace,' he said, and held out his hand to her. 'Would you like to dance?'

'Do you think that's a good idea?' Grace said. It felt as though everyone at the dance was looking at them.

'I do.' He took her hand firmly and led her to the heart of the dancers as Dolly began to sing 'I Will Always Love You'. Jack held her close and she felt his fingers through the soft denim of her shirt, warm against her spine.

She gave in to the feeling of his arm around her, his hand in her hand as they moved together. Her head rested against his collarbone and he turned in to her, his lips against her hairline. 'Jack?'

'Tell me what I can do to make this right.'

'It's me,' she said, thinking of Fraser's words. 'I'm sorry. I always want everything to be perfect,' she said, overcome

331

with tiredness, with wanting him. 'I want . . .' She struggled to explain. 'I know I can do it all by myself. I know I can take care of Harry, and work, and I know I can do everything – but I want someone who sees me, who wants *me*.'

'I see you.' He waited for her to look at him. 'I want you.'

'The way I feel . . .'

'How? How do you feel? I'm not going to let you push me away again.'

'Push you away?' Grace's eyes were bright as she looked at him. 'I don't know what to do, Jack. Harry's heartbroken. I'm not even technically a widow. My husband either killed himself or he cared so little he bailed out on us.' She shook her head. 'It's all such a mess. The Strattons—'

'To hell with the Strattons. It was a mistake not to tell you as soon as we found out, but we were just trying to protect you. You'd been so hurt, and with some creep sending you the stones I didn't think you needed the past dragging up again.' Jack tucked a strand of hair behind her ear. 'Grace, I love you, I love Harry. Let's start from there.'

'Jack, it's more complicated than that . . .'

'I don't know what you want.' He cupped her face in his hand. 'What do you want, Grace? Tell me.'

I love you, she thought. Three simple words. If she said them, the die would be cast, and the future would rise up to meet them.

''Scuse me, miss.' The barman tapped Grace on the shoulder. She gazed at him for a moment, unseeing. 'Young fella left this at the bar for you.' He handed her a manila envelope.

'I have to go,' she said to Jack.

'But Grace—'

She pushed her way through the crowded dance floor to the back of the hall. 'Oh God, oh God,' Grace murmured like a prayer, tearing the envelope open. A fiery blue opal tumbled onto her palm, and a note: *A little early, but I'm running out of time. October's child in darkness oft may grope, the iridescent opal bids it hope.* Grace stuffed the note into her pocket. *He was here. Whoever he is, he was here.*

She pushed her way through a crowd of people in checked shirts and Stetsons coming in and the chill night air cut through her shirt. Her head was swimming with guilt, with emotion. Grace strode around the side of the village hall where it was quiet and she could be alone. She settled back against the stone wall, felt its cold rough surface against her palm.

'You look beautiful, Grace,' a man's voice said. She jumped, and backed away from the shadows.

'Who is that?'

'It's me. Don't you recognise me?' He stepped out of the darkness.

'Sam?' Grace's legs buckled. 'It can't be . . .'

'Hello, baby.' He moved to the light and she saw him clearly now. His hair was dyed dark and it was longer, tied back in a ponytail. He wore a heavy beard, but there, in his clear green eyes, she saw him. They were ringed with new wrinkles that she didn't remember, and she stepped towards him, touched them gently.

'I must be dreaming,' she whispered.

'It's me. It's me,' he said, and tried to embrace her.

'How? Where . . . ?' Grace backed away, trembling with shock.

'Shh, there's plenty of time to explain all that. I'm so sorry, Grace. I'm sorry for everything.'

'The babies,' she said, tears pooling in her eyes, her throat constricting. 'I lost our babies, Sam.'

'I know.' His shoulders hunched. 'I saw you, on their birthday, in Exford.'

'You saw me?' Grace wiped at her eyes with the heel of her hand. 'You've been following us?'

'I wanted to know you were all right. I've been hanging

around Exford on and off. I followed you here from your parents' new place.'

'So it *was* you in the village. Mrs Miller saw you.'

'That old bat sees everything. I thought I was being careful.'

'Where have you been?'

'I'm staying in a B & B in East Wittering now.'

'All this time?'

'No, no. I've been in Spain, Javea.' He raised his chin. 'I'm starting again, Grace. New business, new name.'

'New name?'

'Yeah, Dave Locke.' He took her hand, and she flinched at the intensity of his gaze. 'It's a chance for us, Gracie. New lives, new identities.'

'I *have* a new life.' She stepped away from him, stumbled as she backed into the wall. 'I don't even know who you are any more, *Dave*.'

'Never met a Dave I didn't like. Sounds like an honest name, doesn't it?'

'Honest?' Grace put her hands on her hips, rage rising up in her. 'We lost everything, Sam, the house, my business as well!'

'Jesus, Grace, I'm sorry. I never wanted to put you through this. You paid the creditors?'

'Of course I did.' Her voice broke. 'As many as I could, though the rest didn't give up easily. And I've started again, got myself back on my feet. I used some of the birthstones. Remember them?' Sam looked at his feet, kicked at the ground. 'The ones we put in the chimney. The ones that were meant to bring us all the luck in the world.'

'Yeah, I remember.'

She glared at him. 'But then you would, wouldn't you? It's you, isn't it? You're the one who has been sending me these notes.' She thumped him on the chest with her clenched fist. 'How could you?'

'I thought it was romantic.' He held her wrist firm, pulling her to him. 'I wanted to win you back.'

'To win me? Jesus, Sam, what am I, some kind of trophy? You scared the hell out of me.'

'I'm sorry,' he said, holding her tight. 'I didn't want to scare you. I just couldn't come out in the open, not yet, not until everything was settled.'

'My God, you even bought the ring from Goldstein.'

'He had no idea who I was,' Sam said. 'I was in London and I knew you used to sell your stuff to him before you had the shop, so I went to have a look.' He pressed his hand against the small of her back, holding her close. 'I wanted to have something that you'd touched. Does that sound daft?' Grace turned her face, afraid he was going to try and kiss her. His hold on her loosened. 'As luck would have it, you'd just delivered a new ring.'

'You bought it?'

'Yeah, he was over the moon.'

'*You* bought it?' she said again, struggling free from him. 'Sam, you left me and Harry with less than nothing, and here you are dropping hundreds of pounds on jewellery?'

'Baby, I'm sorry. If I'd known . . . I kept a bit back, offshore, in case everything went tits up.' Grace's thoughts raced back to the day the court order was served for the repossession of her house and her business. Her stomach lurched with anxiety, remembering the incessant calls from creditors, from the bank, the drowning sensation she felt every time the post cascaded onto the mat bringing more bills she couldn't pay. She thought of all the months when she had been looking for change down the side of the sofa just to buy a loaf of bread, too proud to ask her parents for money. How she had stood outside the supermarket one day with Harry, in tears, trying to explain why they would just have to make do with what they had at home because she couldn't get any cash for food.

'Don't touch me,' she said as he reached for her. She felt sick, remembering the constant stress and panic she had lived with for months after he went, the grief she had shouldered alone. 'Just *don't*.'

'I know you're angry. You have every right to be.'

'You weren't the only one who wanted to disappear,' she cried.

'You're stronger than me—'

'I am not stronger. I'm not!' Any relief she felt at seeing Sam alive chilled into cold fury. 'I had no choice. Harry needed me.' Her voice broke. 'I grieved, Sam. Alone. I cried myself to sleep night after night . . .'

'We can start again, be a proper family, with a clean slate. Come with me, Grace.'

'You're not listening to me, are you?' Grace hugged herself. 'Just like that? A new life? You must be mad.' She was shivering with cold and shock. 'This is our home, Sam. I love it here, my parents are here—'

'And your boyfriend.'

'What?'

He leant back into the shadows. 'Who is he?'

'Who?' Her blood chilled.

'Him. That tall bastard you were dancing with.'

'My boss,' she said.

'Your boss? Does he own that estate where you're living? Nice little cottage you're in.'

'You'd know, since you broke in there.'

'Fallen on your feet this time, haven't you?' Sam ran the knuckle of his thumb across his lips. 'To think I was worried about you. You moved on quickly, Grace.' Something in his voice troubled her. She remembered other times when he had picked fights with complete strangers for just looking at her.

'His name is Jack. He's my boss. Nothing's happened.'

'But you want it to. I saw you. I saw how he was looking at you.' He gripped her arm. 'Don't give up on me.'

'You gave up on me, Sam. You walked out on me, on Harry.'

'What was I supposed to do?' He lowered his voice as a group of people walked into the hall. 'What could I do? I had nothing left, Grace.'

'You left me to clear it all up. How do you think I felt? Everyone thought you were dead.'

'Not you, though.' He pinned her against the wall. 'I told you I'd never let you go,' he whispered, his lips against her ear. He smelt the same, of mint gum, of leather and clean linen. He felt the same to her, his powerful, muscular torso holding her close. But he felt wrong. 'It can be the same—'

'It would never be the same again, don't you see that?' She tried to struggle free, but he held her there until she relaxed.

'I love you, Grace.'

'You have no right, no right to say that.'

'Please, forgive me.'

Grace screwed her eyes closed, willing herself not to break down. 'Of course I forgive you. I loved you. All I ever wanted was for you to be happy, Sam. That's why we all took so many risks for you.'

'Loved? You *loved* me?' He buried his face in her hair. 'No. No, you love me.'

'Sam, it's taken me over a year to start to put myself back together.'

'I get it, you're angry. All I'm asking is that you think about it.' He hesitated. 'Can I see Harry?'

'No.' She pressed the heel of her hand against her eye. 'If you want to see her sister, Jemima, or her brother, Rex, you can go to that little white cross in the corner of the graveyard in Exford where you left the pearl.'

'Oh God, Grace . . .'

'I have to go now.'

'When can I see you again?'

'I don't know. Things are . . . They're difficult.' She looked directly at him, her eyes bright with pain. 'I'll be in touch. Where can I find you?'

'No, that's not possible. And don't think about telling the coppers. Sam Morgan is dead.'

'Long live Dave Locke?' Grace dug her hands into her pockets, felt Sam's penknife. 'Here,' she said, shoving it into his hand. 'Take this.' She wrenched off his watch. 'And this.'

'Oh, Gracie . . .'

'Don't call me that. I carried these every day, Sam. Everyone said you were dead, but I didn't believe them.'

'You can believe in me still . . .' He reached out for her, cupped her face in his hands.

'Don't touch me!' Grace tried to push him away.

'Grace?' Jack strode over and grabbed Sam by the shoulder, forcing him to let go of her. Sam took a swing at Jack, clipping his lip, but Jack shoved him hard against the stone wall and raised his fist.

'Stop it!' Grace cried, putting herself between them. 'This isn't going to solve anything.' She put her hand on Jack's chest, holding him back from Sam.

'Who is this?' He stemmed the blood from his lip with the back of his hand.

'Jack, this is Sam.'

'Her husband.' Sam stretched himself up to his full height, but he still had to look up to Jack.

'You've got a nerve showing up, after everything you've done.' She felt the muscles in Jack's chest clench, his arm tense as his fist balled at his side.

'What's it got to do with you, Mr Bigshot?' Sam looked Jack up and down. 'Like screwing around with the staff, do you? With my wife?'

'Don't you dare talk about Grace like that!' Jack lunged at him.

'Stop it!' Grace held him back, their bodies close. 'Stop.' She touched his face, her lips against his cheek. 'Jack, wait for me. Please.'

'You touch her and you'll wish you *were* dead,' Jack said,

glaring at Sam as he backed away. 'I'll be by the car,' he said to Grace, and strode away into the darkness.

'Don't let us keep you,' Sam called after him. When he turned to Grace, his face was set hard with anger. 'Nothing's happened? I don't believe you.'

'Believe what you want.' Grace's voice shook.

'How long have we been together, Grace? Don't throw it away.'

She screwed her eyes closed as the past threatened to pull her away. Memories bloomed in her mind – the first time she saw Sam, their wedding, holding Harry for the first time. She remembered unloading the boxes into the Rectory, Harry's laughter, the sound of her feet racing through the empty rooms. Sam had swung Grace into his arms, carried her over the threshold. She remembered the endless summer days so full of hope.

'I love you, Grace,' Sam said. 'Don't give up on me.'

'It's too late.' Tears seeped through her lashes.

'Think of Harry.'

'Think of Harry? That's all I've *ever* done. Why do you think I stayed with you months, years, after it was good, hoping you'd come back to us?' She wiped at her cheek. 'You left me long before you disappeared.'

'Grace. I don't care about what's happened. I don't care about this Jack.' Sam pulled the collar of his leather jacket up. 'We can be a family again. Start again. I promise you, it'll be how it was at the beginning.'

'Don't you get it?' Grace laughed through her tears. 'It can never, ever be the same. I've grown up, Sam. I had to. I'm not the schoolgirl you picked out at that party to make into the perfect wife.' She started to walk away but Sam grabbed at her wrist. He pulled her to him and forced her to kiss him, his unfamiliar beard scratching her chin, his lips bruising hers.

'There,' he said, as she stumbled back. 'You feel it, don't

you? Don't deny it, Grace. You know, and I know, what we had. You think he can make you feel like that? We couldn't keep our hands off one another.'

'Don't, Sam.' Grace turned away as if she had been struck, but the thought, the idea, of how happy it would make Harry to be back together as a family again took root.

'I'll give you a month to think it all through. The village has a Hallowe'en party down at the beach—'

'The same coast you disappeared off? How poetic.'

'One month. Then you decide what's best, for Harry.' His gaze held her. 'She'll be there?'

'Of course she will. The Strattons invite the whole village. It's a tradition.'

Sam took one last look at Grace. 'You can give me your answer then.'

Jack parked his car outside the cottage and sat in silence beside Grace. *He's alive*, she thought, over and over again. She couldn't face going back to the party and she was shaking so badly that Jack had driven her home. Grace laid her head against the window. *What am I going to do?*

'Grace,' he said, reaching for her hand. Their fingers entwined. 'I know this changes everything.'

'Jack—'

'No, hear me out. Whatever he's done, he's your husband, and Harry's father.' He looked at her, his face full of concern. 'Only you can decide this. You know how I feel about you.' He held her hand to his lips. 'Now you need to choose.'

The cottage door opened, light spilling onto the path, and Ted stepped outside, lighting a cigar. He noticed Jack's car and walked over. His tap on the window made Grace jump and she stared at him for a moment, her eyes unseeing.

'Are you all right, love? We thought you'd be later than this,' he said, opening the door. 'Evening, Jack.'

'Ted,' he said, starting the engine.

340

'Thanks.' Grace squeezed Jack's hand as she stepped out of the car, and he drove away.

'I've got some news,' she said to Ted, and walked towards the house. Her movements felt leaden. Harry was curled up by her grandmother's feet, reading a DC comic as Cilla watched *To The Manor Born*.

'Grandad, *please* can I get some Sea Monkeys,' Harry said. 'They sound amazing. Do you have to go to America to get them?'

'Are you OK, sweetheart?' Grace said.

'Guess so,' Harry said. 'Night.'

'Don't I get a hug?' Grace held her arms open and grudgingly Harry embraced her. Grace buried her face in her daughter's hair, holding her tight. 'Sleep well.' Harry said goodnight to her grandparents and ran upstairs.

'At least she's coming round, eh?' Cilla said, her voice like a paper cut.

'You're loving this, aren't you?' Grace said.

'No, not at all.' Cilla raised her chin and gazed past Grace. 'Just disappointed to be proven right, again.'

'Mum, please, not now.' The look of disappointment on her father's face was a hundred times worse for Grace.

'You always had ants in your pants. Look at what happened with Sam.'

'Stop it, Mum. Just stop.' She put her hands to her face. 'Sam's back,' Grace said quietly, and sat down. She glanced at the stairs to check Harry wasn't eavesdropping. 'Please don't tell Harry, don't tell anyone until I've decided what to do.'

'You've seen him?' Ted's face lit up. 'Is he all right?'

'No, no, not really. He's changed. It's all so hard to take in.'

'Where is he?'

'I don't know. He said he'd find me.'

'It'll all work out now that Sam's back,' Ted said. 'We'll be off now but let's speak in the morning.' He picked up a folded piece of paper from the counter. 'Mr Stratton came by, said something about going to France? He went screeching off into the night.' Grace's heart lurched. Surely Fraser hadn't found out about Margot. 'He left a note for you. Not that it makes much sense.' The message was hurried, his familiar handwriting looping with speed: *Grace. You were right! The missing asteria has surfaced. Up for auction at Drouot. Estate of Emilie someone. Back in a couple of days. F.*

43

Fraser sauntered along the silent forest track, Biba trotting at his side. He hummed an old Tino Rossi tune, 'J'attendrai', his breath pluming in the cold morning air. He swung the basket in his hand, scuffing the piles of golden leaves with his boot, dancing a few steps to the melody. In the canopy of the trees, squirrels leapt and chattered, gathering stores for the winter. At the edge of the woods, Fraser whistled for the dog and set off across the misty field towards Jack's house. He frowned as he grew closer, hearing the crack of an axe chopping through the silence.

'Biba, come.' Fraser quickened his pace. His boots crunched across the gravel driveway and he followed the sound of the axe around to the workshop. Jack was stripped to the waist, his shirt tied around his hips, and he stood beside a large pile of freshly chopped firewood. A bonfire crackled nearby, twigs and dried leaves sparking, filling the air with woodsmoke. Jack placed another log on the block and swung the long axe around, splitting it cleanly.

'You're up early,' Fraser said, walking towards him. Jack looked over in surprise as Floyd raced over to his mother, leaping around her with joy.

'Couldn't sleep. When did you get back?' Jack leant against the handle of the axe, catching his breath.

'Early hours. Felt like stretching my legs after travelling.'

Fraser raised the basket of field mushrooms up. 'Thought I'd leave some of these on the doorstep for your breakfast. Some lovely fairy rings in the usual spot.' He raised his chin. 'Don't catch a chill, dear boy.' Jack wiped the sweat from his face with his shirt and shrugged it on.

'Coffee?'

'Please.' Fraser followed him in to the kitchen. Jack filled the kettle and put it on to the Rayburn. 'Care to tell me how you got that split lip?' Jack's shoulders hunched and his head fell forward as he rested against the rail of the stove.

'He's back.'

'Who?'

'Grace's husband.'

'Good God, really?' Fraser pulled out a kitchen chair. 'When?'

'Night of the Harvest dance.'

'I take it you . . .' Fraser gestured at Jack's lip.

'Yeah, he took a swing at me. I'd have knocked him out if Grace hadn't stopped me.'

'Is she all right?'

'I don't know.' Jack came and sat opposite Fraser.

'One step at a time.' Fraser took a small velvet case from his jacket pocket. 'She was right, you know.' He flicked open the case and turned the star sapphire towards Jack. 'I can't wait to show her.'

'I'm pleased for you – for both of you, after all the work you've done.' He stood and took down a couple of mugs, rifling through the drawer for a spoon.

'Jack, talk to me.'

'What is there to say?' He took a pack of ground coffee from the fridge, and tipped it into a cafetière. He started to close the packet, but his hand fell to the counter, still holding it. 'Frase, I don't know what to do.'

'Here, let me,' Fraser said, coming over. 'Go and take a shower, have a shave, and you'll feel like a different man. We shall talk it through over breakfast.' He reached for the kettle.

'Thank you.'

'By the way, I had a bit of a brainwave while I was away,' Fraser said. 'I've come up with a way to secure the estate for you. If I sign away any right to the Stratton trust money, and we survive on Booth funds, on the estate alone, I think the dreaded cousins will leave us in peace.'

'Are you doing this because of Grace?'

'It's time for a clean break. My hunch is that those chinless wonders will run the family businesses into the ground anyway. I think we will be well shot of them.'

'Fraser, you know I can't bring any money to the table, don't you? The divorce has cleared me out.'

'Jack, you bring yourself. That's all we need. I care about the future of this place, the future of the families who depend on us. I want the estate to be sustainable and I have complete trust and respect for our people and for you.'

'Thank you.' Jack held his gaze. 'I won't let you down. Fraser . . .'

'Yes?'

'What if she leaves?'

'My dear boy, I've no doubt she loves you.' He squeezed Jack's shoulder. 'Give her time. Grace is holding back. She cares about doing the right thing, and she doesn't want to hurt anyone, especially Harry. If I am right about her, I think she returns your feelings completely and a love like that is worth fighting for.' Fraser laughed softly. 'Grace Manners. I knew from her name she'd be a decent sort.'

'Manners maketh man?'

'They go a long way in this world. Decency, kindness, consideration for others. Both you and Grace share many fine qualities. That reminds me,' Fraser said, reaching for his wallet. He slipped out the photograph that he had taken of Jack and Grace at the Lutetia. 'I thought you might like this.' Jack's face softened as he looked at the picture.

'I don't know what's going to happen now her husband is back, but you know, in Paris, Grace chose me. She looked so beautiful and we could have gone anywhere, to any fancy restaurant or show, and she chose to be with me.'

'What more do you need, than to be with the one you love?' Fraser smiled. 'Fight for her, Jack. Don't lose her. Don't let her lose you.'

I didn't know was going to happen now her in some
a look of innocence. In Paris in the hotel, she looked
so frightened, so young, and I remember what I do my heart
recognises she, and she gets lost, and she

What more do I need than to be told that one can keep
to a couple of nights or that day, until later but at her
house.

OCTOBER

Opal

Faith · Confidence · Hope

44

'Fraser, I'm off. I'll see you in a couple of weeks. Good Lord,' Grace said, backtracking quickly from the study door.

'No, it's perfectly all right, we're almost done,' Fraser said, his voice muffled against the massage table. A burly physiotherapist was working on his back and Fraser groaned in pain.

Grace busied herself as they finished, tidying away some papers on her desk. She glanced up as Fraser was dressing, surprised again by what good shape he was in for a man of his age, the elegant line of his tanned legs and toned stomach. 'Are you all right?' she said as he padded over.

Fraser cricked his neck from side to side with a popping sound. 'Bloody back started playing up on the way back from Paris.' He waited for the physio to fold up his table. 'Thank you, Boris,' he called. 'If you pop in to Jack's office and give him your bill, he'll settle up.' He slumped down in the chair. 'Always goes when I'm under stress. My Achilles heel, if you will. Massage is supposed to help with my moods, too, you know, but I still can't get used to the feel of a chap's hands on me, and a girl just seems, well, seedy.' He rattled a jar of vitamins on the desk. 'Ellen's watching me like a hawk, too.'

'There's not much better than a good diet, sleep and fresh air.'

'Sleep?' Fraser laughed. 'Forgotten what it feels like to have a full night.'

'How was Paris?'

'You were right.' He unclipped his briefcase and pulled out a battered jewellery box. 'Go on, open it,' he said.

Grace was grateful that Fraser hadn't asked about her weekend, that he didn't pry into what was happening with Jack. She clicked open the box, and gasped. 'Is this it?'

'The missing Stratton asteria sapphire.' Fraser stood shoulder to shoulder with her, admiring the brooch. 'Fabulous isn't it? Congratulations, Grace.' He put his arm around her. 'If you hadn't deciphered the designs at Bouchet et Fils, I would have carried on looking for a necklace.'

'It makes sense that it was designed to convert into a brooch.'

'No doubt whoever got their hands on it broke up the setting and sold the diamond necklace on.'

'But what happened? How did you get hold of it?'

'As you know, I have had scouts all over Europe looking for it. I rather hoped it might provide a clue to my past, you see. I'd only sent through your sketches a few days before, when an old friend from Paris, an antiques dealer, called on the night of the Harvest dance. He'd spotted the asteria in a Drouot catalogue, but the sale was on the Monday, so I had to get the first flight over there.'

'What did you find out?' Grace sat on the sofa and took the brooch out of the box. 'It's not in its original case.'

'No. It turned up in an estate sale, a real mixed bag house clearance. Drouot reminds me of a jumble sale half the time. There was a lot of tat – paintings of kittens and so on – and then there was this.'

'Did you find out the provenance?'

'No, but it's definitely the piece. I stayed on in Paris to check with Bouchet et Fils. All Drouot could tell me was that it came from the estate of some woman called Emilie Josephine.'

'Josephine?'

'I know. The trail goes cold there. No living relatives, but I spoke to the woman who is her heir, her carer. Apparently this woman, Emilie, wore the asteria every day of her life and she adored it.' Fraser turned it in his hand. 'Makes me feel rather guilty about all the jewels here, tucked away. Jewels should be worn, don't you think? And enjoyed.'

Grace wondered how Margot fitted in to all of this. 'Did you have fun, as well?' she said, hoping to change the subject.

'Yes, it was good to get away, and Paris always feels like a second home.' Fraser stretched his arms above his head. 'But then I suppose it should – I was born there.' He smiled at Grace. 'I finished transcribing my father's diaries in the hotel. I'm so happy, Grace. I had always thought of him as a greatly troubled man, depressed, shell-shocked. I thought – I thought he detested me. All I remember is how he terrified me – that booming voice yelling, "I should have taken the girl!"'

'I remember.'

Fraser tapped the old brown leather diary on his desk. 'He wasn't like that at all at the end, it seems. They loved one another, Grace. He grew to love Clem, and he found peace with her. I'd always assumed he resigned his commission when he was wounded at Mons, but that wasn't the case at all. He adored horses and he went on to run one of the Army Remount Service depots until the end of the war.'

'What did they do?'

'Looked after all the horses that the army needed through-out Europe and the Middle East.' Fraser paused. 'I always thought he deliberately set out to kill himself, riding out on that unbroken horse when he was still lame from the war, but no, his last diary entry is full of high spirits. He was almost demob-happy. He felt like himself again, you see. He wanted to see what he was capable of again. My father died riding – doing what he loved. It was just a damned accident that he fell and broke his neck. If Clem hadn't bundled all his last effects up and stored them in Italy, I'd have found this out years ago. I think it was a romantic gesture on her part because he always wanted to retire to Tuscany.' He shook his head. 'She tried telling me, time and time again, that he loved me. I thought she was just being kind.' Fraser looked at the aquamarine ring on his pinkie finger. 'This was his. It's why I wear it every day. Who knows – if he hadn't taken that fall, perhaps he would have still been with us today.'

'The world is full of what ifs,' Grace said. 'You can waste a lifetime rewriting history. The important thing is you know he loved you.' She handed him the brooch. 'Right, I'd better get on.'

'Please tell me you've changed your mind about leaving?'

'Fraser, I just don't think it is good for me to be here.' She looked down at her hands. 'It's just too complicated.'

'Think of Harry, how happy she is here—'

'Not you too? She's all I think of.' Her shoulders fell. 'Why do you think I've held back from Jack? Why am I even thinking of going with Sam?'

'I understand, but I can't say I approve.' Fraser folded his arms. 'Take some time to really think it through. She would get used to the idea of you and Jack, in time.' He waited for Grace to look at him. 'You can't make her happy, my dear. The only person you can make happy in this life is yourself. It's a decision, a way of looking at life, that she has to make herself. She's a clever girl, but perhaps she is looking at the past through rose-tinted lenses?'

'Perhaps.'

'He hasn't contacted you again, your husband?' Grace shook her head. 'Good. If he tries to pressure you, or hurt you in any way, I want you to call us immediately.' He took Grace's hand. 'In spite of my foolishness trying to hide the truth about the Strattons' involvement in your affairs, I have your best interests at heart.' Grace's chest tightened with guilt. It had all gone too far. Without talking to Margot she couldn't reveal the truth about the link between their families, and she couldn't carry on living a lie, waiting for her grandmother to reappear. *Fraser deserves more, they both do.*

'Do you want me to tidy up before I go?' Grace said.

'Go? You're not leaving already?'

352

She laughed. 'No, you're not getting rid of me that quickly. I have some leave due, don't you remember? I'm going up to London today, to see if I can find some work. Mum and Dad are going to look after Harry. I need a bit of time to think things through—' She broke off as they heard raised voices in the corridor.

'You can't just barge in here, Mr Stratton,' Ellen was saying.

'I'll barge wherever I damn well please.' Tristan strode through the door, a VHS player under one arm.

'I'm sorry,' Ellen said to Fraser. 'I tried to stop him.'

'Not to worry, Ellen. Some coffee perhaps?' Fraser said. 'Tristan. To what do I owe this pleasure?' He glanced at the door as Roger and their father arrived. 'Goodness, the whole family. Splendid.'

'Uncle Fraser, we have something you need to see.' Roger glared at Grace. 'Do you have a television?'

'Jack,' Fraser said, popping his head into the kitchen. 'Do you have a moment?' Jack put down the morning paper. The table was stacked with wooden crates and Ellen was polishing Bramley apples and wrapping them in newspaper for the winter. The kitchen smelt of sweet apple and cinnamon which was stewing on the stove.

'Is Grace around?' Ellen said.

'There's been a delivery for her.' Jack's voice was tight and angry as he pointed at the huge bouquet of red roses on the draining board.

'The husband, I assume? We'll deal with him later.' Fraser gestured for Jack to follow and he walked at Fraser's side along the corridor, still carrying his steaming mug of coffee.

'Have you spoken to Grace?'

'She knows where I am.'

'God, you're as impossible as one other.'

'What's up?'

'I don't know. I just don't know. The bloody cousins have

some bee in their bonnet about a TV programme.' They walked into the playroom to find Roger on his hands and knees in front of the television, wiring up the VHS player. 'It's like pin the tail on the donkey,' Fraser said quietly, glancing at his expansive backside in its straining tartan trousers.

'I thought this thing was a bloody waste of time when Tristan got it. All his wife ever uses it for is to record *Dallas* and the *Antiques Roadshow*,' Sir Richard said.

'Never miss an episode now, more's the pity, all those rich Yanks ...' Roger glanced up as he noticed Jack's boot step forward near his face. 'Ah, our American cousin.'

'Stratton.' Jack leant against the beam, his arms folded.

'There we go. Is that right?' Roger's normally florid face glowed with exertion.

'Don't ask me,' said Tristan. 'My dear wife is the one who knows how to work this thing.'

'What's all this about?' Jack asked. The opening credits of the *Antiques Roadshow* began to play.

'I *knew* I'd seen her somewhere,' Tristan said. 'Then when my wife was fast-forwarding through an old tape, I spotted them.'

'Spotted who?'

'*Her*,' Roger blustered, pointing at the screen as Grace's face flickered into view. 'The tape's knackered. We'd better be careful in case we need it as evidence.'

'Evidence?' Jack's coffee mug rattled as he slammed it down on the windowsill.

'Look, there.' Roger's stubby finger pointed at the close-up of the Bouchet et Fils brooch. 'She's a thief. That's Uncle Fraser's. I remember seeing it when we met at the lawyers. God knows what she has planned – we stripped her husband's company of its assets. She's here for revenge, mark my words.'

'Stop it!' Fraser rounded on him. 'You don't know Grace as we do. How dare you come into my house, bandying these accusations. It doesn't make sense, you fool.'

'No fool like an old fool,' Sir Richard said.

'You'd know, you priapic, pompous ass, with all those wifeys bleeding you dry.' Fraser rounded on Tristan. 'As for you – when was this recorded?'

'How the hell would I know? We could ring the BBC.'

'Excuse me,' Fraser said, striding out of the room.

Jack watched as the camera panned out to show Ted and Margot talking to the expert and Harry standing at her mother's side. He was transfixed, as the cameraman focussed on a close-up of Grace's face, by how radiant she looked. The table did little to disguise her heavily pregnant stomach, but she looked like a different person altogether – relaxed, glowing. *I don't care what she's done. I want her to look like that, to feel like that again,* he thought.

'Right,' Fraser said, coming back in and marching across to the television. 'Thank you for your amateur detective work, but Grace is no thief.' He held out his palm; on it nestled the other Bouchet et Fils brooch. 'Look. Pause the tape.' He held his brooch up to the screen. 'They are a pair, do you see? Move the tape on a little.' He watched as Margot's face swung into view. 'Hold it there.' He crouched down in front of the television and touched it, static crackling against his fingertip. 'It can't be . . .' he said under his breath. 'Grace!' he shouted, running through the house. 'Grace!'

The study was empty. 'What the hell's going on?' Jack caught up with him as he ran to the kitchen and out to the yard.

'Cy,' Fraser yelled. 'Have you seen Grace?' Cy tipped back his Stetson and shook his head.

'Sorry, Fraser. She just left.' He pointed up the driveway and Fraser and Jack stood with their hands on their hips, watching as the Beetle disappeared over the hill.

'Do you know where she's going after London?' Fraser asked Jack.

'She didn't say. Her parents live up in the Meon Valley somewhere.' He turned to Fraser. 'Are you all right? You look like you've seen a ghost.'

'I'm fine. I just – I can't figure out what's going on.' Fraser shook his head. 'I knew there was something about her from the moment I saw her.' He glanced at Jack. 'We shall both just have to be patient. She's coming back at the end of the month for the Hallowe'en party.'

'What if it's too late? What if she chooses her husband?'

'He doesn't deserve her, Jack.' Fraser stared at a goldfinch fluttering in the hedgerow, plucking at the seed head of a bristling thistle. 'Even the toughest, prickliest things have their weaknesses.' He ran his thumb along his lower lip, thinking. 'Do we know where this Sam Morgan, or Dave Locke, or whatever he is calling himself is?'

'Grace said he's staying over in East Wittering somewhere, in a B & B.'

'Right,' Fraser said, and clapped Jack on the back. 'While Grace is away, the mice will play.'

'I don't know what I'll do if she leaves.'

'You'll go on living, Jack. You never get over losing someone you love, you just learn to live with it.'

'Is that how it was with you?'

'Yes. One day you'll realise it's been a day, a week, a month since you thought of her.'

'I don't understand, though. How did Grace have the same brooch as you? Why has she never said anything?'

'Not the same brooch, one of a pair.' In Fraser's mind, the pieces of the puzzle began to slide into place. *Oh, God. Gin . . . the brooch.* He felt the blood drain from his head, a cold sickness spreading through him. 'There's nothing to be done until we talk to Grace.'

45

'Are you sure you'll be all right in here with Harry?' Alice said, flicking on the light in the galley kitchen. Grace gazed down into Andrewsfield market square from the little studio above the Looking Glass Café.

'Of course we will,' Grace said. 'I'm so grateful and it's not forever is it? I think it will be fun working together. I haven't waitressed for years.'

'I don't know how you do it,' Alice said quietly. 'Do you fancy watching *Fawlty Towers*? It's the last one tonight – I could do with a laugh.' She clicked on the little black-and-white television and twisted the dial until she found the channel. She giggled. 'Sybil Fawlty always reminds me of your mum.' She glanced up when Grace didn't reply. She was still gazing out of the dark window. 'Are you all right, Gracie?'

'Hm? I'm fine.' She turned round, resting back against the lukewarm radiator. 'I will be fine.' Grace's voice was brittle, exhausted. 'I just . . . when's it going to get better, Alice? If I give up the job with Fraser, even putting food on the table will be hard. I won't be able to afford to run the car any more.'

'Yeah, well it's that crisis in Iran, isn't it? Oil prices are rocketing.'

'There are no jobs. I tried every jeweller I could think of, Alice, every single one. Not one of them is hiring, even when I offered a silly wage.' Grace forced down her disappointment. 'Anyway, I reckon I'll make more in tips here.'

'Oh you do, do you?' Alice nudged her. 'Are you sure you're doing the right thing, leaving? I mean it's pretty cushy with that little cottage and all.'

'Yes, I am,' Grace said with more certainty than she felt. She missed Jack. *If it weren't for Harry, I'd never even think of going back to Sam.*

'That's decided, then.' Alice reached into a basket on the kitchen counter and pulled out a bottle. 'Fancy a glass? My elderflower wine is just about drinkable now.' She took down two tumblers from the shelf and rinsed them under the gurgling, clunking tap. 'I'll get someone to look at that for you.'

'Thanks,' Grace said, taking a glass. 'To new beginnings, again.'

'Onward and upwards.' Alice chinked glasses. 'If you get a better offer, don't worry. I have people in every day hoping for work.' She grimaced as she drank.

'Bit dry?'

'Sour.' They burst out laughing. 'Give it a few more months, I reckon.' Alice pulled a home-baked loaf of brown bread out of the basket and set it down. 'Do you fancy salmon pâté? Or there's a bit of cheese?'

'Cheese, please.' Grace swirled her glass. 'Is it supposed to be fizzy?'

'God knows. Another one?'

'As much as I'd love to, I've got to pick Harry up from Mum's later.'

'How is she coping?'

'Same as ever.'

'That bad?'

'She just won't let it go. That advice you gave me was good. You're right – I think the only way to survive is to work with what you have right now, do you know what I mean? She's still stuck in all the "what ifs" and "what might have beens".'

'Give her time, Grace. It's not easy for someone of her generation to start again. At least you're still young.' Alice paused. 'Look, I don't want to give you advice if you don't want it.'

'No, go on.' Grace flopped back on the low futon sofa.

'I think it's time for you to let it go.'

'Sam, you mean?'

Alice nodded. 'Say he does come back eventually – it's all changed. You've changed. You need to remember what Sam is really like. I don't think you'd put up with it any more.'

Grace couldn't look at her. 'How do you mean?'

'I think you didn't love him, you were *in* love with him for all those years.'

'And that's a bad thing?'

358

'No, it's amazing, but I think it makes you blind to his faults.' Alice sat down next to her and tucked her leg beneath her. 'I have this theory that when people fall in love, they fall in love with who they think the other person is. They have this ideal lover in mind, and as long as the other person fits that . . .' She waved her hands, trying to express herself. 'That template, or whatever you want to call it, they stay in love. I think your idea of Sam was so strong, you didn't see what he's really like.'

'Go on.'

'Sure, he's always had that dangerous, sexy thing going for him.' Alice looked at Grace. 'So I know why you fell for him when he chose you.'

'But?'

'Don't forget how driven he is, and how moody.'

Grace remembered the bleak days when Sam wouldn't come out of the office, how he would shout at Harry for the slightest interruption. The closed study door was a rebuke, a barrier between him and the world. 'He's tough and selfish, Grace, and that doesn't make for an easy marriage. Is that really what you want?'

Grace leant her head on her hand on the back of the sofa. 'Dad always called him a rough diamond.'

'Rougher than most.'

'He always admired the way Sam had pulled himself up from the council estate, with no qualifications. He can hardly read or write,' she said quietly, as if she were betraying a confidence. She thought of the notes with the gemstones, of how long it must have taken him to write each one. 'It didn't make any difference with Sam, he always found ways round.'

'He was always a fighter. I think it all just got too much for him last year. When you think what he went through, losing his mum as a kid. God knows, his dad wasn't much use.'

'I think that's why this idea of the perfect family, of the perfect home, was so important to him.'

359

'See? That's what I'm talking about. He was trying to create something perfect, and that's not possible.'

'He failed, and I think it broke his heart.' Grace twisted her wedding band on her finger.

'Maybe it's time for you to let go of someone else's dream and see what's in front of you.' Alice took her hand. 'You need to get on with your life.'

'Not you too? You sound like Mum.'

'Face it, Sam's gone.'

Grace hesitated. She longed to confide in Alice, to tell her that Sam was alive and well. *It's not fair*, she thought. *I can't drag her into this, can I?*

46

Sam jogged down the steps of the B & B overlooking the seafront in East Wittering. The rows of bungalows with their fading, flaking paint were buffeted by the cutting wind from the sea. Gulls soared, screeching, overhead, and the beach was deserted. He zipped up his leather bomber jacket and blew on his hands as he walked quickly along the uneven pavement. The nights were drawing in and one by one the street lamps flickered into life.

Fraser tossed down his cigarette and caught up with Sam. 'Mr Locke,' he said, and Sam stopped and turned. 'Or should I say Mr Morgan?'

'Who are you?'

'I'm a friend of Grace's. Fraser Stratton.' He held out his gloved hand.

'How did you find me?'

'It's easy enough when you know roughly where to look.' Fraser tucked his purple cashmere scarf into his coat. 'It's rather parky. Shall we?' He gestured at a nearby pub.

'What do you want?' Sam held his ground.

'I want to make you an offer you can't refuse.'

The pub was deserted, a fruit machine beeping to itself in the corner. 'Thank you,' Fraser said, paying the barman. He carried their drinks to a quiet corner table where Sam sat waiting for him, his hands on his spread knees, fingers drumming. 'Relax, Mr Morgan,' Fraser said, placing his pint in front of him. 'I just thought it was high time we had a little chat.' He raised his glass and sipped his Scotch.

'I'm surprised someone like you carries cash.'

'If you can lay aside that terribly heavy chip on your shoulder, perhaps we can discuss this like adults.' Fraser held his gaze. 'Grace is a remarkable woman.'

'I know that.'

'She deserves better than you.'

'She's worked for you for a few months and you think you know her?' He cocked his head. 'Why isn't that big fellow here, Jack? Is he too chicken to come here himself?'

'Jack has no idea I am here. Nor does Grace.' He glanced at Sam. 'I can assure you Jack is no coward. If he knew where you were, well . . .'

'Does he love her?' Sam's voice was tight.

'Yes, he does.'

'And I suppose you reckon *he's* good enough for her?'

'I know he is. He's a good and decent man. What you have done to Grace is inexcusable.'

'I had no choice.' Sam thumped his pint on the table. 'What was I supposed to do? The banks were after me—'

'What I mean is, you lied to Grace, to all of them. She trusted you, and you abused that. Do you think she wouldn't have gone with you and started again from scratch? Look at what she's achieved, how brave she has been.'

'How could I expect her to take me when I had nothing? When I had lost everything she loved – the house, her jewellery business?'

'She is loyal and strong and generous, Mr Morgan. She

would have stayed with you through anything, I think, but you have proved yourself unworthy of her. I knew there was something remarkable, something familiar, about her the moment I saw her.' Fraser paused, thinking of the videotape. 'We all have secrets, Mr Morgan. It's just a question of who we trust enough to reveal them to.' He looked at Sam. 'Grace belongs at Wittering Manor. We will give her and Harry a safe and loving home.'

'More than I can give them, is that what you're saying?'

Fraser took out his chequebook. 'You're a businessman, Mr Morgan. How much will it take for you to disappear again, this time for good?'

'You think you can buy me out?'

'Everyone has their price.'

'Not me.' He stood up, pushing his chair away. 'There's not enough money in the world to make me leave Grace behind.'

47

'How was your break, love? Did you get your head clear?' Ellen pulled down her witch's hat as the wind caught it. Grace was helping her carry trays of food down to the beach, where Jack and Cy had built a huge bonfire earlier in the week. It was ablaze now, sparks flying up into the sunset. Figures in costume danced in front of the flames to music drifting from a car stereo, children racing in and out of the dunes like quick shadows.

'I did, Ellen.' Grace was dressed as Morticia Addams with a long black wig with a white streak. The ragged hem of her dress trailed in the sand behind her and she had powdered her face a deathly white, with blood-red lips.

'Fraser's been a nightmare since you've been gone. Have you seen him?' Grace shook her head. 'Papers all over the place again, and I can hardly rouse him from his bed. I only got him up and dressed today because of the party.' Ellen raised her finger as she remembered. 'There was a lovely bunch of flowers delivered for you while you were away.' She cocked her head. 'Have you got a secret admirer somewhere?'

'Flowers? They must have been from Mum and Dad.' She lied, trying to cover up quickly. 'It would have been my wedding anniversary.'

'Just as well you had a break, then, love, anniversaries are always hard, aren't they?' Ellen arranged the plates on the trestle table. 'Oh, I hope you change your mind.' The older woman couldn't look at her. 'We've grown to liking you here, everyone has. I was just saying to Cy this morning how much I would miss you if you go.' Grace saw her cheeks colour.

'It's complicated, Ellen.'

'I don't know what it's all about, but look at how Harry has bloomed here – she's like a little plant that's had fresh air and sunshine.'

'I know.' Grace hugged her, felt Ellen's strong arms around her.

'Now, we'll start serving as soon as they get here,' Ellen said. 'Fraser and Jack always like to make an entrance.'

Grace's stomach lurched with nerves. She wondered if Sam was there yet, watching her every move.

'You should eat something, love. Look at you in that dress. Turn sideways and you disappear.'

'I've had a lot on my mind.'

'You're lucky. Every time I'm upset I reach straight for the biscuit tin.' Ellen patted her hips. She raised her head. 'Here they come!' Cy arrived first, followed by Harry on her little pony, then Fraser and Jack galloped side by side along the beach, the wind whipping their horses' manes. Harry's face was painted like a skeleton. 'Is she famine or death?' Ellen said. 'Death I think. Cy is so skinny, they always dress him up as famine.' Fraser brandished a silver sword as they galloped towards the cheering crowd. 'There's war, then. Which just leaves . . .'

Grace caught Jack's eye as he raced past, his black shirt billowing in the wind, his hair lashing back from his face. 'Conquest.' He wheeled his horse around and raised his hand.

'Thank you all for coming,' he shouted against the wind.

'May this be a great and spooktacular night!' Fraser cried to groans from the crowd. 'Eat, drink and make scary!'

'Ellen, have you seen Grace?' Fraser said, helping himself to a drink.

'She was here a minute ago.'

'I'm sure I'll find her,' he said, looking among the crowd. He put his hand in the small of his back and winced. 'A drink, Jack?'

'Later, thanks,' he said. 'I'll get the horses back with Cy in a minute.'

'Have you seen Grace?'

Jack shook his head. 'She only got back this afternoon. I hoped she might have . . .' He paused. 'Well, if she's made up her mind, I hope she tells me tonight.'

'I must talk to her too. It's really terribly important,' Fraser's face was grey, exhausted. He thought about telling Jack about his visit to Sam, but decided not to. 'I visited her parents, did I tell you?'

'No, you didn't.'

'I thought she might have been with them, but it seems she was in London looking for work.' Fraser's face fell. 'I rather hoped she'd stay. I think we both did.'

Jack's cloak billowed in the sea breeze. 'What are they like, her family?'

'I think Grace is more like her father. Charming fellow. He's rebuilding the waterwheel at the Old Mill and I spent an hour or so with him. I told him all about old Cosmo Stratton, that he was an engineer too.' Fraser smiled. 'Rather sad how dissipated we've all become, when you think the baronetcy was earned more through muck than brass.'

'Really?'

'Oh yes. The Strattons aren't an old family, I must have told you that? You'd never know from the airs and graces Dicky's lot give themselves, but you can practically smell the paint on the family coat of arms.'

'I met Grace's grandmother a few months ago,' Jack said. 'She was charming. French, I think.'

'You met her?' Fraser turned to him. 'Why didn't you tell me?'

'It didn't seem important. Don't you remember, I took Grace to that party?'

Fraser ran his hand through his hair. 'Of course you did. Of course. What was he like, her chap?'

'Life and soul of the party type, wealthy.'

'Did she seem happy?'

Jack thought for a moment. 'No. She had that look in her eyes of a horse that's going to bolt at any moment.'

'Did she? Did she indeed.' Fraser smiled, in spite of himself. 'Listen. I'm just going to lie down over there for a spell. Bloody back is killing me. Will you call me when you find Grace?'

Grace spotted him standing alone further up the beach towards the headland. It had to be him. She walked slowly towards him, the noise of the party fading away behind her.

'You look beautiful, like those poncey Italian films you like,' Sam said.

'Fellini?'

'Yeah. Fellini.' He had trimmed his hair, shaved off the beard. He looked, suddenly, like the man she had married.

'Sam . . .'

'Wait. Don't say a thing.' He got down on one knee.

'What are you doing?'

'Shush, Grace. Don't spoil it.' He cleared his throat and

looked into her eyes. 'Grace. Will you marry me?' He held up the ring pull from a drink can.

'You're insane.'

'Please. Let's start again.'

'As Mrs Dave Locke?'

'If you don't like the name we can change it.'

'Why did you do it, Sam? Why did you steal the stones?'

'I thought if you had one gem each month it would make you think of me, even when I wasn't with you.' He got to his feet, stepped close to her. 'Give me another chance. Come with me.'

It wasn't a question, but an instruction. Grace saw it there in his eyes, the blank, focussed stare that he couldn't hide sometimes. It made her think of a snake the moment before it strikes its prey – hypnotic, emotionless. Behind all the swagger, all the charm, there lay a loveless black heart, and this time she had the strength to walk away. 'No,' she said clearly, her voice rising against the wind. She looked back to the party, to the orange glow of the fire. She saw Jack silhouetted against the flames, sure and certain, watching out for her.

'I'll do anything.' He scrabbled in his pocket and took her hand. 'Here, here's the last of them,' he said, dropping the topaz and turquoise stones onto her palm. 'No more games, Grace, I promise. Just you, and me, and Harry.'

'Sam, I can't do it to myself, or her. You conned us all, and I have to make a new life for us.'

She saw his jaw flex, sensed his anger. 'That old guy, Fraser, he tried to buy me off, you know?'

'He didn't?'

'He said that you're in love with this Jack bloke.' Sam glared at her. 'Is that right?'

Grace hugged herself, felt the gemstones digging into her palm. She felt it then, a certainty, a break. 'It's over, Sam.'

'It's not *over*.' Sam's anger flared. 'Why didn't it work, all those little notes? You love that kind of stuff.'

'Sam, it's been terrifying, waiting for the next envelope to turn up.'

'I thought it would be romantic. That you'd figure out it was me, that . . . Look, none of it matters.' He raised his head and she saw that blank stare again. 'This isn't the end, you know.'

'You'll never let me go?' She took a step towards him. 'This time, you will. You will let me and Harry go, because if you don't I will tell the police where to look for you.'

'You wouldn't.'

'Try me.' She held his gaze in the silence, facing him down.

'I'm not going to beg.' He turned to walk away. 'You know where I am if you change your mind.'

'Where are you going? You can't leave without saying goodbye to Harry.'

'I can't do it.'

'You can, and you're going to. That little girl idolised you and right now she hates me because she thinks I drove you away. You're going to make it right.' Grace folded her arms. 'Then, in time, when she is old enough, she can come and stay with you.'

'You'd do that?'

'You didn't think I'd cut you out of her life? However badly we've messed up, and whatever you've done, you're her dad. I want nothing from you, Sam, nothing. We had some good years together, and you gave me Harry, and I will always be grateful for that—'

'I love you, Grace. I'll love you forever.'

'You don't know the meaning of the word.' Grace shook her head. 'You lied to me, you cut yourself off from me, you let me think you were dead. You left me to pick up the pieces, to bury our children, alone.' Her voice caught. 'I forgive you, Sam, but I want someone more than that now. I deserve more.' She hugged him. 'I'll give you a bit of time to get away before I call the police. I won't tell them where you are going, just that you've been in touch. Goodbye – and good luck. I'll get Harry.' She walked away, determined that she wouldn't look back, determined that she wouldn't cry. She tapped her daughter on the shoulder. 'Harry?'

She spun round in surprise. 'Mum?'

'There's someone to see you.' Grace blinked, her throat tight. 'It's a secret, Harry, an important secret.' She pointed into the shadowy dunes, to the dark figure by the seagrass. As Harry walked closer to the man, he called to her. Her face lit up and she began to run. Grace stood and hugged herself, wiping at her cheek with her hand. She saw Sam bend and swing Harry into his arms, spinning her around and around as the surf crashed, ruby in the sunset.

'Are you all right?' Jack was at her side then. He pushed back his skeleton mask and threw it onto the sand. He wore a billowing white shirt beneath the black cape and Grace saw that he'd secured his black cravat with her arrow pin.

'I will be,' she said.

'It's him, isn't it? Your husband?' Grace nodded. She felt him tense. 'Are you going with him?' he said, unable to look at her.

Grace took his hand. 'No.' She waited, holding her breath to see what his reaction would be. When he laced their fingers tightly together, held their hands close to his side, she exhaled. Everything would work out; she felt it now. She watched as Sam crouched down to Harry's level and spoke to her. She couldn't make out what they were saying, they were too far away, but she saw Harry's shoulders stoop and shake as she started to cry. 'I should go to her.'

'Leave them,' Jack said. 'This is between them. We'll be there to pick up the pieces.' He held tight to Grace's hand. 'God, I want to kiss you.'

'We can't, Jack. Harry's going to be broken-hearted. We have to wait.' She stopped talking as Harry ran back towards them. 'Harry, darling?' Grace called.

'Leave me alone!' She cut away towards the car park.

'Grace, hold on a minute.' Jack turned to her. 'I need to ask you something. While you were away, those chinless twats Roger and Tristan turned up with a videotape.'

'I don't understand.' Grace followed Harry with her gaze.

'Grace, they had a recording of some antiques show.'

'Did Fraser see it? Oh God, I can explain!'

'He needs to talk to you. Hold on. What's she doing?' Jack let go of her hand and ran towards the car park. 'She's taking Felix. Harry, wait!'

Grace saw Sam raise his hand in farewell and disappear into the falling darkness. She ran after Jack, sprinting towards the car park where the horses were tethered. She saw that Felix had already gone. Jack leapt into the saddle and wheeled his horse around. 'I'll find her,' he said. 'Follow in the Land Rover. She'll be taking the bridle path back to the house.'

'I know it.'

Grace's hand shook as she tried to get the key into the ignition. The engine roared and she sped up the lane, then cut off-road along the bridle path. She saw Jack's horse not far ahead. His shoulders were lowered, powerful and strong, as the horse thundered up the lane. Her headlights illuminated a tunnel of wind-whipped trees. Within seconds, Jack raised his hand and she stopped. He leapt down. 'Harry!' Grace yelled as she caught a glimpse of a leg on the path up ahead. 'Harry!' She ran from the car, the engine still running.

'Mummy,' Harry sobbed, turning her head towards her.

'Stay still, sweetheart,' Jack said.

'I'm sorry, Mummy.'

'Grace, go and get a hold of Felix,' Jack said. 'You can tie him up to the gate there. I'm going to get Harry into the back of the Land Rover, then you'll need to take her to A & E. I'll follow once I get the horses back to the stable.' He glanced up at her, his hair blue-black in the night. 'She's going to be OK, but she's broken her collarbone.'

'It was a bin bag, in the hedge, he hates them,' Harry said. 'Felix reared up and I just couldn't stay on.'

'You're a real rider now, Harry.' Jack brushed her hair away from her tear-stained cheek. 'You've had your first proper fall. Welcome to the club.'

Grace ran up the lane towards Felix. 'Come on you,' she said. She hesitated, afraid, remembering the sudden, shocking pain of the bite from the horse on the farm when she was a toddler. Then she grabbed for the reins and led the pony back, tethering him at the gate. Jack swung Harry up easily, careful not to move her shoulder. He waited for Grace to open the back of the Land Rover and laid her down gently in the back, kissing her forehead.

'It will be all right,' Jack said. 'I promise you.'

NOVEMBER

Topaz

Sincerity · Clarity · Friendship

48

'It's over, Alice,' Grace said, the phone crooked beneath her jaw. She placed the topaz and turquoise stones in their spaces in the little wooden box and clicked it shut. *It's over.*

'I don't believe it.' Alice leant against the counter of the Looking Glass Café, gesturing at the next customer to wait a moment. 'I can't believe that Sam would do that to you.'

'I wish I could have told you earlier. I just didn't want you getting dragged into this mess.' Grace put the box into the packing case and started taking down Harry's paintings from the fridge.

She heard Alice exhale. 'You didn't need to go through all this alone, Grace.'

'We'll be fine.' Grace paused by the dresser and took down the photo she had taken of Harry by the pool. *Am I doing the right thing?* she wondered. *There's no choice, is there?*

'Do you need a hand moving?'

'Thanks, but there's not much. I'll move everything into the flat later, if that's OK?'

'Of course. How are your parents coping with all this?'

'They're pretty cut up, as you can imagine.'

'Have you told the police?'

Grace cupped the phone, glanced over at Harry. 'Yes. I gave Sam a bit of time, but I've let them know it's all over.'

'Good. You can tell me all about it later.'

'Thanks, Alice.'

'Get away with you. Good luck with Fraser, it's not going to be easy is it?'

'You have no idea,' Grace said quietly, before hanging up.

Harry sat on the sofa watching *Blue Peter*, her arm in a sling. 'Mum,' she called out, her voice muffled by an Opal Fruit. 'They say we've got to check the bonfire for hedgehogs.'

'All right darling,' Grace called, her hand still resting on the phone.

'Why aren't we having a fireworks party at Grandma and Grandad's like every year?'

'Because . . .' Grace remembered her difficult confrontation with Ted and Cilla, telling them that Sam had gone. 'Because we're busy packing this year.'

'Do we really have to move?' Harry shuffled through from the living room. 'Now I know Daddy is OK, it's different.' Grace closed her eyes and took a breath before she turned to Harry.

'Go and rest your arm, sweetheart.'

'But, Mum. I love it here. Please can we stay?'

'Darling, it's complicated. It's for the best.' She thought of Jack, wondering if that was true. *I have no idea what's going to happen now Fraser knows about Margot.* 'It may not be forever, and it will be fun living above Alice's café,' she said, trying to sound cheerful, her heart sinking at the thought of the shabby studio flat.

'If it's about you and Jack, I'm sorry. Daddy explained that it was his fault, that he'd made you sad, and that he wants you to be happy.' Harry put her good arm around her mother's waist and laid her head on her chest. 'Jack makes you happy. You're always all sparkly around him. I like it. You should marry him.'

'Harry, that's getting a bit ahead of ourselves.'

'What will happen to Felix?'

'Jack will look after him for you and you can come and visit.' Grace looked away as she saw her daughter's eyes welling up.

'Pleeeeease! I can't leave Felix. Pleeeease can we stay?'

'Not death by whining, not now,' Grace said, trying to laugh when she felt like weeping herself.

'Has Daddy really gone?'

'Yes, he has, sweetheart.' Grace checked her watch, feeling sick with nerves. It was ten to ten. 'Darling, it's time. I have to go to work.' She straightened her back, and took a deep breath as she walked to the door. 'If you need anything, I'll – I'll be with Fraser.'

'Ah, Grace.' Fraser padded round to his desk, and tossed down a copy of *The Hitchhiker's Guide to the Galaxy*. His thick grey hair was wild, unbrushed, and a silver stubble scattered across his tanned, sallow cheeks like snow. He couldn't look at her. 'Did you enjoy the Hallowe'en party?'

'It was . . . eventful,' Grace said.

'I heard about Harry's fall. Is she all right?'

'Week off school, strapped up with a sling.'

'They're like little saplings at that age, the bones heal quickly.' Grace waited, butterflies in her stomach. She knew he would get round to talking about the videotape in his own time. Fraser busied himself, stacking papers on the desk. 'I broke my collarbone when I was forty and it was a nightmare. Weeks in bed with a back brace a medieval torturer would have been proud of.' Grace's heart went out to him. Fraser looked exhausted and dark circles bloomed beneath his eyes.

'Fraser, I just came to say goodbye. I think it's easier if I go now.'

'You must stay for the fireworks tonight. Come, sit down for a minute.' The lightness of his voice made her stomach lurch with anxiety. He grimaced, easing down to the sofa, and Grace tucked a cushion behind his back. 'Thank you.' He patted the seat next to him, and Grace sat on the edge. 'I need to talk to you about something. Something important. I saw a most interesting recording.'

Grace closed her eyes. She felt as if she was at the top of a roller coaster, caught in a weightless moment before plunging down. 'I know. Jack told me.' She hung her head. 'I'm sorry. I wanted to tell you about the brooch, but I had to hear

375

the truth from my grandmother first.' Grace chewed her lip. 'I still don't know everything.'

It was as if he hadn't heard her, like he was running through a speech he had prepared. 'Yes, those helpful cousins of mine have one of those newfangled video recorders, and they happened to tape an episode of that charming antiques programme.'

'The *Roadshow*, in Newbury?'

He started, seemed to come back to her. 'Precisely. They were kind enough to come around and share it with me.'

'I really didn't want you to find out like this.'

'How did you find me?'

Grace took a deep breath. So much had happened since the day she had found the receipt in the Bouchet et Fils jewel box and followed the trail to Wittering Manor. *If it hadn't been for that little slip of paper*, she thought, *none of this would have happened.* She had come to the house expecting to be in and out within minutes. But then there was Jack, and the cottage, and the chance to start again. And she owed it all to Fraser. 'There was a receipt in the original box. The day I turned up here for the interview, I was hoping to ask you about the brooch. But when I heard there was a house as part of the package . . .'

'You took your chance?'

'I just haven't known how to tell you.' She looked at her hands. 'It all went too far. How could I hurt you, and Jack, and Harry?'

He pulled the Bouchet et Fils wing from his pocket. 'Where is it, the other half of the tiara?'

'My grandmother has it,' she said, her voice a whisper.

'Ah yes, your grandmother. A beautiful woman, still.' He turned the wing over in his hand. 'Where is Gin, now?'

'I don't know. She's been travelling, but she lives near Andrewsfield.'

Fraser shook his head. 'All this time? I've searched the world for her and she was on the doorstep. Don't you see what a marvellous sense of humour God, or the universe, or whatever you call it, has?' His eyes were full of pain when he looked at Grace. 'I trusted you. The bloody cousins thought I'd give you the sack for being a thief; little did they know there are two brooches, two halves of the tiara.' He rubbed his eyes, his brow furrowed. 'What that tape really revealed was Virginia West. What it showed was the woman who stole my heart, my happiness, my peace of mind.' His voice shook. 'So, what have you got to say for yourself? It's a bit rich you laying into me for hiding information.'

'Fraser, I had good cause.' Grace felt sick. 'My grandmother's real name is Margot.' She saw the colour drain from his face. 'Virginia West was just a stage name.'

'Oh, God.' He pressed his hand to his mouth. 'Margot? My sister, Margot Helene? So, it's as I feared.' His hand shook as he ran his fingertips over the sparkling diamond wing. 'I – I had a horrible feeling when I saw the other brooch. I thought, I *hoped*, that Bouchet et Fils had made another.' His head sank. 'I was fooling myself, of course. They only made two, and Albert took one for me and Clem, and left one with Margot. My sister. Has she even been to America?'

'No.' Grace's eyes filled with sympathy. 'She was born in Paris . . .'

'With a twin brother, to a woman called Josephine.' The silence seemed to vibrate and Grace felt her head spinning. 'I don't think I ever got over it, really. When I lost Clemmie, and then so soon after was jilted by Gin – by your grandmother – that's why I buried myself in my work, why I never married, why I never had children of my own.' He screwed his eyes shut. 'She is the only woman I have ever loved – Christ!' Fraser gasped for breath. 'She's my sister?' He leant his elbows on his knees and buried his face in his hands, the diamond wing against his forehead.

'I'm sorry, I'm so sorry.' Grace put her arm around his shoulders.

377

'Tell me what happened to Margot,' he said, his voice muffled.

'She had never seen your brooch until the night before the wedding. That's why she ran away. She guessed you must be the boy her mother had talked about.'

'Poor girl. Poor, dear girl.'

'Eventually, she returned to a small village south of Paris and raised her daughter Priscilla there.'

'Daughter?' Fraser looked up, shocked. 'I always knew she was hiding something.'

'Cilla, my mother, was ... from a previous relationship.' Grace couldn't bring herself to tell Fraser about the rape.

'Then what? What has Gin – Margot – been doing all this time?'

'She helped the Resistance during the war.'

'Good for her. She was always brave. Always.'

'Then, Priscilla met Ted, my father, on VE Day in Paris – it was love at first sight.'

Fraser did a quick calculation. 'Margot must have been a child when she had her, then?' He waited for Grace to explain, but then went on, 'The child is the secret Margot was hiding all along – she had a young daughter.' They sat in silence for a time, letting the revelations sink in.

'I always wondered why Margot settled down here, and now I know,' Grace said. 'She wanted to be close to you. I don't know why she never contacted you—'

'Think, Grace. She's my sister!' Fraser cried. 'Imagine the conflict she must have felt – wanting to be close, and yet that shame, that revulsion.'

'I've been waiting to talk to her.' Grace sank back on the sofa. 'But she's run off again.'

'She's rather good at disappearing.' Fraser pressed his lips together.

'She had an argument with her – well, with Ben. When she comes back, you can—'

'No, my dear, it's time to warm up the fat lady.' He tried to smile.

'I'm so angry with her, I'll never forgive her for using me like this.'

'My dear,' Fraser said, 'if I can forgive her, you damn well will.' He looked away. 'I'm sorry too, Grace. I couldn't possibly bear to see Margot again. I loved her with a great passion, you see. Fortunately I was old-fashioned enough to think that a man should make love to his wife on his wedding night. Not quite the Greek tragedy it might have been, but not far off.' His jaw flexed. 'I thought writing my memoirs might lay some ghosts to rest, but instead it's destroyed everything. What is it they say? Be careful what you wish for? I found her.' He took a deep breath. 'We found her. Well, your grandmother is now my closest living relative and heir. This changes everything, of course.'

Fraser looked up at a knock on the door. 'Ah, Jack. You'd better sit down.'

'Is everything all right? What can I do to help?' Jack glanced at Grace, then turned to Fraser.

'Sadly, my dear boy, there's nothing any of us can do to undo nearly seventy years of secrets.' He explained the story as Grace watched Jack's every reaction.

'Let me get this straight . . .' Jack ran his thumb over his lips and turned his gaze to Grace. She saw the anger and confusion in his eyes. 'That means this woman, Margot, your grandmother, is now heir to Wittering Manor.'

'She's my sister,' Fraser said.

'And your ex.'

Fraser took a deep breath. 'You have every right to be angry.'

'But why should it affect Jack?' Grace said.

'Because, my dear, he loses everything.'

Her eyes widened as she realised the implications. 'Oh, Jack – no! That isn't right at all. Margot won't want this, I promise you.'

'Tell me you haven't planned this all along?' Jack stood, towering over her.

'How can you even think that?'

'Jack, don't say anything you'll regret.' Fraser looked up at him.

'What do you think I was doing? Just stringing you along in case my little scheme didn't work?' She stood slowly. 'I'll make this right.' Grace looked at Fraser. 'I'll prove to you that I was only trying to protect you.' She turned to Jack. His face was etched with confusion, with hurt, but he reached out to her still, touched her face.

'I'm sorry,' she whispered, covering his hand with her own, leaning in to his touch. 'Trust me. Please, trust me. I may have lied about why I came here, but I've never lied about loving you.'

49

Grace drove as fast as the Beetle could manage all the way to Exford, the windscreen wipers at full speed swishing aside the tumbling leaves and rain.

'Ow!' Harry said as they went over a pothole.

'I'm sorry, darling.' Grace glanced up in the rear-view mirror. She swung the car into the driveway of the Old Mill and Cilla ran out to meet her, holding a pink umbrella.

'Whatever's happened? I just tried to call you.' Cilla put her hands on her hips. 'I found her.'

'Gogo's back?'

'After you told us all about Sam, and what's been going on at the Manor, I thought it was about time she came back and faced the music. I rang every friend I could think of in France and tracked her down.'

'Where was she?'

'In London, doing some antiques fair, if you can believe it.'

Cilla pursed her lips. 'I told her she's put you through enough. You idolise that woman, but it's time for her to sort out her own mess. I can't believe how she used *my* daughter—' Her words were stifled by Grace's hug.

'Thanks, Mum! Where is she now?'

'At her cottage.'

Grace helped Harry out of the car. 'Can you look after Harry for a couple of hours? I have to go and talk to Gogo.'

'Hello, love,' Cilla said, sheltering Harry under the umbrella. 'Come inside.' She glanced at Grace. 'Go on then, and don't let her run rings around you.'

Grace pulled up in the driveway of her grandmother's cottage and jumped out of the car. 'Gogo,' she called, striding up the path. She rang the bell and waited. 'Gogo?' She hammered on the door. The rain stung her cheeks, plastered her hair to her face. Grace heard an inner door unlatch and the sound of music – a Chopin nocturne. Margot swung open the front door.

'Grace, darling, I have missed you. Did Harry get my parcel?'

'Where have you been?' Grace pushed past.

'It's lovely to see you, too.'

'You look ...' Grace waved her hand up and down. 'Wonderful.'

'I am a new woman.' Margot touched her freshly waved hair. 'I saw old friends, walked for miles, went to galleries ...' She gestured towards the living room.

'And Ben?' Grace stood in front of the crackling fireplace.

'He's already shacked up with his barmaid. No hard feelings.'

'How convenient. Gogo, he knows.'

'Who knows?'

'Fraser. He saw the *Antiques Roadshow* and he put two and two together. He asked how I was connected to the mysterious Virginia West.'

'Sarcasm doesn't suit you. Do sit down, you're making me dizzy pacing backwards and forwards.'

Grace threw Harry's birthday card on the coffee table and the cinema ticket Margot had drawn drifted out. 'Lovely calligraphy, Gogo, but then you always were a good forger.' Grace paused. 'I wondered where I had seen that beautiful copperplate script before, and then I remembered. The receipt in the tiara box.'

Margot regarded her coolly, her violet eyes clear. 'I'm surprised it took you so long to figure out.'

'What were you thinking? My God!'

'I needed to know. When I guessed Ben was going to ask me to marry him, I needed to put my past to rest. I had to let go of Fraser, of us. I had to know if Fraser knew the truth about me.'

'You were seriously thinking of marrying Ben?'

'Look at my life. I have been alone all this time. Frightened to live, to love – what kind of life is that?' Margot sighed. 'But knowing Fraser was still there, alive, so close ... when I was forced to choose between the past and the future, all these feelings came surging back.'

Grace threw her hands in the air. 'Why didn't you just ask him?'

'How could I, after what I did to him?' Margot's eyes were bright. 'You don't know what he was like when he was younger. Everything was black and white. He never forgave, and he never forgot – my God, when I think of how he talked about his father. I couldn't bear the thought that he hated me like that.'

'You let me stay there, all these months ...'

'When I saw how happy you and Harry were, how could I tell you? I had no idea you would end up working for him, Grace. I thought you would be in and out quickly.'

'You used me. You faked the Bouchet et Fils receipt, and you set me up.'

'I needed you!' Margot shouted. She collected herself. 'I was scared. I couldn't go myself. I just wanted to know if he was happy. If he thought of me.'

'I trusted you.' Grace tore her hands through her hair. 'I feel so stupid.'

'How – how is Fraser?'

'How do you think? Fraser's destroyed, Gogo. And Jack asked if I did all this to steal the estate away from him.' Grace put her head in her hands. 'I wish I'd never started any of this. I wish Fraser didn't know he was in love with his sister.'

'His sister?' Margot fell silent. 'God, how dreadful. He thinks I'm his *sister*?'

'You're not?' Grace paled with shock.

'It was all a misunderstanding . . .'

Grace leapt to her feet. 'Oh God, what have I done?'

'Where are you going?'

'I have to tell Fraser. Do you have any idea what you've done, running off to France without telling me the whole story?'

'Now hold on, what *I've* done?'

'I love you, Gogo, but you've been so wrapped up in your own drama you didn't think what this would do to Fraser.'

'I didn't think of Fraser?' Margot cried. 'I have thought of him every day for the last forty years. Every day. I thought so much of him that I gave up my own happiness.'

Grace closed her eyes, pinched the bridge of her nose. Finally, she looked at Margot. 'Do you love him?'

'I have loved him for a lifetime.'

'Then tell him. That's what this memoir is all about. You. He never got over you.' Grace picked up her car keys. 'I wouldn't hang around, though. That old friend of his, Cesca – I reckon she has her sights set on him.'

'Cesca?' Margot's violet eyes seemed to change, to darken. 'Her?'

'Come with me now, talk to him.'

'No. I can't. I can't just turn up after all these years. I have to prepare myself.'

'Like the Little Prince?'

'You remember?' Margot's face softened. 'I loved reading that story to you. He always reminded me of Fraser.'

'Gogo, he loves you. Prepare your heart, or do whatever you need to do, but you started all this – now you have to make things right.'

'Darling, I have carried that man in my heart for over forty years. I hurt him terribly.' She looked down at her hands. 'Besides, I have perfect memories. What if he were to reject me, now? I couldn't bear it.'

'You owe him this.' Grace's voice was low and clear. 'Maybe, just maybe, if for once you can put someone else first, you'll go and see Fraser tomorrow and apologise, and tell him the truth. Tell all of us the truth, for that matter. If you're not his sister, then who the hell are you?'

50

Grace's little car bumped along the familiar rainswept drive to Wittering Manor. A few valiant fireworks were already flaring up into the darkening sky above the village and she heard the scream of rockets. The moment she drove into the stable yard, she noticed the light was on in Jack's office and she ran straight there, draping her coat over her head.

'Grace?' Cy said, looking up from the armchair by the fire. 'You looking for Jack?'

'Have you seen him?'

'Try the stables.'

Grace ran out into the night, her feet splashing in the puddles, rain and wind lashing her face, her hair. She heaved open the stable door, light from the lantern above spilling into the dark space inside.

'Who's there?' Jack's voice called from the shadows. 'Close the door, damn it.' One of the horses whinnied and stamped its feet as another firework screamed into the night.

'It's me,' Grace said, dragging the door closed. 'Where are you?' She looked around the row of dark loose boxes. The rain drummed steadily on the roof, only the breath of the horses, the soft shift of their feet among the straw, breaking the silence. 'Jack?' She looked up as a pool of golden light swung across the rafters. He stood above her in the hayloft, holding a storm lantern high.

'Did you forget something? Deeds to the estate?'

'Don't be mean. It doesn't suit you.' She scrambled up the old wooden ladder to the loft and Jack leant down, taking her hand. It was warm in the eaves of the stable and sweet-smelling. Among the hay bales she saw Jack had laid out a dark blue wool blanket and a book lay open beside a steaming flask of coffee. 'Why are you camping up here?'

'I was worried about the horses with the fireworks,' he said. 'And I wanted some peace and quiet.'

'Sorry.' She felt the tension, the pain in his voice.

'You're soaking,' he said, and put down the lantern. 'Come here before you catch cold.' He shrugged off his jacket and draped it around her shoulders.

'I don't care.' Grace laughed, shivering with adrenalin and cold, pulling the coat around her. 'I've never felt better.'

'Do you take anything seriously?' Jack lifted the lantern again to see her, the light gilding his face. 'Why are you laughing?'

'You have every right to be angry with me, but I've found out something wonderful. I'm so relieved.' She sat down on the blanket. 'Is there any coffee left in there?'

'Sure.' He poured her a cup.

'Eugh.' She grimaced. 'How many sugars are in this? You're as bad as Fraser.' Jack stretched out beside her, the lantern at his side. 'It's all going to be all right,' she said, reaching for his hand.

'How can it be?' He looked down. 'So, what do you want,

the estate and me, like some sort of eunuch?' Grace burst out laughing. 'This isn't funny. I've just seen my whole future go up in smoke.'

'I'm sorry,' she said. 'You're just about the least likely eunuch I've ever met.' She knelt in front of him, took his face in her hands. 'I love you, Jack Booth. Do you love me?'

'You know I do.'

'Even if you are a wealthy landowner and I am a penniless, divorced, single mother, will you love me?'

'I don't understand?'

'Margot, my grandmother, is not Fraser's sister.'

'You're kidding me?' She felt the tension in his jaw, his neck relax. 'Thank God. Then who is she? What's the connection with the brooch, or tiara, or whatever it was?'

'I don't know the whole story yet, but Fraser should hear this too. I'm going to force Margot to come over tomorrow and talk to you both.' She leant down and kissed him. She felt him give in to trusting her. 'We are free now, Jack, we're free,' she murmured, her lips brushing his. 'I love you,' she said. 'I love you.'

Jack took her in his arms, kissed her passionately, her hands in his hair. Through the stable skylight, golden fireworks lit up the night sky. The feel of him, new and powerful, thrilled her. She traced the hard muscles of his shoulders, his back, his stomach. She wanted to learn him by heart, slowly, every muscle, every fibre that she had imagined, alive now and loved. 'Stay with me tonight,' Jack said. His hand slid over the small of her back, down to her thigh, his fingers pulling at the soft cotton of her dress.

'I can't, not tonight. Harry's at my parents and I've got to pick her up.'

He groaned with longing. 'Christ, I can't stand the thought of a night without you. I just want you in my bed.'

'Or your hayloft?'

He made space for her to lie beside him, her hair spilling

gold across the warm wool rug, the soft hay. 'Stay with me,' he murmured, kissing her neck.

'Jack,' she said, and kissed him, felt his tongue slide against hers, her body wakening, quickening in answer to his. Her back arched as he undressed her, unbuttoning her dress one slow button at a time, his lips tracing her breastbone, her stomach. He knelt back into the shadows, pulled his shirt over his head. Grace watched him undress, her arms flung above her head, fingertips brushing against the soft hay in anticipation. The rain drumming above them seemed far away. Here, she felt they were the only people alive.

'God, you're beautiful,' he said. Jack lay down beside her, waiting, taking his time. Eye to eye, the night shimmering between them, alive and electric, now there was nothing but the darkness keeping them apart, and the night was theirs alone.

'Come back with me.' Jack held her close, his breath steadying, her spine curving against his stomach. The rain had stopped and moonlight spilled silver across the blanket covering them. Her arm lay against his, their fingers entwined.

'I wish we could stay like this forever,' she said.

'We can, soon.' He kissed the nape of her neck. 'Marry me.'

Grace took a strand of golden hay, and bound the ring fingers of their left hands together with a looping figure of eight. 'I don't need the white dress and the marquee, Jack,' she said, his hand closing over hers. 'It's enough just to be with you.' She rolled over to face him, her body aching, deliciously bruised. 'We have all the time in the world.'

'You'll stay now, won't you?' He brushed her swollen lips with his thumb. Grace kissed the swell of his palm and Jack pulled her to him again. 'I understand. I don't expect you to move in with me straight away if that's not what you want.'

'We have to give Harry some time.'

'I know. But come home to the cottage. I need you near me, we all do.'

'Talking of which, I think we should go and break the good news to Fraser, don't you?'

Grace could see a shard of light from underneath the study door. Jack pulled her to him in the darkness, kissed her a last time. 'Do you want to tell him the good news?' she said. Golden light flooded out as Jack threw the door open. Biba stood by the desk, growling, her teeth bared, snapping.

'That's odd? Why's he left you in here by yourself?' Jack strode round the desk as the dog raced through the house barking, and lifted up the final page of the completed manuscript of Fraser's memoirs. At the end, Fraser had added a handwritten note:

Jack, Grace. I lived, and I loved, and those I loved live on in you. Remember me kindly. Fraser.

'Oh God,' Grace said. 'That sounds – it sounds like a—'

'Fraser!' Jack shouted, running after the dog.

Grace sprinted after him, hearing Jack's shouts echo around the empty house. She found them in the kitchen, Jack searching the scullery drawers for a torch. 'You don't think . . . ? Fraser hasn't done something stupid, has he?'

'That bloody prophecy. He's been obsessed, lately.' Jack flicked on the beam of the torch and unlocked the back door, releasing the frantic hound. 'Find him, Biba,' he said, running after her. 'Get Cy,' he shouted back to Grace. 'Get all of them. Something's wrong, I know it. We have to find him.'

DECEMBER

Turquoise

Prosperity · Happiness · Success

51

2014

The branches of the Christmas tree in the porch trembled in the breeze, its white lights bobbing gently. Grace paused at the door of the estate church and pulled on a pair of soft kid leather gloves. The churchyard was coated with snow and the sky clear turquoise blue. The others were taking their time and she began to feel the cold, so she walked cautiously along the slippery path to a white gravestone. She squatted down, the hem of her deep blue coat brushing the snow, and she cleared away the dead flowers, carrying them back to a bin at the church gate. She took a spray of holly and deep red roses from the pedestal she had arranged in the porch and went back to the grave, tucking them into the mesh pot in the earth.

'There,' she said. 'That's more festive, isn't it? You'd have loved the christening, Fraser. The whole gang are here. Even Harry's husband has come over from the States for the holidays with the children. You have three great-great-grandchildren, now. It's a real houseful.' Grace brushed the snow from the gravestone, clearing the letters. 'I still miss you, though,' she said, tears pricking her eyes. She glanced back at the church as the family began to troop out into the snow. 'See you next week,' she said, patting the headstone.

Grace thought back to 1979, to the hours after they found Fraser. She remembered Jack pacing the corridor in the hospital. The hissing strip lights drained the colour from his face, and dark circles ringed his eyes. Fraser had been unconscious since they brought him in. The morning cleaners were just coming on shift and a janitor listlessly mopped the lino floor, the smell of pine disinfectant cutting through the air. Jack looked up as he heard the click of Grace's boots approaching. She carried two steaming polystyrene mugs of coffee, and handed one to him.

'Any news?' she said. She was pale with lack of sleep, her hair messily piled up into a bun, tendrils of hair framing her face.

Jack shook his head, rubbed the dark stubble on his jaw. 'He still hasn't come round.'

Grace settled down on her haunches, her back resting against the wall. 'I called everyone. Harry's fine with Mum and Dad.' She looked down at her hands. 'He's going to make it, isn't he?'

Jack sat beside her, leaning his head against hers. 'I hope so.'

'It's my fault, Jack.' Grace bit her lip, trying not to cry. 'If I'd gone straight to him and told him what Margot said about not being his sister, maybe I would have been in time. He was heartbroken. What if I could have caught him?'

'No, no, it's not your fault. God knows what he was thinking.' He put his arm around Grace, kissed the top of her head. 'We've just got to pray he pulls through.'

The minutes stretched into hours, and they tried to sleep in the waiting room, the constant noise of the A & E department whirling around them. Finally, just before lunch, a doctor appeared at the door. 'Mr Booth?' he said.

Jack jumped to his feet. 'How is he?'

'He's stable now. Luckily he's fit for a man of his age and you found him in time.'

'Thank God.' Jack turned to Grace as she took his arm.

'Can we see him?' she said.

'I'll ask someone to take you up,' the doctor said, beckoning to a petite brunette nurse.

'Mr Booth?' she said. 'I'm sorry, I hadn't realised you were waiting in there. Mr Stratton already has a visitor. Perhaps you'd both like to follow me?'

'Do you mind if I join you?'

Grace turned at the sound of her grandmother's voice. 'Gogo?'

'I don't want to intrude.' Her brow furrowed. 'I heard what happened and I feel responsible. If only I'd told you the whole story before I left for France, none of this would have happened.' She looked at Jack. 'I'm so sorry.' She held out her hand.

'So, you're the one that got away.' Jack held her hand in both of his. 'He's going to be pleased to see you.'

The blinds were drawn in Fraser's room, a weak sliver of light wavering across the bed as the material shifted in the air conditioning. He lay on his back, his eyes closed, and he breathed softly, his arms above the covers. Cesca sat beside him, holding his hand.

'Jack, Grace,' she said, standing as they came in. Her face set hard as she saw Margot waiting in the doorway. 'You?'

'Yes, me.' Margot glared at Cesca.

'Oh, Fraser,' Grace murmured. She took Jack's hand. 'He looks like a marble tomb.'

'I'm not dead, yet,' Fraser said, his voice croaky and dry. His throat was raw, and the pain in his stomach felt like a leaden weight. His eyes flickered open. 'What the hell happened?'

'You gave us quite a scare.' Jack leant down and kissed his forehead. 'How are you feeling?'

'Not bad for a chap who came off worst in an argument with a stomach pump.'

'What on earth were you thinking?'

'I was drowning my sorrows, that's all. After Grace's

bombshell my back seized up, and I thought some of Cy's special cigarettes might help the pain as well.'

'Some? Do you have any idea how strong that stuff is?'

'I do now.' Fraser grimaced. 'That's why I left Biba at the house. I didn't want the poor dog getting stoned.'

'Honestly, Fraser, it looked like a smokehouse when we hauled you out of Cy's shed.' Grace tried not to laugh with relief. 'Thank God you'd been playing with his CB radio. Cy heard you rambling on round at a friend's house and he came running back to the house to fetch us.'

'I'm glad you all find it amusing,' Fraser said.

'You were lucky,' Jack said. 'When we found you, you'd passed out. If Biba hadn't raised the alarm, and Cy hadn't come back, you could be dead.'

'We thought ...' Grace paused. 'Well, when we read the note you left on the manuscript, and found you wearing the Bouchet et Fils wing, we thought you'd tried to kill yourself.'

'Ha! It was the bloody dedication, for the book – I thought you'd both be pleased.' He looked up at Jack. 'I'm sorry, my dear boy. You know I'd never do that to you, though I had good reason.'

'No, you didn't,' Margot said quietly. She stood in the doorway, the light a halo of gold around her soft white hair. At the sound of her voice, Fraser tried to sit up.

'Gin? I must be hallucinating. These painkillers are good stuff.' To Fraser, it seemed as though she floated across the room, a vision from the dreams he longed for and feared with equal measure over the years. A moment with her, even in his imaginings, was worth the emptiness, the loss, he felt each time he woke alone. 'Gin? Is it you? Is it really you?'

'Hello, Fraser,' she said. Her face had a softness that Grace had never seen before, her violet eyes shone.

'Gin, oh my darling.'

'Margot, now.' She tilted her head. 'As I was then, really.'

'What's happened to your voice?'

'Do you prefer this?' she said, slipping fluidly into an American accent.

'No, you'll do.'

Grace glanced at Cesca, who stood against the far wall, her arms folded. She was glaring at Margot. *What's this all about?* Grace thought. 'Fraser, there's something you need to know,' she said. 'Gogo's not your sister.'

He looked at Margot. 'Is this true?'

'Yes, my love.' She stroked his cheek with the back of her fingertips. He closed his eyes at her touch, exhaled.

'Then why did you run away? Why didn't you come back to me?'

'Don't you think you've done enough damage?' Cesca said, her words clipped and tight.

'Damage?' Margot's eyes darkened. 'You are a fine one to talk. I wish I'd never listened to you.'

'I don't understand,' Fraser said.

'I came back,' Margot said. 'When I found out the truth from my mother's friend, Josephine, I came back to Paris to tell you, to beg you to forgive me. I went to the British Embassy, but you had taken some time off. Alec – he was a decent man – he took me home when he saw I was so upset, but she—' Margot pointed at Cesca. 'She convinced me that you would never forgive me, that you hated me. She told me to let you go.'

'I convinced Alec it was for the best, that he should never tell Fraser you had returned. For someone like *you* to leave a man like Fraser at the altar?' Cesca sneered at Margot. 'You were never good enough for him.'

Margot raised her chin. 'That was not for you to decide. You were always a little in love with him, weren't you, all these years?'

Fraser's head turned towards Cesca. 'Is this true?'

Her face contorted as she tried to restrain her emotions. 'I'm sorry, Fraser.' She looked at him, her eyes brimming with tears. She picked up her coat and handbag from the chair by the bed. Grace saw the look of triumph on her grandmother's face as Cesca ran from the room.

'Come,' Fraser said to Margot, patting the bed. 'I think you owe us all an explanation. If you're not my sister, then who on earth are you?'

52

Margot settled on the bed at Fraser's side, and took his hand. 'You've been to Josephine's apartment in Paris, haven't you?' she said. 'Well, picture the scene. As Albert Stratton climbs out of his taxi on the way to break off with Josephine, there is a woman begging by the café. "Spare a few centimes for a blind woman and her child, sir," she says, raising a pale hand. Maybe he notices the baby swaddled tightly to her chest and takes pity, drops a few coins into her palm, and she scurries away into the building.'

'A beggar woman?' Fraser said.

'My mother, Helene,' Margot said calmly. 'Josephine's best friend, who told me the story of the babies, a girl called Margot and a boy called Fraser, whose father gave them each a diamond wing.'

'Hold on – your mother *Helene*?'

'I was born around the same time as you and your sister. Helene and Josephine came up with a plan. They thought Albert would want to take both children because Clementine was barren. An instant family.' Margot turned his hand over in hers, traced the lines of his palm with her index finger. 'In the end he only wanted the boy, an heir. But they weren't to know that. Josephine and Helene swapped girls. Josephine couldn't bear the thought of giving up both of her children, and Helene was more than willing to give up her daughter, me. God knows, she never wanted me, and no doubt she

396

thought she could get some money out of it. She took Josephine's daughter, Emilie – your sister – with her that day, begging.'

'Begging?' Grace said.

'Yes, my dear. As I told you, your great-grandmother was a con artist, a petty thief, and whore.' Margot folded her arm over her narrow ribcage. 'Her favourite trick was the blind woman with the baby – she had a little pair of opaque black glasses she hid her violet eyes behind.'

'Do you know what happened? After Albert took me?' Fraser said.

'You can imagine how distraught Josephine was, losing her son and the man she loved,' Margot said. 'She had trusted Albert – in the throes of passion he said he would leave his wife for her. As so many men do.' She shook her head. 'At least she still had Emilie.'

'Emilie?' Fraser said, the name ringing a distant bell.

'The asteria,' Grace said. 'The woman with the sapphire brooch.'

'Emilie was safely with Helene while Albert was breaking up with Josephine,' Margot explained. 'When Josephine realised Albert wasn't going to take you, and me.' Margot said to Fraser, 'she decided to do the best for both girls. Stratton left most of the tiara and some cash, but while he was busy admiring his son, Josephine pocketed the sapphire necklace, hid it in the coal scuttle.'

'Ha,' Fraser laughed, setting off a coughing fit. Margot lifted a glass of water to his lips. 'Good for her,' he said, settling back.

'Josephine let Helene keep the diamond wing, and no matter how hard up she was, my mother never sold it. On her deathbed, she said she wished Albert had taken me with you.'

'What a different life that would have been,' Fraser said.

'Was it just a coincidence, then, that you met before World War Two?' Jack said.

'It was the art school, dear boy,' Fraser said. 'I took an evening class at the same school where my father met Josephine. I suppose I was hoping to feel closer to his memory, somehow.'

'And Josephine had found me some work there, through her old contacts,' Margot looked at Fraser. 'She had a hard life, but she was a good woman, and took care of me and Emilie.'

'What happened to her?'

'I don't know.' Margot looked at her hands. 'She and Emilie left Paris in 1915 to make a new life in Bordeaux. That was where I went in 1939, to ask her the truth about you and me and Emilie. Then, when war came, I lost touch. Who knows what happened to them?'

'You really believed I was your twin brother when you saw the matching brooch on our wedding eve?'

'I couldn't risk it. I loved you so much – it was horrifying to think we might be brother and sister. I couldn't bring myself to tell you what I thought, so I left.'

'It broke my heart,' Fraser said. 'I've spent my whole life wondering why you left me.'

Margot closed her eyes and lowered her brow to his for a moment. 'I'm so sorry,' she whispered. Fraser squeezed her hand. 'I had to be sure, in case we were making a terrible mistake, but I didn't want to get Josephine in trouble. She stole from your father and I know she always felt bad about that.'

'But Josephine gave him the child and heir he longed for.'

'A prize more precious than jewels?' Grace said.

'Exactly what I wrote recently,' Fraser said, turning to her. 'You kids run along home. You both look as if you could do with some sleep.' Grace leant over and kissed him, then took Jack's hand and walked away.

Margot slipped off her shoes and tossed her coat onto the armchair. 'Would you like some more water?'

'Rather have a whisky.'

'Same old Fraser,' she said. Margot held the weight of his head in her hand as he drank thirstily.

'Thank you.' He gazed up at her. 'I can't believe it's you. I've held you in my heart all this time and you haven't changed a bit.'

'Neither have you.' She smoothed back his hair from his brow. 'You're still the most attractive man I ever saw.'

'If you knew we weren't brother and sister, why didn't you ignore Cesca and Alec? I know you. I know how strong you are. Why didn't you find me?'

'Because I loved you too much. Everything is terribly black and white when you are young, isn't it?'

'I get the feeling you haven't mellowed much with age.' Fraser narrowed his eyes, smiling.

'Oh, it seems crazy now.' Margot rubbed the bridge of her nose. 'I was so ashamed for running away like that, of how much I must have hurt you. Even if you forgave me, I had taken something perfect and broken it.' She looked down at their hands, entwined. 'Meeting you, loving you . . .' Her eyes pricked with tears. 'It was the most beautiful thing that ever happened to me in my life.'

'And mine. And it is still ours, even after all this time.' Fraser smiled. 'Perfection becomes less important with age. It's the cracks and faults, the things that almost broke you but you survived, which make people and relationships beautiful.' Fraser gestured to the table at his side. 'Look in that drawer.' Margot slid it open, and saw his watch and wallet, and there, resting on top, the Bouchet et Fils wing. The diamonds shone as she lifted it into the light. 'We have Grace to thank for putting the pieces together.'

'It was all my fault, by the way,' Margot said. 'Grace had no idea.'

'I adore that girl. I knew she reminded me of someone.'

'She's so angry with me. She thinks I used her, to find out about you.'

'Well you did, didn't you?'

'I guess . . . I guess I did.' Margot reached for her handbag and clicked it open. 'Look,' she said, holding up the other wing. She handed Fraser his and lay down gently beside him. They held the two together above them, the diamonds sparkling in the light from the lamp.

'Just think,' Fraser said, 'we may have lain in our cradle like this once.' He rested his head against hers. 'I have spent my whole life looking for you ever since.'

'I'm back,' Margot said. 'And this time, we never have to be apart again.'

53

1980

'Where are we going?' Grace steadied herself as the Land Rover bumped off-road. She touched the blindfold covering her eyes. 'We seem to have been driving for miles. Jack, is this going to take long? We've got a stack of orders to finish for Christmas, and the rest of the decorations to do before the carols tonight.'

'Relax, it all looks beautiful,' he said. Grace's team at the farm shop had been working overtime to get the café and boutiques decorated with twinkling lights and fresh pine and holly swags. Cy and his men had put up a large Christmas tree at the heart of the courtyard, and that night Harry's school choir was going to sing carols while people shopped for Christmas gifts. The old barns had been transformed, and smelt of orange, cinnamon and mulled wine. Over the last year, Jack had turned the derelict buildings into boutiques full of character. There were artists, craftsmen, and Margot had taken one of the shops for her antiques. Grace had taken another space to sell her jewellery designs, and she had just been putting the finishing touches to her window display when Jack surprised her. She had seen his reflection join hers, his smile, the Christmas lights shimmering, reflected in the glass as if the glittering jewels on display were creating the colours themselves.

'Jack, we have hundreds of people coming tonight,' Grace said now as the Land Rover sped across the field. 'It's going to be the busiest night of the year.'

'You can afford to take a couple of hours off.' He reached across to her, his hand sliding along her thigh. 'I hear your boss is very understanding.'

'Hey! Concentrate on driving,' she said, laughing. 'Anyway, why are you all dressed up?' When Jack had slipped the blindfold over her eyes she had turned to him, felt he was wearing a suit and the turquoise tiepin she had made for him the year before. Now she heard the crunch and hiss of snow beneath the wheels, sensed shifting sunlight through the blindfold. 'Comfortably Numb' played quietly on the stereo.

'Nearly there,' Jack said, putting on the brake. 'I'll come round and help you, OK? No peeking.' Grace heard him slam the driver's door and his footsteps trudging around the car. There was something else, a rushing, roaring sound she couldn't place.

'Take my hand,' he said, guiding her out of the car and across the field. The cold pinched her cheeks, but her hand was warm and safe in his. 'Are you ready?' He untied the blindfold and the silk scarf slipped away.

'Oh, Jack,' she said, 'it's beautiful!' A red hot-air balloon soared above them, the flame roaring gold against the pale blue winter sky. A flock of geese wheeled above, the cries of the birds clear and true.

'Morning, Mr Booth, everything is ready,' the balloon pilot said.

'Thank you.' Jack helped Grace up into the basket, and

jumped easily in. 'Hold tight,' he said, putting his arm around her.

The balloon swayed and lifted, carrying them effortlessly up into the morning sky. West Wittering fell away beneath them. 'There's the house,' Grace said, pointing out the estate in the distance. The sea was a shimmering blanket before them. 'This is wonderful, Jack.'

'You're always saying you wish you knew what it was like to fly. This is the closest I could get.' He kissed her, his cheek cold against hers. The balloon drifted closer to Wittering Manor. Grace made out all the familiar roads. The cars seemed like toys beetling backwards and forwards. 'Look! You can see the horses,' she said to Jack. 'Hold on a minute, who's that? Oh look! It's Harry!' She could make out her bright turquoise puffa jacket against the snow, and she waved frantically from the basket. Grace narrowed her eyes against the sunlight. 'What are they doing? Gogo and Fraser are with her.' She turned to Jack. 'Did you plan all this?'

He shrugged, a smile playing on his lips. As the balloon drew closer, Grace could see Margot and Fraser running hand in hand with Harry, clearing a message, the letters showing green through the crisp white snow:

Marry Me?

'I love you, Grace,' Jack said. She touched the simple gold arrow pinned above his heart, the small turquoise stone smooth beneath her fingertip. 'What do you say?'

'Do you think she will say yes?' Fraser said to Margot.

'I do hope so, but you never know with Grace,' she said.

'If she doesn't, you can only blame yourself for brainwashing her. All those years of telling her she doesn't need a man. Honestly.'

Margot turned to him and pulled the suede collar of Fraser's tweed coat closer around his neck. 'That's because I only ever met one man I wanted to marry and I had to wait forty years for him.' Fraser cupped her jaw in his gloved hand and kissed her as Harry ran on behind them.

'I adore you, Lady Stratton, you've made me the happiest man alive,' Fraser said. 'If I had to wait forty years again for you, I would.'

54

2014

Grace smiled as Jack wheeled Margot's wheelchair from the chapel, with Harry and her family walking behind. Jack's hair was white now but every time she saw her husband, Grace still felt a visceral shock of pleasure. He still rode every day, and though his broad shoulders had grown stooped, he was still strong. Their two sons were like carbon copies of their father and each other, identical twins that even Grace had difficulty sometimes telling apart. They helped Cilla negotiate the church steps, one on each arm. Even after ten years, Grace still expected to see Ted at her side.

She glanced back at Fraser's tombstone. 'You'd be proud of your family,' she said. *Thirty years together with Gogo, but it was still too soon when you went.* She pulled off her gloves and twisted her new eternity ring around. It was one she had designed herself, baguette diamonds banded with one of the gemstones – the peridot, her birthstone. The garnet, Margot still wore as a cocktail ring. The other stones, Grace had fashioned into rings that bound the family together wherever they were in the world. Only the pearl was untouched, nestling still in Jem and Rex's grave. Grace waved as her eldest granddaughter looked over at her. *I'm so glad Phoebe has the same beautiful violet eyes as Harry and Margot.* She glanced down at her eternity ring. *Twelve lucky stones, just one with me now,* she thought, running her thumb across the jewel. It seemed like a lifetime ago that she had chosen the gemstones to hide in the old house. Most days she did not feel like a pensioner. She didn't know where the thirty-four years of their marriage had gone. It was hard now to remember a time before Jack, to remember the young girl she had been when she met Sam.

'Excuse me,' a young woman approached. She was carrying a clipboard, and had a BlackBerry clamped to her ear. 'Can you tell me who owns the Manor?'

Grace smiled. 'We do.'

'That's fabulous.' She shifted the phone against her ear. 'I'm going to have to call you back,' she said, clicking it off. 'I'm a location scout,' she said to Grace. 'We're looking for venues for a new antiques programme and I think the Manor would be perfect for next year's Christmas special.'

'Leave me your card,' Grace said. 'Our sons run the estate these days, so it will be up to them.'

The young woman slipped a card from her clipboard and pointed at the two brooches on Grace's lapels. 'You should bring those to the show, they're gorgeous.'

'Thank you, but no, I don't think so. They're a private family item.' She glanced over at Harry and her family. 'My daughter wore them as a tiara for her wedding, as I did at mine.' She raised her hand in greeting as a slender woman with pale blonde hair walked over. 'It will be your turn next with the tiara, Phoebe,' she said to her.

'That was a great christening, Grandma,' she said, hugging Grace. An amethyst ring glinted on her finger.

'Do think about it,' the location scout said and walked away, already dialling a new number on her phone.

'What did she want?' Phoebe asked.

'They're making some new antiques programme and want to use the Manor,' Grace said.

'Hasn't the family had enough adventures with antiques shows already?'

'Oh, it is good to see you.' Grace took her arm. 'You look so like your mother when she was your age.'

'That's what everyone says.' They walked back towards the church. 'How does it feel having three grandchildren now?'

'I think Jack hopes we'll have enough for a football – or soccer – team soon.' Grace looked at her family with love. 'The more the merrier. I think this little chap was a bit of a surprise for your mother.' She caught Harry's eye, smiled at how happy she looked. Harry's husband carried his newborn son proudly from the church and a photographer gestured for them all to stand closer together.

'Can we have a photograph of Lady Stratton and her great-great-grandson?' the photographer said, looking up from his camera. Jack wheeled Margot to the front of the group and Harry laid the baby in her arms. 'Looking gorgeous, Lady S.' The photographer focussed on her.

'I'll be a hundred soon,' she said.

'Never! Can I ask, what's the secret to your long life?'

Margot's laugh was throaty, infectious. 'Love, chocolate, sex, good genes – and a glass of red wine a day.' She tilted her head coquettishly. 'Or two. I was a dancer, you know, once upon a time. I could still do a high kick into my eighties.'

'Gogo, behave,' Harry said, laughing. She smoothed out the christening gown. 'He's not too heavy is he?' The family gathered round.

'Not at all,' Margot said. The wind caught her silver hair, lifted it gently as she stroked the baby's cheek. He gazed up at her with violet eyes and gurgled happily, clasping her finger in his hand. 'Hello, Fraser,' she said.

Phoebe looked from Jack to Grace. 'I love the way Grandpa looks at you, still.'

Grace laughed. 'Oh, we've had our moments, like all couples.'

'Thank you,' the photographer said, and everyone started to walk towards the cars.

'I hope one day that I have a relationship like yours,' Phoebe said to Grace. 'I mean – you've still got *it*, Grandma.'

'You've made my day,' Grace said, her eyes sparkling.

'How did you and Grandpa meet?' Phoebe asked, taking her arm.

'It's a long story, darling.'

'Go on.'

'Well, it was an icy day, like this, and I was driving an old banger. I had this mad old lurcher at the time, Jagger.' Grace's eyes glistened at the memory of him. 'I was stuck in the snow and ice, trying to chase after that silly old dog.' Her breath caught. 'Jack just appeared like a miracle, when I needed him most.' She looked over to him. Jack felt her watching and turned to her. Even in a crowd of people, he could still make her feel like they were the only people alive. 'It felt . . . it felt like he really saw me. You don't meet many people like that in a lifetime, Phoebe. If you do, take my advice, you treasure them.' Grace smiled at Jack. '"Take my hand," those were the first words he said to me. "Take my hand".' Grace reached out to him as he walked towards her now. 'And I did.'

Acknowledgements

It was a pleasure learning more about tiaras from Geoffrey Munn of Wartski and the *Antiques Roadshow*, and my thanks go to him for generously sharing his expertise, and Vicky Mitchell, Michele Burgess and Pam McIntyre for their help researching the early days of the show. My thanks also go to Patrick Baty for his generous help during my research of the Lancers. Thank you to: The Wartime Memories Project; Charlotte Soehngen, Christie's; Lyn Mills, the Goldsmiths' Company; Liz Higgins, Cowdray Park Polo Club; Judy Rudoe, the British Museum; William Lobb, John Lobb Ltd; Jane Bartholomew, Goodwood estate; Katherine Phillips, Imperial War Museum; Alan Hirst, the Insolvency Service; and Daniel Magson, Missing People.

Every book published truly is a team effort, and I am lucky to work with a remarkable group of people. Thank you to Sheila Crowley, Rebecca Ritchie and all at Curtis Brown, and to Kate Mills and all at Orion. Finally to my husband and children – for your love, support and all the times you've been patient when I am 'typing', thank you.